Leviathan with a Fish-hook

S. L. Russell

Bright Pen

Visit us online at www.authorsonline.co.uk

A Bright Pen Book

Text Copyright © S.L. Russell

Cover design by S.L. Russell and Jamie Day ©

Scriptures and additional materials quoted are from the Good News Bible ©1994 published by the Bible Societies/Harper Collins Publishers Ltd UK, Good News Bible ©American Bible Society 1966, 1971, 1976, 1992. Used with permission. www.biblesociety.org.uk; and from the Revised Standard Version of the Bible copyright ©1946, 1952 and 1971 by the Division of Christian Education of the National Council of Churches in the USA. Used by permission. All rights reserved. Extracts from the Book of Common Prayer, the rights in which are vested in the Crown, are reproduced by permission of the Crown's Patentee, Cambridge University Press.

ISBN 978-07552-1181-4

Authors OnLine Ltd
19 The Cinques
Gamlingay, Sandy
Bedfordshire SG19 3NU
England

This book is also available in e-book format, details of which are available at www.authorsonline.co.uk

*With special thanks to
Derek, for his endless patience
and Nikki, for her unwavering loyalty*

A M D G

Can you catch Leviathan with a fish-hook
or tie his tongue down with a rope?
Can you put a rope through his snout
or put a hook through his jaws?
Will he beg you to let him go?
Will he plead with you for mercy?
Will he make an agreement with you,
and promise to serve you for ever?

Job 41: 1-4

Friday 17th May 1996

A few minutes before midnight Eileen snapped awake. She lay still, her breathing shallow, and felt her blood pump and surge. Anxiety lay over her heart like a clammy hand. She groaned quietly as she forced herself to sit up. What had awakened her? A dream? The cry of a hunting owl? Rags and tatters of memory floated across her conscious mind, gone before she could grasp them.

Then she remembered, and in the warmth of her quiet bedroom she shuddered in sudden cold.

Eileen glanced at the kitchen clock. Four thirty. Marie would be home.

She dried her hands on a ragged bit of towel and went to the phone in the hall. After the bright sunshine in the kitchen it was quite dark, and the stone floor felt agreeably cool under her bare feet. She dialled, and waited. 'Marie? Hi, it's Eileen. How long have you been back?'

'Oh, an hour or two. Stan came for me after lunch.'

'So, what did the consultant say? Is he happy with the way it went?'

'He seemed to be. You know how they are. He must do hundreds of these operations. Bit of a bore for the poor chap, really.'

'Even so, it's your body, your uterus. You've got to live with it, not him. Or without it, rather.'

'Good riddance to the blessed thing, I say. It's given me nothing but grief. Well, apart from producing Stephanie.'

Eileen laughed. 'And how is Stephanie?'

'She's just this minute handing me a cup of tea.'

'She has her redeeming qualities, whatever her hard-hearted mother would have you believe.'

'Hm. Maybe.'

'Marie, shall I come and see you in the morning? I can pick up a few things for you from the shop if that would help.'

'That would be great. A loaf and a drop of milk is all I need. I stocked up before I went into hospital.'

1

'All right then. I'll be over about ten.'

'That's lovely. How are things with you?'

'Much as ever. Christina's home for the weekend.'

'Have you heard from David?'

There was a barely perceptible pause. 'David should be phoning tonight, as usual,' Eileen said, her voice bland. 'As far as I know, he's well. He always rings when he knows Christie's here.'

'Of course he does. Whatever else, you know, he loves his children.'

'I'm sure you're right,' Eileen said. She frowned. Did she know any more what David thought, felt, liked, hated? 'Well, my dear, I don't want to wear the invalid out, so till tomorrow, all right? If you think of anything you need, call me.'

'I will. Thanks for ringing.'

'Bye.'

Thinking about Marie, Eileen turned back down the hall and almost tripped over her old dog, who had been lying quietly by her feet.

'Right, old girl, I think there's just about time for a stroll. Let me find some shoes.'

Eileen stuffed her feet into her old beach shoes and stood by the open door, blinking in the strong sunlight. The back garden sloped gently downwards, part of the general fall towards the river as it wound its way slowly to the sea, opening out into a broad and sluggish estuary just visible now between the trees. The afternoon sun sparkled on the water.

The old dog grunted and sighed a little as she rose to her feet and followed Eileen down the overgrown garden path and through the gate. They turned right along the footpath as it led down towards the woods. The dry weather over so many weeks had left the paths deeply cracked and rutted. Everything had come early: the bluebells were gone, leaving only the crushed and sad-looking stalks, and much of the blackthorn blossom had fallen or turned brown round the edges. Off the path and under the trees, ground ivy, campion and wild garlic grew in abundance. Among the clinging honeysuckle with its nascent buds even the odd dog-rose was beginning to unfold, and along the edges of the wood cow parsley and stitchwort grew in white banks.

Eileen's path ran downward, sometimes steeply, sometimes more gently. The afternoon sun, still very warm, slanted through foliage already dense, and a tiny breeze ruffled the topmost leaves. The elms that had once dominated here had gone, ravaged by Dutch Elm disease twenty years ago. The massive oaks had fallen to the great storm almost a decade before. Because they were old and shallow-rooted, the hurricane-force wind had ripped them up and tossed them aside. Those

2

that survived had lost branches or been torn from the earth. There were ash in the woods too, hosts in the damper seasons to dish-shaped fungi which grew high up the trunks.

Eileen breathed the balmy air and smiled, at home and at peace. The old dog flopped at her feet and sighed deeply.

Then, in the deep quiet, she heard a sudden crash, crunching footfalls, breaking branches, and, softly but unmistakably, a string of curses. The dog cocked her head and growled in the back of her throat.

'Hush, Tillie.' Eileen stood still, staring into the green thickets. She caught sight of a hand, a grubby white tennis-shoe, and then a man came into her field of vision. She had time to notice his dark hair and vividly-striped jumper before his head came up and he saw her—and froze. A sickly half-smile wavered on his pale, dirty young face. A long moment stretched out, suspended. Eileen cleared her throat. She felt she should say something. But then the stranger raised a hand, not so much in greeting, it seemed to her, as in self-defence. In one movement he pulled himself up, turned his back and hared down the path, almost immediately disappearing into the bushes.

Eileen gazed after him, shaking her head and frowning. *How odd.*

She continued on down, her shoes making little sound on the dry mud. Before coming out onto the rough heath above the marshes she took another path that angled off to the left, taking her back on herself into another part of the wood. There was hawthorn here, and many fallen trunks, some caught up in their parent trees. In a thicket off the path a fluttering of foreign colour caught her eye, and the dog ambling by her side raised her head and sniffed, whining. A shifting patch of yellow and blue moved behind a rough tarpaulin camouflage, then a glimpse of hair and a muffled laugh.

Eileen smiled as she moved quietly on. 'It's all right, Tillie,' she murmured to the dog, gently brushing the smooth black head with her fingers. 'It's only Michael and Stephen. Don't let on we've discovered their bivouac.' She glanced at her watch. 'We'd better move, old dear. I've got to be at the station at five thirty, and we shouldn't be late for choir practice.' Nevertheless she stood still for a moment. The memory of her dream, if such it was, brushed against the edges of her consciousness, reviving her anxiety. The oddity of the man in the woods, the vulnerability of two heedless little boys, the uneasiness seeping from some dark unconsidered region of her mind, combined to create an ambiguous sense of insecurity, as if, barely noticed, the world was beginning to rock and sway under her feet.

But time was pressing on, and they had to hurry home. The station

3

was at Caxford, six miles away. Holton had never had a railway service and the buses were few and unpredictable.

Tillie flopped down panting onto the hallway tiles. Eileen, changing her shoes, looked at her with concern. 'It's still too hot for you, isn't it? Perhaps I'd better leave your walks till later while this weather lasts.'

She scrabbled in her handbag for car keys and sunglasses, then left the house by the front door. Her ancient Citroen stood on the gravel drive, its flaking bilious yellow looking tawdry in the early evening sun. The first clouds in weeks were beginning to form overhead, and what little wind there was had died to a sultry stillness. Crickets buzzed and clicked in the overgrown hedges, and swallows feasted on the myriad hovering bugs.

Eileen looked at her watch again as she started the engine. The road to Caxford was narrow and winding, and there was every likelihood of meeting a tractor or a herd of cows going home for milking. She roared off down the road in an explosion of exhaust fumes, past two other cottages which had once been similar to her own but were now more modern and smartly painted; then into the main village street, past the church, the pub and the bit of green; past a few more houses, the village shop and the lane up to Marie's cottage, then out of the village. The road to Caxford followed the line of the fields and was quite dangerous at night, especially for the unfamiliar or those the worse for drink. Cars upended in the ditches on either side were a not-uncommon sight. Not so long ago the road had been bordered only by trees and fields and the odd cottage, but more recently clusters of new developments had sprung up, and some gloomy souls predicted that before long Holton would be a suburb of Caxford. Eileen bristled at this thought. Holton was a backwater, the end of the line, not on the way to anywhere else, and seldom visited by anyone except the occasional party of ramblers or bird-watchers. This suited her very well.

Eileen met no tractors and covered the six miles in thirteen minutes, clattering into the small station forecourt at Caxford just after five-thirty. Christina was waiting for her, sitting cross-legged on the pavement in a pair of washed-out denim dungarees, her overnight bag and sandals beside her. She had her headphones on, and her eyes were closed, but the sound of her mother's car was noisy enough to drown out the loudest music. She scrambled to her feet, removing the headphones, and waved as Eileen ground to a halt and got out of the car.

'Mum, hi.' She gave Eileen a hug. 'The train got in early for once.'

'Hello, darling. How are you? Good journey?' They threw the bag onto the back seat, retrieved the sandals and got into the car.

'It was terribly hot and crowded in London. The station was a nightmare. Remind me not to travel on Fridays.'

Back on the road to Holton, Eileen drove more slowly.

Christina glanced sideways at her mother as they bowled along the road. 'Heard from Dad lately?'

'Oh yes, he telephones once in a while and speaks to Natasha.'

'All right, is he? Not lonely?'

'He seems fine. But you can ask him yourself. I always know he will ring when you're home—nothing surer.' She glanced at her daughter. 'I like your new haircut, by the way.'

'Do you?' Christina ran a hand over her spiky fair crop. 'It got so hot, I couldn't stand it around my neck any more.'

'Well, it suits you.'

For the last mile or two they travelled in silence. The sun was going down, and the trees alongside the road were beginning to cast long shadows. A breeze sprang up, cooling the air. The clouds Eileen noticed earlier had moved to the horizon.

As they came into Holton Eileen said, 'What time is it?'

'Ten to six.'

Eileen brought the car to a noisy halt outside the front door. 'Right. Michael should be in at six, and we'll just have time for a bite to eat before we go. I must have a wash before I go out. I'm so grubby and dusty after the woods and rooting around in the garden.'

'No problem, mother dear,' Christina said. 'I'll wash a bit of salad while you turn yourself into something more like a chorister.'

'Well, I've given up all pretence of great musical contributions, but I can at least be sweet-smelling.'

'Do you ever play these days?'

'No. I hardly dare to. Philip is such a gifted organist, I depress myself if I try to compete.'

She fished for her key and let them both in.

'It's always seemed a bit of a mystery to me,' Christina said, following her mother into the hallway, 'why a musician like Philip could wind up somewhere like this. I should think he'd be more suited to a cathedral.'

'Yes, I know,' said Eileen. 'There's a story behind it somewhere, I think, but nobody knows what it is. Unless Marie does.'

'Is that still going strong?' Christina raised her eyebrows.

Eileen shrugged. 'So it would seem. Marie doesn't say a lot, except for dark hints and occasional quite scurrilous references to his…how shall I put this delicately? Um, amorous accomplishments.'

5

Christina burst into peals of laughter. 'Mother, you have a wonderful way of putting things.'

'Well, you know,' Eileen said, perfectly deadpan, in a very bad Irish accent, 'I don't want to shock you, you being so young and all.'

'By today's standards,' Christina called down the stairs as she took her bag up, 'nineteen is quite elderly. I'll be down in a jiff to help.' She vanished, humming, behind a carelessly-slammed door.

Eileen smiled to herself as she pulled things out of the fridge and began washing lettuce, tomatoes, cucumber, red pepper, radishes and a rather sad-looking head of celery.

The back door creaked open and a blond head appeared in a shaft of low sunlight.

'Hello, Michael.'

'Hello, Mum. Is Christie home?'

'Yes, she is. Wash your hands first, Michael. You look filthy, and it's choir practice tonight.' But the latter part of the sentence was lost. Michael was already hurtling noisily up the stairs, shouting for Christina.

As she laid the table Eileen thought about Michael, how he had altered out of all recognition from the hunched, defensive, school-refusing five-year-old who had first come home with her. Then, his overburdened, young single mother, with two younger children to care for, had been unable to cope. Now, apart from being several inches taller, Michael had grown into a good-natured, patient and thoughtful boy. Or perhaps he had merely retrieved what had always been his.

A few minutes later he and Christina came downstairs together, arms round each other's shoulders. Looking at them Eileen thought how odd it was that Michael, someone else's son, was more like her than her own natural child, at least superficially. She and Michael were both tall, fair, slow-moving, sometimes clumsy, while Christina was tiny, slim, wiry, deceptively strong, with small, pointed features.

'You're nearly as tall as me,' Christina said. 'It shouldn't be allowed.'

Michael giggled. 'That's because you're a midget.'

Eileen put a loaf of bread, some cold meats, cheese, pickles and salad on the table. Michael buzzed about like an excited bee, chattering and getting in their way. Eventually they sat down and in a tiny quiet gap managed to say grace before starting to eat. The front door opened and banged shut. Heavy determined footsteps sounded on the thinly-carpeted stairs. Everyone looked up.

'Natasha's home,' Christina said.

Eileen put down her fork. 'Natasha!' She frowned. 'Food on the table.'

6

'Not hungry. On a diet,' came the distant reply in decidedly cranky tones.

'Don't worry, Mum,' Christina said. 'I'll talk to her later, when you and Michael are out. She'll be OK, she always is. It just takes a while.'

'Things are improving a bit with Tash,' Eileen said with a sigh, 'but there are still times when she behaves as if I were her bitterest enemy, for no reason that I can think of. And until recently she's seemed to delight in knocking about with the village dregs.'

Christina's eyebrows shot up. 'What a snob you are, Ma.'

'Well, it does seem about time she started acting like an adult instead of a thirteen-year-old at the mercy of her hormones.'

They ate for a while in silence, then Christina said, wiping every last smear of mayonnaise from her plate with a crust of bread, 'Maybe she needs to get away from here.'

'She can't afford to, not on her pittance. I suppose it's something she's stuck that job so long, but oddly I think she's grown to like it.'

'At least she's got some independence.'

'Michael, have you finished? Do you want some ice cream?' Eileen pushed back her chair and went to a curtained alcove in the kitchen behind which lurked an elderly and loudly-humming freezer. She thumped the door hard, then opened it with difficulty. 'This blessed door's sticking again,' she muttered. 'Will strawberry flavour be all right? I'll do a bit of shopping tomorrow while you're down at Charley's.'

'Strawberry's OK. Am I seeing Mummy tomorrow, then?'

'Yes. Had you forgotten?'

'And Harry and Ellie?'

'I guess so.'

'Will Christie still be here?'

'She's here till Sunday afternoon. You'll have plenty of time. Anyway, you haven't seen Mummy for a few weeks. It'll be nice. Christie and I can go shopping while you're there and get some things you like.'

Michael nodded. 'That's OK, then.'

'Finish up quickly now, and go and get washed. I don't want to be late.'

When he had gone Christina said, 'Doesn't he ever go to his mum's flat any more?'

'No,' Eileen said. 'That's never been reinstated. The visits at the Family Centre seem to go better, so we're sticking with it.'

'Is the boyfriend still around?'

'What, the one Michael took against? I don't think so. I think Denise is on her own again. Poor Denise. She doesn't seem to have much of a life.'

7

'Did Charley ever hear what happened to Michael's dad?' Christina said, filling the kitchen sink with hot water. 'It's like he vanished off the face of the earth.'

Eileen shrugged. 'Charley and I both have our suspicions, but I won't go into that. Little boys have very long ears.'

'Point taken. Why don't you go and get ready? I'll finish tidying up.'

'Right. Thanks, love.' Eileen paused by the stairs. 'I'm just thankful Michael seems so happy now. But, you know, it can't last for ever.'

'Can't it? Why not?'

'That's just not the way it works.'

'Couldn't you adopt him?'

'Somehow I don't think Denise would ever agree to that. Would you, if Michael was yours?' She called up the stairs. 'Get a move on, Michael, will you?' As she reached the landing, the phone rang. 'That'll be your dad, Christie.'

Ten minutes later Eileen and Michael left the house in a hurry, having remembered at the last moment that Bill, Michael's guinea-pig, had not had any supper. They waved goodbye to Christina who was still on the phone. It was dusk but still warm as they crunched across the drive and onto the pathless road for the five-minute walk to the church. Michael took Eileen's hand and swung it as they walked. The church bells had been ringing; they left a tinny echo in the still air.

'Mum.'

'Mm.'

'What are dregs?'

Eileen smiled slightly, then sighed. 'Sorry, Michael. That was not a very nice way to talk about people.'

'Why not?'

'Dregs are the bits you find at the bottom of a classy bottle of wine, so calling people dregs means they are the sludge at the bottom that nobody wants.'

'Are Tashie's mates like that, then?'

'No, of course not. Nobody is, at least, that's what we are told to believe, because God values everybody even if we don't always.'

'Is Tashie a dreg?'

'No, of course she isn't! I wish I'd never said it now. It wasn't a very kind thing to say anyway. Forget it, there's a love.'

'OK.'

After the gathering shadows outside, the church was brightly lit as they pushed open the heavy door. A knot of people stood at the back of the nave, by the bell-tower, talking as Eileen and Michael entered. On the far side of the church, behind the half-open door of the vestry, more voices could be heard: the choir, sorting out books and music, gathering for practice as the bell-ringers, finished with theirs for the week, made their way unhurriedly to home or pub.

Some bell-ringers were choir members too, and were even now detaching themselves from one group and making their way to join the other. Arthur Thompson, small, frail and elderly, his white hair immaculately combed, his old, dark suit and shining shoes formal, leant on the arm of his granddaughter, Georgina Quilley.

'Good evening, Eileen,' he said.

'Hello Arthur, hi Georgina,' Eileen said. 'How are you feeling today, Arthur?'

'A little better, thank you,' Arthur replied in his shaky voice. He had been in church choirs almost all his life, and although his voice was reedy now, nobody minded. A tenor who could sing in tune was a precious thing in a tiny choir.

Bell-ringers greeted Eileen as they ambled off towards the door. The two church-wardens—retired farmer Frank Aherne, red-faced, with bristling sideburns and corkscrew hair, port drinker's nose and dusty tweeds, and Richard Dyer, a businessman in his fifties, out of his city suit now and dressed for the rural weekend in balding corduroy—were the first to leave. Rumour had it that Richard Dyer was having an affair with Anita Bloodworth, wife of one of the bell-ringers, and had been for years. Eileen wondered where they were supposed to conduct their trysts. Don Bloodworth was usually at home, working in his huge greenhouse; and Annette Dyer, a woman of fragile temperament given to bouts of depression, likewise rarely left her house. Eileen, making her way up the nave in Michael's wake, suppressed a brief and shameless vision of Anita emerging from behind a haystack with straw in her hair and laddered tights. If the stories were true, though, she was sorry. Don was a bit of a bore, but well-intentioned. And she liked Annette Dyer, and pitied her, with her huge untidy house and garden, her crushing moods, and her relentlessly cheerful, loud and popularity-seeking husband. The Dyer children, two sons who had long since married and moved away, resembled their father, not least in treating their mother with blithe and patronising insensitivity. Privately Eileen wondered, as she often did looking at long-married couples, what had brought them together in the first place, and what, in Annette's case, had kept her from flight all these years. For a moment she thought of her own situation, and how it must appear to others. Mysterious, probably: a husband permanently away from home, and three children only one of whom she had given birth to. She walked into the vestry. Everybody was chattering, and Philip was calling from the organ, chivvying them to start.

Eileen took her place in the choir-stalls next to Georgina.

'Right, everyone, quiet down now, please,' Philip said. The little girls had a last snigger and came to order. Though he was never unkind, their respect for Philip had an element of fear in it. 'For Sunday, I thought we would do the Wesley. We all know that quite well, and perhaps Georgina can do the solo verses. All right, Georgina?' He glanced up momentarily from the lectern, his dark eyes seeking the girl out. 'Good. And the Stone setting of the Lord's Prayer. That's reasonably familiar. But we'd better begin working on something for the induction service. It's bound to happen sooner or later, and we might as well start preparing now, and decide what we're going to sing before half term.' At the mention of the induction there was a buzz of speculation. Philip quelled it by a tap of his baton on the lectern and an inscrutable glance that swept over every member of the choir. 'I thought we'd try this Bach anthem, "God is our hope and strength." It's not beyond us but there are some tricky bits and you'll have to count.' He smiled fleetingly. 'You get very little help from the accompaniment as I have a lot of twiddly semiquavers. Right—the music's in your folders, so let's give the Bach a run through and see how we get on.'

The first effort was, predictably, a shambles. It had no shape, and nobody could make much sense of it. But by the end of an hour it was hanging together; the steady four-crotchet beat had been hammered home; the foundations were laid. In addition, they had warmed up the Wesley and the Lord's Prayer for Sunday and run through an alternative to the Bach, an anthem by Ouseley which they had done a few times before. Sunday's hymns were given a cursory play-through, and then they were released.

'Anyone taking music home, please sign the list as usual,' Philip said as they disappeared.

Gillian Clayton, the only adult treble in the choir and mother of one of the little girls, cornered Eileen in the porch. 'Do you think he knows something about the new Rector?' she said. 'Seeing as he's dreaming up music for the induction.'

'I haven't a clue,' Eileen said. 'He'll know before we do, I suppose. But surely he's right. It can't be much longer.'

'Hm. Frank and Richard have been having their own way long enough, if you ask me,' Gillian said. 'I for one will be delighted when we get someone permanent. Oh well. No doubt we'll find out in good time. Are the children in the churchyard again? Joanne!'

After some hooting and shoving, four girls appeared from among the

10

gravestones and were taken away by Gillian. Michael was still inside. A moment later he emerged with Philip, who switched off the lights and locked the door. There was still light in the churchyard.

'Philip.'

Philip looked up. He looked nervous, embarrassed, ready to bolt. Eileen noticed his elderly jacket, chalk-flecked baggy trousers, scuffed brown shoes, a new maroon shirt at odds with the dusty tweed, the loosely-knotted tie.

'Marie came home from hospital this afternoon,' Eileen said. 'The operation went all right.'

Philip stared at his feet, then at Eileen, a dark stain spreading upwards from his collar. 'Good,' he muttered. 'I'm glad to hear it.' He made a visible effort, clearing his throat. 'So, um, when will she be able to sing again, do you think?'

'They said six weeks' convalescence, but I guess once her wound is healed singing will be OK. It hardly constitutes violent activity. I guess she'll be back in two or three weeks.'

'Yes. Well, um, give her my best wishes, won't you.' Michael started clattering about impatiently. Philip seemed relieved to be interrupted. 'Goodnight,' he said, making off down the path. 'See you on Sunday.'

'Come on, Michael. Let's go home.'

'What a strange man Philip Elsdon is,' Eileen said to Christina, after Michael had gone to bed. 'I told him about Marie, because I knew he wouldn't have asked. You'd think he'd make some polite enquiry at least. She's in his choir after all, quite apart from anything else.'

'I don't think you're supposed to know about the *anything else*, are you?' Christina said.

'That doesn't seem very realistic to me,' Eileen said. 'He knows Marie is my friend, he knows we talk. How can he think I don't know?'

'He probably thinks you disapprove,' Christina said, stretching her legs the length of the sagging sofa. 'He always seems uncomfortable, doesn't he? Guilty, even. Maybe he thinks you're going to stand in the vestry doorway and demand to know if his intentions are honourable.'

'I think it's all gone beyond the realm of intentions,' Eileen said, pursing her lips. 'Anyway, Marie's a grown-up. She's quite capable of making rotten decisions, just like the rest of us.' She smiled suddenly, kicked off her shoes, and flopped into a chair. 'How about making me a cup of coffee? You probably have no idea how exhausting Bach can be.'

'Sad, but true. I am such a Philistine. I'll put the kettle on.' Christina dragged herself up from the sofa and ruffled her mother's hair as she went into the kitchen. 'So, tell me, what's Philip really like?'

'Well, as you rightly said earlier, he's a fantastic organist, far too good for a backwater like Holton.'

'Bit of a mystery, then,' Christina said.

'Mm. But he's a good teacher too, though maybe you wouldn't expect that. He gets an amazing standard out of our little choir, considering there are only two men, three women, no, four if you count Georgina, four small girls and Michael. But he is a bit of a mystery, you're right. Sometimes I go up to the church to change the flowers or do a bit of dusting and he's there, practising. Only it isn't like practice, because there's nothing wrong with it. And I've played that organ, and I know I couldn't make it sing like he does. But if he notices me there, he packs up and leaves. It's odd, as if his gift is an embarrassment to him.'

Christina came in with two mugs of coffee. 'It doesn't seem to hang together, what you've told me about him, with having a fling with Marie.'

'I know what you mean,' Eileen said. 'I get the impression he hasn't had too much female company, and Marie's just knocked him off his feet.'

'So where does he go when he's not here?'

'Oh, he has a job. And a flat, I believe. He teaches at that private boys' school the other side of Caxford. I can't remember its name.'

Christina sipped her coffee. 'And we have an idea what Marie sees in *him*,' she said with a wicked grin.

'He's actually not bad-looking,' Eileen said. 'Anyway, people are peculiar. Who knows anything about why one person is drawn to another?'

'Who, indeed? I'm going to take my coffee upstairs, Mum. My dear sister has persuaded me to go to the pub with her tonight. She's paying, so I'm not arguing.'

'Oh, OK. Try not to roll home drunk, won't you?'

'Chance would be a fine thing. Knowing Tash we'll probably have to make a half last all night.'

Eileen lay propped up in bed, her Bible open at Romans 12. With her reading glasses on the end of her nose, beneath her bent head the small print glowed in the light of her bedside lamp.

"So then, my brothers and sisters, because of God's great mercy to us, I appeal to you: offer yourselves as a living sacrifice to God, dedicated to his service and pleasing to him. This is the true worship that you should offer."

Eileen looked up, catching a dark glimpse of herself in the mirror across the room. St. Paul was a single-minded idealist and a hard taskmaster. Inspired by his own great vision, he had given up all dedication to self. And who could contest his argument? God has been merciful to us, and we, in responsive love, must sacrifice ourselves to him. *But there's something in me that's fighting this inch by inch, even though I think it's right. What is it? Something atavistically wicked? Pride? The old Adam? Or just a desire to survive as a self?* As she pondered this puzzle, not for the first time, it occurred to her that what she read and, indeed, believed, instead of meshing smoothly with her thoughts, seemed to shriek and grind like a machine devoid of oil.

She went back to her reading.

"Do not conform yourselves to the standard of this world, but let God transform you inwardly by a complete change of your mind. Then you will be able to know the will of God—what is good and is pleasing to him and is perfect."

That must be it. I am resisting that complete inward transformation. Like everything else, I want to do it by myself.

Thinking about this independence of spirit, her thoughts drifted, and she found herself mentally picturing her mother standing at the back door of the house where Eileen had grown up, a house not unlike the one she lived in now, but neater, with a well-ordered garden. Her mother stood, one hand shading her eyes against the sun, the other shaking a duster, wearing a floral apron, tall, broad and fair like her older daughter, with that same dancing light in her eyes.

It was she who has made me the way I am, in great measure. She taught me, both in what she said and how she just was, to depend on myself. Those early habits take some breaking, and I haven't done it yet, if I ever do.

She tried again.

"And because of God's gracious gift to me I say to every one of you: do not think of yourself more highly than you should. Instead be modest in your thinking, and judge yourself according to the amount of faith that God has given you."

But that was the hard part, simply because those standards were not of this world, which was always trying to persuade us to judge ourselves and others by any number of different criteria. And the world used methods both fair and foul, whereas God's were always an appeal to the better bits of us.

She read on. There was the passage about being part of Christ's body and working harmoniously with the other parts, followed by the right use of one's gifts. She sighed. What were her gifts exactly? They all seemed so nebulous, so commonplace. Perhaps she was suffering from some kind of spiritual blindness, so that any way ahead was featureless, devoid of signposts.

She gathered herself with an effort and finished the chapter. Full of instruction about living the Christian life out in practice and defeating evil with good, she had no trouble with it theoretically, hard as it was to do.

She closed her Bible and let it rest in her lap.

So what was this obstacle? The orthodox would have said it was sin, no doubt. Perhaps it was her whole situation of rebelliousness. Perhaps she should have gone dutifully off to Scotland with David. Maybe that was what some people thought. Was it what God thought?

Weariness settled on her like a weight. She put the Bible on her bedside table and closed her eyes. A thirty-year-old scene rewound itself before her mental vision: herself aged eighteen, coming home from her secretarial course, walking up the garden path, putting her key in the lock, and finding her father inexplicably home early from work, sitting on the sofa with his younger daughter weeping beside him. As soon as Eileen entered the room, before she had time to utter a word, Marilyn had leapt up and flung herself into her sister's arms, spilling out between sobs the terrible news: how she had come home from school that afternoon to find their mother collapsed by the kitchen range, a broken milk-jug in her hand, dead of an aneurysm at forty-one.

Everything changed after that. Her father seemed shocked into immobility; Marilyn, always rather childlike, began to treat her sister as if she were another mother. Eileen felt years older than either of them. She had informed what few relatives there were, organized the funeral, paid the bills and run the house. Everything her mother had said to her was true. Other people were kind, charming, lovable even, but not very reliable. They seemed, in Eileen's experience, to lack stuffing. Only she and her mother were rocks of strength, and her mother was gone.

Eileen thought of her family, how distant they seemed. Her father had died of lung cancer barely two years after his wife's death, his body emaciated, his spirit crushed. Marilyn emigrated to Australia with her new husband and baby son. She had been there now twenty-five years, and never once returned. Nor had Eileen visited her. The sisters exchanged Christmas cards and photographs of children and grandchildren. But it seemed to Eileen that a door had shut firmly on her early life, and now it was alien, like someone else's story.

Eileen leaned over and turned off the lamp. She resettled her pillows and lay down with a sigh. In the darkness she contemplated her twenty-one-year-old self as if she was a stranger from another world.

Perhaps I coped so well because I was so ignorant.

Marilyn was gone, her parents were dead. Eileen settled the debts, sold the house, disposed briskly of the contents, sent half the proceeds to Marilyn and banked the rest. Then she took a week off from college to consider what to do, and went to the coast for a holiday.

She looked forward to that week as an oasis of calm: the chance to look back, gather her thoughts, and, free of duties, to grieve for her parents. She grieved too for herself, young and alone; but the part of her that was her mother's doing exulted. If there had been more time, young would have meant full of hope, and alone would have been another word for free. As it was, life picked her up and whirled her about before her feet fairly settled on the ground. One warm afternoon, on the crowded pier of the little seaside town, she met a young sailor called David Harding.

And the rest, as they say, is history.

In the warm darkness Eileen tried to pray. She asked God to open the eyes of her spirit so that she could see what it was he wanted of her. More truthfully, she prayed for the desire to change. She prayed for the world, her church and her children. She prayed especially for Natasha. Then her mind wandered, undisciplined, back into the past.

Eileen had never fathomed what David had seen in her, but she had a clear recollection of what had attracted her to him. She smiled to herself in the darkness of her quiet bedroom, remembering the twenty-four-year-old David, his compact frame, his skin tanned from months of tropic sun, his worldly-wisdom—or so it seemed to her—his sheer ease and lack of awkwardness, his naturalness, the life in him that was as powerful as a magnet. He had travelled, he had seen exotic places and met uncommon people, and for Eileen he was a revelation. Every day, and soon every night, was spent together. David was an intense, hungry and demanding lover, and Eileen, dazed and overwhelmed, discovered something akin in herself.

How things change.

Why hadn't it ended there? Perhaps it should have. But after his leave was over David wrote letters from sea, long, literate letters, telling her about his life and the things he saw, particularly the animals and birds, which even then were his deepest interest, and begging her to wait for him. He was full of plans. Almost overnight her world took on a very different hue. So long grey and circumscribed, now it seemed to abound with promise. How could she have withstood him?

The dream came back to her. She was running through the woods in unsuitable shoes. The trees were rain-soaked and the paths slick, and she slipped and slithered and fell to her hands and knees. Plastered with mud, she struggled back to her feet and ran on, tears rolling down her face, her breath coming in painful gasps. Michael was missing, and she feared for his life. Someone had taken him. Who? Why? He was someone else's child, and she had failed to protect him. She felt the weight of responsibility like a roof suddenly caving in.

Saturday 18th May 1996

The weather had broken in the night. When Eileen woke she was aware of the sound of water dripping gently from the branches of the apple tree as they moved in the freshening wind. She opened the curtains and saw a day of rolling cloud; beyond the garden the trees were shaken and restless.

She dressed and went downstairs. Tillie heaved herself from her basket and ambled towards her, the black plume of her tail waving lazily in greeting.

'I thought we'd go out early this morning, old girl,' Eileen whispered. 'Before too many people are about. Before it gets too hot.'

As they left the house Bill let out a volley of squeaks, anxiously enquiring after his breakfast. Eileen collected her boots from the garden shed; the long grass was wet.

The rain had slimed the long-dry paths and she had to walk carefully. The low hawthorns and hazels dripped water steadily, letting loose a sudden shower every time the wind strengthened. Today she went a different way: entering under the trees, after a short distance she turned left, and before long stood at the beginning of a broad ride bordered with oak, ash and chestnut, big trees in full summer foliage, looking this morning rather forbidding under the cloudy sky. A jay broke cover and swooped ahead of her, weaving from side to side of the pathway till it found refuge. For a while the path was level, then it narrowed and began to descend. On each side, under the bigger trees, a tangle of lower bushes grew and among the leaf litter from previous years a blackbird foraged noisily. A little further down, in a small open space round a spreading oak, she disturbed a flock of long-tailed tits, following each other in a crowd from tree to tree.

This part of the woods was narrower than elsewhere, and before long Eileen came out from the cover of the trees into a descending belt of heathland, peppered with gorse bushes flowering yellow. Above, the grey sky was more broken, and tiny gleams of sunlight were beginning to break through. The air was cool, but warmth was already rising from the ground.

17

As she approached, several woodpigeons left the trees with a loud clatter of wings. Behind her the dog was beginning to pant. Eileen perched on a stump and waited for her to catch up. She looked down and stroked the dog's smooth black head. 'Take it easy, old dear,' she said. 'Have a bit of a rest, then we'll go back.'

After a while they turned left again, skirting the trees. They climbed the steep hill dotted with ragwort and ox-eye daisy, and after a few minutes arrived at the back wall of the church. Eileen closed the gate behind them. As she did so she heard a sound from the woods behind her, like a cracking of dry twigs. She turned quickly, her skin tingling, half-expecting to see that pale, dirty face, and the striped jumper; but there was no one there. She looked up at the squat tower as a sudden gleam of sunlight broke from the cloud. Over the church roof two herons flew, their long lazy wingbeats deceptively swift. She shivered, and caught herself thinking paranoid thoughts about lurking stalkers. Then she shook her head crossly and turned towards home.

When Eileen returned from the woods she found her daughter sitting at the table, sipping a cup of black tea, with a book propped up against her cereal bowl.

'You're early,' Eileen said. 'What's this?'

Christina made a face. 'Shakespeare. Exams on Monday week, so I figured I'd better do some work, instead of fooling around having sex and taking drugs like I do the rest of the year.'

'Ha, ha.'

'Well, you know what we feckless students are.'

'I thought you all had business plans these days,' Eileen said. 'I wouldn't have thought there'd be time among all that ambition for normal activities like sex and drugs.'

Christina laughed. 'Maybe I'm an old-fashioned student, you know, all-night parties and left-wing politics.'

Michael appeared, and in five minutes he demolished a mountain of toast, fed Bill, begged for his pocket money and disappeared to collect Stephen. Then it was Natasha's turn, mumbling her greetings and farewells before haring off to catch the 8.10 bus to work. Peace returned. Eileen ate her breakfast, flipped through the post, cleaned out Bill's hutch and washed the dishes.

'I'm going to the shop for Marie,' she told Christina. 'I'll be back before lunch.'

Holton had one tiny crammed shop which doubled as a post office. It was run by Nora Meadows, with the help of a tremulous pensioner, Mrs. Pickett, who manned the shop while Nora took charge of the post office. Nora's husband Reg had been postmaster until struck down by emphysema. Now he was confined to bed, dependent on oxygen, any exertion causing bouts of wheezing breathlessness which left his lips blue and hands shaking uncontrollably.

When Eileen pushed open the oak-and-glass door, jangling the bell, the shop was already crowded, though there were only two other customers: Peter Quilley, father of Georgina, and Kit Muldoon, a lady of questionable reputation who presided over her two equally unsavoury sons in a ramshackle and insanitary cottage at the end of an unmade road behind the shop. Kit kept chickens and a goat and her house was full of half-feral cats which had never known the benefits of house-training. Consequently it, and she, smelled.

She was swathed in dusty, shapeless black, her feet in ancient slippers. She turned to Eileen with a grin that was almost wolfish. 'Morning, dear. How's the world treating you?'

'All right, thank you, Kit,' Eileen said. 'How are you?'

'You know me, dear, a martyr to my gout and my boys.' She picked up her newspaper and rolled it under her arm. 'How's your friend Marie?' she asked slyly.

'Recuperating,' Eileen said. 'Good morning, Peter.'

'Course, I've always had trouble with my women's parts,' Kit said, patting herself vaguely around the midriff. Eileen smiled to see Peter Quilley wince. Nora Meadows and Doreen Pickett simply looked at one another with eyes ever so slightly raised towards the ceiling.

'Mind, dear, they do say as that operation mucks you up inside,' Kit went on. 'Still, I suppose,' she said with an air of false innocence, 'that won't matter to her, being on her own.'

Peter Quilley picked up his change, smiled painfully and left the shop.

'A loaf and a pint of milk, please, Nora,' Eileen said.

'Getting a few supplies in for Marie?' asked Nora. 'Coming along all right, is she?'

'Yes, she said she was fine. How are you, Nora? You look tired.'

'You know how it is, dear,' Nora said quietly. 'But thank you for asking.'

'Well, you know things can go wrong with them operations,' Kit said, showing no sign of going about her business. 'She's still young enough to find herself a feller; she don't want to muck herself up.'

'Your lad was in here earlier,' Mrs. Pickett told Eileen.

'I hear,' Kit said, 'he can't read yet. That so, dear?'

'No,' Eileen said, compressing her lips against an acid reply. 'He can read. But yes, he does have some difficulties.'

19

'I had a cousin once, he never learned to read or write, but it never did him no harm. Well, I'm off. Give my regards to Marie, dear, won't you? Tell her from me not to move around too much or she might muck up her insides. Cheerio, all.' She left, laughing wheezily under her breath.

'That woman!' said Nora after Kit had rounded the corner. 'She's got a tongue like a viper. Open the window, will you, Doreen. It smells diabolical in here.'

How was it, Eileen wondered, that in a village such as Holton almost everyone felt they must know everyone else's business? Marie's relationship with Philip was a matter of common speculation despite their discretion, though few would have pursued their interest as openly as Kit Muldoon.

As Eileen was leaving Doreen Pickett said, 'Any news of a new vicar yet, do you know, Mrs. Harding?'

'No, nothing's been said apart from a lot of gossip. But it can't be too long, I'd guess. The Armitages have been gone almost nine months now.'

'Do you hear from them at all? How are they getting on?'

'We chat on the phone sometimes,' Eileen said, smiling. 'They're well. It's a nice peaceful life for them at Lambury.'

'He was a lovely chap, that Mr. Armitage,' said Nora, stacking piles of newspapers on the shop counter and ticking off deliveries in her notebook. 'Always had such lovely manners, didn't he? He was good to Reg too. Came by and saw him a few times. Reg isn't much of a believer, but he was glad of the company.'

'He even looked like you imagine a saint might look,' said Doreen Pickett. She giggled suddenly. 'Mr. Armitage I mean, dear, not Reg.'

'Not much saintly about him, you're right there,' Nora said. 'I'll go and make him a pot of tea while it's quiet. Bye, dear.'

On her way to Marie's Eileen thought about Geoffrey Armitage. She knew what Mrs. Pickett meant: with his calm, lined face and rather long white hair he always looked somehow other-worldly, and his soft voice, with its hint of a country accent, must have been soothing to the sick and dying. But Eileen knew that behind the gentle face was a keen intellect and an ability to argue equal to anyone she had encountered, whether face-to-face or in print. He, and his wife Celia, had helped Eileen in her own tortuous journey to God, never minding challenging questions and often vehement doubts.

Eileen pictured Celia now, in her beautiful garden with an armful of flowers, a battered sunhat shading her eyes, in baggy trousers and a grass-stained shirt of her husband's, nodding thoughtfully as Eileen

20

propounded her theories, as if she had all the time there was; and Geoffrey, who was a scholar, had been patient with her amateurish struggles, absorbed all her angry resistance, and explained points of Scripture with quiet conviction. Their self-giving humility and generosity of spirit had been for Eileen, more than anything else, a signpost to the master they served. Even now, telephoning to chat and exchange news, she could ask Geoffrey about things that had arisen from her study of the Bible. But there was a shadow on their friendship, though it was never mentioned openly. Eileen knew that Geoffrey and Celia were troubled by the situation with David, clearly seeing it as an impediment to her spiritual progress, something in need of repentance and forgiveness. They were right. But she couldn't do anything, not now.

She came to Marie's white-painted wooden gate. She walked up the garden path, bordered by straggling fuchsia bushes and jam-tart daisies, and knocked softly on the door.

Eileen pushed open the door onto a small hallway. The place was as neat as always. 'It's me, Marie.'

To the left of the hallway was a kitchen, to the right a small sitting-room. Marie sat with her legs up on a sofa patterned with huge pink roses.

'I'll put these in the kitchen.' Eileen held up the milk and bread.

'That's lovely. Thanks, Eileen.'

Marie's soft Irish voice matched her appearance. She wore her wavy brown-going-grey hair long, and her body was generously proportioned. Had her features been harder she might have appeared a trifle tarty, but Marie Clements had a face as soft, round and innocent as a child's and clear, guileless eyes. 'Come in dear, do. It's lovely to see you.'

She was looking a little pale and tired, but otherwise Eileen saw no reason for alarm. She sat in a squashy armchair that matched the sofa. 'How are you feeling this morning?'

'Well, I woke up a few times in the night, and it's a bit sore, especially trying to get out of bed to go to the loo, but not bad, thank you.'

'Had any visitors?'

'You're my first, bar one.'

'Oh?' Eileen said, thinking it was a bit early for Philip to have driven over from Caxford.

'Our Michael dropped by,' said Marie. 'He must have come from the shop, because he gave me a packet of mints.'

'I'm sure they'll aid your recovery no end,' Eileen said with a smile.

'Well, actually, you know, I rather think they will. Put the kettle on, would you? I've a terrific thirst. I think it must be an after-effect of the anaesthetic.'

Eileen made coffee in Marie's spotless, matching, floral-patterned china mugs and brought it into the sitting-room on a tray.

'Is Stephanie home?' she asked as she and Marie sat drinking.

'Asleep, I think. She doesn't usually appear before midday, unlike Christina.' A note of disapproval crept into Marie's voice; it jarred with her habitual gentleness and tolerance.

A vision of Stephanie, Marie's eighteen-year-old daughter, rose unbidden in her many guises before Eileen's inner eyes: green hair-dye, ghoulish eye make-up, metallic skirts, aggressive boots, and as Eileen had once, startled, seen her, coming out of the bathroom draped in a towel, her face bland and ordinary. On that occasion she had scuttled without a greeting into her bedroom, there, presumably, to recreate herself behind a closed door. Stephanie's movements were always mysterious. After a school career in which she had excelled only in terrorizing her fellow-pupils and facing down the teachers, she had no job but plenty of money. Eileen, sipping her coffee, wondered uncomfortably where she got it from. But she did not ask. Marie worried enough about her hard, rebellious child.

'So, how was choir practice?' asked Marie with an air of naivety, belied a moment later by a broad grin.

Eileen told her what they had practised. 'I've an idea Philip knows something. He actually mentioned the induction in an off-hand sort of way. Incidentally, I told him you were home, and he wanted to know when you'd be back. He seemed terribly embarrassed.'

'He's getting fed up with all the daft chit-chat in this place,' Marie said softly, stretching her shapely legs on the sofa. 'We don't make a big thing of it, you know, and it's not as if either of us is cheating on anybody.'

'True,' Eileen said. 'People just love to feel they're in there with their neighbours' business, don't they? But it has its plus side too. They help as well as interfere.'

'Yes, I suppose so.'

'And also people are intrigued by Philip. They don't know what to make of him.'

'He's not so mysterious,' said Marie. 'Not as a man, I mean. As a creative person, I grant you, he is baffling, but anyone with a gift like his is hard for us lesser creatures to fathom, don't you think?'

'Hm. He certainly appears to be on a different plane from the rest of us at times. Maybe that's why he seems so awkward with ordinary life.'

'Have you got a bit of a down on poor Philip, Eileen?' asked Marie with a mock frown.

Eileen sighed. 'Not really. I would hate to see you come a cropper, but I suppose you're old enough to make your own decisions.'

'Just about, though not quite as old as you.'

Eileen made a rude face.

'So,' Marie said, 'you don't see me as the painted *femme fatale* and Philip as the poor innocent caught by my wiles?'

'I can't say that I've thought of it like that, no.'

'Perhaps you are just the teensiest bit prejudiced against men generally.'

'Perhaps I am.'

'I'm not sure I know why, though. David didn't do anything so very bad, did he? He didn't beat you, or fool around with other women, as far as I know.'

'He did nothing worse really,' Eileen said with a stab of pain, 'than disappoint me.'

'Ah, well,' said Marie softly, 'that may be a commoner experience than you realise.'

'Maybe I disappointed him.'

'I think you puzzled him, but that again is nothing unusual, is it? I don't suppose he has ever understood why you didn't happily up sticks and go off to Scotland.'

'Do *you* understand?'

'I think so. Perhaps not entirely. I guess it's down to what happened over the years, the way things just go bad.'

'I thought it would be different. I was young and stupid then, maybe. As opposed to middle-aged and stupid. It's hard to believe things can go so sour, though. It was great at first.'

'But then, you had...what? Seven years of trying to have a child? That puts pressure on people.'

'Mm.'

'Then you adopted Natasha, and almost at once you were pregnant with Christina. That happens oftener than you think.'

'I know. And two babies under a year old is a bit of a challenge.'

'You must have been exhausted.'

'I was. And the house was falling to pieces, and when David came home after months at sea he was for ever swanning about in the woods all day with his sandwich and his binoculars, and coming home full of all the wonderful things he'd seen, and I was not impressed.'

'He certainly was away a lot.'

'I got very hard and mean.'

'Nonsense. You are never hard and mean.'

'I was to him.'

Marie sighed and put her cup on the table. 'Well, dear, it's water under the bridge. I can't see you changing your mind now.'

'No. Too late for that. I do wonder sometimes, though, whether I have been terribly wrong.'

Marie shook her head. 'It's probably too late for such thoughts as that, too,' she said gently.

'You are braver than me, I think,' Eileen said after a moment.

'Whatever makes you say that?'

'You had a much worse time of it than I did. With Ray. But here you are, apparently willing to give the whole risky business another shot.'

Marie laughed, her eyes crinkling up. 'I can't think of two people as unlike as Ray and Philip. And I'm so much older now. Maybe not wiser, no, but certainly more carefree. Philip's a dear, I'm happy and so is he. What more do you want?'

Walking home later that morning Eileen thought about the oddity of marriage and its many permutations. In Marie's case it had certainly been disastrous. Marie had come over from Ireland is search of work, a naïve twenty-year-old who had known little but a large, loving family and a few careless affairs. Against such a man as Ray Clements she was defenceless. His pride and guile and bitter cleverness were all hidden, at first, beneath a veneer of attentive charm and good looks. But, with the honeymoon barely over, the real Ray had surfaced. Marie had endured six years of abuse at his hands, abuse which had worsened after the birth of Stephanie, when Marie had suffered a bout of post-natal depression. Ray had used her vulnerability to torture her with a sense of abject failure.

In the end it was he who brought the fragile edifice of their marriage crashing down. One horrible day, when some plan of his own had sunk, stinging his pride and feeding his frustration, he had beaten Marie and wrecked the house. There was even some hint that he had ill-treated Stephanie, then aged four, but Marie had never enlarged on this, as if it was too painful to admit to conscious consideration. That night he went from the house leaving wreckage behind him, and he never came back.

Eileen was so deep in her thoughts as she entered the house that she barely noticed Christina, who was making a stack of sandwiches at the kitchen table.

'You look as if you'd completely forgotten I was even here!' Christina said. 'What were you thinking about with such a gloomy expression?'

24

'Not gloomy exactly. I was thinking about Marie's ex, Ray Clements.'

'Stephanie's dad.'

'Yes. Rather a nasty character.'

'No wonder Stephanie's so weird. Marie's really nice, but Stephanie is a head-case.'

'I don't suppose she's all bad.'

'Well, as you know, Tash and I haven't forgiven her for being cruel to Tillie when she was a puppy.'

'Christie, that was years ago! You can't have been more than five or six.'

'Well, I know. I hope she has improved. But she was a horrible child. Marie deserves better. Someone nice like me, who kindly makes sandwiches for lunch.'

'Thank you, dear. But, you know, Marie would say Stephanie deserved better than to have Ray for a father.'

'Hindsight is a great thing. Poor Marie, up to her ears in guilt. I hope you don't feel at all guilty.'

'Occasionally.'

'Well, Tash and I aren't especially monstrous, so I guess you've done OK. When are you due at Social Services?'

'Three.'

'I'll come with you. I could do with a bit of a break.'

In the end it was a rush to get ready. Michael came back from the woods late, hungry and dirty. Christina was sent in search of a clean T shirt while Michael demolished sandwiches with blinding speed and little refinement. Then they bundled into the car and set off for Caxford. The sun came out through the watery clouds in long, slanting beams. The heat was building up again, and it was windless and sticky.

Eileen parked in the car park of the small supermarket and from there they walked the short distance to the Social Services building. They saw Michael in at the front door and left him, promising to pick him up at five. He knew the way and bounded up the stairs two at a time. From an upstairs window a face appeared and someone waved.

Eileen waved back. 'Charley,' she said. Charlotte Robbins had been Michael's social worker from the beginning, before his placement with Eileen.

'I've never met Charley,' Christina said. 'What's she like? You've never said much about her.'

'Hm…young, not tall, keen and chatty, long curly blonde hair, bouncy and bubbly, big boobs. But bright and professional. And she

25

really listens. That's unusual. I have noticed, though, when there are any men present their eyes are out on stalks, even the older ones who should know better. Sometimes looks like Charley's are a disadvantage.'

'How depressingly predictable.'

'Why, are students any different?'

'Not at all. Even the lecturers have a tendency to ogle the blonde and buxom.'

Eileen sighed. 'Not much hope for us, then, is there? Though I suppose we are blonde. Ish.'

Christina looked at her mother with eyebrows raised, and there was an edge to her voice. 'Why, are you getting lonely in your old age, Mother?'

Eileen grinned. 'Aren't we all?'

Christina shook her head. 'No, I'm not. I'd rather be self-sufficient. I see such a lot of damage done and time wasted with some of my friends, hanging round the phone, mooning over some silly youth who's probably forgotten her and gone off to football.'

'You sound like someone twice your age.'

Christina laughed. 'I am twice my age. Shall we shop first, or go for a cup of tea somewhere?'

'Tea first, then if we get anything frozen we won't be leaving it to defrost in the car.'

On their way to the tea shop they crossed a small side road, wide enough for only one vehicle, at the end of which was a shabby-looking building.

'We're thinking of going there tonight,' said Christina. 'Hang out with the locals, have a few drinks, last fling before exams.'

Eileen looked at the now-extinct neon sign, which said *Hotspot Nite Club*.

'Rather you than me. It looks like a real dive. And who's *we*?'

'Natasha and me. I think she knows a few people there.'

'Well, I hope you'll keep an eye on each other.'

'Don't fret. We'll keep our hands on our money, our legs tightly crossed, decline all suspect substances and come home by taxi.'

'Very sensible.'

They pushed open the door of the little café, ordered, and sat down at a table near the window.

After a sip or two Eileen said, 'How was your dad last night?'

'OK. He gave me a rundown on all the new birds he's seen. They're having a big open day soon, with press and TV coming, so he's very busy.'

There was a thoughtful silence for a few moments, then Christina said, 'It's very beautiful up there, you know.'

Eileen looked up, startled. 'What? You've actually been there?'

'Yes. I went there for a few days during the Easter vac., just before I went back to Exeter.'

'You never said.'

'I suppose I wanted to take it all in and mull it over first. Then other stuff got in the way.' She gave her mother a long, level look. 'Do you want to know what it's like?'

'Why not?'

'Well now. Glen Achuil is surrounded by mountains. It's in a narrow valley, with trees going up on each side, pines of course. There are goldcrests and firecrests there, and hawfinches and crossbills. There's a small loch, with hides round the edges, lots of water-birds, and some exotic species visiting from time to time. It's very peaceful, full of birdsong, and with that wonderful smell pine trees have, very fresh.'

'And your dad?'

'He has a solid little timber cottage, back from the main entrance, with log fires, all very cosy, and a small garden. He seems settled.'

Eileen stirred her tea thoughtfully. 'Will you go there again, do you think?'

'Probably. When the exams are over, maybe. Dad doesn't come down here any more, does he? I like to see him, he likes to see me, I think.'

Eileen felt that she was being tested. Something like fear began to close in around her.

Christina said, 'I was thinking of asking Natasha if she'd like to come with me. Do you think she would?'

'Well, she isn't much into wildlife, but I think she'd like to see her dad, and how he's living.'

'I'll ask her. By the way, I'm definitely travelling this summer.'

'Oh? Where are you thinking of?'

'Just Europe. I'm going with my friends Jenny and Isabel. We're going to get those cheap rail tickets. I thought I'd spend a few days in Scotland first.'

'It sounds like fun.'

There was silence for a while as they finished their tea. The little café was filling up.

'Mum.'

'What?'

'Will you ever go to Scotland?'

'What, to visit, or to live?'

27

'Either way.'

'I don't know.'

'You don't want to think about it, do you? Is it because if you did you'd find no reason not to go?'

Eileen felt suddenly as if her heart had plummeted into her stomach. 'Christie, the fact is, I don't know if I could live with your dad any more. It's gone on too long.'

Christina's expression gave nothing away, but her eyes seemed intensely blue. 'Yes, I've noticed that. Sometimes things seem to start small enough, and grow out of all proportion as time passes.' She took a deep breath. 'Well, Mother, it's your life. Never say I interfere. But the chances are, as you say, it's too late now.' She smiled. Eileen felt sympathy there, but also sadness. 'What do you want out of life, Ma? You never say.'

'I'm not sure I want anything.'

'Doesn't everyone want something?'

'I suppose so. I can't think of anything I want, though, not for myself. Apart from some space to think my own thoughts, a bit of peace perhaps. I'll think about it and let you know, shall I?'

'I'll hold you to that,' Christina said. She looked at her watch. 'We'd better go and get the shopping, or we'll be late collecting Michael.'

They paid the bill and left. Across the road from the café was the florist's where Natasha worked.

'Who's that?' Christina nudged her mother.

'Who?'

'In the shop, talking to Natasha.'

Eileen looked across the road. Natasha was standing at the shop counter, writing something in an order book. Leaning on the other side of the counter was a man.

Eileen shook her head. 'Never seen him before. Why?'

'Oh, nothing. He's rather good looking, isn't he? And Natasha is grinning quite idiotically.'

'I can't keep up with Natasha's boyfriends. She's seemed quiet recently, though.'

'I'll see if I can dig some info out of her tonight.'

'You're a terrible tease to your sister, Christie. You, of course, are immune to such simple girlish things.'

'Like I said, Mother,' Christina said lightly, 'I look after myself, and I'm careful.'

'Very wise,' Eileen said. But inwardly she felt a wave of sadness, and wondered if her own example had made Christina so prematurely sober and wary.

'Here we are,' Christina said. 'Have you got your list?'

In the end they had to hurry to get the shopping done in time to collect Michael. The sunshine had brought more people out, and the checkouts were crowded. Eventually they threw the bags into the boot of the car and headed back to Social Services.

Michael was waiting by the reception desk. He had a carrier bag in his hand.

'Hello, Michael. What have you got there?'

'Oh, stuff from Mummy,' Michael mumbled.

Eileen was immediately aware that something was wrong, or at least different. Michael was always rather quiet after he had seen his mother and siblings, but today there was a discomfort about him that was almost palpable. It was evident in his downcast eyes, the way he slouched, his fidgeting feet.

Christina was aware of it too. 'Come on, curly,' she said. 'I've bought you some sweets. You can eat them in the car, but you have to share them with me. Or else.'

'Or else what?' shouted Michael, his usual self returning as he squared up to Christina. 'You don't scare me!'

The two of them teased and sparred all the way back to the car, but during the journey home Michael was quiet, as if sunk in deep thought.

'Mummy all right?' asked Eileen. 'How are Harry and Ellie?'

'OK. We played a bit. Harry's not too bad now.'

'How's Charley?'

'OK. She said to tell you she'd ring you Monday.'

'Oh? Why?'

'I don't know.'

'All right. We'll talk about it later.'

Christina and Natasha planned to leave at eight thirty, taking the last bus into Caxford. Another bus returned at about eleven, but that was too early for them. They put the shopping away, fed the animals, walked the dog, and had a meal. The two girls were upstairs, shrieking with mirth at each other's proposed outfits, putting on makeup, monopolising the bathroom. Michael fidgeted, hanging around the kitchen.

'Is it bedtime?'

'It is nearly. Shall I read to you?'

'Yes, in a minute. Can I get Bill out?'

'All right, for a little while.'

Michael sat at the kitchen table, stroking Bill, who lay against his shoulder, a black furry blob.

'Mum.'

'Yes.'

'Today, when I went to see Mummy, there was a man with her.'

'Oh? Has Mummy got a new boyfriend?'

'No.' Michael looked up at her, his expression inscrutable. 'It was my dad.'

'What!' Eileen felt as if she had physically reeled, though in reality she was standing quite still, dishcloth in hand. 'You mean Andy, your real dad?'

Michael nodded. 'That's why Charley is going to ring you. Monday morning.'

'I wonder why she didn't tell me he would be there. Then I could have told you, and it wouldn't have been such a...surprise, would it?'

'Charley didn't know he was coming. He just came along with Mummy and Harry and Ellie. I didn't remember him.' He said this with an air of puzzled disappointment.

'Of course you didn't.'

'But he remembered me. It felt funny to see him.'

'Funny nice, or funny nasty?'

'Funny nice, I think. He gave me stuff.'

'What stuff, Michael?'

'A football shirt, a red one, and some sweets.'

'Heavens, your teeth will drop out. So, did Daddy talk to you much?'

'Yes, lots. Mummy was talking to Charley, and the kids were mucking around with the toys.'

'What did you talk about?'

'Oh, like where he's been and what he wants to do.'

'I see.' Though clearly she did not.

'He said he wants to come back. To be with Mummy and be a family. He said he wants me to come back too.'

Eileen looked at Michael, her brain racing. He seemed anxious. She forced herself to speak calmly.

'So where has he been all this time, Michael? Do you know?'

'Yes. He's been in prison. He robbed a place, a factory or somewhere, and he hurt someone, a security man it was, but he said he didn't mean to hurt him, it was an accident. Then they put him in prison for a long time, but they let him out because he was good in there. He said he thought about things in prison, and now he's sorry he did a lot of wrong stuff. He says he's different now and he wants to look after us.'

'What do you think?'

'I don't know. Mum, will they take me away?'

30

Eileen sat down beside him and put her arm around his shoulders. Bill squeaked in protest. 'Nothing's going to happen that you don't agree to,' she said firmly, hoping it was the truth. 'What would you like to happen?'

'I don't know. I want to be with Mummy and Daddy and Harry and Ellie, but I want to be here with you as well.'

'Don't worry about it for now. Nothing's going to happen straight away. I'll talk to Charley about it on Monday, and I'll give you any news after school.'

'OK.' Michael was quiet for a moment, resting his head on Eileen's shoulder. 'Mum.'

'Mm.'

'If I had to go back to my mummy and daddy, would I be allowed to take Bill with me?'

'Of course. Bill is yours. But first you'd have to make sure that was all right with your family.'

'Yes,' said Michael, obviously deep in his thoughts. 'Because Bill would pine without me, wouldn't he?'

'I expect so. Now, Michael, let's not worry about it now. Between us we'll get it all sorted out, you'll see.'

Later as she hugged him goodnight Michael said, 'If I go back with them, will you miss me?'

Eileen felt something like a tiny electric shock prickle her skin. *Good heavens, in his mind he's already gone.* 'Of course I would. But if you were happy, I would be too.'

'Would they let me come back sometimes?'

'I don't know, Michael. I'll talk to Charley on Monday. Now it's time to go to sleep.'

She sat at the kitchen table. Michael was asleep. Tillie dozed in her basket. It was very quiet. Only the table lamp was lit, making a circle of yellow light on the tablecloth. Eileen had closed the curtains, and the house felt like a cave. She had been trying to patch a pair of Michael's jeans, but had come to the conclusion that they had been mended once too often, and that she would have to cut the legs off them and make shorts. Beside the crumpled denim lay also her Bible. She was struggling on with her study of Romans, but chapter thirteen, with its instructions on how to behave towards state authority, did not seem at this moment to speak to her condition, and she had laid it down with a sigh. Her brain felt clogged, her thought-processes unwieldy, as if too much information, undealt with, lay there stagnant, rotting, giving off noxious fumes, causing this sense of unappeased worry, this buzzing stomach-sick anxiety. She shook her head, as if to get something moving.

My mind is like a dark alley full of dustbins, in a torpid city where the refuse collectors have gone on strike.

Michael's news had caused a disturbance somewhere dark and usually shunned. She had always known that he would probably not be with her for long—a year, perhaps eighteen months, to see if his mother could sort out her life. The surprise was that it had been so long. But somehow, among all the possibilities that she and Charley had contemplated, Andy's return had never really been considered.

I wonder what happened to Andy in jail. Something obviously did.

Michael worried her. His dogged faith in the rightness of the traditional family, its power to confer security and identity, even though, in Eileen's eyes, it flew in the face of all the evidence, was a source of concern, and now the problem, once little more than an oddity, had broken out of the egg and taken wing.

Michael was going to be terribly let down. How could she warn him? This was one message he would not, *dared not*, listen to. What kind of a guy was Andy, anyway? Had he really changed? Or was this another project, to be dropped when something more interesting or profitable came along? And when Michael realised all this, when he was disappointed and betrayed because he had hoped for too much, who could he turn to? They wouldn't let Eileen see him. Michael would go backwards. Soon there would come a time when she no longer had any input into his life. But what could she say to him? Nothing. All she could do was pray for him, for strength and safety, for God's protection.

She wondered if, perhaps, with Michael gone, her own relationship with Natasha might be easier. Natasha could be prickly, unreasonable, jealous of her sister and Michael, though she was as much loved. Eileen thought of the verse in Romans 13 where the early Church was told that if you loved someone you would never do them wrong, and that therefore to love was to keep the whole spirit of the Law.

But that's perfect love, in an ideal existence. Of course I love Natasha, but I don't love her perfectly. How could I? I don't know her perfectly. Only God does that. What about human ignorance, or moments of weakness, later regretted? I don't think I have ever intended to do her wrong. But that's not what Scripture says.

Wearily she returned to the passage and read on doggedly.

"You must do this, because you know that the time has come for you to wake up from your sleep. For the moment when we will be saved is closer than it was when we first believed. The night is nearly over, day is almost here."

Am I asleep? Is it urgent? Should this reassure or depress me? Am I about to be rescued? Are the last days upon us?

She smiled at the thought, but it was a smile without humour or joy. She paid lip-service to the dictum that humans can do nothing in their own strength, yet every hour of every day she behaved as if her own strength was all there was to rely on. Even if she discounted the external world with all its complications, actions and interactions, just thinking about the world inside her head, her life was like that Old Testament monster of the deep waters, huge, implacable, untameable, and indifferent. How could she hope to bring it to order? Only one human being had ever done that, and he was God. He alone had the charisma, the power; his was the ultimate word of authority.

She went to the Gospels and turned pages, noticing passages at random. It was not like before, when she had first felt the light beyond the world shining on her blindness. Then, more and more, she had been like a person starved of nourishment, eating till she was satisfied. Now, already well fed, she flitted from dish to dish, seeking some special flavour. But although she sought in the wrong way, and knew it, and although no one message answered her question, still the authentic voice shed some kind of understanding and peace on her troubled mind.

"...your heart will always be where your riches are."

"And so I say to you: ask, and you will receive; seek, and you will find; knock, and the door will be opened to you. For all those who ask will receive, and those who seek will find, and the door will be opened to anyone who knocks."

Is that all that's really required of us? Simply to imitate him, in our limited way? To keep on asking, and not to despair? Perhaps so.

Her mind wandered for a moment, back to a time when David was still coming home, and the girls were too young for school. She had been doing something in the garden, and Celia Armitage had passed by the back gate, followed by her lumbering black labrador, Jasper, on her way to the woods. The Armitages had not long come to Holton, and Eileen did not know them, but after a few minutes of chatting to Celia she had found herself agreeing to bring the children along to Sunday school; and so it had begun.

When, after some while, Geoffrey and Celia had turned their attention, gentle but implacable, upon Eileen, she had resisted fiercely. Thinking about it now she smiled. She had found out later, much later, that the Armitages and others had been praying for her all through that time. They met her where she was, answering her questions, lending her books, gently encouraging and guiding. Along the way somewhere Eileen had met her Saviour for herself. How could there be any contest after that? And his voice still spoke to her, more strongly now that she recognized it instantly, claiming that part of her that was beyond ego, or insecurity, or fear. With his strength behind and around her she could bring the beast to heel.

But all things must be paid for, and the price of her conversion had been David. It was neither so simple nor so stark as that, of course. Other things had lent themselves to their estrangement, but David, returning from sea, had found her altered, at once more and less approachable, kinder, perhaps, but no longer his.

I wasn't anyway. But he didn't notice it till then.

At first David had seen only the positive side of Eileen's new loyalties and different acquaintances. He probably thought it was some kind of harmless phase. But as the years passed, and her involvement grew, he became suspicious, and in his insecurity derided her beliefs at a time when they were very green and vulnerable. She had tried to make him understand, but when he began to scoff and sneer, she turned on him with scalding indignation. Proud and scornful words were exchanged, bitter insults traded, the hurts and disappointments of the years brought out to view, where they wriggled, ugly and pathetic. What marriage, with even one honest partner, could have survived?

From the outside, it had seemed to struggle on, as well as anybody else's, and if not a huge success, then whose was without strife and stress? The reality was bleaker. David never really understood what he had done; and for Eileen it was as if he had been supplanted by a suitor with whom he could never hope to compete.

She remembered another passage, and searched for it.

"I am the Good Shepherd. As the Father knows me and I know the Father, in the same way I know my sheep and they know me. And I am willing to die for them."

Eileen closed her Bible. *And so he did.* She remembered hearing that passage read in church one Sunday morning years ago, and Geoffrey preaching on it, and the overwhelming love and gratitude that rose up in her then so powerfully that it still had resonance for her.

She sighed and got to her feet, wincing a little at creaking joints. *I've been sitting too long. Getting old.*

The kitchen clock said eleven thirty. Suddenly she felt very tired. She turfed the unwilling dog out briefly, then locked up, doused the lights and went to bed. Her legs felt heavy and the stairs creaked.

34

A few hours later she surfaced blearily from sleep as she heard the stairs creak again. She heard a car leaving the village, and muffled laughter from downstairs. Christina and Natasha were home. She sank back into the unconscious dark.

Michael and another figure, larger, shadowy, the face indistinct, both in identical grey herringbone overcoats, are walking slowly up the garden path, hand in hand, in torrential rain. Eileen is standing at the front door, watching them approach. As they come level she takes the towel that she has ready and rubs Michael's dripping hair. But the man with him, whom she recognises as his father though she has never met him, or even seen a photograph, pulls him onward into the house, into the back room, where a meal is laid on the table. All this takes place in silence. Eileen stands at the front door as if immobilised, damp towel in hand, wave after wave of desolation breaking over her.

Sunday 19th May 1996

After church Michael, never a socializer, hared off to his school friend Stephen's. He had been distant all morning, in some far-off place where he wanted no disturbance. Eileen herself felt a heaviness in all her limbs, as if she had been plagued by exhausting dreams which had cost her hours of rest, though there was little now she could recall. If she had dreamt, most of it was gone, shut up in the cobwebby cellar of her unconscious mind. But she remembered Michael and Andy in the rain, and she shivered even in the sticky heat, feeling as if somehow things were swinging out of control.

Leaving the churchyard, she decided that she had time to call at Marie's before getting home to cook lunch. She found Marie in the front garden, kneeling on a frayed mat, hoe in hand.

'Are you supposed to be doing that?' she asked, more crossly than she had intended.

Marie got up carefully and brushed the hair out of her eyes. 'Probably not, but the weeds are getting rampant.'

'I've got news for you,' Eileen said. 'Frank announced it in church just now. We have a new Rector at last, one Edward Jescott, and the induction's on the fifteenth of next month.'

'Well, well.' Marie seemed unsurprised.

Eileen's eyebrows shot up. 'Did you already know?'

'Philip has dropped the odd little hint,' Marie said. 'Do you want to come in for a bit?'

'No, thanks, I'd better get home and peel potatoes,' Eileen said. 'Remind me another time not to give you any news.' She smiled, shaking her head. 'I should know you are a repository of secrets.'

'That's the trouble, isn't it?'

'What is?'

'It's no use having a secret, because nobody knows you have it, unless you tell, and then it's not one.'

'Your logic defeats me. I'm going home. For goodness' sake, take it easy. You don't want to wreck your insides, not even to please Kit Muldoon.'

'All right, if you insist. Will I see you tomorrow?'

'Probably. Bye.'

Eileen walked home slowly through the gathering midday heat. Entering the house she kicked off her shoes, enjoying the coolness of the hallway tiles under her hot feet. A smell of roasting meat came out of the kitchen, and when she went in she found the two girls up and dressed, and the potatoes peeled. 'Thank you. What angelic children.'

'Think nothing of it, Mother,' Christina said.

'Pour me a glass of something, please.'

'What is madam's fancy today? A tot of meths, perhaps? An exotic cocktail of my own devising? Gin and paraquat?'

'Mm, delicious. What did you drink last night?'

Christina laughed. 'Nothing so imaginative, I'm afraid. We can only afford beer on our pitiful pittances.'

'Good thing too. So how was your evening?'

Natasha slouched in from the other room.

'Rather eventful, as it happens,' said Christina. 'What's in this bottle?'

'Mrs. Pickett's elderflower. You can open it if you like.'

'Is it safe?' Christina held it at arm's length and looked at it dubiously.

Eileen shrugged. 'Who cares? It tastes all right and is probably very alcoholic indeed.'

'Three glasses and a corkscrew please, Tash.'

'So tell me,' Eileen said. 'What happened? Was there a shoot-out? Or did you meet some paragon who changed your life in an instant?'

'You are full of sparkling wit this morning,' Christina said. 'Has something disturbed the Holton millpond of dullness?'

Eileen sat down at the kitchen table. 'Actually, yes. Frank announced it just now, made everyone sit up and take notice. A new Rector has been found for this erring flock.' She took a sip of the elderflower. 'He arrives in a month, complete with a wife and three children. There'll be a young family at the Rectory, which will make a pleasant change. Moral direction returns.'

'It would take more than that,' Natasha said. She sat down opposite her mother.

'You should know, dear,' Christina said, looking at her sister meaningfully.

'What's that supposed to mean?'

'Oh, you know. In with the cool crowd, etcetera.'

Natasha lobbed a dishcloth at her. 'Ha bloody ha, Miss Know-all.'

'So?' Eileen said, resting her arms on her elbows. 'Give me the bottom line, will you, before I die of curiosity.'

Natasha leaned forward, more animated than Eileen had seen her for some time. 'I didn't realize, because I haven't been to the Hotspot in ages, but it's real Stephanie Clements territory.'

'She was there, was she?'

'Very much Queen of the Hill,' Christina said. 'Or the dung-heap, if you prefer. Going around as if she owned the place, with a gang of cronies who all look positively spectral.'

'You know how Stephanie looks sometimes?' said Natasha. 'Made up like some kind of ghoul? Well, next to those mates of hers she looks quite healthy.'

'Wholesome, even,' said Christina.

Eileen digested this unlikely thought for a moment. 'So what was she actually doing?'

'Propping up the bar,' Natasha said. 'Or going from one group of people to another having deep conversations. Oh yes, and the Muldoons were there, and Neil Quilley, acting like the five-year-olds they are when they've had a few too many. But she ignored them. Sometimes she disappeared into the back room, the one marked *Private*, you know. She stared at us, but she didn't say anything. You'd think she didn't know us. Maybe we're too uncool for her.'

'Which is funny, when you think we had the doubtful pleasure of her acquaintance for years, including going to the same school,' Christina said. 'Mind you, I noticed she gave Sean a good looking-over.'

Natasha looked uncomfortable. 'Shut up, you mouthy cow.'

'Children, please! Elderly ears are present. Am I allowed to know who Sean is?'

'A blond hunk who thinks Natasha is the most desirable female since Cleopatra.'

'Give over, will you!' Natasha aimed a blow at the sniggering Christina.

Eileen held up her hands. 'All right, let's pass over the heavenly Sean and get back to Stephanie.'

'She's up to something,' Natasha said. 'It looked as if she was doing deals. Drugs, probably. Quite a few of the people there were out of their heads.'

'What about Stephanie herself?'

'Oh, no, not Stephanie,' Christina said. 'She was very much in control, I thought.'

Eileen shook her head. 'No wonder she always seems so flush. No sign of the law, I suppose?'

'They did make a brief appearance at one point,' Christina said. 'But it all looked fairly routine.'

'Anyway, Mum, that's not the end of the story,' Natasha said. Her eyes sparkled. 'We decided to leave and go to Sean's for some coffee.' At the mention of Sean she looked embarrassed again.

'Oh, he lives nearby, does he?' Eileen asked.

'Not specially, but he's got a car. Anyway, some of the people at the club were getting really tanked up, and we were worried in case things got out of hand, like they do sometimes on Saturday nights, so we decided to go. About one, it was.'

Christina took up the story. 'There's a little side-road next to the Hotspot. It doesn't go anywhere. I think it's used for deliveries, that sort of stuff. As we were leaving we noticed movement, and there was Stephanie and two men, who I'm sure are connected with the club somehow, talking to some other blokes who'd been in before but hadn't stayed long. One in particular I noticed, in a very sharp suit, sitting on the bonnet of a red sports car, and there were three or four others, real heavies they looked, in a black van of some kind, and it was pretty obvious they had all had a falling-out.'

'Yes, we saw some pushing and shoving and they were acting big and threatening,' said Natasha.

'Then Sir Sean the noble knight whisked us away from trouble,' Christina sighed. 'Before we had a chance to find out what was going on, poor innocent damsels that we are.'

Natasha scowled.

'Good for him,' said Eileen. 'I am warming to this man by the moment. He seems to have some sense, unlike others I could mention.'

'Anyway, that wasn't the end of it,' Natasha said. 'We were on our way to the car park at the other end of the High Street, and the two cars, the red sports car and the black van, came up behind us doing about sixty.'

'There was a screaming of tyres and people were leaning out of the windows and shouting,' Christina said. 'It was like something on TV. Not that I have time to watch TV, of course.' She grinned at her mother. 'Too busy with Shakespeare, Milton, Chaucer and all that bunch.'

'So what then?' asked Eileen.

'Well, it all fizzled out after that,' Christina said. 'No car chases, no guns. We are talking about Caxford here, remember. After that we all went to Sean's for a cup of coffee, and then the dear lad brought us home.'

'Better and better,' Eileen said. 'Sean sounds like a real find. You want to hold on to this one, Tash.'

'Maybe I will, maybe I won't,' Natasha said, 'but it won't be either of you two who makes up my mind.'

Despite this Eileen could see that Natasha was gratified by their approval.

'Right, enough of this idleness and levity,' Eileen said as she got up. 'We've got to get the lunch. Someone can do some vegetables if they will. Christie, what train are you thinking of catching?'

'The four-twenty, I thought. That has the best connection. It'll get me back around ten.'

'OK. Now what shall we do for pudding?'

'Can't we just have fruit? Neither of us wants to get any fatter.'

'Neither of you needs to get any thinner, either,' Eileen said. 'All right, I'll be lazy. There are carrots and broccoli in the fridge, and I'll do the table.'

Michael appeared magically for lunch, helped perfunctorily with the dishes, and vanished again.

'Say goodbye to Christie, Michael, because you won't be seeing her for a while,' Eileen said.

Michael gave Christina a bear-hug and she ruffled his hair fondly. 'I'll ring you soonest, Mickey Mouse.'

'And Michael,' Eileen said as he paused at the back door. 'Home at five, please. You must have a bath tonight, or the school will think they've got a new boy with considerably darker skin.'

Michael waved and disappeared down the garden.

Natasha got up. 'I'm just going to ring my friend Lisa, Mum, OK?' She went into the hallway, letting the door slam behind her.

Eileen sighed. 'I've just remembered, I've got a meeting tomorrow morning with the Head and Michael's class teacher.'

'Why, has he been up to mischief?' asked Christina, who was folding the tea towels.

'No, but they are very concerned about his progress, or lack of it,' Eileen replied. 'I think they're going to tell me he needs specialist help.'

'Does he?'

Eileen shrugged. 'Probably. One problem is, Michael isn't terribly motivated when it comes to school work, which is a shame, because he is far from dim.'

'Can't the school help him?'

'Up to a point, I guess. But they have children with all sorts of needs there, and some who are a real headache. Michael keeps a low profile at school, and it's only in the last year or so that they've really got concerned.'

'Would a special school help?' Christina leaned back against the sink.

'It might do, but the nearest one is just outside Lambury.'

'Too far to travel.'

'I'm afraid so. Well, I'll see what they have to say tomorrow. Anyway, with Michael's dad back on the scene, anything might change in Michael's life.'

Christina frowned. 'Do you really think he might go back to his family? I mean, he's happy here. Won't they take that into account?'

'Michael wants to go, Christie. He's totally sold on the redemptive power of "Mum, Dad and the kids." That's what really worries me. And when it comes to a situation like this, anything might happen. If Charley and her bosses think Andy really has reformed, and if Michael really wants to be with them, the chances are it'll happen. After a trial period, of course.'

'How would you feel about that?'

'Of course I'd miss him. But what I feel doesn't really count. It's got to be what's good for Michael.'

'There could be a number of opinions on that score,' Christina said. 'I hope they look into this jail business you were telling me about at breakfast, for a start. Do you have any idea what happened?'

'Not really, except the little Michael has told me. I hope to find out a bit more from Charley tomorrow. I know about Michael's early life from before, when I was going through all the preparations for fostering him. Denise and Andy were way too young to have kids then, but such things happen. Denise had trouble coping, she had a few unsuitable friends, and there were times when Michael was neglected. I think she did her best, honestly. But once the other two kids were born it was all too much, and Michael's insecurity came out in some difficult behaviour.' She became aware of the kitchen clock ticking. 'I need to stroll the dog before I drive you to Caxford. She was really dozy this morning, so I didn't walk her. Do you want to come?'

'No, I think I'll get my stuff together, thanks, Mum. Not to mention my head.' Christina gave Eileen a hug as she passed. 'It's been great to see you guys. But now I have to plunge back into the hot academic rat-race. Poor me.' She grimaced theatrically.

'Poor you, I don't think! I'd swap in a micro-split-second.'

'Would you?'

'No question.'

'It's not all beer and skittles, actually.'

'Nor is anything. Anyway, beer and skittles aren't exactly what I'm after.'

'What are you after, if one may enquire? Have you given it any thought?'

'Kind of, but it's still inconclusive.'

Christina smiled broadly and shook her head. 'Mother, you should have been in politics.'

'Anyway,' Eileen said, 'you have to pack, I have to exercise the dog, so there's no time to pursue this line of conversation, fascinating as my half-baked aspirations might be. Be off!'

Under the trees it was fractionally cooler. A light breeze ruffled the leaves, but lower down it was still. Eileen walked slowly, in time with Tillie, who ambled and stopped and sniffed and ambled on again. They went down in a straight line, and soon came out into a field of grasses and sun-baked overgrown weeds. Eileen flopped down on the dry ground for a few moments to give the dog a chance to rest. The afternoon sun beat down on her closed eyes. From the trees behind her came the sound of a turtle dove's bubbling call; otherwise there was silence.

Lying there almost dozing, she wondered what Marie was doing, and then thought that Philip was likely to be there with her in the neat little cottage. She sternly squashed her imagination at this point, remembering how she had felt when she first realised what was going on between Marie and Philip. It should have been obvious before, but it was a time when things were troubled in Eileen's own life, and she hadn't noticed the tiny clues in her friend's behaviour. Marie, always so candid, had sometimes been evasive, and there were times when she didn't answer when spoken to, as if her mind was far away. Then one afternoon Eileen had been out walking Tillie and had decided to call on Marie on the off-chance. She had recognized Philip's car, parked in the lane outside, but for a moment she simply didn't understand what she was seeing. As realization broke, she looked up at Marie's upstairs windows, and saw the curtains drawn; and she felt a kind of hot shock course through her body.

There was no human reason, she told herself, why it should not be so, or why she should disapprove. But she felt stupid, not having realized, and she was puzzled that Marie had said nothing. She turned thoughtfully away and went home. Later, trying to understand her own feeling of discomfort, recognizing the stirring of unworthy fear and jealousy, she decided to say nothing, mind her own business, and carry on as normal.

It was Marie herself who opened the way, walking home one Sunday after church, with Michael running on in front, sending up clouds of pollen from the long grasses.

'I guess you must know by now that Philip and I are a bit of an item.' She glanced sideways at Eileen.

'It took me a while to cotton on. I must be dimmer than most.'

'So what do you think?'

'Why should it matter what I think? It's your life.'

Marie stopped and laid a hand on her arm. 'Of course it matters what you think, probably more than anyone. You are my dearest friend. I don't know what I would have done without you these last years.'

Eileen swallowed. 'Well, are you happy? Is it working out?'

'That's why I haven't said anything till now,' Marie said. 'In case it was just a flash in the pan.' She giggled. 'Sorry, poor choice of words.'

'Marie, you are disgraceful. I suppose you're going to tell me it was your mutual love of Bach that brought you together.'

'No, dear, I'm afraid it was more to do with lust. On my part, at least. Certainly to begin with.'

'I see.' Eileen tried to sound concerned, but her grin gave her away. 'Well, make sure the tabloids don't get hold of it. They love that sort of thing.'

'Discretion it shall be. You have to be discreet in Holton, anyway.'

'Philip's younger than you, isn't he?'

'Yes. He's a mere youth of thirty-five. I expect I'm leading him astray, but he doesn't seem to be resisting overmuch.'

'Marie, you are shameless.'

'I know. But don't begrudge me my thrilling little liaison. I've not had too many thrills in my life recently, apart from the nasty kind. And I have to say that Philip's not just fantastic at music.'

Eileen held up her hands. 'Enough! Off you go, then, to your afternoon of passion. Don't let me hold you up.'

'Please,' Marie said. 'Not till after lunch. We must keep up some appearances.'

They had parted giggling like schoolgirls. But Eileen was anxious. What if things were to change for Philip? What if he were to return to the world where, musically at least, he really belonged? What would happen to Marie? Would he simply drop her and move on? Eileen did not know Philip well enough to answer her own questions, but when she thought of the pain that Marie had already suffered, she wanted to stand between her friend and any repetition of the past.

Two puzzles came to Eileen's mind. How Marie squared her current activities with her faith was one which Eileen could not investigate. But the issue of Stephanie, and her reaction to her mother's affair, was to be answered not long after. A few days after that Sunday's revelation, Marie phoned, obviously agitated.

'Eileen, it's Stephanie. She's gone. Packed all her stuff, and gone.'

'But Marie, she's done it before, hasn't she?'

'This is different. She was in a terrible temper, yelling, banging doors, swearing. It was dreadful.'

'What happened?'

'That's the thing. She found out about me and Philip.'

'Did you tell her?'

'No. I'm such a coward. I thought this was how she'd be, so I kept quiet. I don't know how she found out. She is just furious. But you know, I think it's because she's afraid. She's terribly insecure under all that hardness and bravado.'

'You don't deserve this, Marie.'

'She thinks I do. She obviously blames me.'

'And you blame yourself.'

'Well, she has been the victim of my choices. She's so bitter, Eileen. She can't forgive Ray for all the things he did, and for abandoning her. I'm the only security she has, and I've betrayed her with Philip. That's how she sees it.'

'She's got to grow up some time, you know,' Eileen said gently. 'Kids do leave home. I guess it wasn't the best way for it to happen, though.'

'The worst of it was Philip walked in right in the middle of the row. There was so much noise we didn't hear him. I was so ashamed of her, Eileen, flinging insults and shrieking like that. I was almost glad to see the back of her. But now I'm so worried. Where can she have gone?'

'She has friends in Caxford, hasn't she? I expect she's gone to them. There's not much you can do, I'm afraid, my dear, except wait, hope and pray. She'll be back, Marie, I'm sure. She'll cool off. Whatever else, Stephanie is no fool.'

'I hope you're right.'

'And Philip? How has he taken all this?'

'Oh, Eileen, he was brilliant. I had to fill him in a bit more about my past. I hadn't said much about Ray. But Philip was great, so calm and reassuring. He's going to ring me later.'

It was around then that things had changed between Philip and Marie, and Eileen had to acknowledge that Philip really did seem to care for her friend. As for Stephanie, she stayed away for two months, and phoned her mother once during that time, curtly telling her she was not to worry. Then, one hot August day, she came back, bag in hand, and with very little explanation moved back in.

Marie told Eileen a few days later that she seemed altered, almost subdued. 'Something happened to her while she was away, but she won't say where she's been, or what's going on. She's got her own phone now, so she's even more secretive.'

'How's Philip coping with her?'

'You're not going to believe this, Eileen, but she actually apologized to him.'

'Good heavens.'

'He came round the day after she came home. She stopped him in the hall. You know the belligerent way she has, arms folded, all that. Philip took it well, as he does. He just greeted her civilly, and then she seemed to drop her gaze, as if she couldn't look at him, and actually blushed! She mumbled something about being sorry for her rudeness, that it wasn't his fault, he said it was perfectly all right, and she dived back into her bedroom.'

'How extraordinary.'

'But something's not right, Eileen. I hear her sometimes, shouting out in her sleep. I can't help worrying.'

'You've got her back, Marie. That's the main thing. I think you're going to have to be very patient.'

'I've had plenty of practice in that department.'

Now, with the hard ground under her back and the sun beating on her face, Eileen was roused from her thoughts by a sudden low growl from Tillie. It was such an unusual sound from her peaceable dog that Eileen sat up, shading her eyes with her hand and blinking away the sunspots that were dancing in front of them.

Coming up the hill below her, head down, hands in pockets, was the stalker. Eileen was struck by his odd creeping gait, and then his jumper, brightly striped in orange, black and green. He had obviously not seen her, intent on his own thoughts, and he was only yards away when he looked up and faced her. Seeing him so suddenly, her skin prickled, but she held her breath and forced herself to smile. 'Hello,' she said. 'Warm, isn't it?'

The man seemed to twitch, and he stopped dead, as if frozen. For a moment he stared at her, his eyes wide. Then he mumbled something she did not catch and shuffled sideways, as if to avoid entering her space. He was young, no more than in his early twenties, with dark, wavy, longish hair and several days' growth of beard. His hands and clothes were filthy, and he was plainly terrified. As soon as he had gone sideways far enough to avoid Eileen and the dog, he loped towards the trees and disappeared. For a while Eileen could hear him crashing around in the undergrowth.

Eileen sat still for several minutes, struck by his strangeness. Who was he? He didn't look like a birdwatcher or a rambler. Perhaps he was living rough out here. He was certainly dirty. But somehow he didn't look organized enough even for a tramp.

'And what do you think spooked him?' she murmured to the dog. 'You? Anyone in their right mind can see you're about as threatening as a raspberry jelly.'

Tillie looked up at her and yawned, as if in agreement.

'Oh, well. Time for home,' Eileen said. 'We'd better get Christie to the station.'

On her slow way home she puzzled about the young man in the woods. What was he doing there? His behaviour had been very odd. Was he drunk, drugged perhaps? It had not seemed so. His fearfulness had struck Eileen forcibly; it seemed so out of proportion to the circumstances. Perhaps he just didn't like dogs. But the woods on a sunny Sunday afternoon in May were probably not the best place to avoid them.

Just before four they got into the car. Natasha had decided, casually it seemed, to come with them, but Christina's raised eyebrows seemed to indicate that Natasha had an agenda of her own. Eileen knew better than to enquire too openly into her older daughter's business.

As they left Holton Christina let out an exclamation. 'Tash, look who it is!'

They were passing a layby. Several people and vehicles were gathered there. Eileen recognized Neil Quilley astride his motorbike, and Colin and Danny Muldoon. A black van, windowless and dusty, was parked alongside, and leaning against it were two youngish men, heavy-set, wearing dark suits with white T-shirts underneath, shiny boots and sunglasses. Their hair was cut very short, almost shaved.

'They look like comic-book gangsters,' Eileen said.

'They're the same guys we saw last night!' Natasha said. 'What on earth are they doing here?'

Eileen had to drive very slowly because they were following a tractor with a laden trailer. 'More to the point, what on earth is Georgina doing with them? I can't believe Angela and Peter know what company their daughter is keeping.'

'We don't know anything bad about those guys,' Christina said as

46

they finally overtook the tractor and picked up speed. 'Just because someone kits himself out like a Hollywood mafioso doesn't mean he's necessarily up to no good.'

'No, theoretically that's true,' Eileen said. 'But I don't know about you, I've got a most uncomfortable feeling seeing Georgina there. I hope her brother is keeping an eye on her.'

'I doubt it,' said Natasha. 'Neil is an idiot.'

'Well, I don't like it,' Eileen said. 'If she's still there when I return I shall be an interfering old busybody and offer her a lift.'

'Did you see what the silly kid was wearing?' said Natasha in tones of disbelief, as if she herself was well known for her conservative style. 'I know it's hot, but all she had on was a little skirt and a boob tube.'

'What was she doing exactly, did you notice?' Eileen asked.

'She was talking to one of the mafiosi,' Christina said. 'From the little I could see it was all giggles and cow eyes. And she was smoking.'

At ten past four they pulled into Caxford station forecourt. Christina found her train ticket, hoisted her bag onto her shoulder, hugged her mother and sister goodbye, and disappeared into the station.

'Time to get back?' Eileen said.

Natasha fidgeted a little, coughed and squirmed. 'I'll come back later, OK, Mum? I thought, as I'm here, I'd go and see a friend.'

'Oh, all right then. Have a good time, and don't forget the last bus goes at eight.'

Natasha mumbled something about not needing the bus. Then she was gone, her long, slim legs striding out down the High Street, full of purpose and hope. Some primeval fear stirred in Eileen then, something deep and atavistic, and for a fleeting moment she wished both girls were babies again, asleep and safe.

No, I don't. She chided herself as she got back into the car. *Remember how trapped I felt back then. They can look after themselves, and if they can't, there's not a lot I can do about it.*

Driving back to Holton she looked out for Georgina Quilley and the black van, but they were gone.

Later that night she lay stretched out on the sofa, thinking. Michael was bathed and sleeping, his clean school uniform folded on the chair beside the bed, ready for the morning. But before he went up to bed he said something which added to Eileen's sense of unease, of things beginning to unravel, to get loose from her grip.

Eileen said, 'I didn't see you and Stephen down in the woods today. Did you decide to stay at Stephen's?'

'No, Steve's mum chucked us out. Danielle had to have a sleep after lunch, and me and Steve were making too much noise, she said.'

'So where did you go?'

'We did go to the woods. But you didn't see us because we've made a new secret camp in a different place.'

'Oh. Did the old one fall to bits?'

'No, we gave it away.'

'Pardon?'

Michael rambled on, oblivious to the look on Eileen's face. 'We met this tramp down there, well, he's sort of a tramp, and he didn't have anywhere to sleep, so we let him have our camp. We wanted to make a new one anyway.'

'This tramp, Michael—what did he look like?'

'Quite young, a bit scruffy, like you'd think a tramp would be.' He caught sight of Eileen's expression of horror. 'It's all right, Mum. He's nice, honestly. We gave him our crisps. He was really starving.'

'Was he wearing a striped jumper?'

'Yes, that's him! Why, have you seen him too?'

'Yes,' Eileen said. 'Today. He seemed afraid.'

'Steve and me reckon he's on the run,' Michael said. 'Hiding out from the police, or something.'

'You've been watching too much TV. All the same, you mustn't go down to the woods any more, not on your own or just with Stephen, not for a while anyway.'

'But Mum, why not?'

'Because, if your theory is right, and he's running away, he knows you know where he is, and he might want to do something to stop you telling anyone.'

'No, Mum, really, he isn't like that. He's nice. His name's Christopher. Chris.'

'I shall have a word with Stephen's mum at the school gate tomorrow. Meanwhile you and Stephen can play in the back garden. It's about time you paid more attention to Bill. Why don't you make him an assault course? He's getting too fat, and the exercise will do him good.'

Michael protested for a few more minutes, but Eileen was not to be moved, and in the end he accepted defeat.

Now she lay, eyes closed, as if sleeping, her hands folded on her stomach, her feet propped up on a cushion. Her body was still, but her mind was busy.

What ought to have been the day's big news, the coming of the Jescotts to the parish, was eclipsed by other, darker happenings. The story of Stephanie at the night club, the rather sinister strangers in the layby, and somehow the very presence there of Georgina, made her feel that the village itself, the church, the people, all its innocence, was vulnerable.

That's daft. Holton's not innocent. It's as worldly and corrupt as anywhere with people in it. But the thought would not go away.

And now this man, sleeping rough in the woods. Who was he? Even the woods, which had been so natural and full of untouched beauty, now seemed tainted and faintly menacing. Suddenly it felt imperative that she should keep Michael safe, safe for his family to claim him.

She sighed deeply and shifted position. Thinking of Michael and his parents brought another twist of anxiety. Tomorrow Charley would be on the phone, and decisions would have to be made. She swung her legs to the floor. She wanted to ring Marie, to hear her quizzical voice and banish these comfortless, fearful feelings, but it was late, and maybe Philip was there. A vivid, unwelcome picture, of Marie with Philip, and Natasha with Sean, flashed up before her eyes, and a cold pang struck her.

She got up heavily, went to the understairs cupboard, took out the ironing-board, plugged in the iron, and began to assail a backlog of neglected laundry, as if a routine job might quell for a moment that feeling of unease that was creeping through the corridors of her mind.

Monday 20th May 1996

She came into the house and shut the front door behind her. After the sunlight outside it was dark, and her eyes had trouble adjusting.

The telephone rang before she had even taken her shoes off. She picked up the receiver and leaned against the staircase.

'Eileen? Hi, it's Charley.'

'Hello, Charley. Have you tried to ring before? I've just got back from the school.'

'Right, yes, I remember. How did you get on?'

'I saw an educational psychologist. Michael is severely dyslexic, he says.'

'Expand on that, can you, Eileen? What does it mean practically?'

'Well, Michael is above average intelligence, but this is holding him back. He's not concentrating in class, younger children are beginning to outstrip him, and his teacher is afraid he'll soon be quite negative about school as a whole.'

'They can't help him?'

'There are thirty-two in the class, Charley, with three year groups together. It's only a small village school.'

'Hm. Not good news. Do they have anything to suggest as a way forward?'

'They told me about a specialist school in Lambury, Hartridge House. They reckon they could get Michael a place there in September.'

Charley was quiet for a moment. 'Let me think about this, Eileen. If I come up with anything I'll let you know, of course. Meanwhile, I guess you heard about Andy.'

Eileen pulled up a stool and sat down. Her legs were aching. 'Michael said his dad was there on Saturday.'

'Yes. He appeared with Denise and the children, unannounced. You can imagine, I was gobsmacked. Denise seemed a bit sheepish, mumbled something about trying to ring me, but basically it's pretty obvious who's in charge. She and the little ones are totally under his spell.'

'So what's he like?'

'Different from what I imagined, and from what Denise has told me. I'd always thought of Andy as a rather pathetic, easily-led teenager who got into trouble, a bit of a drifter. Well, if he was ever that, he isn't any more. He's quite a tough character now, not nasty, but determined: knows what he wants, got an answer for everything. When I first saw him I thought, "My God, who's Denise taken up with now?" You know her taste in men isn't exactly spectacular. In comes this guy, in jeans, boots and a skimpy vest, shaved head, tattoos and an earring, and when Denise said who he was I nearly passed out with amazement.'

'Extraordinary. So did you find out his story?'

'Up to a point. He's been in Rackhampton jail. Apparently he's been back with the family some time, but Denise has kept him quiet. I guess they've been sorting themselves out, deciding what to do. Denise obviously idolizes him and is quite willing to let him make major decisions, and even the little ones seem happy with him.'

'So how does he feel about them—a couple of cuckoos?'

'That's another odd thing, Eileen. And one of the reasons why Denise is all goofy and grateful, I suppose. He's taken them on as his own. I must say I was quite impressed. This guy knows what he wants and is very persuasive.'

'Being in jail has done some good, then, do you think? That's unusual, from all I hear.'

'Very. Rackhampton has quite a good reputation, though. And apparently Andy did go downhill when he was first inside, drugs, the lot. He was young and gullible, and some real villains were on to him straight away.'

'If my sums are right, he's been inside for…what, almost seven years?'

'About that. He got mixed up in a burglary at a factory, and the security guard was very badly injured and unfortunately actually died during the trial. You can imagine public feeling was very high against this little gang of antisocial yobs. The security guard was well known in the town, a popular bloke, did a lot for charity, left a widow, you know the sort of thing. I don't think Andy meant to hurt him, but he panicked. Out of his league, I'd say.'

'So they clobbered him with a heavy sentence.'

'Yes. Then, as I say, he went from bad to worse in jail—at first.'

'So what changed him? It all seems so unlikely.'

'I know. But weird things sometimes happen in extreme circumstances. Apparently Andy saw the error of his ways.'

'This is all sounding more and more apocryphal.'

'You said it. But if you heard Andy talk, I think you might feel differently. I certainly did, and I've come across a few real hard cases in my time.'

Eileen frowned. 'Are you telling me that Andy, unaided, became a reformed character?'

'No, he had help. I was coming to that. I think he had something like a breakdown in prison. Rackhampton has a Listeners' scheme. It's a bit like the Samaritans, with inmates trained to listen to other prisoners' troubles. Andy didn't go into that bit much, the time he was suicidal, but some of these other guys helped him, and he also got to know the prison chaplain, a bloke called Jerry Wilson. I've met him, and he's a bit of a charismatic character himself. Not like a vicar at all, long hair and tight jeans.'

'Charley, are you telling me that Andy actually saw the light in prison?'

'Yep. And he really is different, from what Denise tells me. He's been out just a few months, in which time he's decorated the flat and got a job in a garage, and his employers seem happy with him.'

'I am having trouble taking all this in, I have to say.'

'Me too. But meet Andy, and see what you think. By the way, I actually rang Jerry Wilson at the prison, and he confirmed it all. Andy did a complete turnaround and became a Listener himself. He and Jerry apparently worked through his sense of terrible guilt, and he even wrote a letter to the security guard's widow. I don't think Jerry's a fool, and anyway Andy behaved himself for several years before they let him out. If it wasn't genuine it sure was a very long time to keep up a charade, and to be frank I don't think Andy could hack that kind of long-term deception. He isn't all that bright.'

Eileen was silent for a moment, thinking. What could she say, she who knew the revolutionizing power of the Holy Spirit? Who was she to say that Andy was beyond redemption? Nobody was. But it did all seem quite astonishing.

She stretched her legs. 'So, Charley, what next? He wants Michael back now, I hear.'

'That's the idea, to rebuild the family, with nobody missing. He's determined to make up for being a useless father. What they want is to have Michael over half term, just to see how they all get on, and go from there. How do you feel about it?'

Eileen sighed. 'You know, Charley, I think I must be led by you on this. I know Michael, but you know the whole situation and all concerned. Michael himself seemed very keen, and was obviously impressed by his dad. But I do worry about him.'

'In what way?'

'Well, it's this belief he seems to have, that your mum and dad can't be wrong, that once he's back where he belongs, as he feels, it will all be happy ever after. Even if Denise and Andy do their utmost, Michael is going to be disappointed. His expectations are way too high. I've tried to talk to him about it, but I got nowhere.'

'I know. I've noticed it too. Actually I've seen something similar with other kids in care, even when their foster family is plainly far better for them than their birth family. It's a sort of unspoken creed, that you can't criticize your mum. Michael has generously included his dad and siblings. I do understand your concern, Eileen. But I don't think resisting this situation is the way through. The fact is, with guidelines as they are, unless Denise and Andy were deemed a danger to their children in some way, policy is to keep families together, if we can. Money also clearly has a part to play in that, not to be too cynical. Obviously I will have to monitor progress for quite a while. Andy understands and accepts that, which in itself makes me hopeful. And Eileen, kids are resilient. Michael will be OK. He has to learn to cope with disappointment. It's one of the basic requirements of growing up.'

'Of course it is. I guess I tend to be a bit over-protective of his feelings. He's had a few knocks in his short life.'

'But think how he's gained in confidence over the last three years. You've helped him enormously, you know that. He's a different kid.'

'I will miss him, Charley. He's part of the family. The girls will too.'

'I know. But we all knew it wouldn't be for ever.'

'Yes. So, what next?'

'I'll say he can go to Denise's for half term, then. Can you bring him down here for eleven on Saturday? We'll see how it goes. I'll arrange a meeting the following week with you and me and Denise and Andy, and probably my supervisor, just for another viewpoint. You know Eric, don't you? He's always taken an interest in Michael. We'll talk through all the angles and go on from there.'

'All right, Charley. I'll tell Michael after school. He'll be delighted.'

'And I'll tell Denise and Andy what the school says. They need to know about his educational problems.'

'Yes.'

'Eileen, don't be too downhearted. You've done a brilliant job, and this might just be the moment for Michael to take off.'

'You're probably right. I'll see you on Saturday.'

'OK. I'll call you if anything comes up.'

'Likewise. Bye, Charley.' She put the receiver down and sat for a moment, gnawing at her fingernail. Her brain was in turmoil, and she had no energy to clear the paths and set things in order.

Eileen stared unseeing at her cup of coffee as she sat at the kitchen table. Her mind was turning over with painful, leaden slowness. The issues raised at Michael's school had been eclipsed, since they would soon be someone else's problem. But even though Michael would before long cease to be her responsibility, or so it seemed, her concern for him was just as keen as it had ever been. Things went on for a while in their humdrum way. Then, suddenly, everything changed, so quickly and so randomly that feelings could not keep up.

She rested her head in her hands and tried to clear her mind.

God, are you there? Of course you are. You cannot be elsewhere. Are you tuned in to me? You must be. It's me that switches off the set, just when you get uncomfortably close, so close that I might actually have to change. You know the situation. You can see into my mind more clearly than I can myself. What am I to think, feel, do? Is this right for Michael? Can I trust Charley, Andy, Jerry Wilson? Even if I can't, what can I do about it? She took a sip of coffee. It was almost cold. *Help me, please. Help me to be there for Michael. He's happy, but it's still going to be tough for him having to adjust and readjust. Be with him, Lord. Wrap him round, protect him from danger, guide him. He is a precious life.* She rubbed her eyes. *Keep me on my feet, Lord. Strengthen me, because all this makes me feel weak, tired, confused. Help me not to judge, but to look at everything and everyone with an open mind. Let me be available to be the channel of your grace in this complicated human web. Thank you, Lord. Please keep with me, though I drift off the track.*

On an impulse Eileen decided to visit Annette Dyer. Richard, she knew, would be at work, and Annette would be in her big house, alone, neglected and miserable. Eileen washed up her coffee cup, put on her shoes, and left the house. She crossed the road and walked up the lane bordered with cottages. One of them belonged to the family of Michael's friend Stephen, whose mother Nancy was hanging out washing as Eileen passed. Eileen waved to her, and she waved back. Her toddler daughter was playing on the lawn with a fat tabby cat.

Eileen walked on up the lane. The sun was warm but there were clouds building up low on the horizon. To her left, between the houses and over the trees, she could just see the river. The houses petered out after a while, giving way to fields full of rape and linseed. On either side grew tall cow-parsley and ragged mallow, overhanging the dusty roadway. In a hawthorn tree a robin sang his sharp, surprising song. Except for him it was quiet.

The Dyers' house lay at the end of a long gravel drive that wound between tall shrubs: deutzia, philadelphus and lilac. Although the garden was well-tended, the house itself had a neglected look. Windows needed painting, and the outhouse where Richard kept his car was in a state of picturesque decay. The house itself, though large, was unremarkable, foursquare, pebble-dashed in part, with a lean-to scullery. Eileen climbed the two steps and rang the bell, which clanged forlornly in the echoing hall. She waited several minutes, tried again. There was no response.

I know Annette is here. She never goes out. Perhaps she is still in bed.

She looked at her watch. It was eleven fifteen. A cold thought struck her: Annette suffered from bouts of black depression. Had she ever been really suicidal? Eileen did not know, did not know how to tell. She went round the side of the house, and peered in through the grimy scullery window. The scullery led into the kitchen, a huge barn of a room, high-ceilinged. She could see Annette, still in her ancient dressing gown, sitting at the kitchen table, her head resting on her arms.

Eileen tapped on the window. 'Annette! It's me, Eileen.'

Annette slowly raised her head and looked blearily in Eileen's direction. A glimmer of recognition passed over her face, then the beginnings of a smile. She heaved herself to her feet, painfully it seemed, and opened the back door. 'Eileen. It's good to see you.' Her voice sounded croaky, as if she had not used it for some time.

'Hello, Annette. How are you?'

'Lousy, I'm afraid. Come in. I'll put the kettle on. If I can find it. I'm completely mental. I can't find a thing. It drives Richard mad.'

Eileen sat down at the kitchen table, watching Annette drift aimlessly about in search of the kettle. *I'm not going to do it for her. I don't want to become one of those busybodies that takes over other people's lives and makes them feel more helpless than ever.*

Annette eventually found the kettle, filled it and plugged it in.

'Have you eaten today, Annette?'

'I can't remember, dear. Food is a total drag.'

'Are you cooking for yourself and Richard?'

'No, I can't manage even simple things at the moment. Richard has a good lunch in town and makes himself a snack in the evening.'

'What about you? I'm sure you've lost weight.'

'The thought of food makes me sick.'

'If I make the tea, will you have some?'

'I'll do it,' Annette said. 'I must do something, or I might as well be dead and buried.'

55

There was a pause, punctuated only by the sound of boiling water and a whine on the other side of the door.

'Can I let him in?' Eileen said.

'Yes, if you like. He's probably a bit smelly and will dribble all over you, but I know you don't mind the ways of dogs.'

Eileen opened the kitchen door and was immediately besieged by a large springer spaniel, all scrabbling paws and lolling tongue.

Annette, as if in slow motion, found a large teapot and filled it.

'The garden is looking lovely, Annette.'

'Yes, Richard works hard at it,' she said, sitting down again languidly. 'You can't blame him. Gardening saves him from having to talk to me.'

'It's a beautiful day. Why don't we take a stroll outside? Sam would appreciate it, wouldn't you, old fellow?'

A tiny smile appeared on Annette's pale face. 'Are you bullying me ever so slightly, Eileen? I suppose you'll tell me I have to get dressed next.'

'Yes, and you could take a shower first.'

'What! I don't know if I've got the energy.'

'Just try. Then I'll pour this tea.'

'All right. Do you know, I think you are the only person who doesn't think I am a completely hopeless case. Even Dr. Powell is bored with me.'

'Dr. Powell is bored with everything. He is a bored sort of man. Although I think I've noticed a gleam of interest when that new receptionist is about, you know, the one with the legs. Go on, off you go.'

Annette went. Eileen made herself useful. The kitchen was an odorous tip, but she managed to find cleaning materials and give the sink area a going over. Now it was more or less on a hygiene level with her own: mildly grubby, but not an active hazard to health. She poured the tea, scratched around in the fridge, and put a sandwich together for her friend.

Annette reappeared. She looked less dishevelled, but still slightly odd, in stained jodhpurs, a jumper with holes in and a faded scarf hiding her lifeless fair hair. Her face was very pale, her eyes dark and sunken. Annette Dyer had once been a pretty woman. Life, marriage and misery had obliterated her looks.

She eyed the sandwich. 'Must I?'

'Try. You are like a piece of string.'

Annette forced down half a sandwich and a cup of tea. It was painful to watch.

Eileen looked out of the window. 'The clouds are building up. Let's take this bouncy dog out into the garden and smell the roses.'

Annette seemed weak. She took Eileen's arm as they went outside and gasped as the strong sunlight beat on her face. 'I think I need sunglasses. I've got used to dark rooms.'

'Have mine for now.'

They walked slowly round the garden. The excited dog dashed in front and behind, his tail wagging.

'Well, you've made someone happy, at least,' Eileen said.

Annette smiled sadly. 'The trouble with Sam, he's a hundred and ten per cent canine, if you know what I mean. How's Tillie?'

'Getting old, creaky and slow.'

'That's the trouble with animals.'

'And with us.'

Eileen stayed with Annette for an hour or so, gently chivvying and encouraging her. After a while she seemed more animated, though still fragile. Eileen, with great difficulty, using all her powers of persuasion, made her promise faithfully to walk the short distance down the lane to her house the next day, bringing Sam with her, to drink a cup of coffee together, simply to have a change of scenery from her four dull walls.

Eileen gave her a hug as she left. She felt thin and wispy. 'You will come, won't you? Don't let me down.'

'No, I won't, and yes, I will. No, the other way around. I'll see you tomorrow. Thank you, Eileen. Thank you for caring.'

'Of course I care, nitwit. Till tomorrow.'

After leaving the Dyers', instead of going back down the lane to her own house, Eileen crossed a stile and followed a footpath along the edge of the woods which would lead her after ten minutes or so to the end of the dead-end lane where Marie lived. It was hot, dusty and quiet. Nettles overhung the path. She found a stick and beat them back as she walked. The woods were on her left, fields on her right, and she could just see the roofs of the houses ahead. As she came to the end of the footpath and climbed another stile into Marie's lane, she looked back in the direction of Annette's house. A movement by the trees made her focus. Standing in the field by the footpath was a figure in a striped jumper.

An extremely odd feeling came over her, like a fist clenched in her chest. She stood still and watched him. He too did not move.

Why should I feel afraid? Perhaps this is not fear, but something else for which I have no name.

She saw him disappear into the trees. Had he seen her?

She went on down the lane and knocked on Marie's door, then pushed it open. She found Marie in the kitchen, washing salad. 'Hello, you're on your feet today.'

'Got to keep the circulation flowing, so the medics said. You're in time for lunch.'

'I timed it well, then.' After Annette it was a relief to be with Marie, who somehow kept her sense of humour through the vicissitudes of her life. 'I've just been to see Annette Dyer.'

'Oh? How is the poor dear?'

'Awful. But I made her promise to come and see me tomorrow.'

'That'll be a great achievement, if she comes. I haven't seen her out for weeks.'

'No. You all right?'

'Going in the right direction, I think, thanks.'

Eileen helped her prepare lunch, and they sat down together at the tiny kitchen table. 'Marie, have you noticed anyone about? Anyone you don't know?'

'No, I can't say I have, but I haven't been out for the last few days. Why, is there someone?'

'I've seen this young man, yesterday and again just now. I think he's living rough in the woods. He's very dirty, and he seems frightened. He wears a striped jumper. It's very distinctive.'

'How odd. A young man, you say?'

'Yes, no more than twenty-something. Michael and Stephen have actually met him in the woods.'

'What!'

'Yes, I know, I felt the same. I've banned Michael from the woods for the moment. He says this fellow is OK, but children just wouldn't know if he wasn't, would they? They've given him their old camp and fed him with crisps.'

'I wonder what he's doing there.'

'The boys have this romantic notion that he's hiding out from the law.'

Marie put down her fork. 'From what you say he doesn't seem organized enough for that. He may be hiding from something else, something not even real.'

'What do you mean?'

'Haven't you been to London recently? Seen the poor down-and-outs in cardboard boxes, in shop doorways, parks, under bridges?'

'I hadn't thought of that angle.'

'This chap could be an alcoholic, though from your description I doubt it, or suffering from some form of mental illness.'

'About which I know nothing.'

Marie picked up the water jug and offered it to Eileen. 'I've heard about people like him. They tend to drift in a sort of downward spiral, until nobody knows who they are or where they've come from.'

'What do you suppose he is afraid of?'

Marie shrugged. 'I've no idea, but paranoia is not uncommon.'

'Where would he have come from, do you suppose?'

'Well, now that the institutions are closed and mentally sick people are living in the community there's no way of telling.'

'There's nowhere like that in Holton, is there?'

'No, but there may be in Caxford.'

Eileen shook her head. 'I am having so many odd things said to me today I am feeling quite bewildered.' She told Marie about her conversation with Charley and about Andy's reappearance.

'Well, well,' Marie said. 'So jail can sometimes be beneficial. I'd always thought that doing time would make a bad man worse, give him new ideas, but it seems I've been unduly cynical.'

'I don't think so,' Eileen said. 'In most cases I think you are right. The drug element can't help either.'

Marie sighed. 'I wouldn't be at all surprised to hear that my not-so-dear ex. has spent a few years held at public expense. And I can't see him reforming, not at any price.' She shuddered. 'It must be terrible to have to go to jail.'

'Anyway, according to Charley, Andy has had to prove himself over a number of years.'

'Let's hope so, for Michael's sake.'

'Marie, do you think I ought to say something about this man in the woods?'

'Who to, exactly? The police?'

'I don't know. He hasn't done anything wrong that I know of, but he still makes me uneasy. If he is one of those poor sick souls, is he likely to be a danger?'

'From the little I know, probably not, except to himself. You do get the odd awful incident, but they are grabbed and blown out of all proportion by the media. And usually it's down to a sheer lack of understanding and care of these poor creatures.'

'What do you think is the matter with him?'

'Who knows? And what help is a label anyway? Let it be for now, I would. He may disappear of his own accord. Still, I think it's probably sensible to keep Michael out of the way. Perhaps it's a good thing he's going to spend time with his family. Do you want any more?'

'No, thanks. That was just right.'

They talked of other things. Stephanie was not often at home. Eileen decided not to mention that Christina and Natasha had seen her at the nightclub. Marie needed no new worries about Stephanie.

Eileen started to stack the dirty plates. 'Has Philip been over since you came home from hospital?'

'Of course. He was here yesterday evening. I am discovering more and more that he is a jewel among men.'

Eileen grinned as she pushed her chair back and took the plates to the kitchen. 'There speaks a bit of Irish poetry. But I am glad to hear his devotion to you is not on the wane.'

'Quite the reverse, I assure you,' said Marie.

Eileen, catching Marie's mood, swallowed her momentary mirth. 'Do you think you might be fit to sing at our new Rector-to-be's induction?'

'I am hoping so.' A glint appeared in Marie's innocent blue eyes. 'And if my voice is getting a little rusty from lack of practice, I have the very person on hand to give me private lessons.'

Eileen laughed out loud. 'From all I have heard, you should be the one giving lessons. Though probably not in singing.'

'I don't know what you mean. Goodness, Eileen, shouldn't you be at the school gates? It's after three.'

'Is it? Heavens, you're right. Sorry, I shall have to leave you with these dishes. Thanks for lunch. I'll catch up with you soon.'

'Sure. Don't rush now, it's bad for a woman of your age.'

'If you weren't in a delicate state of convalescence, I'd thump you for that.'

'Dear me,' Marie said. 'Such violence. Go and pick up that poor abandoned boy, for goodness' sake!'

Eileen half-ran down the road to the school, not so much to be in time for Michael as to catch Nancy Potter before she became too embroiled in gossip with the other mothers. As it happened they met on the corner and crossed the road together. 'Nancy, has Stephen mentioned this man in the woods?'

'He did say something, but when I quizzed him he clammed up. Probably thought he'd be in trouble.'

'Apparently our boys have made their camp over to him and have been feeding him crisps.'

'No, Stephen never said anything about that, or I'd have fetched him one.'

'I don't know who this guy is or anything about him, but I've banned Michael from the woods for the time being.'

'OK, I'll tell my Stephen the same. I mean, they can always muck around in the garden, can't they? Stephen moans that Danielle always wrecks their games, that's the only thing.'

'They can play at my place,' Eileen said. 'But I'm puzzled about this man. Have you any idea where he might have come from?'

Nancy shook her head. 'If he's some kind of nutter, there's at least one of them community homes in Caxford. He might have done a bunk from there. My mum used to be a carer for one of those people, a young girl it was, a complete fruitcake from what Mum said. She only stood it for a while, then she packed it in. She said if she kept on with it any longer she'd be barmy herself. Not but what she didn't feel sorry for her as well,' she added hastily. 'And she said most of the nutcases were harmless.'

'I'm afraid I'm pretty ignorant about mental illness.'

'Me too. I keep away from all that. Got enough to worry about.'

'Yes. By the way, Michael won't be around for half term. He's going to visit his family.'

'Oh. That's nice. Stephen will miss him though.'

They were interrupted by a sudden clatter and babble of voices as the children began to pour out of the school. The two boys appeared out of the noisy crowd.

'I'll send Stephen home in time for his tea, Nancy.'

'Yes, thanks. Be a good boy, Stephen.'

Stephen pulled a face at his mother's retreating figure, then both he and Michael ran home at full pelt, giggling, their school bags banging on their backs.

'It looks like Michael will be going to his parents for half term,' Eileen said to Natasha later that evening as they washed dishes. She told her about the conversation with Charley.

Natasha raised her eyebrows. 'Lots of changes on the horizon, then, Mum. Was Michael pleased?'

'Very. But he's more concerned about this man in the woods. He seems to think he'll starve without his and Stephen's supplies.'

'It does make you wonder what he's living on, doesn't it?'

'Tash, do you think he might be dangerous? I just wish I knew more about these things.'

'I don't know either. But Sean might. I'll ask him when I ring him later.' She paused for a moment, thinking. 'I might know where he's come from, though.'

61

'Where?'

'You know those big Victorian houses, down Denbigh Street, opposite where the old cinema used to be? There's a house there for those people. They're OK to look after themselves, but they have people they can call on when they need something or can't cope. Sometimes you see them in the street or in the shops. Some of them are really weird, shouting out at thin air, a lot of rubbish usually, but sometimes they look perfectly normal.'

'Why do you think Sean might know something?'

'Oh, I don't know, he just knows a lot of stuff.' Natasha spoke with affected casualness, but every word gave her away. 'I'll ring him now and ask him.'

A few moments later Eileen could hear her voice, low and breathless, from the hall. There were silences, interspersed with chatter and bursts of sudden laughter.

'Sean has a cousin who is a manic depressive,' she said when she reappeared. 'She goes through times when she's really high, and she starts up all sorts of schemes, and has loads of energy and does daft things, sort of on impulse. Then she goes way down and is depressed for ages, especially if she's blown a lot of money in the high time. She doesn't get out of bed, and lets everything go to ruin, including herself. Sean said the last time she was really in a bad way her husband took her two little boys away because they couldn't stand living like that. Then I think someone talked her into getting some treatment so I think she's more or less on an even keel now.'

'Poor thing,' Eileen said. 'Did her husband bring the children back?'

'Oh yes, they're fine now. Her mum helps her out and they all make sure she sticks to her medication. He doesn't really know much more. Perhaps you need to go to the library and read up about it if you're that interested. I'm going to watch TV now, OK, Mum?' She disappeared into the living room.

Eileen shut the door to dull the noise from the television, and opened her Bible on the kitchen table. She delved into the mysteries of Romans 14.

"So then we must always aim at those things that bring peace and that help to strengthen one another," Eileen read. And a little further on, "Keep what you believe about this matter, then, between yourself and God... Anything that is not based on faith is sin."

But that, taken to its logical conclusion, implied that nothing, in moral or spiritual terms, was neutral. Nothing was simple, innocent, earthly. Everything had spiritual significance. Perhaps, if you went along

62

with the notion of the Fall, that was logical. When people were innocent, so was everything else in the natural realm; as soon as people went wrong, everything in creation was tainted, and became, like the human race, in need of redemption. She thought of another passage that she had read a few weeks before.

"Yet there was the hope that creation itself would one day be set free from its slavery to decay and would share the glorious freedom of the children of God."

Eileen dwelt on this thought for some time. What a responsibility it was. And what a mess humanity had made of it. But it was right, because it flowed from God's original mandate to the heirs of Adam in Genesis:

"Then God said, 'And now we will make human beings; they will be like us and resemble us. They will have power over the fish, the birds, and all animals, domestic and wild, large and small.' So God created human beings, making them to be like himself. He created them male and female, blessed them, and said, 'Have many children, so that your descendants will live over all the earth, and bring it under their control.'" So all nature shared in the Fall, in earthly corruption, and in eventual redemption. How awesome a destiny! And when she looked at people, what did she see? Such a blend of the divine, and the diabolical, and the paltry.

Her thoughts strayed to the woods, sumptuous in the foliage of early summer, leaves clattering against each other in the wind, hedgerows bright with stitchwort and campion, secretive celandine in the thickets, the sweet breath of green things. And she thought of corruption living there in the body of a human being, twisted out of shape by a sickness that seemed spiritual in its manifestations. But was that man corrupt in himself? Surely not, surely his illness was a symptom of that fall from grace all people shared. Can minds, like bodies, be made whole? She thought of the people Jesus had healed with a touch of human compassion and divine power. Were some of the demons he had banished in fact the demons of mental affliction? Some of the stories, she knew, referred to epilepsy. Perhaps not all. She thought of the demons that were driven out into the herd of pigs, freeing the man who had spent his life wandering naked among the tombs, screaming, and cutting himself with stones. That didn't sound like someone with fits. She felt the need to find books to help her understand. There were so many questions with no answers.

Her train of thought was interrupted by Natasha, who came in from the living room, yawning and stretching. 'You should have watched that, Mum. It was really funny.' She peered over her mother's shoulder. 'What

63

are you doing? Oh, reading your Bible. What can you get from that? Honestly?'

'Is that a rhetorical question?' Eileen asked. 'Or do you really want to know?'

'Go on, tell me. I want to know. But I'll put the kettle on. Do you want something?'

'Yes, I'll have tea if you're making it. OK, what do I find in here?' She laid a hand on the closed book. 'Everything, really. It tells you about how to live to your full capacity, your destiny as a child of God, all about sin and evil and redemption, even about the end of the world as we know it. And more.' She said nothing more for the moment, waiting for Natasha to finish clattering in the kitchen, leaving her time to ponder.

Natasha sat down opposite her mother, putting two mugs of tea on the table. 'Heavy stuff. Is there anything in there about marriage?'

'Plenty. What did you have in mind exactly?'

Natasha studied her teacup. 'Oh, stuff like whether to get married or not.' Eileen waited. Natasha looked up at her. Her eyes were dark and intent. 'Sean is talking about getting married,' she said at last.

'I see. Well, the Bible is in favour of marriage in principle,' Eileen said in as neutral a voice as she could manage. 'But it doesn't say much about who to marry, or when, or what colour dress to wear. St. Paul reckoned it was better to stay single, if you can, but if you can't cope with that, go ahead. And it seems fairly clear that it's the best situation for children to grow up in.'

Natasha sighed deeply. 'Yeah, that sounds OK. But I still don't know what to do.'

'You haven't known each other long, have you?'

'Almost three months.'

'And you're still only twenty.'

'Yes, but Sean's older. Twenty-six.'

'How do you feel about it? Is he putting pressure on you?'

'Oh, no. But it's what he wants. Do you think I am a bit pathetic to want what he wants?'

'Not necessarily. But it can be dangerous.'

Natasha brooded for a moment. 'How can you tell if you love someone? If I'm going to see Sean I feel really excited, but does that mean I love him?'

'I don't know. It sounds more like lust to me.'

'Mum! You are embarrassing me.'

'Why? It's all perfectly normal, isn't it? The only trouble is, lust doesn't last that long, and you need commitment, plenty of will-power,

64

to get you through the rotten or boring bits that come with every marriage, to equip you for the long haul.'

'Do you think I ought to wait then?'

'You must do what you think is right for you. I'm no great role model anyway, as far as marriage is concerned. Maybe, if you're feeling doubtful, you do need a bit more time.'

Natasha finished her tea and got up. She went to the sink and slowly rinsed out her mug. 'Do you think I'm too young?'

'Definitely. Nobody should get married before the age of fifty.'

'Mum, you are daft.'

'Probably. Anyway, love, I'm going to bed. Don't forget to switch off the lights. And keep me posted on your wedding plans, won't you? I don't want to be the last to know.'

'Go to bed, Mum. You obviously need your sleep. I think you are definitely cracking up.'

'On that happy note,' Eileen said, 'I shall wish you good night.'

Drifting off to sleep, she remembered what she hadn't told Natasha. *Just as, I imagine, there is plenty she hasn't told me.*

After Stephen had gone home for his tea, Michael hovered about, plainly building up to something. He had talked little about the impending visit with his parents, though Eileen knew he was looking forward to it. Something else, more immediate and urgent, was on his mind.

Eileen paused, a saucepan in one hand, the other on the tap. 'Well?' She looked at him enquiringly.

'Mum, I'm really worried about Chris,' Michael said in a rush. 'Without Steve and me he'll starve. He hasn't got anything to drink except a mouldy old bottle of water we took him. And if it stops being hot he's going to freeze to death at night. We can't just leave him, Mum, we can't.'

'You're not going down there, Michael.'

'I know. But Mum,' he said, moving closer, 'we could go down to the woods, you and me. It would be all right if you was there.'

'He's very frightened. I'd probably scare him away.'

'You could just be somewhere near, to make sure it's OK. I could take him some sandwiches, something to drink. Please, Mum.' He gazed at her searchingly.

'Michael, this is crazy.'

'Mum, doesn't it say in the Bible, you know, that bit about giving people food and drink and clothes and visiting them in prison? It's a bit like that, isn't it?'

Eileen was silent. He was right. How could she duck it?

She sighed. 'All right, Michael. Tomorrow after school you and I will go to the woods. Just you and I, not Stephen or anybody else. We will leave food and drink for this poor man. And after that we will stay at home. You won't go on about it. Not a word. Is it a deal?' The boy nodded, clearly relieved. 'If he is there, you try to persuade him to go home. People will soon notice him hanging about, and he'll get into trouble. We don't want that to happen.'

'OK, Mum,' Michael said. 'We'll take plenty, won't we, so it lasts a while.'

'All right. But no more of it now. I don't know how you persuaded me into this lunacy.'

Michael came up behind her and put his arms round her middle. 'Because you are kind and like helping people, like me and Chris.'

'Go on, now. Wash your hands before we eat.'

I must be out of my mind. Poking around in the woods after some head-case at the whim of an eight-year-old. It's a good job nobody knows. They would think I had completely lost my reason.

As she slithered down the dark road to unconsciousness, she prayed. *Keep us safe, Lord, Michael and me. Let nothing bad happen, for the sake of his trust in your commands. Not just tomorrow, but every day, especially when soon I will not be there, don't let that little flame of his be extinguished. We both need saving from ourselves, and only you can do it.*

Tuesday 21st May 1996

Ten thirty came and there was still no sign of Annette. Eileen busied herself with other things, but she could not settle for long. Her mind was agitated and restless, like the surface of a dark lake ruffled by conflicting winds.

At eleven she rang the Dyers' number. It rang and rang, but no one answered. A feeling of dread began to creep up from her stomach, encircling her throat, making it difficult to breathe. She found the house oppressive, and the growing heat did not help. She went out into the front garden, crossed the road and stood in the lane that led up to Annette's. There was nobody about.

Then, suddenly and to her great relief, Sam the spaniel appeared out of nowhere, hurtling down the road towards her in lolloping bounds, tongue hanging out, whining with delight. Behind him some way Annette crept, his lead dangling from her hand. When she saw Eileen she managed a feeble wave. Eileen, Sam at her heels, walked up to meet her. 'I thought you'd chickened out,' she said, taking Annette by the arm.

'I nearly did,' Annette said. She sounded breathless, panicky. 'And this wretched dog was so excited he slipped his collar and rushed away. So I had to follow. I couldn't let anything happen to Sam, even if he is a class-A pain.'

They walked slowly down the lane.

'Do you want to sit in the garden?' Eileen asked. 'It isn't as posh as yours, but the breeze makes it a bit cooler than indoors, and we can keep an eye on the dogs.'

Sam greeted Tillie with overpowering enthusiasm, almost leaping into her basket with her. She grunted her disapproval, heaved herself up, and went outside, lying down under the apple tree with a disgruntled sigh. Sam raced round her in circles, trying to tempt her to play, but she resolutely ignored him, and finally he gave up and contented himself with rooting around among the vegetables, savouring the various smells of an unfamiliar garden. He tried to make Bill's acquaintance, but Bill scuttled squeaking to the back of his hutch and hid under a pile of hay.

Eileen put two garden chairs on a fairly level bit of grass and took out a tray of coffee. 'How are you feeling today?'

Annette hesitated. 'I was going to say awful, or lousy, or some such word. But then it came to me how sick I am of saying that. I can't tell you how much I want to say, "Fine, never better, thank you," and mean it.'

'Is that a new feeling?'

'No, but it's something I haven't felt for a long time, a really desperate desire to get well.'

'That sounds hopeful, doesn't it?' Eileen said. 'I confess my ignorance. You are the expert here.'

'I hardly know myself,' Annette said. 'I seem to have been confused for years. Dr. Powell prescribed me some pills two Christmases ago. They made me feel totally spaced out. I thought I was literally going mad. So I stopped taking them.'

'Did you tell him that?'

'No, I was too cowardly. He thinks I am a hypochondriac anyway. He probably talks to Richard at the golf club. Do you think a new doctor might be more sympathetic?'

'It's certainly worth a try. What about that rather glamorous lady doctor I've seen at the surgery—what's her name?'

'No idea. Would it be all right to see somebody else?'

'Why not? Get an appointment when you know Dr. Powell is playing golf.'

Annette attempted a smile. 'I am terribly feeble, I know, but would you come with me? Just to the waiting room, I mean.'

'Of course.'

'I want to do everything I can to get better, but I feel very unsure of myself. I seem to have no confidence at all. I know it's been very hard on Richard and the boys, having me like this.'

You are loyal, Annette. But I think I would have gone down the drain if I'd had to live with Richard all these years, and raise those two loud, insensitive, ungrateful, rugby-playing, beer-swilling, money-mad sons of yours. Then she gave herself a mental slap on the wrist. No, Annette was ill even when the boys were young and still quite charming in a puppyish sort of way. And Richard wasn't really a bad man, just oafish at times, with that crass, hobnailed sense of humour. Even so, the three of them had not helped her one bit.

'Eileen, do you remember that group I went to, in Caxford, a few years ago?'

'Vaguely. It didn't last long, as I recall.'

68

'No. I wasn't ready for it, I suppose. Something went wrong. I expect Richard made some derogatory remark and I never went back.'

'Was it any good?'

'At the time, I didn't take much in. But just lately I've been thinking. At night, you know. I don't sleep well, so I just lie in bed or wander round the house. I feel now it could have been helpful, if only I'd given it a proper chance. What do you think?'

'If you feel up to it, why not? Can you remember who ran it?'

'Amazingly, yes. It was a young man called Mark Pepper. He was a sufferer too, he'd been depressed for a long time, but he had benefited from something called cognitive therapy. Have you heard of it?'

'I think so, but don't ask me to define it.'

'When I stopped going after one or two sessions, he rang me up to ask me to carry on coming. I just ignored it then, but now I think it was kind of him to take the trouble.' Annette leaned forward and spoke more urgently. 'I must be getting better, Eileen, because when I am really in a bad way I can't think of anything but myself and this awful blackness. Somehow just lately I've been more aware of other people.'

'I certainly haven't heard you say so much at one sitting, if ever,' Eileen said. 'But please, be careful. Don't go for the marathon yet. And let me help, if I can.'

'You already have, and I thank you for that,' said Annette, squeezing Eileen's hand. 'But if I do manage to get hold of Mark and go back to the group, will you drive me? I don't feel I could quite cope with the bus yet, and Richard always has the car for work.'

'I'd be glad to.'

'Eileen, this may seem an odd question, but do you do a crossword?'

Eileen was startled. 'No, but I dare say I could find one. There are plenty of old newspapers under the stairs. Michael uses them for Bill's hutch.'

'I just thought it might be a start. You know, crank up the old brain a bit. I am sure it's beginning to atrophy.'

'I can't believe I am hearing all this. What has happened?'

'Nothing really, at least not outwardly. After you went home yesterday I sat and thought for ages and I told myself it was up to me to sort my life out, to put myself back together again, even if other things get broken on the way. I sound brave, don't I? I don't feel it, in fact I am scared. But I remembered something Mark Pepper said, about depression being a prison, but some of us stay in there because it's safe, even if the key is on our side of the door.'

'Well, champ,' Eileen said, 'I'm with you, and I'm all admiration.'

She found a crossword in an ancient faded paper and, after half an hour of laughter at their own ineptitude, and continual reference to the dictionary, they completed it.

'Eileen, you make me feel almost normal,' said Annette. 'And I haven't asked how things are with you.'

Eileen told her about Christina's visit, Natasha and Sean, and the latest news of Michael. Then, rather hesitantly, she mentioned what had been on her mind since Sunday. 'Annette, do you know much about mental illness in general?'

'A bit, not much. Why?'

'There's someone living rough in the woods, and I don't think he's a tramp.'

'Oh yes, I've seen him. A young, dark-haired fellow in a striped jumper.'

'Yes, that's him. I haven't scared you by mentioning him, have I?'

'No. He doesn't look very violent to me. I feel afraid for him, not of him.'

Eileen nodded. 'I know what you mean.'

'I noticed him because of the shouting,' said Annette.

'Shouting?'

'Yes. I was in the bathroom one day last week, I had the window open, and suddenly I heard someone shouting. I looked out, and there he was in the rape field, arms raised to heaven, shouting.'

'Weren't you afraid?'

'Only for a moment. Then I realized. A long time ago I had a spell in hospital.' She trembled visibly. 'There were some very strange people in there. After a while I got used to them. But some of them yelled and shouted like that. There were the poor souls who had hallucinations. They saw and heard things that weren't there, not that anyone else could see, anyway. One of the nurses explained to me that they were shouting at voices they could hear inside their heads.'

'How horrible.'

'It must have been, although not all of them were miserable. Some used to shriek with laughter, as if at a private joke. There were others too, people with what they called drug-induced psychosis. And a host of other oddities. I hated that place, though I knew they tried to be kind. It was literally Bedlam.'

'I had no idea.'

'I never want to get that ill again, Eileen.'

'Of course you don't. Between us we've got to make sure it doesn't happen.'

'What do you think,' Annette said. 'I thought I might ring that woman who does your hair at home. The trouble is, I can't let anyone in to my filthy, neglected tip.'

'You book the hairdresser, and I'll come by the day before and help you clean the place up,' Eileen said.

'That would be wonderful,' Annette said. 'You really are a dear, putting yourself out for me like this.'

'It's a pleasure. In fact, if I find you the number, why don't you ring that hair woman now? You know, take the first step.'

'Do you think I can?'

'Absolutely. When you're ready, the phone is waiting.'

An hour later Eileen walked Annette up the lane to her own house. She felt uneasy, looking round at the empty fields where only the wind and butterflies moved, wondering if the strange young man might appear, but Annette seemed unconcerned. She had booked the hairdresser for Friday afternoon.

'Fine,' Eileen said. 'On Thursday we clean the kitchen and the hallway. She won't need to see anything else.'

Returning from Annette's Eileen made herself a hasty sandwich, locked up, put on sandals and sunglasses and went out. Her mind was busy. She barely noticed anything in the physical world and drove like a robot. Just before two o'clock she parked in Caxford in a side road off the High Street and walked along to the library. Despite the weather few people were about, apart from some shift workers and elderly men who lounged at tables on the pavement outside the town's two High Street pubs. After the sticky warmth of the street, Eileen was glad of the cool tranquillity of the library.

For a small market town, the library was surprisingly well-stocked. It took Eileen less than twenty minutes of searching and browsing to find at least some of what she wanted. She found nothing on cognitive therapy, but came away satisfied with a commentary on St. Paul's Epistle to the Romans and a slim handbook for laymen on schizophrenia and associated conditions.

On the way back to where she had parked the car she made a detour to Denbigh Street. It was a quiet cul-de-sac, a row of substantial houses down one side, the boarded-up cinema and a coal yard on the other, and at the end a high railing and a grass bank on top of which, behind dusty fencing, ran the railway line. She walked slowly up and down the street, feeling conspicuous but trying to look casual and insignificant. She saw nobody, and there was no way of telling which, if any, was the house she had come to see.

71

Still in a state of abstraction, she drove home. She was jolted back into the world of quotidian reality when, approaching Holton as the road passed through a small wood, a young fox broke from cover and ran across the road in front of her, making her brake suddenly. The fox sat on the far verge and watched as she restarted the car. Then with a flick of its tail it vanished into the hedgerow. She drove sedately after that, trying to keep her mind on the present and particular.

She made a cup of tea. There was half an hour before she had to pick up Michael from school. She opened the book on schizophrenia and began to read.

Twenty minutes later she closed the book and walked down to the school, still completely absorbed in her thoughts. Her mind was full of unfamiliar terms: core symptoms, course criteria, exclusion criteria, differential diagnosis. The case histories that she had read, though fictitious, had opened her imagination to a world of fractured thinking, unintelligible speech, inappropriate responses, hallucinations and delusions. She shivered as she thought of the harrowing effect these things must have on a sufferer's family and friends. But this, apparently, was not all. In addition to these dramatic symptoms were the more insidious and perhaps even more debilitating reduction of normal mental processes and emotional responses, the absence of will to act, the inability to feel pleasure, the lack of self-care which could characterize acutely ill patients.

At this point Eileen had been obliged to stop and go to the school to collect Michael, but it was more than enough. She was horrified, but fascinated. What could cause such a catastrophic breakdown in normal thinking and behaviour? How could anyone cope if a member of their family fell ill? It so often affected young adults on the brink of independent life, and there seemed no cure, only treatment and the possibility of remission. It was the end of all hope, all ambition. Eileen thought then of the young man, standing in a field of rape, shouting to the wind. What could he see or hear that was visible or audible to no one else? What was he afraid of? Who or what had driven him to seek refuge, if such it was, in Holton woods? Despite the caveats of her rational, cautious, adult self, Eileen was not entirely sorry that she had promised to take Michael in search of the mysterious young man in the striped jumper.

'Mum, do you think Chris would like peanut butter?' asked Michael, frowning with concentration as he spread a thick slice of bread. He had hardly stopped talking since they entered the house.

'I don't know what he likes, and neither do you,' Eileen said. 'Make

72

lots of different kinds, then there's bound to be something to suit him. There's plenty of stuff in the cupboard.'

She made a flask of coffee, filled a plastic bottle with water, added apples and chocolate, then helped Michael finish the sandwiches. She put them in a large plastic box and put everything into a carrier bag.

'Ready?'

Michael nodded, wiping buttery hands down the side of his school trousers.

'I think I'll take Tillie,' Eileen said. 'She hasn't had a walk today, and if that poor young man is afraid, it will seem more normal if I am seen as a dog-walker.'

They set off down the back garden. Eileen felt very peculiar, as if she were walking in a dream. Her feet seemed barely to feel the ground, defying gravity. There was an atmosphere of unreality, almost as if she had stepped into another dimension. She felt a curious buzzing in her ears.

Michael, quiet at last, led the way, down through the fallen oaks and the hawthorns tangled with honeysuckle. The woods were silent, heavy under the afternoon sun, still, hot and stuffy. As they came to the bottom of the path, with Tillie lumbering behind, Michael turned and put a finger to his lips.

The feeling of unreality persisted, and the buzzing became a hammering. She followed Michael reluctantly as he disappeared into the thickets at the side of the path. For a moment she lost sight of him, then, after some rustling, she heard a low cry. He came back to her, his face troubled. 'Mum, he isn't here. He's gone.'

Eileen thought for a moment. 'Perhaps he's in some other part of the woods. I saw him yesterday, remember, near the end of Marie's lane, and Mrs. Dyer has seen him in the rape field. He must wander about a lot.'

'I know. But this is his base-camp. He always leaves his things here. He hides them in this patch of brambles.'

'What things?'

'Oh, he has a silver tin with his special things in, things he likes. And he has an old grey blanket. He keeps it rolled up round the tin. I've looked, and they're not there.'

A thought struck Eileen. 'Does he have anything like medicine in this tin, Michael?'

'No, he does have pills, he told us, they're to make him feel better. But he keeps them in his pocket. He said he doesn't want anyone else getting hold of them.' He looked up at her, anxiously plucking at her sleeve. 'Where do you think he's gone? I hope he's all right.'

'Well, *I* hope he's seen sense and gone home,' Eileen said. Normality seemed to be returning. The ground felt solid again. 'Why don't we leave the food here, just in case he comes back? Look, we could put it on this tree-stump near to the hiding place. Do you want to leave a note?'

The boy shook his head. 'He'll know it's for him, if he does come back.'

He seemed disappointed, and dragged his feet all the way home.

'You know, Michael, if he has gone home, it's better for him,' Eileen said, trying to sound encouraging. 'It can't be good for anyone to live in the woods.'

'But what if he ran away from home in the first place?' Michael said. 'He couldn't go back there then.'

'Did he say anything to you about where he'd come from?'

'No, he just said he'd walked and kept out of sight. Sometimes he was like that, just talked ordinary, then sometimes he went a bit funny and said queer things.'

'What sort of queer things?'

'Nothing really, like lots of jumbled-up stuff. Steve was a bit scared but I wasn't. Chris is OK.' He was quiet for a moment, considering; then he brightened. 'Can I go down to Steve's?'

'Yes, but keep out of Mrs. Potter's way, don't tease Danielle, and the woods are still off-limits.'

'We'll go to the playground and muck around with Steve's football.'

'All right. Be back by six.'

Eileen was gazing distractedly at the disordered, iced-up contents of the freezer, trying to think of something for dinner, when the phone rang.

'Eileen, hi, it's Charley.'

'Hello, Charley. How are you?'

'I'm fine, thanks, just in a rush as usual. End of the day, desk smothered in paperwork, the normal situation. I just wanted to tell you about some talks I had with Denise and Andy earlier today. I'll have to be quick, though. I've got a meeting in ten minutes.'

'Fire away.'

'Well, as you know, I wanted to let Denise and Andy know about your visit to Michael's school, so I called them this morning early. Andy was at work, so I talked to Denise, mentioned this special school, and left it with her. She must have talked to Andy at lunchtime because he then rang me. Whatever else, Eileen, you have to hand it to him for keenness, because he's now talking about applying to the council for a

74

transfer to Lambury so that Michael can go to Hartridge House. Andy said the flat would be too small anyway, with both Michael and himself there, and also he was talking about the kids needing a garden.'

'I see. Do you think the transfer is a possibility?'

'Oh yes, especially with backing from this department.'

Eileen was silent for a moment; the trickle of implications was rapidly becoming a flood. 'It seems everything is working out, doesn't it?'

'It does, but we, you and I, must make sure it doesn't go too fast. It's good that Andy is showing so much commitment, but our responsibility is to Michael, and I don't want his future to come crashing down round his ears because we haven't thought it all through properly.'

'Good. I'm really relieved to hear you say that.'

'Don't worry, Eileen, really. I'm not a complete moron, nor do I want to have too many blots and blunders on my CV.'

'Point taken. And of course you're not a moron.'

'Look, I'm thinking of setting up a meeting straight after half term. If Michael comes back to you on Saturday the first, you can talk to Michael, also Denise and Andy can chew over how it went, then we can all get together. I'll set it up and let you know, of course, but can you pencil in, say, eleven on Monday the third?'

'Yes, that's all right.'

'Good. Now I must fly. See you on Saturday. Bye.'

After she had put the phone down, Eileen stood for a moment in the hallway, automatically scratching one leg with the other bare foot, her thoughts slowly churning. Although Charley's caution had comforted her, she still felt as if control of the situation had left her hands, and it made her uneasy. The clattering of the back door brought her back to the moment.

'Steve had to go in, so I came home early,' Michael said. 'What are you cooking?'

'Nothing yet. I can't make up my mind.'

'Can we have pizza?'

'All right. Go and wash your hands then.'

Michael paused at the foot of the stairs. 'Steve's dad, you know, Jim, he's seen Chris.'

'Oh? Where?'

'He was going down the main road in his tractor, Jim, I mean. I expect he was going to that big field near the woods.'

Eileen nodded. It was close to where the fox had run out in front of her.

'Steve's dad saw him walking along the side of the road, but when Chris heard the tractor he went into the trees.'

'Which way was he going?'

'Towards town. So it looks like he really has gone.'

'Well, Michael, I hope he has, for his own sake. I hope he is safe somewhere. When did Mr. Potter see him?'

'Yesterday, about tea time, Steve said. He heard his dad talk about it to his mum when he came in.'

'That's probably the end of it, then. I'll go and collect the things we left in the woods when I walk Tillie tomorrow. Go and get ready now, because this doesn't take long to cook.'

Natasha came in from work, ate hastily, bathed and changed. Sean collected her, and waved to Eileen politely from his car. Eileen had an impression of a well-built, fair-haired, soft-featured, smiling young man; and Natasha's every movement and gesture, her impatience to be gone, haring down the front path and losing a shoe, betrayed her eagerness to be with him. Eileen smiled to herself.

When Michael had gone to bed, she switched on the TV for the news. It was dominated by the sinking of a passenger-steamer in Africa, with a thousand people dead. Eileen switched off the set and sighed. She wished she could not imagine the scene, the terror, the confusion, the washed-up bodies, the sickened emergency workers, the distraught relatives. She felt tired suddenly, heavy, deflated, sour. She made a cup of coffee. The house was hot, and she opened the back door to let in cooler air. An owl took off silently from the apple tree and swooped away in a soft flurry of feathers. The peace of the woods, the darkness itself, flowed up to meet her. The only sounds were late birds, Bill fidgeting in his hutch, muted merriment from the pub, an occasional burst of laughter from people sitting outside, enjoying the warm summer evening. Then the phone rang. Eileen shut the back door and went to answer it.

'Hello, Eileen. It's David.'

The sound of his voice came back to her instantly as if the three years since they had last met had ceased to exist. She thought she had forgotten, and perhaps she had; but the tone of his pleasant tenor voice, warm, friendly and enquiring, with a hint of reticence, coming so unexpectedly, gave her a physical shock: tiny prickles ran down her arms and she shivered involuntarily. Realizing that she had not yet replied, she gathered herself with an effort.

'David, what a surprise. But I'm afraid Natasha has gone out.'

'It's not Natasha I want to speak to, it's you, as it happens.'

'Oh.' Surprise gave way to alarm. Why did he want to speak to her?

The only thing she could think of in that moment of confusion was that he was going to ask her for a divorce.

I can't make any big decisions, not right now. She tried to quell a rising tide of fright. She could not clearly identify the reason for her fear, but it felt as if judgment was at hand, complete with drum-roll.

David was explaining. 'I am coming down to London on Sunday for a conference which starts on Monday. Our evenings are free, and I was hoping I could drive down and talk for an hour or so. When you aren't too busy, of course,' he added politely.

Eileen was regaining her composure. She was not sure she wanted to talk to him. But what on earth could he want? And there was a twinge of curiosity as well. Had he altered, aged, gone bald or grey? Despite the conflicting feelings she answered calmly enough.

'All right, if you like. Would Tuesday suit you? Any time after six-ish would be fine.'

'Good, Tuesday, yes. How are things with you? Are you well? Are the girls all right? How about the young lad, Michael isn't it, is he still with you?'

'Yes, but he will be away for half term. And we are all quite well, thank you.'

'Good. Till Tuesday, then. I'll be driving down, so I'll probably be with you about eight.'

'All right. Goodbye, David.'

She put the phone down and sat in the kitchen, puzzling over the meaning of David's call. Clearly it was no impromptu whim on his part; he had rung *to make an appointment.* He had something specific in mind, and the manner of its delivery, pleasant, polite, implacable, only added to her feeling of defensiveness. She felt she had been somehow, obscurely, wrong-footed. For a moment she thought of asking Natasha or Christina if they had any inkling of their father's mind, but she rejected the idea. Whether they knew anything or not, her own ignorance, unsurprising as it was, made her feel uncomfortable, even humiliated.

Bother David. Why does he have to be so mysterious? I shall banish him from my mind, and go and wrestle with St. Paul. Mentally and metaphorically.

Sitting at the kitchen table, she started again with Romans 12. The commentary lay open beside her Bible.

"Paul's mind sweeps the infinite, but is also practical and pragmatic. Its theology searches the depths, but always he concludes with the ethical imperatives that spring from them. For Paul the body as well as the soul is acceptable as an offering in God's service; after all, Jesus himself took on human flesh and lived as a man. The greatest works of art, and the least, including those created specifically for the glory of God, are made by hands and seen by eyes. God's true service, therefore, is the offering to him of the life and work of every ordinary day, seeing all of creation, and the self as part of it, as God's holy temple.

"The change of which Paul speaks in verse two is truly radical, a change of the inward person, no longer living according to the dictates of the fallen human world with its low standards of conduct and high expectations of selfish satisfaction, but living a life taken over, dominated, irradiated by the spirit of Christ.

"Self-knowledge is a primary prerequisite, and with knowledge acceptance, not coveting another's gift but humbly recognizing and using one's own in the service of God and his Church. All are gifted, and all gifts, whether they be humble or noteworthy, hidden or obvious, are from God himself. In the end all gifts are God's, and their use must be his also."

She looked again at the list of gifts, shaking her head gloomily as her eyes passed over prophecy, teaching, leadership. Perhaps there were others, less elevated, less demanding. Surely she could manage to be kind to people and do things to help them, at the least. But when she read on, the guidance given by St. Paul for Christian living made her quail before its sheer disdain of compromise.

For the Christian, it was better to suffer evil than to do it; persecution must be met with prayer. Rejoice with the happy, weep with the sad. *Harder to rejoice, if someone has succeeded where you have failed, or got something easily for which you have been unsuccessfully striving. What it means, over and over, is the death of self.*

Christians should live in harmony, because nothing good could be achieved where there was strife. Pride and snobbery were definitely out; birth, wealth, status were of no interest to God. Our conduct must not only *be* good, it must be seen to be good. *Oh dear. Even here in our own little church community we have fallen somewhat flat.* She thought of petty quarrels, of undignified jostling for rights, of offence taken at being neglected or insufficiently thanked, and shuddered at the contrast between such smallness of spirit and the great demands of the Apostle.

She read on.

Christians must live in peace with all people. But here there were two provisos. St Paul allowed for fighting for a principle. And he conceded that some people find peace more difficult than others: the fiery must expend more effort in restraining temper than the naturally mild. But vengeance should not be touched in any circumstance. First, because it was solely God's province and privilege; only he had the total knowledge that allows just judgment. And second, to move, change and win the hearts of men and women, kindness was more effective. But perhaps above all other considerations, the Christian person must not stoop to evil, for so was evil increased; hate itself was a chief among evils, and only love was the antidote to its poison.

Eileen sat back in her chair, trying to blink away the beginnings of a headache. As always, when she read and thought more deeply, the sheer magnitude of the demands of her faith hit her hard. And yet how else could it be? Given the vast insidious grip of evil, and the enormous sacrifice of God in its defeat, how could the expectation of the Christian person's contribution not also be huge? But how could these great commands be injected into a little, limited, tedious, inconsequential life like hers?

The headache had now taken hold. She made a cup of tea and took two painkillers. It was eleven o'clock. She did a few last chores and locked up. She was thinking of going up to bed when she heard the soft scrunch of tyres on gravel, whispered voices, an engine starting up, the front door opening and closing quietly.

'Hello, you're early,' she said to Natasha as she came into the kitchen.

'Work tomorrow, Mum. Got to get plenty of sleep, or I'll be baggy-eyed and cranky.' Natasha seemed in an excellent mood.

'Did you make a pot?' she asked, eyeing her mother's tea.

'No, but the kettle's only just boiled. Had a good evening?'

'Yeah, OK, thanks.' Natasha hummed as she poured boiling water onto a teabag.

Eileen noticed a smell about her, faint but instantly recognizable, slightly sweaty and something else besides. *Everybody's at it, it seems. Marie and Philip, Natasha and Sean, and I dare say Christina is not above the odd fling, whatever she tells me.* A thought struck her. Maybe David too, maybe that was what he was coming to tell her. She wondered how she would feel, and realized she didn't know. But, considering the circumstances, how she might feel was more or less irrelevant.

'Your dad rang me tonight,' she said. 'He wants to come down and see me. I can't imagine why.'

Natasha seemed oblivious to any significance her father's call might have. 'Oh yes, he's coming down to London. He rang me too. I meant to tell you. Sean and I are going up to London on Sunday night, meeting Dad at King's Cross, going for a drink. It was his idea.'

'I thought he was driving.'

'I think he's planning to hire a car and maybe see a few people while he's down south.'

'Oh.' She paused a moment, started to say something, stopped. 'Oh, well, as you say, time to get some sleep. Goodnight, love, see you in the morning.'

'Yeah. 'Night, Mum.'

She lay on her back, thinking. *I don't want to think. I want to go to sleep. Everything is getting muddled, messy and mysterious.*

When she did eventually sleep it was shallow and fitful, and she woke several times. Under chemical influence her headache receded, but it was still there, hovering and threatening, like a storm on the horizon. The bed was too hot, and she kicked off the covers. Then the breeze from the window cooled her sweaty skin and she pulled them back on. The sheets were wrinkled, and it felt as if she was lying on stones. She got up twice to go to the bathroom. At last, by this time extremely frustrated and losing the battle against ill-temper, just as the darkness was beginning to lighten outside, she fell into a sleep of utter exhaustion. But even then the gremlins of her unconscious were busily, maliciously at work.

She stood on a short stone pier gazing out towards the sea. It was low tide, and the shining water lay beyond an expanse of flat, grey mud. She leaned on iron railings, and a cool breeze lifted her hair.

After a short while, prompted by she knew not what, she descended a narrow flight of steps at the side of the pier, treading carefully because of the lurid green seaweed, until she reached the bottom and stepped down where the sand of the beach met the gleaming wet mud. Coming towards the shore out of the sea were deep footprints, already filling up with water. They were not human prints, but much bigger, with four widely-spaced toes. She did not know to what sort of creature they belonged, but as she looked at the long, straight line of prints coming towards her out of the sea, something contracted in her chest, a surge of deep primeval fear. She turned and looked shoreward, and the prints continued, fainter in the narrow stretch of sand, then making wet marks on the concrete promenade, and fading altogether as they marched away into the streets of the little seaside town. She clutched her heavy winter coat about her. Her bare legs and feet were wet and cold and crusted with salt and sand. Reluctantly she turned and followed the footprints. Whatever it was that had risen unseen from the sea was now in the town, and it was up to her to apprehend it. What she would do when she found it she had no idea. She only knew that she was afraid, alone, and full of doubt.

Saturday 25th May 1996

After breakfast Michael roamed restlessly round the house, picking things up, putting them down. He switched on the TV, watched for ten minutes, then left it blaring and went out into the garden. He pestered Eileen for drinks, biscuits, crisps. She realized that he was boiling up over the half term visit, partly excited, partly apprehensive, but in the end his fidgeting wore her down. 'Michael, love, can't you find something to do instead of buzzing around like an angry bee?'

'Mum, I'm fed up, there's nothing to do and it's years till eleven o'clock. Can't I go out for just a little while? I'll keep clean.'

'Who are you trying to kid? Clean isn't in your power to deliver, or I'm the fairy queen.'

'You don't look like a fairy queen.'

'No, you are right, but we won't go into that. What's Stephen up to this morning?'

'Just hanging around, I guess. Couldn't we please go down to the woods, just for a little while? It's OK now, you said it was, you said Chris has really gone.'

Eileen sighed. It was true: every day she had walked Tillie there had been no sign of anyone near the boys' camp or elsewhere, and she had deliberately covered a different part of the woods each day. On Wednesday she collected the untouched picnic. On Thursday she went to Annette's to clean, and took the long way round through the woods, approaching the Dyers' house from the orchards and the rape fields. Not only did she meet no one, she found no sign that anyone had been there. On Friday she visited Annette again, to be with her while she had her hair done, and this time she went via Marie's lane, covering another area of woods as she did so. It certainly seemed that Christopher had gone.

'Oh, all right,' she said. 'Only if Mrs. Potter agrees, though. And please, be back here by ten thirty at the latest. That'll give you time to clean up before we leave. Is it a deal?'

'Deal,' Michael said, beaming.

81

'Be careful,' Eileen called after him as he dashed out of the door, banging it shut behind him.

When he was gone she packed a suitcase with his things. She had taken particular care over washing and ironing his clothes so that he would not have to feel like a scruffy poor relation, but she guessed he didn't really care.

She thought about Annette. Cleaning her kitchen had been a herculean task, with Annette apologizing for the dirt every few minutes, and not able to offer much real help. She was very slow and disorganized, and Eileen was glad she had taken her own cleaning materials because they would have spent half their day finding things. Searching for a bucket, with frequent diversions and distractions, had taken half an hour or more. Eileen worked harder on Annette's house than she had ever worked on her own, and by the time she was obliged to stop to pick up Michael from school it was quite presentable.

'Richard won't know the place,' Annette said, looking round with her sad doll's eyes.

'Never mind Richard. We are doing this for you.' Annette gave her a strange look but said nothing. 'Would you like me to come up tomorrow and be around while the hairdresser's here?' Eileen said.

'Oh, yes, please, would you? I feel so awkward. It's been ages since I went out socially. I hardly know what to say to people any more.'

'All right, but I'll have to go about three, like today.'

'Thanks, Eileen. What would I do without you?'

Eileen smiled. 'Shall I come up early and bring us some lunch?' To this Annette agreed. She had done very little, but already she looked tired. 'Go and put your feet up now, and I'll see you about midday tomorrow.'

'All right. Thanks for everything. I really do feel shattered. Still, the place looks better, doesn't it? It seems less gloomy when it's clean and tidy, but normally I just can't summon up the energy to tackle it.'

'I know.' Eileen patted her friend's arm. 'Till tomorrow.'

She rang Marie that Friday evening. Marie reported good progress with her convalescence. She was doing more, getting less tired, and generally returning to normality. Without going into detail Eileen told her what was happening with Michael and Natasha.

Marie sighed when Eileen told her about Sean. 'I wish Stephanie would find some man to take her on. But she's too much for any of them at the moment. They seem to follow her around like little dogs, panting with their tongues hanging out, looking at her adoringly. Or perhaps it's fear, not adoration.'

'Just think how long it's taken Natasha to find herself a reasonable boyfriend,' Eileen said. 'She's had a string of very odd characters. With some of them I couldn't understand what she could possibly see in them.'

'Perhaps that was just the point,' Marie said wryly. 'So tell me, is Michael looking forward to his home visit?'

'Yes, I am sure he is.'

'You will miss him, Eileen. We all will. He is a dear fellow.'

'Yes.' There was a silence for a few heartbeats, then she said, 'How's Philip?'

'I've not seen him for a day or two. He's been very busy at school. They're doing their annual production this week and he's very much involved with the music. But he'll drop by tomorrow after choir practice.'

Eileen thought for a moment. 'Marie, something quite odd has happened. David rang me the night before last, and he wants to come down and see me.'

'Not before time, wouldn't you say?'

'How do you mean?'

'Well, this whole situation with you and David has been hanging in mid-air for years, hasn't it? Full of questions with nobody volunteering any answers. Perhaps David wants to sort things out. Don't you?'

'No, not really. I feel most uncomfortable about the whole visit idea. It's all far better where it belongs, under the carpet.'

Marie laughed. 'Nonsense. Perhaps David wants his freedom.'

'He is free. The girls and I are no hindrance to him.'

'Has it occurred to you he might want to embark on a more rewarding relationship?'

'It has.'

'How would that strike you?'

'I don't know.'

'Well maybe you need to ask yourself a few awkward questions, before he does.'

'Bother. I was quite happy ignoring it all.'

'Somehow, I doubt that.'

'Pardon?'

'Perhaps you need your freedom too, Eileen. Officially, openly, up front and acknowledged.'

'I thought you were the champion of love-ever-after these days.'

'You know, sourness doesn't suit you. Anyway, let me know how it goes, and don't be too beastly to poor David. He hardly deserves it.'

'I will be all charm, I promise you.'

'Hm. I'd rather have beastly, on second thoughts.'

'He wouldn't. He never could cope with my demonic side. I will be reasonable, fair, open-minded and even-tempered. Will that suit madame?'

'It will. Give young Michael a hug from me and wish him a happy time, won't you?'

'Of course.'

'I shall see Natasha myself before too long and give her the benefit of some matronly advice.'

'Best of luck!'

'Bye, Eileen. Look out for yourself.'

'Bye, Marie.'

Eileen put the phone down, realizing that she had said nothing to Marie about the man in the woods.

It's over. There's nothing to tell her.

She shut Michael's suitcase, and found him a change of clean clothes. Then, suddenly remembering, she went upstairs to find his swimming trunks. There was a public pool on the road between Caxford and Lambury, and with the weather remaining fine there was every chance that Denise and Andy might take the children there. As she started back down the stairs there was the sound of running feet and the back door banged.

'Mum! Where are you?' Michael's voice was cracked and full of panic.

She ran down to find him standing in the kitchen, fists clenched, clothes torn and dirty, his face streaked with tears, his chest heaving, and babbling incomprehensibly. A terrible cold fear struck her. 'What on earth is the matter?' She took him gently by the shoulders. 'Are you hurt?' She could see a tiny scratch on his knee oozing a trickle of blood, but nothing else.

Michael could not answer for crying. She put her arms round him, gently sat him down in a chair, and got him a drink. Meanwhile her own thoughts were whirling and she was trying to fight down a rising tide of alarm. 'Now, come on, love, calm down a bit and tell me what's happened,' she said, keeping her voice level. 'Whatever it is, we can handle it.' *I hope.*

Michael took several deep breaths, drank a little, hiccuped. 'I done something I shouldn't,' he said brokenly. 'Now I'm in dead trouble.'

'What trouble?'

'You'll be really cross.'

'Try me.'

'I went down the woods with Steve.'

'I know that.'

'But I took Bill.' His soft blue eyes were huge, overflowing with tears. 'I know I shouldn't, but we wanted to make a little camp for him. We was careful, I watched him, honestly I really did, and then there was this noise, and he ran and we looked and looked but we couldn't find him.' His voice rose to a wail. 'It's all my fault, I lost my Bill, now he's going to be eaten by a fox and I'll never see him again.'

Eileen hugged him and stroked his blond head. A wave of relief washed over her. *Bill. And I had in mind something altogether more sinister and violent.*

'Come on, Michael,' she said. 'I'll put my shoes on and we'll go and have another hunt for him.'

Michael looked up at her, his streaked face both pitiful and comic. 'Aren't you really cross?'

'Well, I'm not exactly thrilled, you've done something very silly, for sure, but we'll have to think about that later. Right now we have to try and find one scared little guinea pig. Not to mention getting you to Caxford to meet your mum and dad.'

'Oh. Yes, I forgot that.'

'Come on then. Let's wipe your face and go.'

Michael ran over to the back door and pulled it open. Then he gave a sort of strangled squeak and stood completely still. As the door swung wide, there, on the doorstep, a few feet from Eileen, staring at her intently, stood the man from the woods. For a stunned moment Eileen froze, immobilized, incapable of speech or action. Michael was gaping up at him, mouth open, eyes popping. Slowly the young man reached inside his jacket, and gently thrust something into Michael's hands, something wriggling and snuffling. Then, still in silence, he backed off a few steps, turned, and ran down the garden path.

'Mum, it's Bill,' Michael said. 'Chris has brought Bill back. He's OK!'

Still clutching his pet, he ran after the retreating figure. 'Chris, come back!' Then, 'Thanks, Chris!' as the dark shape disappeared into the trees.

Eileen's heart was thudding too loudly and her skin felt hot. Michael ran back to her, his face alight, holding Bill out for inspection. 'See, Mum? He's all right! Chris found him, isn't that great? I told you Chris was OK, he's a mate.'

Eileen took a deep breath. The shock of seeing Christopher on the doorstep was beginning to fade, but she was sweating. 'It's a big relief, Michael. Thank goodness Bill is found and he's come to no harm. Put him in his hutch now, give him a piece of apple, and make sure you secure the doors properly. Poor old fellow, he's had a big adventure.'

'Chris is a hero,' Michael said, glowing with triumph. 'I knew he was OK. I must tell Steve.'

'Not now,' Eileen said. 'Now you are going to wash and change, and we are going to Caxford. Five minutes is all you've got. I'll let the Potters know about Bill.'

Ten minutes later they were in the car, speeding along the Caxford road. Michael was still in the clouds and hadn't stopped talking. 'Chris came back just in time, didn't he, Mum? What did you tell Steve?'

'I spoke to his mum,' Eileen said. 'I just told her Bill had been found unharmed. I didn't mention Christopher. Yes, it's good that he found Bill, but Bill shouldn't have been in the woods anyway, and they aren't a good place for a person to live either.'

Michael seemed chastened and was silent for a few miles, but evidently his mind was very much still on Christopher. As they drew in to the Social Services car park he said seriously, 'Mum, now that he *is* back, you will look after Chris, won't you? Steve won't be allowed down there on his own, and he's a bit scared anyway. Chris will be hungry if we don't help him. And now especially after he's done this for me, finding Bill and everything.'

Eileen took Michael's suitcase out of the boot and locked the car. 'Michael, I will promise you nothing except that I will do what I think is right. You will have to leave it at that. Now let's go and meet your family. Forget everything for the whole of this week if you can. Forget me, Bill, Holton, Steve, the woods, everything, and concentrate on getting to know your family and having a good time. I dare say we shall all still be here, just the same and waiting for you, when you get back.'

Despite Charley's description, Eileen's first sight of Andy came as a surprise. He stood in the family room with hands on hips, waiting for his son. Eileen paused in the doorway holding the suitcase, while Michael went hesitantly into the room. 'Hello, Dad,' he said shyly.

'Mikey, boy!' Andy enveloped Michael in a bear hug. His arms were covered in tattoos from shoulder to elbow, intricate designs of snakes and wolves' heads, fiercely grinning. His reddish skin was freckled, his close-cropped hair a gingery blond, and his eyes were like Michael's, but a harder, glinting blue. He looked over the boy's head, and stretched out a hand.

'Mrs. Harding—or can I call you Eileen? Good to meet you.' His tone was confident, almost brash. There was a hint of a challenge in his greeting, as if to say, *This is my boy, and don't forget it.*

Eileen shook his hand briefly, murmured hello, was introduced to Denise and smiled at the children. They did not look like Michael's siblings, partly because of the way they were dressed: Harry wore a matching set of T-shirt and shorts which seemed several sizes too large, and trainers with huge orange soles, while three-year-old Ellie was got up as a doll, her hair in tiny bunches with pink hair ties, socks with lace edges, a pink spotted dress and gold studs in her ears. Evidently Denise had considered the occasion special enough to dress her children up in their summer best. By contrast Michael seemed quite plain in his unaffected jeans and T-shirt. Released by his father, Michael hugged Denise and was soon involved, a little reluctantly, in a game with Harry. Charley stood beside Eileen. 'Come in, Eileen, won't you, for a while?'

'I'll get back, if you don't mind. I've a few things to do.' It wasn't particularly true, but she felt she had done her duty, and it was beginning to be a painful one, as she had known it would. 'I'll see you all on Monday week. I hope you have a good half term.'

She waved a hand to Michael, who stood looking confused and awkward, unsure of the protocol, not knowing whose feelings to consider. She smiled with as much warmth and encouragement as she could muster. 'Be good, Michael, have fun. See you soon.'

He nodded, speechless, his eyes fixed on her face, as if trying to read her thoughts. Then he raised a hand in salute.

Charley followed her down the stairs. 'You OK, Eileen?' she asked at the front door.

'I am sure I shall be.'

'This bit's not easy, is it?'

'I could cope better if I had some magic spyglass which could look into the future and tell me that Michael was going to be all right. Of course he will be all right—I'm sure Denise and Andy will do their best for him, I don't mean that—but Michael is special, somehow.'

'Yes, he is,' Charley said. 'To them as well as to you; and he is their son.'

Eileen nodded, half-smiling. 'I hadn't forgotten. See you, Charley. Monday the third at eleven, yes?'

'Bye, Eileen. Thanks for bringing him.'

Eileen did not go straight home. She felt a need to be alone in neutral territory, and on an impulse she drove the twenty miles to Osewick and spent an hour of peace in the Abbey, sitting, wandering among the tourists, admiring the stained glass and the monuments, the dead bishops reclining on their marble tombs, hands folded in prayer. She noted that evensong was at three thirty, and she decided to return. She did a little desultory window-shopping and ate lunch in a pub garden overlooking the river. With Michael gone there was no reason to hurry home, and she felt a curious blankness, as if all feeling were temporarily suspended.

By three fifteen she had taken her place in the quire, where evensong was to be sung. Her eyes ranged languidly over the gilt names of long-departed canons above ornate seats and discreetly-shaded lamps.

As the organ began the opening voluntary, she thought of Philip, and how he sat at the organ, in complete concentration, his dark eyes fixed on the page, the assurance of his fingers creating music from blobs on paper, recreating the composer's mind. The choir processed in, little boys in starched ruffs, men behind, solemnly in step as they took their places. Eileen was reminded of Michael in his choir robes, and the thought came to her that that part of his life, his voice, was lost. She felt a dull pain in her chest, and wondered if she had been wise to come to the Abbey. But in the end it was a calming experience, although she could not sing, for her tight throat would not allow it, and she was mute in the prayers, because of the thundering in her ears. But it did not matter: evensong at Osewick did not require much participation from the congregation.

The service wound its stately way: she heard the thin, accurate tenor of the Precentor, then the unmistakably Elizabethan sound of the Byrd responses, which she knew slightly. After the canticles came another hymn, and then the choir was all attentiveness, eyes glued to the conductor, a tall thin man with heavy glasses and intractable hair, as the organ gave them a single note and they launched into the psalm. Eileen glanced down at her service sheet, printed in pale purple: Psalm 119, verses 73 to 80, a dull pedestrian chant, but the words crisp and clear:

"Thy hands have made me and fashioned me: O give me understanding, that I may learn thy commandments...

I know, O Lord, that thy judgments are right: and that thou of very faithfulness hast caused me to be troubled.

O let thy merciful kindness be my comfort: according to thy word unto thy servant...

O let thy loving mercies come unto me that I may live: for thy law is my delight.

Let the proud be confounded, for they go wickedly about to destroy me: but I will be occupied in thy commandments."

As all rose for the Gloria, Eileen wondered at the thought of trouble being part of the faithfulness of God; but it made a kind of sense. If trouble was what opened your eyes, then even trouble must be welcomed. But she was only half-convinced.

The choir had launched into the concluding anthem. It was a superb choir by any standards, singing as one body, perfectly in tune, with such diction as cost no effort to take in. The price of this excellence was vigilance, concentration, so that the visual element was secondary and suffered. Eileen wondered, as she had done before when watching some musical performance on television, whether it would be better to close one's eyes, to blot out the spectacle of wobbly lips, raised eyebrows, tonsils. She was reminded of a particularly satisfying performance of "Messiah," using old instruments which must have been at the very least temperamental to play, and the hair-raising trumpet solo, played by a red-faced, crop-haired man with gnarled and scabbed fingers. The contrast between the celestial sound and the puffed cheeks awash with sweat was almost ludicrous. The thought came to her then, surrounded by the hearty droning of the final hymn, that perhaps this was what was meant by incarnation: that miraculous *piano* playing of an antique trumpet, produced against the odds, was the work of this creature of pumping breath, twitching muscles, flashing electric signals across spongy grey stuff fed with blood. Perhaps here lay the human creature's glory: music, inspired by the praise of God, composed by genius, performed by people of great gifts and extraordinary dedication, work whose end result was bliss of the highest order, and all achieved with fingers, lips, vocal cords, sawing arms, swelling lungs and orchestrating brains. Was this some statement of creation, was this how she was to understand, in part at least, the word made flesh? God in man, the eternal resident in the temporal, the creator in his creature.

The organ was playing, the choir departing, people around her were shuffling books, rising from their knees, making ready to go. She blinked, returning to the everyday in a kind of haze.

When she emerged from the Abbey into the sunshine, the streets were still crowded with shoppers. Osewick had several upmarket shops, but Eileen ignored them. The closing voluntary, an intricate, loud, insistent piece of Bach with which she was unfamiliar, was still echoing in her mind as she got into the car. The seats were hot, and the metal buckle of the seat-belt burned her hand. She still felt in the mood for the peculiarly melancholy sense of elevation that church music, superbly rendered, sometimes evoked in her, and she found a few battered tapes and put one on as she drove home. The country roads were sunlit, overarched by the shadows of the trees.

"To thee all angels cry aloud, the heavens and all the powers therein..."

The rolling phrases of the Stanford Te Deum filled the car. "O Lord, save thy people, and bless thine heritage; govern them, and lift them up for ever."

As the last verse sounded, both pleading and confident, she felt a tear leaking from the corner of her eye. Almost imperceptibly the words slipped from the communal to the personal, and it felt for a moment as if she were being pierced with several sharp knives.

"O Lord, let thy mercy lighten upon us, as our trust is in thee;
O Lord, in thee have I trusted; let me never be confounded."

Mawkish fool! Get a grip, for heaven's sake.

She drove on with clenched teeth and stinging eyes, resolutely trying to banish the image of Michael standing in the family room at Social Services, hand raised in farewell.

As she pulled into her own road she saw a smart red Japanese car parked outside the house, and recognized it as Sean's. Her eyebrows metaphorically raised, she locked the car and went into the house, kicking off her shoes in the hall to feel the cool tiles under her hot, cramped feet.

A voice hailed her from the living room. She opened the door and put her head round. Natasha was lounging on the sofa, and Sean stood by the window, looking out into the garden. They looked oddly posed, like people on a stage set, or models arranged by photographers.

'Hi, Mum,' Natasha said with uncharacteristic brightness. 'This is Sean.'

Sean turned from his contemplation of the garden with an engaging smile and shook her hand. 'Nice to meet you, Mrs. Harding.' His voice had a soft country twang, and when he smiled he blinked, showing long, dark eyelashes.

'You too, Sean,' Eileen said, returning his smile. 'You're home early, love,' she said to Natasha.

'I've been home since lunchtime,' said Natasha. 'I told you, don't you remember, Daphne shut the shop at midday. She had that cousin's funeral to go to this afternoon.'

'Oh, yes, I remember now, you did say.'

'We thought we'd come back here, see how you were, and then, hey presto, you weren't here.'

'Why did you need to find out how I was?' Eileen said, puzzled.

'Well, you know, taking Michael to his parents must have been a bit awful.'

90

'Oh. Yes, of course. Thank you, darling, that was a kind thought. But he'll be back after half term. It's not as if he's gone for ever yet.'

'I know. But in a way this is the beginning of the end, as they say in books.'

She is right. The beginning of the end. Words, even trite ones, make it much worse.

'Do you two want a cup of tea?'

Natasha unfolded her long legs from the sofa. 'I'll put the kettle on.'

When she had gone, there was a friendly silence, full of unspoken questions.

'Have you got the afternoon off too, Sean?' Eileen asked.

'I don't work Saturdays,' he said. 'Saturdays I normally lie in, do a few chores.' He grinned comically, as if the thought of duster and dishcloth in his hands was ridiculous. 'Then sometimes I pop into the shop and waste Natasha's time, but I have to be careful, because her boss doesn't approve.'

'Of you, or of timewasters?'

'Of anyone who takes her mind off her work, I suppose. She's a bit of a dragon, is Daphne. But lunchtimes are often pretty quiet, and you can put flowers in bunches and chat at the same time, can't you?'

'I would have thought so.'

'Then in the afternoon sometimes I go to a football match, if there's one on. After that I meet Natasha from work.'

'Ah.' Why was he telling her all this?

But Sean seemed determined to chat, to make an impression. 'Natasha's very good at her work, I think. Have you seen some of the stuff she's done?'

'Not much, I'm afraid.'

'Don't you like flowers, then?'

'Yes, I do, but you wouldn't think so, would you, looking at my garden.'

He smiled. 'That's one thing I don't have to worry about, living in a flat.'

'Whereabouts is your flat?' Eileen asked.

'I live near Lambury, on the outskirts. It's handy for work.'

'Oh.' Should she ask him what he did for a living? But she needn't have worried.

'Do you know Maxted's, the engineering firm, on the road out of here, about a mile from Lambury? I'm a draughtsman there, have been since I left school.'

'Do you enjoy it?'

91

'Yes, I suppose so, as far as you can enjoy work, that is. They're a nice bunch of people there, anyway.'

Natasha came in with a tray bearing three cups of tea, and they were spared further conversation. 'You all right?' she said anxiously to Sean.

'Course I am, what do you think your mum's going to do to me, eat me alive?'

'Don't be daft.' Natasha punched him, smiling coyly.

They sat side by side on the sofa, drinking their tea, leaning forward, nobody knowing quite where to look, smiling amiably when their eyes met.

'Mum, would you like Sean and me to walk the dog?'

'Oh. Yes, all right, thanks.'

'We thought we'd get a take-away, save you cooking.'

'You don't have to do that. It's a bit of a trip to Caxford and back.'

'It's no trouble,' Sean said. 'None at all.'

'We were thinking of going to the cinema tonight in Lambury,' Natasha said. 'I'll probably stay over, come back some time on Sunday, if that's OK with you, Mum.'

'Why wouldn't it be?'

Natasha shrugged. 'I'll need to come back and change before we go up to London to meet Dad.'

'You are certainly running the gauntlet of Natasha's relations this weekend, aren't you, Sean?' Eileen said, grinning.

Sean grinned back. 'It had to be done sooner or later.'

Eileen laughed. 'So why don't we really go for it, and you two come back here tomorrow for Sunday lunch? I'll put on Grandma's pearls and crack open the sherry.'

'Mum!' Natasha said, clearly finding her mother's levity premature.

But Sean beamed. 'Sounds a good idea to me. I'll put on a collar and tie and bring a bottle of wine.'

Natasha looked from one to the other. 'You two are as bad as each other. Come on, Sean, let's take the dog out.'

They got up, and Natasha took his arm possessively.

'See you later, Mrs. Harding,' Sean said.

'Call me Eileen,' she said. 'You can be formal tomorrow, if you feel it goes with a collar and tie.' Sean was still smiling to himself as Natasha led him from the room.

After they had gone Eileen went upstairs and wandered round Michael's room, half-heartedly tidying. Then she ran a hot bath and wallowed till the water cooled. She was still soaking when Natasha and Sean came back.

'Mum, Sean's going for the take-away. What do you want?'

'Anything. You choose.'

Presently, hearing the front door close and the car start up, she thought it was probably safe to go down in a bathrobe with a towel round her head. Natasha was feeding the still-panting Tillie. 'What do you think, then, Mum?'

'Of what?'

'Of Sean, of course, what else?'

'I think he is quite delightful. And he obviously thinks you are the bee's knees.'

'Do you think so?'

'Definitely. But it's what you think that counts. It's not me that'll have to put up with his bad temper and rotten socks.'

'I've never seen him bad-tempered. And he can wash his own socks, thanks.'

'Fair enough.'

Sean came back whistling, bearing a savoury-smelling brown paper carrier. The makeshift meal was merry, lubricated by alcohol. Without being in the slightest over-familiar, Sean made himself at home, and Eileen felt that he was, almost, an old friend.

When they had gone, the house felt doubly empty. Eileen was used to being alone in the evenings, but she knew that Michael was there, even though he was asleep. Now the place seemed to echo dully, and she could not look into his empty room.

The chairs were still in the garden, under the tree, from Annette's visit. As the shadows of the trees and bushes lengthened, lending an air of undeserved mystery to their straggling overgrown shapes, Eileen sat outside, enjoying the cool air. The house was still oppressively hot. She was trying to read: Romans again. *Nobody could accuse me of lacking perseverance.* It became steadily darker, but she felt reluctant to move. There was a rustling in the apple boughs, and she wondered if it was the owl, and whether perhaps her tree had become a favourite roost. Eventually, resisting the moment when she would feel compelled to go indoors, she lit an oil lamp and put it on the table; but in the flickering shadows it was impossible to read, and presently moths and other nocturnal bugs became attracted to the light and started whizzing round her in frantic circles.

She sighed and gave up, extinguished the lamp and went inside. When she turned the lights on, the garden seemed plunged in darkness. She drew the curtains at the front of the house, made a cup of coffee, and sat down heavily. She was restless, disturbed, and she knew why. There was too much happening, too much changing, too much to think about all at once. Well, all these things would have to take their turn for attention. First she was going to crack on with Romans. It had been a bit like Paul's race of life in miniature, and she was nearly at the finishing post. The rest of them would have to wait.

"We who are strong in the faith ought to help the weak to carry their burdens. We should not please ourselves. Instead we should all please our brothers and sisters for their own good, in order to build them up in the faith. For Christ did not please himself."

You can't argue with that bit, at least. She read the commentary, but found it less than helpful. Her own thoughts were beginning to come together. Perhaps someone else's thoughts and words had provided the spur. St. Paul needn't have gone a step further in his argument. After all, what was good enough for the boss had to be OK for his disciples. He had the strongest faith and the clearest conscience of all time. How could it be otherwise? And yet he also had the tenderest sympathy, consideration for frailty, love for tainted and imperfect souls. But of course, St. Paul didn't stop there. It might have been obvious, but he had to hammer it home.

"And may God, the source of patience and encouragement, enable you to have the same point of view among yourselves by following the example of Christ Jesus, so that all of you together may praise with one voice the God and Father of our Lord Jesus Christ."

She got up and started to walk around the room, as if movement might help her brain to function. She knew better than to expect her reading of the Bible to furnish answers for the present concern. Others claimed such direct guidance, but for Eileen it had never worked in that way, and her sceptical self said, *Too easy.* It was a part of faith to struggle on, believing that soaking up Scripture would so inform her thinking, life itself, the very heart of her, as a constant nourishing background, that right actions would proceed and flow as a natural consequence. This idea, she knew, had not reached its fruition. It often let her down. What she knew and believed often seemed useless. But she felt that if she ceased to believe it, everything else might come unpinned and start to unravel.

As she wandered round the house, picking things up, examining them without seeing, faces began to intrude into her conscious mind: Natasha and Sean, David, Michael, Christopher.

Go away! I'll deal with you later. I haven't finished thinking yet.

She sat down again, opened both Bible and commentary, and read

94

and thought with deep concentration for half an hour. Then she shut the books, leaned back in the chair, and closed her eyes.

So, there were two principles at work here, as far as she could see. St. Paul looked on strong faith as the desirable goal, and in his view it was shown in lack of fear, freedom, not worrying about special days and food rules, for instance. The weaker brethren needed to educate their tender consciences, perhaps, in order to grow in true Christian liberty. Because hadn't Christ said he had come to set people free, to give them life in all its fullness? But all must be done according to love, because all fellow-Christians were brothers and sisters for whom Christ died, and so they should be honoured and served, and their consciences should be respected. It all seemed to boil down to this: in fundamentals, faith must be paramount, and no one could use love as an excuse for sloppiness. In non-fundamentals, like food and feast days, love must be paramount, and faith could not be used to excuse a failure to love the brethren. The exercise of the freedom of faith was limited by love.

But there was another question lurking behind the first. What was fundamental, and what wasn't? No wonder nobody in the church could agree. But for the sake of the unity so prized by St. Paul and his master, answers had to be sought.

She stretched. *Another day. I've done enough.*

She went out into the garden, gave Bill enough food to last the night, and turfed out the reluctant Tillie. Then she locked up and closed the curtains at the back. 'Goodnight, old dog. See you in the morning.' Tillie's tail flapped lazily as she curled up in her basket, sighing deeply. Eileen switched off the lights and went upstairs.

David came back to plague her as she stood in front of the bathroom mirror, cleaning her teeth.

What did he want? Did he have another woman, as Marie was hinting? Did he want to separate formally? She could hardly object, given the circumstances. The only other possibility that she could think of was that he might want to make a move to patch things up, a prospect she frankly found more alarming still. Why didn't she want to be with him? She did once. Was it just an instinctive revulsion at the idea of the dutiful little woman trotting mindlessly round the country in her lord and master's wake? Maybe she was a complete idiot, a sulky child, because she would undoubtedly have loved Glen Achuil. No, it was David himself she didn't want, or any imaginable husband. He was too big a presence, too dominating and influential. He needed keeping at a distance. She missed sex, though. She could almost forget it, push it into the background, but she was surrounded by it and she couldn't escape.

There were Sean and Natasha, quite plainly in a state of erotic intoxication, so obvious that it was practically oozing out of their pores, and where were they heading? To the altar, she supposed. Understandably, perhaps, at their age; for them it was connected with the apparent freedom of adulthood, having their own home, establishing their own life, their own family eventually. But what about Marie and Philip? Where would they end? They seemed to be settling into a very agreeable pattern, and as far as she knew they were still at it hammer and tongs. Lucky them. But would that, too, inevitably lead to some kind of institutionalized, conventional, publicly-endorsed situation, if it didn't end in tears? She didn't envy them that, though for them perhaps it was different, something they'd never had. *It's a shame that I am forbidden the middle way.* She grinned at her reflection in the mirror as she rinsed her toothbrush. *Have a lover and keep my freedom. Ha! Who'd want me anyway? Keep it real.*

She switched off the bathroom light, closed the bedroom curtains, and got into bed. Her legs were aching, and it felt good to stretch them out. Mentally she probed the tender spot that bore Michael's image. It still hurt, but she knew the pain had to be lived with till it eventually faded and became more manageable. Michael was out of her hands now, effectively. He'd be back, but he'd be in winding-up mode, preparing for his new life. All she could do now was pray for him.

David and Michael were taken care of, whether she liked it or not, out of any control of hers; for good or ill dead as projects, though they both took a bit of her away with them. But what should she do, if anything, about the young man Christopher? Perhaps she should have nothing to do with him at all. But as she was a striving Christian, so he was a needy soul, on her very doorstep. His life has crossed with hers, and it was almost as if she could not resist.

Of course, that wasn't really so. She could ignore him. She could contact any one of a number of authorities and tell herself—maybe rightly—that it was for his good. But that felt like betrayal. Maybe she had it all wrong. But she felt she must find out first, before she did anything far-reaching, who and what he was, why he was hiding there, what he was afraid of, what he needed, how, if at all, she could help him. *I will do it because I want to, because I must. There are all sorts of rational and charitable reasons, and all sorts of irrational ones. I know that. I will sleep on it. But in the morning, I will decide. Whatever it is, I will do something.*

Sunday 26th May 1996

When Sunday morning came, it brought back Eileen's misgivings, and the deep influence of her rationalizing self. Ill-at-ease with her conscience, with herself and the whole situation, even though it barely existed save in her own mind, she put Christopher on the back burner. There simply wasn't time. She had to see to herself and the animals, and get to church soon after ten. Sean and Natasha were coming for lunch: food had to be thought of, potatoes peeled, pudding prepared.

Then, once she got to church, robed, in the choir stalls, books open in the right places, mind far away, there was Frank, pleading again for people to help with cleaning and decorating the rectory and tidying its garden. She felt a spasm of guilt, and as soon as the service was over she scanned Frank's lists and signed up for duty on the following day. Another day gone; and yet she had to give Christopher time. *I can't just go down there, find him and dump him again. I must have time, to be prepared for whatever might be needed.* But she was frustrated with life and irritated with herself.

After church she did not stop to chat but went straight home, and after two glasses of sherry and banging a few saucepans about began to feel better. Sean and Natasha duly arrived, looking as if they had made an effort. Natasha was quiet and did not eat much. She refused pudding, complaining of a headache, and at Eileen's suggestion she went upstairs to sleep it off.

Sean was anxious. 'Is she all right?'

'It's probably something premenstrual,' Eileen said. After a glass or two of the wine that Sean had brought she was past making allowances for any sensitivity of his. But he was unruffled.

'Then I guess it's you and me for the dirty dishes,' he said. 'Lead me to my apron.'

While they washed up they talked about his family. He was, he told her, the younger child and only son. His sister Caroline was married to a man who worked in the Council offices in Lambury. 'Pen-pusher Graham,' Sean referred to his brother-in-law dismissively. 'She used to work there too. It's where they met.'

'Are you close to your sister?' Eileen asked.

Sean considered for a moment, tea cloth in hand. 'She's all right, Caroline is. A bit sharp-tongued, but not daft, which makes me wonder what she sees in dear old Graham. A duller man I never met. Predictable as clockwork, washes the car on Sundays, tells the same three jokes, that sort of thing. You don't believe such people exist, do you? Then you meet Graham. He's all right, of course, he's a decent bloke who wouldn't hurt a fly, and a loving husband and dad, but he bores you to death. Maybe my sister doesn't want any excitement. I think she was more knocked out when our dad died than anybody realized, and went for the safe option.'

Eileen was quiet for a moment, concentrating on an encrusted saucepan lid. 'So how old were you when your dad died, Sean?'

'Fifteen.'

'What was he like?'

Sean sighed. 'He was a great bloke. We all thought the world of him. A big, gentle, soft-spoken man who never lost his cool. Not like me, I'm afraid.' He smiled sadly. 'Cancer, of course. He was only forty-six.'

'I lost my parents in my teens and early twenties,' Eileen said. 'It makes a big difference to the rest of your life, I've found.'

'How do you think it's changed you, then?' Sean asked.

'Well, I was always a bit of a loner, but not having them around made me very independent. I missed my mother terribly, though, for years. She was the strong one in our family. She held everything together.'

'Just like you.'

'Well, I don't know about that. My children seem very capable in their own right. What about your mum?'

Sean dried a wine glass with thoughtful thoroughness. 'My mum fell apart when Dad died. My sister and I held her up and put her back together. Then Caroline met Graham and got married in six months. I think she needed her own place and her own life. Mum and I were on our own for five years, then I got my flat. But I still go round there and fix things up for her. She depended on me. She still does. I was the man of the house. You know the sort of thing? I guess I was spoilt. I reminded her of Dad, she said. She's all right now; she's got her life and her friends, even a man friend, but she's very coy and close about him, refers to him as Mister Draycott, as if she's trying to make out he's just an acquaintance. Then when Caroline's babies came along she had a new interest, of course.' He smiled ironically. 'Caroline has two little girls, four and two, and I'm a doting uncle.'

'So has Natasha met your family?' Eileen said.

98

'Yes, she gets along fine with Caroline and Graham and the kids.'

'And your mother? She might just object to someone taking her beloved son away.'

Sean was silent for a moment, his face flushed. 'I don't know if I really should say this to you.' His face took on a miserable, bewildered look quite foreign to the smiling, affable man Eileen had seen up to now.

'What? Has Tash put her foot in it?'

'Oh, no. It's my mum that's putting a spanner in the works.'

'Maybe she's jealous.'

'Maybe. But I don't think so. She's been going on for a while about me finding myself a nice girl and settling down to breed like some old ram. Fair makes you sick after the first few thousand times.' He took a deep breath. 'No, my mother, who is normally a decent, kind enough sort of woman, says things about Natasha that I don't know if I'd care to repeat.'

'Like what? What is she objecting to?'

'I am ashamed even to talk about it.' And he looked ashamed, embarrassed, humiliated, confused and angry. Light began to dawn in Eileen's mind. 'Are you telling me, Sean, that your mum objects to Natasha because she is black?'

Sean nodded dumbly.

Eileen couldn't think of anything to say. Natasha was herself; Eileen hadn't really considered her colour in twenty years. Rarely had any mention been made of it, apart from occasional playground sallies, and it was years since the subject had crossed Eileen's conscious mind, except sometimes when she was struck by Natasha's particular beauty: her slender height, her long legs, her smooth skin, her glorious smile.

'I see,' she said. 'Poor old you, what a horrible cleft stick you must feel you're in.'

Sean nodded. 'It makes me so mad sometimes, I just can't be in the same room as my mum. Don't get me wrong, I love her dearly and I'd do anything for her, but she makes me feel so ashamed. If she ever said anything to Natasha I think I'd do something violent.'

'So Natasha doesn't know?'

'No. She guesses Mum doesn't approve, but she doesn't know why. It's just so bloody unreasonable. Sorry, I shouldn't swear. All this stuff like, "But Sean, have you thought, your babies will be coffee-coloured, think of them, they'll get bullied at school." It's like out of the ark. I just can't believe I'm hearing it.'

Eileen put her hand on his arm. To her surprise he was shaking.

'Don't worry, Sean. Tash is a lot tougher than you imagine. She won't let it get to her.'

'Can't Mum understand?' Sean broke out. 'I mean, I love the way Natasha looks, I think she is beautiful, but if she was green with antennae and came from outer space I'd still feel the same. It wouldn't make a blind bit of difference.'

'Of course not. But I guess you'd much rather not be angry with your mum.'

'That's right. But if Mum can't behave, she'll be the loser.'

'So how about your sister? What does she think?'

'She says Mum will come around. I've had to stop Caroline giving her a piece of her mind. Very forthright is my sister. I don't want to cause trouble in the family. We've had enough grief. My poor old dad would be turning in his grave.'

'Let's hope your sister is right. Give your mum a bit more time, perhaps, to get used to your having a black girlfriend.'

'You don't seem too upset.'

Eileen shook her head. 'You two will be OK, I see that. And I guess your mum will see sense and keep quiet, even if she can't change her mind, especially if she thinks both her children are on the warpath. For her, there's too much at stake. Perhaps you need to have a chat to the mysterious Mr. Draycott.'

Sean grinned suddenly. 'I get the impression Mr. Draycott is well and truly under Mother's thumb. But I couldn't really say, because I've never been allowed to meet him, and neither has Caroline. Perhaps he's a midget or something.'

Eileen laughed. 'Or a figment of her imagination.'

'I'd never thought of that,' Sean said. 'Anyway, I'm glad it hasn't made you angry or upset.'

'I reckon Tash is pretty safe with you, Sean.'

'What about her dad? Will he give me a heavy inspection?'

'I doubt it. He'll probably assume you're just another of Natasha's many admirers. Till he finds out otherwise.'

'Oh, has she had lots of other blokes then?'

Eileen laughed. 'No pumping, OK? If she hasn't told you, you won't find anything out from me.'

Sean smiled broadly, his eyes full of merriment. 'Fair enough. I shall have to do some digging on my own.'

'Prepare to be disappointed. Tash can be as close as a clam. You might have to be content with knowing you are number one at the moment.'

Eileen made some coffee, and they drank it in the garden. Tillie lay on Sean's feet, growling in her sleep. A little while later Natasha came down, looking puffy-eyed, saying her headache had subsided. 'I'll just get changed, OK, Sean?' she said, lolling against his chair.

He put an arm round her waist, hugged her affectionately. 'Go on, then.'

She looked at him with her eyebrows raised, as if surprised by this show of feeling in front of her mother, then cast a covert glance at Eileen, but seeing no particular response shrugged and went upstairs.

Shortly afterwards they left for London. Sean kissed Eileen's cheek as they went. 'Thanks for a lovely meal. And for listening to me burbling on.'

Eileen noticed the queer look Natasha gave him. *I'll bet she'll be giving him the third degree all the way to London.*

Monday 27th May 1996

The air seemed cooler as Eileen set off for the rectory. The faint mist was blown off early by a brisk wind which set the trees rustling and shaking. Tillie had flatly refused to come out of her basket for a walk and seemed uninterested in breakfast. Her eyes appeared a trifle bloodshot. Eileen studied her closely for a few moments, trying to decide if the dog's malaise was worthy of veterinary attention. *Perhaps not yet.*

Holton Rectory was a low, rambling house from the turn of the century, partly ivy-covered, architecturally unremarkable but comfortable and homely. What had once been an enormous garden had shrunk over the years, as parcels of land had been sold to various developers. There had been more than one attempt to sell the house itself and build a more modern, purpose-designed rectory, but something had fouled the plans every time.

The garden had been kept down in the months of the interregnum by the same handyman that mowed the churchyard, but the finer points of trimming and weeding had been neglected. As Eileen arrived a group of people were already deployed around the garden, armed with hoes and shears, while Frank Aherne directed operations from the overgrown patio. 'Good morning, Eileen, how are you?' he boomed.

'Fine, thanks, Frank,' Eileen said. 'Where can I help?'

'Angela Quilley's indoors doing a spot of painting. She could probably do with another pair of hands, if you're happy with that.'

'No problem, though I'd never call myself an expert.'

'All the stuff's in the hallway. Angela can tell you what she's tackling.'

Cans of paint, brushes and white spirit stood on a neat square of newspaper in the hall. As Eileen went in the open front door she heard crashing and voices from upstairs. Angela Quilley's head appeared round the living room door. 'Hello, Eileen. What on earth are they doing up there?'

'Sounds like furniture removal. Who is it, anyway?'

'Don, I think. Bill Mottram as well.'

'Don wants to take it easy. If he's doing anything heavy he'll be putting a strain on his heart.'

'Have you come to help paint?'

'If you'll have me.'

'Great. Do you want some overalls?'

'No, I put old stuff on. Not that I've got much that isn't old, of course.'

'Come on, then. I'm doing skirting boards and window frames. You can have a go at the doors if you like. We've rolled back the carpet.'

They worked for a while in amicable silence. Then someone shouted, 'Coffee in the kitchen!' They cleaned paint off their hands, stretched kinked backs, and wandered outside into the sunshine, cups in hand.

'The weather's changing,' Angela said.

'It certainly seems breezier,' Eileen said. 'We need rain. Everything's dry as a desert.'

For a moment they sipped in silence, then Angela said, 'How are things with you? Kids OK?'

Eileen sighed. 'I think I'm going to lose our Michael.'

'No! Really? How come?'

'It's always on the cards, of course, with foster-children. I knew he couldn't be with me forever. His dad's back on the scene, and wants to make a go of the family. Michael's there now.'

'How does he feel about it?'

'Mixed, I guess. But mostly excited and happy.'

'It will be strange for you without him.'

'Yes, it will.'

'How are the girls?'

'Fine, thanks. What about Neil and Georgina?'

A frown settled on Angela's face, and she shook her head. 'My Neil is a worry. He keeps rotten company, and he is such a baby under all that loud-mouth stuff. He runs after his so-called mates like a puppy. I think if they told him to jump off a motorway bridge he'd do it.'

'So what is he doing at the moment?'

'Oh, he's working, it's not that he's idle. He's got a job at that garden centre on the other side of Caxford. D'you know where I mean?' Eileen nodded. 'He's got money, and of course he's out most nights drinking with his mates, sometimes here at the Ash Tree but more often out of our sight. He hangs out at that nightclub too...what's it called? The Hotspot. Goodness knows what they get up to there.'

'Christina and Natasha said they saw him there recently, but they didn't mention any misbehaviour, as I recall.'

103

Angela shook her head. 'You get stupid boys and alcohol together, and a gullible lad like Neil doesn't stand a chance. I'm just waiting for the day when I find he's into drugs, in a fight, or in the cells.'

'They all do seem to have a wild period,' Eileen said.

'It's getting them through it undamaged,' Angela said. 'Peter's just about given up with Neil, and I can't really blame him: Neil's such a slob at times, and his language is appalling. But I can't just wash my hands of him. He worries me sick.'

'What about Georgina? She always seems a level-headed sort of girl.'

'Well, she used to be, but even she is getting a bit flouncy now, you know the way teenage girls do. I just hope she doesn't get in with her brother's crowd. She doesn't like me keeping her on a short rein, but she's still very young and a lot less mature than she'd like us to believe.'

Eileen thought of what she had seen in the layby, the afternoon she'd taken Christina to the station. She wondered if she should say something to Angela, but decided it was really not her business to report on other people's activities. What, after all, had Georgina been doing? And it sounded as if Angela had enough to concern herself about. The moment passed, and Eileen said nothing.

Angela finished her coffee. 'Do your girls go to that night-club much?'

'Christina doesn't. She's hardly ever here, of course. I've no idea what she gets up to in Exeter, and in a way I'm glad I don't. At that age there's not a lot you can do about them except worry yourself into a coronary. Natasha might have gone there a fair bit at one time. I don't really know. She certainly had a few friends I didn't care for much. I think that's one reason she kept them up, to get at me. But now there's a new boyfriend on the scene, and she seems steadier these days.'

'Oh? What's he like?'

'Lovely. If she doesn't hold on to him she wants her brain examined.'

Angela seemed sunk in thought for several moments. 'I reckon there's all sorts of things go on at that club. Marie's daughter hangs out there as well, so I'm told.'

'Yes, I heard that too.'

'She's a very strange kid, isn't she? Stephanie, I mean. I have a lot of sympathy for Marie. How is she, by the way?'

'Progressing well, I'm glad to say. Time to get back to work, I think, Angela. Frank is looking at his watch.'

'OK. It's not too bad, the old place, is it? Just needs a lick of paint to brighten it up.'

'Anyway, three young children will soon wreck our efforts.'

'I wonder what he'll be like, the new bloke?' Angela said as they went back indoors.

'Different.'

'That's the only thing you can be sure of, isn't it?'

'What?'

'That nothing stays the same.' They went back into the living-room and Angela dipped her paintbrush into the can of paint. 'Your charming children turn into yobs and trollops and your waistline disappears.'

Eileen smiled. 'Yes, but by the same law, by the time your waistline has completely vanished your yob and your trollop are respectable, middle-aged and solvent. Round the wheel goes.'

Angela sighed. 'Maybe you're right. Oh well, let's get this room finished and then we've done our bit for today.'

When they left in the late afternoon the change in the weather was becoming more ominous. Clouds rolled turbulently across the sky, chased by a freshening wind, and it was noticeably cooler.

'Rain tonight,' Angela said as they parted.

Walking on towards her own house Eileen pondered on what Angela had said. How was it that some children seemed to go into self-destruct mode so wholeheartedly, and others merely skimmed the surface? There seemed to be a particularly dangerous age for young people, when they were too old to control but young enough to be feckless and foolish. It was more by luck than superb parenting if kids got through those years unscathed. They wanted to live and breathe and be free, and all their dull elders wanted was for them to be safe. Safe! It was laughable, really. Who was ever safe?

Later that evening, sitting in the lamplight nursing a cup of tea, listening to the wind hurling heavy raindrops at the windows, she thought of Christopher with a twinge of guilt. As far as she knew he was down there somewhere in the wet woods, trying to shelter, probably hungry, maybe desperate.

Tomorrow I will go and find him. God willing, unless I have a heart attack and peg out in the night, I will find him if he is anywhere to be found.

At three in the morning she woke suddenly. Her heart was thumping, but when she listened, ears straining in the darkness, the house was quiet. After a while, she drifted back to sleep.

She was standing in a bare garden in front of a house, a bleak farmhouse on a lonely moor. Lights were on in the house, but outside all was dark. At an upper window a face appeared, the face of her father, George Bennet, lined and yellow as she remembered him from his last illness. He looked distraught, mouthing soundlessly, pleading to be let out. But Eileen had no key, and all the doors were locked. Then she became aware of a presence behind her. She didn't know who it was, but she knew that whoever it was had the key. She turned round to plead with the unknown person, but there was nobody there. She looked down and found she was holding a yellow scarf which she recognized as David's. She felt powerless, overwhelmed by guilt and fear.

Tuesday 28th May 1996

By morning the rain had stopped, but it was much cooler. Heavy clouds still hung round the horizon, as if biding their time, and water lay suspended on the leaves, waiting for a breeze to shake it down in showers.

Eileen stood by the back door, her eyes ranging over the wet woods. It was still early and quiet, but she had already made sandwiches and coffee for Christopher. She had debated packing other things too, a sleeping bag, a plastic sheet, but these she decided to defer. *I will see how the land lies. Maybe he won't even be there. Maybe he's gone again.*

With the drop in temperature Tillie seemed to have revived, and pushed past Eileen to stretch and shake in the garden. Bill squeaked in answer, rushing round his hutch in a spurt of early morning energy. Eileen opened the cage door, offered him a piece of celery, and stroked his coarse black head with one finger as he munched it.

On with this, no more delays. She shut Bill in, locked the back door, picked up the bag and went down the garden, followed by Tillie. She stopped at the shed to put on her boots. As she went through the gate she looked at her watch. It was half past seven.

She went quietly, almost crept, through the long rain-soaked grass under the trees. The air was still, heavy with moisture. There was little birdsong. Tillie sauntered along behind her, pausing to sniff at various clumps of weeds, but there had been few dogs about so early, and the rain had diluted any lingering scents.

As she neared the boys' camp Eileen found herself going even more stealthily, almost holding her breath. *This is crazy. What are you trying to do, frighten the poor boy to death?* She could feel her heart thudding. Deliberately she called to Tillie to catch up, and brushed aside the branches noisily, ducking under low vegetation which drenched her in sudden spray.

But there was nobody in Christopher's camp. Eileen stood still and looked around. She could not see any sign of habitation, nothing that might have been his. Only a soggy chocolate wrapper clung feebly to a tree stump. She felt relief, then disappointment.

107

Then she heard a small sound behind her, and a whine from Tillie. For a moment she froze, the skin on her forearms prickling, her breath suspended. With a great effort she turned round slowly, trying to summon up a friendly smile. Her face felt stiff, and her eyes seemed too big.

He was squatting on his haunches on the narrow, muddy path she had just left. Tillie was sniffing his knees, her tail wagging lazily. He scratched her ears and stroked her head, but his eyes were on Eileen's face, and his expression was unreadable.

'Hello, Christopher,' Eileen said, very quietly.

At once a look of wariness crossed his face. He bit his lip, started as if to rise and run. Then he cleared his throat, and when he spoke, his voice was crackly, as if it was some time since he had used it. 'How do you know my name?'

'Michael told me. You know the two little lads whose camp this was? He's the fair one. And I'm Eileen.'

'Oh. Is he your son, then?'

'No. But I look after him at the moment. I came down here to find you, to say thank you for bringing Bill home. You saved Michael and me a lot of trouble, not to mention heartache.'

Christopher seemed to relax a little. He put his arm round Tillie's neck. 'The boys didn't know I was here.' He had a pleasant voice, a light baritone, hesitant, a little clipped, with well-rounded vowels and no trace of the local accent. 'I was up a tree, watching. I didn't feel like talking that day. I saw them looking, then running off. Then I saw the little fellow. He hadn't gone far, but being black he was well camouflaged in the leaf mould.'

'It was kind of you.'

Christopher was silent for a moment. He blinked several times, as if the growing light was bothering him. Then he said, slowly and rather mechanically, 'I had a rabbit once, when I was about Michael's age. She was a little Dutch one, very pretty, with grey and white fur. My grandfather gave her to me for my birthday. She died of some gut trouble. One day she was all right, the next she was dead.'

Eileen nodded sympathetically. 'Rabbits are such vulnerable creatures. They just seem to give up. That's why we got Michael a guinea pig. They seem tougher. Did you have other pets? You obviously like animals.'

'No. I wanted a cat. But I was so upset when the rabbit died it was considered unwise to replace her.' A bitter note had come into his voice.

Eileen decided to change tack. 'I wondered if you might be hungry. I brought some sandwiches and coffee.' She held out the bag.

Christopher rose to his feet, his arms wrapped around his body. For a moment it seemed he was undecided whether to accept her offering or run for his life. She held the bag out to him, smiling encouragingly, then, when he did not move, she put it down on the ground, backed away and sat down on a tree stump.

He came forward cautiously, squatted down by the bag and undid the wrappers, every few seconds glancing up. She stayed still and continued to smile, trying to look unthreatening. He took a sandwich, prepared to bite, then paused and looked up again. 'Thank you.'

'You're welcome.'

He ate as if he were starving. As he unscrewed the cap of the flask Eileen said, 'Be careful. It's hot.' He nodded, poured carefully, left the cup to cool, took another sandwich, then, as if again remembering long-ago training, offered one to Eileen.

She shook her head. 'I already had breakfast, thanks. I hope you like peanut butter. Michael thought you would.'

Christopher glanced around, still chewing. 'Michael? Where is he?'

'Oh, he's not here. He's away for half term. But we brought you some sandwiches a few days ago. Michael was very worried about you; he was afraid you would starve. It was his idea. But you weren't here. I left the stuff on the tree stump, but when I came back the next day it was untouched, so I guessed you had gone elsewhere.'

Christopher brushed crumbs from his fingers, took a deep draught of coffee, shuddered, and licked his lips. 'I went for my injection.'

'Your injection?'

'Yes. I have one every month. I have to, or I would be crazy. I know that. I am not crazy now, am I?' His look was a challenge.

Eileen shook her head. 'You look OK to me.'

'That's because I've had my injection. Sometimes it doesn't work too well. But this time it seems to be all right. So far.'

'Where do you go for your injection?'

'The county hospital, near Osewick. My carer, Jackie, comes in her car to take me. I went back to my house to change my clothes and shave and shower. I walked through the night. Jackie came at nine. She didn't know I'd been here. The others were all still asleep. When she dropped me off afterwards I just said goodbye. I pretended everything was all right. Then I came back here. Nobody saw me. Nobody knows, only Michael and Stephen. And now you, I suppose.' While he had been telling her how he had carried out his plan, he had sounded triumphant. Now a note of doubt crept into his voice.

109

'What would have happened to you if you hadn't had your injection, Christopher?' Eileen asked gently.

'They would have known I wasn't there. They would have started looking for me. Maybe I would have caused a lot of trouble.' He sounded fearful.

'I mean, what would you be like if you didn't have it?'

He tensed. 'Why do you want to know?'

'I just wondered. I'm just interested. It's no big deal.'

'I would be mad, of course.' His eyes narrowed. 'That's what the injections are for, to stop me being mad.'

'I see.' Eileen felt she had gone as far as she could, that he would tolerate no more questions along this line. 'Are you planning to stay in the woods for long?'

'Why? Are you going to tell someone? I won't let them find me. There are plenty of other places.'

Eileen shrugged. 'I know. And I wasn't planning to tell anybody. Why should I? But I just thought it can't be very comfortable for you down here, especially now that the weather's changed. If I come down tomorrow when I walk the dog, would you like me to bring you some stuff? A plastic sheet to keep the rain out, and perhaps a sleeping bag or blankets?'

He looked at her sideways, not wanting to meet her eyes, but as if trying to read her thoughts. 'Why do you want to help me?'

'I don't know. I just think of you living out here in the woods, cold and wet and hungry, and I can get you things to make it a bit better.'

'I can't give *you* anything.'

'I don't want anything.'

He considered for a moment, scuffing the leaf mould with the toe of his filthy trainer. 'All right. A plastic sheet would be good, and a sleeping bag. Thanks.'

'I'll bring them down later.'

'I might not be here.'

'I'll just leave them here, then, in a bag.'

'If I decide to go away again, that's where I'll leave them too.'

'OK.' She got up, stretched her legs. 'I'll go home now. Take care of yourself.'

He backed away, once again hugging himself tightly as if he feared something might escape from inside. 'Please don't tell anyone I'm here.'

She looked at him directly, and saw him flinch. His dark blue eyes, full of fear and misery, stared out from among the dirt and stubble.

'I won't. But there are others who have seen you. I don't think they

110

will say anything, but maybe you'd better lie low. Then they'll think you've gone.'

'All right.' His voice was barely a whisper.

'See you later, maybe. Come on, Tillie.'

She went back up the path, deliberately not turning round. But when she reached the top of the path and turned right along the lane, she caught a brief glimpse of him, still standing where she had left him, gazing after her.

She sat drinking coffee in the kitchen, her eyes staring at the wall, but seeing nothing, absorbed in her thoughts. The sunlight had broken through, and was shining in at the sitting room window, casting odd shadows.

Christopher was, after all, not scary, menacing or violent. Or at least, he didn't seem so, even allowing for her very limited knowledge. She felt no sense of threat. She could be wrong, of course. But all she felt was his immense vulnerability, his fragility, his neediness. He was a curious cross between a well-raised human being and a flighty wild creature, like a deer. All she could think of was to help him, but she knew she must be careful. He was very suspicious. If she struck a wrong note he'd be off. But what was he afraid of? He seemed so anxious to stay in control. Sneaking off for his injection, now, that had taken some planning, and he was quite clear about his need of medication. He didn't seem crazy, but there were some peculiar things about him: his fearfulness, and his oddly flat and mechanical way of talking. She did want to help him, that bit was true, but almost as much she wanted to find out what was behind this strange young man. She wanted to learn what it felt like to be him. Where had he come from, what was his illness, where was his family, when had it all started? Did she have a right to this knowledge, or was she guiltily buying it with food and blankets? She couldn't pursue this line of thinking, because she didn't understand it herself. He needed her to help him, but perhaps just as much she needed him to tell her about himself. Somehow she just had to know. Was it a fair bargain? Was she harming him in some way? She didn't want that. Should she tell someone he was there? According to him, nobody knew he was missing. Perhaps she was being infected by his fear, but she didn't want anybody to find him, not yet. She felt he needed to be free, for a while at least. Why did she feel that? She knew nothing about him. Was she being crazy herself? Irresponsible even? She didn't know.

The telephone rang. She went into the hallway and picked up the receiver.

'Hello, Eileen.' It was Marie.

111

'Hello, Marie. How are you?'

'Pretty fair, thanks. I just thought I'd see how you were, all on your own.'

'Oh, I'm coping somehow.'

'Was it tough on Saturday, leaving Michael?'

'Yes, it was a bit. I went to evensong at Osewick Abbey afterwards.'

'That's where Philip used to work.'

'What, as organist?'

'Yes.'

'That answers a lot, doesn't it? I wonder why he left. What must it be like for him, playing at Holton, after that?'

'I think it's better than playing nowhere.'

'Whatever went wrong, Marie?'

There was a brief pause, then Marie said, 'I've promised not to talk about it, not even to you, Eileen.'

'Oh. It's his business, of course. Anyway, the singing was beautiful. I think it was a visiting choir.'

'So, how are you feeling today? A bit nervous, maybe?'

'Why should I be feeling nervous?'

'I am talking about the visit from David. Your husband—remember him?'

'Right. I had forgotten he was coming. Momentarily only, of course.'

Marie sighed. 'Eileen, you are hopeless. Poor David, he hardly stands a chance.'

'Maybe that's not what he's coming for. But as to that, I am no wiser than you. I'll let you know, if it's repeatable.'

'How's Christina doing? Isn't she taking exams this week?'

'Yes. I spoke to her over the weekend, wished her luck, told her about Michael. I won't ring this week. She needs to concentrate. When it's all over I'll call her.'

'What did she say about Michael and his news?'

'She was as philosophical as ever. She'll miss him, though. I'm sure she'll manage to get back to see him before he finally goes.'

'So you think it will really happen?'

'Yes, I do. I can't see why it wouldn't. The pressures are all working in that direction.'

'Whatever will you do?'

'I dare say I'll find something to keep me off the streets.'

'Hm.'

'How's Stephanie?'

'I haven't seen much of her. She's been staying with her friends in Caxford. Eileen, there goes the doorbell. I'll catch up with you later.'

'OK. Bye, Marie.'

She put the phone down, feeling vaguely irritated. Marie seemed to be going the way of all unthinking humanity, wondering what her friend would do if deprived of husband and children, with no work to fill the hours. Was it perhaps the influence of her own situation with Philip, that she was unconsciously thinking of Eileen, not as a free-standing individual, but in terms of her relationships? Eileen felt at once cross and lonely. On Marie, if on no one else, she had always been able to rely, until now, to see things from her own angle, to be free of conventional wisdom, to see, understand and love her friend simply for what she was herself.

She sighed. Perhaps it was just a passing phase. She hoped the old Marie was under there somewhere, dormant perhaps, but ready to emerge again once this cosy blanket of love got a touch too stifling. *Would I be the same? God forbid. Well, I'm on my own all ways round now, and perhaps that's the way it has to be.*

She grinned to herself. Marie was trying to persuade her to behave well towards David, as she would see it, but what she was doing, whether she knew it or not, was making Eileen more likely to resist any blandishments of his. Still, what did she know? He was probably coming to give her the push. That would take away the necessity of making any decision, at least.

She did a few chores, very half-heartedly, repeatedly looking down the garden as if she expected Christopher to appear from the woods. Finally, after lunch, she could resist no longer. She found a piece of stout plastic sheeting in the shed, and cleaned it up a bit. She put a sleeping bag and an extra blanket in a bag. The sun was out now, and hot, drying up the night's rain. It was beginning to feel sticky again.

When she got to the camp there was no sign of Christopher. She left the bag on the stump, feeling surprised by the strength of her disappointment.

As she walked home she spoke to herself sternly in the silence of her mind. *You are becoming a stupid woman, flapping about like this. You have always been, if not patient, then self-controlled. You need that now. Back off, keep a clear head. There are things in your life that need attending to.*

But it didn't feel like that. It shocked her that everything else seemed pale and insubstantial. All the people around her were living their own lives. This pathetic little bit was all that was her own, and it may well prove illusory. As she entered the house by the back door she felt angry with herself. She was behaving like a fool. What on earth was she doing, creeping round the woods, helping a sick man to run away from the people who cared for him? I will phone Social Services now. No, she couldn't. She had said she wouldn't. Why had she done that? She must be going senile.

Her train of thought was interrupted by a strange sound from the dog. Tillie had been lying in her basket, snoozing off the morning's exertions. Now she looked strange: her eyes were rolling and her breathing was noisy. At once Eileen forgot Christopher and everything else and knelt on the floor beside Tillie's basket. She ran a hand over the furry body. Tillie's tail flapped very slightly, acknowledging her, but too weak to wag.

'What's up, old dear?' she said, gently stroking the warm, smooth head. 'You don't look right.'

During the afternoon she kept an eye on Tillie, who seemed to be neither better nor worse. But when she refused food Eileen rang the vet in Caxford and was given an appointment for six o'clock. She could just make it, as long as she didn't have to wait too long in the surgery. She should be back in time for David, but perhaps she would leave a note on the door in case she was late.

David arrived promptly at eight. From the kitchen Eileen heard the soft scrunch of tyres coming to rest on gravel. She looked out as David got out of the car and locked the door. He was the same but different: older certainly, thicker round the waist, with a peppering of grey in his dark hair, of which there was still plenty. As he turned towards her, she saw his face, weathered and lined from his outdoor life, still familiar, especially when he smiled, as he did now. He looked prosperous, well-fed, content with himself, and quite well turned out, for him, in a green polo shirt and beige trousers. The muddy wax jacket and boots he had no doubt left at home.

'Eileen, hello, it's good to see you,' he said, bending to kiss her lightly on the cheek. His voice was the same, warm and friendly.

'Hello, David. Come in, sit down.'

He looked at her searchingly. 'Are you all right?'

'No, as a matter of fact, I've had some rotten news.'

'Since we spoke on the phone? What is it?'

'I've just got back from the vet's in Caxford. Tillie is ill.'

'Oh, dear. What's the matter?' David rose from his chair, squatted down beside the dog's basket, and gently stroked her. She looked up at him, blearily grateful.

114

Don't be so sympathetic. I wish you hated animals and thought Tillie was a smelly nuisance. Say something dismissive, please. It's bad enough knowing she's poorly. If I cry while you are here, I will die of shame.

She cleared her throat, summoned up every fibre of will. 'The vet didn't know exactly. He thinks it's probably her liver, a tumour or some kind of calcification. Either way it's to do with her age. He's taken a blood test and is going to let me know as soon as he's got the results.'

'Poor old dog. Is she in any pain, do you suppose?'

'The vet says not. I wouldn't even have brought her home if I'd thought she was suffering.'

'Of course not. I'm truly sorry, Eileen. She's been a good friend.'

'Yes.' She turned abruptly away. 'Would you like some coffee?'

'Thanks. That would be nice.'

Eileen busied herself with the kettle. 'How is the conference going?' Heat rose in her cheeks as she saw him looking at her steadily, not saying a word.

'Oh, yes, very interesting. Quite a few people from overseas. It's good to hear what they're doing, exchange news.'

'Christie was telling me about Glen Achuil. She says it's very beautiful.'

'Yes, it is. You would love it.'

What does he mean? 'Would I?'

He seemed not to notice her reply. 'It's in the winter I love it most, when there's six inches of crunchy snow, the mountains and the trees are white, and I go to look for ptarmigan. At night you can see the owls flitting about.'

'It sounds wonderful.' She made two mugs of coffee and put them down on the table.

There was a silence as they sipped their coffee. Then David said, very quietly, 'So why don't you come and see it?'

Panic hit her like a wave. *This is it. What can I say to him?* But her voice was calm when she answered, as if she had it all thought out. 'Why do you say that?'

David leaned forward in his chair. He rested his arms on the table and spoke with some intensity. Eileen suddenly became fascinated by the light catching on the dark hairs on the backs of his hands.

'Think about it,' he said, quiet but compelling. 'Christie has her own life, she'll graduate, get a job, travel, whatever. I've seen Natasha and Sean. She seems very settled with him, don't you think?'

'Yes, I suppose so. But they've only known each other a few months. What did you think of Sean?'

115

'I liked him. Don't you?'

'Yes, I do. I think he is a dear, and quite devoted to Tash.'

'Eventually they will get married, I guess.'

'Probably.'

'She's already rarely here, isn't that right? If she's not at work, she's with him.'

'Yes.'

'And then there's Michael. I've heard from Natasha what is going on there. The chances are in the next few months he will have gone to live with his natural family.'

'Yes.'

'Surely that's a success story for you, isn't it? A satisfactory conclusion?'

'Nothing is unmixed.'

David frowned. 'Of course you'll miss him, I understand that.'

Do you?

'And now, there's poor old Tillie. I'm not trying to be unkind here, but you could have a dog in Scotland.'

'I could have a dog here, if I chose.'

'Eileen, forgive me, but I feel we've wasted so much time. You said, years ago, you didn't want to leave Holton. You talked about the girls' schooling. I thought it pretty pathetic at the time, but I accepted it, though I felt hurt, rejected even. But I'm willing to put all that behind us, make a new start. What is there to keep you here?'

Eileen looked at him stonily. *What indeed?* 'You really don't know about my life here.'

'So tell me.'

'Why, so that you can sit in judgment on whether it matches up to what you're offering? What exactly are you offering, anyway?'

'Please, don't let's argue, that's not why I'm here. I asked you, what is keeping you here?'

Eileen was silent for a moment. 'I cannot tell you that.'

'Are you hinting that there's some other man?' David asked, looking suddenly vulnerable.

'Not in the way you have in mind.'

'What's that supposed to mean? Why do you have to be so mysterious?'

'I cannot explain.'

David groaned in exasperation. 'Look, I came here prepared to be honest and straightforward with you.' *Bully for you.* 'So I might as well tell you that I have a lady friend in Scotland, somebody I am very fond of, but I haven't let it get too far, because I don't feel it's fair. I wanted to see if you and I could patch it up, start over. Surely we had something going for us once? Are you saying that it's too late? I need to know, for Margaret's sake.'

Eileen took a deep breath and let it out slowly. 'David, as ever, you have done what you felt to be right. You have been honest and I thank you for that. All this is my fault, I don't doubt. If it helps you to think that, then think it. There is more to me than home, husband and children, or if there isn't now, there will be, because I am going to make it happen.'

I had no idea I was even thinking that. But as it happens, I am.

David stared at her, frowning. 'I don't understand you.'

'No. I know you don't.'

'So whose fault is that? Is it that I'm thick?'

'Of course not. As to whose fault it is, if it's anybody's, maybe both of us have been clueless and obstinate.' She smiled at him, suddenly seeing the farcical nature of it all. 'Look, David, why don't we just wrap it up now, while we can still be civil? You go and do right by Margaret, and good luck to both of you. For heaven's sake don't let me plague your conscience. I've made my bed and I'm lying in it. Maybe I'll live to regret it, who knows, but at this moment I'm not sorry.'

'Are you sure? I mean, all thought out and no more to be said?'

Of course she wasn't sure. But what she was saying to him was still true. There were real temptations in what he was laying before her. Scotland sounded lovely. In other circumstances it would have been completely up her street, without question. And yes, her life here was ended, in a way, if you considered the family had been her life. And David himself was still a very attractive man. She was far from immune to that, but she was keeping it quiet. In lots of ways there was something very tempting about letting go of lonely decisions and responsibility. Not to mention sex; that would be good too. But then she thought of the weeks, months, perhaps years of explanations, descending into recriminations; and then Margaret would be on his conscience, and he would have regrets which she would know about even if he never voiced them. *No, I don't think so. And anyway, there is Christopher.* With a sickening pang she heard her own thoughts, clear and unequivocal. *What am I saying? This is total nonsense. I have no relationship with Christopher, of any sort. Delete that.* 'Not all thought out, no. But again, perhaps it's enough. Is that what you wanted to hear? *Carte blanche* for your new life?'

He frowned in puzzlement. 'I don't know what I wanted. I just felt it was right. As to my "new life", it doesn't exist yet. I think, I hope, I can make it exist.'

'Then do it. I'll see you, won't I? At the very least, at Natasha's wedding, Christie's graduation. Bring Margaret.'

David shook his head. 'You are a very odd character, Eileen. How come I never really noticed it before?'

Eileen laughed out loud. 'I'll leave you to ponder that little conundrum on your way back to London.'

In the end he seemed curiously reluctant to leave, and it was almost dark when he climbed into the shiny dark blue hire car.

'I'll have to be in touch again,' he said. 'To sort out the business side of things.'

'Of course. I won't be going anywhere just yet.'

He hesitated, as if searching for the appropriate words. 'You know I will try to be fair.'

'I hope we both will. There is no need for grudges, after all.'

'No. Well, I'll call you. Goodbye, Eileen.'

'Goodbye, David. Have a safe journey.'

She watched the car disappear down the rutted road, and shivered despite the lingering warmth.

How is it that anyone can behave like that, like I did, so unfazed, cool, thought-it-all-out, know-what-I-want, and yet inside be a complete wreck? It's as if there are two distinct people locked in one mind, as if I am my own Siamese twin.

She went back inside, shut the door, trailed listlessly back to the kitchen, and washed the coffee cups. Her mind ranged back over the day impassively, as if watching a film of somebody else's life. Her bones ached and her heart felt like a rock in her chest. She sat on the floor next to Tillie's basket, put her arms round her dog, and wept.

Later, drained of all feeling, empty and blank, she lay propped up in bed and searched the Psalms, poems of a fragile man who was also the nation's leader chosen by God, songs of triumph and despair, glory, vindication, shame and defeat. She fell asleep with the words still speaking inside her head.

"Save me, O God!

The water is up to my neck; I am sinking in deep mud, and there is no solid ground;

I am out on deep water, and the waves are about to drown me.

I am worn out from calling for help, and my throat is aching.

I have strained my eyes, looking for your help."

118

Wednesday 29th May 1996

The phone rang twice while Eileen was eating breakfast. First it was Natasha, ringing in haste from Sean's flat before dashing off to work. Eileen had not seen her since she had waved her off to London on Sunday. Now Natasha was saying she would be home that evening. 'I need to do some washing, get myself together. And have a bit of space to breathe. What with seeing Dad this week as well, it's all getting a bit heavy.'

Ten minutes later Annette was on the line, sounding agitated, but perhaps for once more excited than fearful. 'Eileen, you'll never believe this, but I actually rang that young man I was telling you about, Mark Pepper.'

'What did he say?'

'He wasn't there, so I left a message on his machine. I'd almost given up on him. Then he rang me late last night. He was very charming, full of apologies for not ringing sooner, but he'd been away. He remembered me from before, said he was delighted I'd called and to come back to the group any time.'

'Are you going?'

'I rather think I am.'

'Wonderful. So when is it?'

'This afternoon. I was hoping you would drive me.'

'Of course I will. I said I would. What time do you need to be there?'

'Two o'clock, finishing at half-three for the people who have children at school.'

'All right, my dear, I'll be outside your front door at half past one or soon after.'

'Thanks, Eileen, you are a life-saver.'

'Hardly that. See you later, Annette.'

She packed food for Christopher and made soup. Tillie seemed quite peaceful, but obviously disinclined to get out of her basket, so Eileen went to the woods alone. It was another beautiful morning. The sunlight

119

slanted down through the branches from a well-washed sky, the birds were busy and full of song, and the woods smelled fresh and earthy after the recent rain. She descended the grassy path, noting the pink campion growing tall at the foot of the oaks and wild garlic opening its myriad white flowerlets. She approached Christopher's sanctum with caution. She still thought of him as a wild creature, apt to run if startled.

He was perched on the tree stump, his knees drawn up, smoking a homemade cigarette, his eyes squinting in the sunlight. His bedding was neatly rolled and stowed, his belongings, few as they were, carefully arranged beside him. For a moment Eileen felt like a subject bringing offerings to a monarch on his throne, nervous in case what she laid before him was not acceptable.

'Hello,' she said.

He did not answer, simply went on smoking and looking at her intently.

'Did you keep warmer last night?' she asked.

He unfolded his legs, encased in grimy jeans, stood up, carefully ground out the stub of his cigarette, then picked it up and put it into a flat tobacco tin. 'Yes, thank you. The stuff helped.'

'I've brought you some supplies.' She handed him the bag.

He ate squatting on the ground among the damp leaves, leaving Eileen the tree stump. Once again she was struck by the peculiar combination of modern human and something wilder and older, an animal, or perhaps a member of some ancient culture. The dirt was blurring the signs that Christopher belonged to the twentieth century. He was gradually becoming a denizen of the forest, a being from another time. But when he spoke, the illusion shattered.

He brushed crumbs away. 'It's nice of you to help me like this. But I don't know why you should bother.'

'Is it wrong, then, do you think, to help people?'

He paused and pondered for a moment. 'No, not wrong, but unusual.'

'Don't people help you, as a rule?'

'I guess they think that's what they're doing. Some of them are doing what other people say they should, and all of them are trying to do me good, but there's a lot they don't know, and they don't ask me if I want it.'

Eileen nodded. 'What do you want, I wonder?'

'To be left alone. Maybe I can sort myself out.'

'Do you really think you can?'

'I'd like to try.'

'Do you mean you don't want to live on drugs?'

He frowned. 'They tell me I need them, and I keep to it to get them off my back, but I'm wondering more and more how effective it all is.'

'Are you saying the medication isn't working?'

'It doesn't work as well as it used to. And sometimes one drug works against another.'

'What difference does that make to you?'

'Do you know much about drugs?'

'Not a thing.'

'Well, the injection I have every month is to stop me hearing things and seeing things.'

'What kind of things?'

Christopher gave her a considering, sideways look. 'Why do you want to know all this stuff?'

'I don't know. But I find it all very interesting for some reason.'

He rose to a crouch. 'They haven't sent you, have they? To spy on me, to find things out, so they can come and get me?'

'Christopher, of course not. I don't know any of these people. I just saw you in the woods, Michael did too, I live here, don't I? You know where I live. I promise you, I am not trying to harm you.'

He subsided into a squatting position, but his eyes were watchful. 'It just seems funny,' he muttered. 'I don't know why you want to have anything to do with me. I'm just a nutter hanging out in your woods. I could be dangerous, for all you know.' He sounded bitter.

'Well, are you?' Eileen asked. 'Do you feel a need to knock me about?'

Christopher bent his head, hugged his knees. His voice was muffled; it was almost as if he was crying.

'No,' he answered. 'I never hurt anyone in my life. The idea makes me sick.'

'That's what I thought. I am not afraid of you, and I don't want you to be afraid of me.'

'We are equal, then.'

'Of course we are.'

'Except that you are helping me.'

'Look,' Eileen said. 'It was Michael, if you must know. He rather shamed me into remembering what I should be doing. He told me that it says in the Bible I should feed the hungry, clothe the naked, take in the stranger. I guess he must have been thinking of that bit from Matthew, the division of the sheep and the goats.'

'Yes,' whispered Christopher. 'I know. "I was hungry and you fed me, thirsty and you gave me a drink; I was a stranger and you received me in your homes, naked and you clothed me; I was sick and you took care of me, in prison and you visited me.'"

Eileen gaped. She had not expected this. 'Yes, that's it.'

'So you are telling me,' said Christopher, 'that I represent your duty as a God-fearing person? Is that what you are, a God-fearing person?'

Eileen was at once alarmed and irritated by his suddenly aggressive tone. 'I wouldn't put it quite like that. I feel that God has forgiven and blessed me in many ways, and if he says I must pass this on to other people, then I think I should. As to your being an object of duty, it isn't quite so cold and mechanical. I don't know much about you, and I don't want to interfere, but I see you are in need of help, and if I can help you I would like to. I hope, out of love, not duty.'

Christopher was silent for several long moments. 'OK. I'm sorry if I sounded ungrateful. I get twitchy when people quote the Bible.'

'You did it yourself, rather accurately, I thought.'

He laughed, but it was not a joyful sound. It was hollow, full of sneering and self-disgust. 'Yeah, well, so would you, if you'd been brought up in a vicarage.'

'I see. You make it sound a less than happy experience.'

'My father,' Christopher said, giving the simple words a contemptuous irony, 'is a canon of the church, a scholar, a pastor, a truly wonderful man. Ha, ha.'

'Who says he's wonderful?'

'Oh, everybody. The bishop, my mum, his dear sister, my dear sisters, his parishioners.'

'But not his son.'

'No. But I'm beyond the pale. I'm stupid, sick, mad, a disgrace to the family.'

'Did he say that?'

'No, he didn't. He's far too careful and Christian for that. He wouldn't ever let himself get so heated over anything. Very measured and even-handed is my father. It must make him sick to have an unbalanced son.' He loaded the adjective with sarcastic loathing.

Eileen looked at him silently for a while. Clearly he was fighting with some strong emotion; the battle was being played out on his face and body in front of her.

'What about your mother?' she asked. 'Is she any more sympathetic?'

Christopher winced visibly, and his tone changed. 'She's OK,' he mumbled. 'She did her best. It was hard for her, having me around as I was.' His eyes filled with tears, and he hung his head.

122

What Eileen wanted then was to put her arms around him and hug him, but she didn't dare. In his distress he reminded her of Michael in the early days. 'Do you still live at your parents' house, Christopher?'

He shook his head. 'No, that's something at least. They don't have to watch me every day, going crazy before their eyes; they don't have to be reminded. I live with five other headcases, in Caxford.'

'Where do your family live, then?'

'My dad is vicar of All Saints, Barnwell. It's about three miles south of Osewick. I go there once in a while, not so much lately.'

'Did I hear you have sisters?'

'I'm afraid so. They are younger than me, and twins. They are very clever, unlike their big brother. *They* aren't a disgrace to the great Arrowsmith tradition.'

'Are you happier living away from home?'

Christopher shrugged, as if the matter were of no importance. 'At least where I live the others don't hassle me. Because they're mad themselves, of course. Would you like to know more about my charming house-mates?' He grinned mirthlessly, mockingly.

'Yes, I would.'

'Well, there's Dave. He's about forty, and he has a system for winning the lottery, only of course it doesn't work, but he'll talk to you about it for hours if you let him. I think he's actually quite clever but he can't hack it any more, normal life, I mean. He's better than he used to be. He used to rant and rave at night, and bang on the walls, and sob loudly. Poor bloke, I think he suffered from nightmares. Then there's Rita. She's very odd, quite young but looks ancient, like a bag lady or a crone. She walks the streets all day, muttering and singing to herself. She's spent most of her life in and out of hospital, but they don't seem to be able to help her much. Then there's Chuck. He really fancies himself, thinks he's very flash, but he's totally incapable of relating to the real world, whatever that is. When he's really ill he's a gibbering wreck, just huddles in a corner of his room for days, moaning. He doesn't even come out of his room to go to the toilet, which is quite revolting. If he gets like that they take him in, but he's not been bad for a while now. Maybe they've got his drugs right, who knows. Then there's Sylvie. She's like a little girl, all coy and cute. She thinks she's everybody's girlfriend. She's tried to attach herself to all the men in the house at one time, even Maurice, and he's quite old.' He paused for a moment, grimacing as if fighting for mastery of some inner demon. 'It's a shame really. She is terribly lonely, and people take advantage of her. Once, ages ago, she turned up in my room in the night with nothing on except a pink ribbon. It was horrible.

I locked my door after that. But I feel sorry for her; she's such a mess. Someone said she had a baby once. That's not surprising, the way she carries on. I guess it was adopted. Poor Sylvie. And then there's me. You know what our place reminds me of?'

Eileen shook her head.

'Gormenghast. Have you read it?'

'Yes, but it was a long time ago.'

Christopher smiled sadly. 'A Gothic house of horrors, that's us.'

'Are you left to your own devices? I mean, can these people look after themselves?'

'Most of the time we help each other and muddle along. But there's always someone in the background anyway, looming like a big black cloud, armed with drugs and ready to haul you off to hospital. I have a psychiatrist, Dr. Partridge. I keep out of his way. Then there's Sandra, she's my CPN, that's a community psychiatric nurse. And my carer, Jackie. She's the one that takes me for my injection. I even have a social worker, Mick Cohen.'

'What are they like?'

'Oh, they're all right, I suppose. Want to sort you out, all that. I keep my head down. I want to keep away from shrinks and hospitals. They do my head in worse than it already is.'

'I have a friend who spent time once in a psychiatric ward,' Eileen said. 'She suffers very badly from depression. She'd do anything to keep out of hospital, like you. I'm taking her to a sort of self-help group this afternoon.'

'Yeah, they tried to get me involved in that sort of thing, but I felt really freaked, I wouldn't go. I'm all right if they leave me alone. But they don't, nobody does, not for long.'

'Is that why you're here, Christopher?' Eileen asked. 'In the woods, hiding perhaps?'

Christopher shrugged and looked away without answering. After a while he looked up cautiously, met her eyes, and looked away again. He got up, stretched his legs, and walked around kicking the leaves. 'Where's your dog?'

'She's ill,' Eileen said. 'She won't get out of her basket, and she's not eating. I'm waiting for a call from the vet with some test results. If I don't hear, I'll ring the vet myself before I take my friend into town.'

'She's old, isn't she?'

'What, Tillie? Yes, she's almost sixteen.'

'Are you very worried?'

'Yes. Talking to you has taken my mind off it for a while, but I'm not

124

looking forward to the vet ringing. It gives me a sick feeling in my stomach. I'm dreading having to make a decision. I would almost rather she just died, though I will miss her terribly.'

To her enormous surprise Christopher shambled over, squatted down beside her, and took her hand in his own filthy one. He looked very young, despite the stubble on his cheeks and chin. 'You really like animals, don't you? Do you like them better than people?'

'No, not really,' Eileen said. 'But they are a lot easier to love and receive love from than people.'

'And they aren't usually mad.'

'I guess not, though Tillie as a pup was a bit daft.'

'My rabbit was like that,' said Christopher sadly. 'She used to kick up her heels and tear about her run, just for the fun of it, I suppose.'

'Didn't you say your grandfather gave her to you?'

'Yes.'

'Do you see much of him?'

'I used to. But he's dead.'

'Oh. I'm sorry. He sounds like a good friend. You must miss him.'

'I do. He was the only real friend I ever had, I think.'

'That's very sad, to hear you say that. Didn't you have any friends at school?'

'They all thought I was peculiar, a freak. I didn't think like them.'

'What about the people you live with?'

'The trouble with mad people, they're often so self-absorbed. I am myself, a lot of the time. I guess they just don't have the energy to relate to other people. They're too busy fighting off the weird things going on in their heads. Have you ever felt crazy?'

Eileen shook her head. 'Not in the way you mean. I felt I was going mad sometimes after my mother died and my father was so ill. But that was grief, it can do that to you.'

Christopher nodded forlornly. 'Yes, that's how I was when my grandad died. Only I guess I never got over it. I went mad and stayed mad.'

'You don't seem mad to me.'

'I know. It's because I don't feel frightened. You are not threatening, somehow.'

'I'm glad of that.'

'But I am mad, of course. Or rather, I have a mental illness. That's how they prefer to describe it.'

'Does this illness have a name?'

'Yes. But who cares? I'm mad. That's all you need to know.'

125

Eileen looked at her watch. 'Christopher, I have to go. There are a few things I have to do before I take my friend to Caxford. Is there anything I can get you while I'm there?'

Christopher shook his head. 'No. Just don't tell anyone you've seen me.'

'I won't. Would you like me to come back later? I could bring you some tea.'

'I might go for a walk.'

'If you are not around I could leave it here. This is your base camp, isn't it?'

'I suppose so. But I could go anywhere.'

'I know. You are a free man.'

'I am, aren't I? That's what I am, here in the woods. Free. Maybe I'll see you later, then.'

Eileen got up from the tree stump, creaking a little. She collected the bag. 'Take care, Christopher.'

He nodded. She turned away, pushed her way through the bushes onto the path, and headed home.

After lunch she rang the vet. The receptionist told her that the test results were not yet available, and that she would telephone later. Thinking of bringing Annette back, and of taking food to Christopher, Eileen asked her to ring after five. As she left the house Tillie raised her head and wagged her tail slowly in farewell, then sighed deeply and went back to sleep. The image of her, suddenly aged, stayed in Eileen's mind as she drove up to the Dyers' house, and she felt a blanket of heaviness descend upon her, an ache in her chest, a greyness before her eyes as if the world were temporarily drained of its rightful colour.

Annette was waiting at the door. For a moment Eileen blinked speechlessly: Annette looked so different. She was wearing high heels and a suit of lemon linen, and carrying a patent leather handbag. Her hair was stylish, and she had makeup on. 'What do you think?'

'The men need to watch themselves, it seems to me,' Eileen said, smiling. 'You look terrific, Annette.'

'It's taken me all morning to get organized,' Annette said. 'I feel dreadfully nervous. Stupid, isn't it.'

'Get in, then. We'll take it nice and easy.'

They drove to Caxford mostly in amicable silence, punctuated by desultory comments on the weather and local residents. Annette was evidently preoccupied with her afternoon session, trying to argue herself out of her fears. Eileen thought of Tillie, and Christopher, and Michael.

126

Michael will be all right. Everybody will be on their best behaviour. It's still the honeymoon.

She dropped Annette outside the meeting hall.

'What will you do?' Annette asked her.

'Oh, I'll probably do a bit of shopping, or call in at the library. See you back here at half past three. Good luck, Annette.'

There were few people about on the streets of Caxford, just elderly folk and mothers pushing prams. The supermarket was empty and Eileen did her shopping very quickly. She strolled up to the library, pulled books off the shelves at random; but she couldn't concentrate. Her brain felt overloaded, her eyes blurred, and she felt the beginnings of a headache.

Her thoughts circled back to Christopher. On the face of it he seemed so normal, or at least rational. But there was an undefinable undercurrent in him, something fragile and unpredictable. It was unusual, certainly, uncomfortable, no doubt, but was it really irrational to want to live rough in the woods? She felt certain that something had happened to drive him there, but whether it had occurred in the daily life that we quaintly call real or whether it had happened inside his head— was such an event less real?—she could not tell. More and more she wanted to find out what drove and powered him, but she was aware how tenuous her link with him was, and how easily it could be broken. *I think I am leaving the path of so-called reality myself. I am becoming obsessive. Still, there is nobody to care about how batty I become, except me.*

When she pulled up outside the meeting hall to collect Annette the headache had taken hold in earnest. Annette was excited and chatty, and did not seem to notice Eileen's monosyllabic replies. 'I think it might actually be going to do me some good. Mark is such a helpful young man; he's given me some ideas on how to cope till next week. "Building on my achievements", he calls it. I have to say the others in the group were a bit dead-and-alive. Still, I suppose that's how I was till just recently. There's one poor girl there, she's got six children and her husband knocks her about. The way she talks, when she talks at all, you'd think she deserved it. Then there's this man; truly, Eileen, he is quite repellent: tall, skinny, with broken teeth and greasy grey hair in a ponytail, grubby clothes and yellow fingers from years of smoking, and all he goes on about are his three failed marriages, which I can sympathize with, of course, but I do wish he wouldn't insist on giving us all the gruesome bedroom details.'

'Will you go again?'

127

'Oh, yes. I feel I've found my voice at last, with Mark's help. And yours, of course.' She patted Eileen's arm timidly. 'Maybe in a week or two I'll be brave enough to try the bus.'

'Don't worry, Annette. I don't mind taking you.'

'You are very kind, Eileen. But soon I must make myself branch out a bit. I have to practise being a bit more independent. If I don't make the effort now, I don't think I ever will.'

Eileen drew up outside Annette's house. 'Fair enough. Just let me know if you need me for anything.'

'I will. Many, many thanks, dear.'

'You're welcome. Be in touch.'

Tillie managed to get up out of her basket and walk slowly and creakily to the front door to greet Eileen as she let herself in.

'Hello, old girl,' Eileen said, bending down to stroke her head. 'Have you had enough sleep yet, lazybones?'

She stowed the shopping and made a cup of tea. Tillie condescended to eat a few mouthfuls, and went out into the garden to flop on the grass. Eileen put a picnic together.

'Are you fit enough for a stroll?' she asked the dog. 'Just a short one, down the hill and back?'

To her delight Tillie followed her down the garden, through the gate and into the trees. Progress was very slow, but eventually they made it to the camp.

There was no sign of Christopher. His things were either gone or well hidden. Only the disintegrating chocolate wrapper betrayed a human presence. Eileen frowned, puzzled, then shrugged resignedly. She left the bag of food and the flask of tea on the tree stump. Tillie was lying down in the soft grass by the side of the path. She didn't look too ill, just old and tired. She heaved herself up and followed Eileen back up the hill. But by the time they got to the gate she was plainly exhausted, whining with bewilderment that her legs were refusing to carry her. With some difficulty, for she was not a small dog, Eileen gathered her up in her arms and carried her indoors. She was struck by how light and bony and fragile she had become; her solid frame seemed to be melting away. She laid her gently in her basket, and put a dish of diluted milk within reach. She was beginning to prepare a meal for herself and Natasha when the vet called.

'Unfortunately the tests weren't totally conclusive,' he said. 'It's definitely her liver, but what's causing it we aren't sure. If you like you can bring her in some time over the next day or two and we can give her a shot to stimulate the system generally and alleviate symptoms. I'm afraid it won't last for long, of course. At her age deterioration is likely to be faster rather than slower.'

'So it's really down to me, to keep an eye on her and make whatever decision I must.'

'Yes. You know her best, of course. It's never easy, when an animal gets old and sick. We're here if you need us.'

'Yes. Thanks for ringing.'

Natasha arrived on the six o'clock bus, looking tired.

Eileen was surprised. 'No Sean?'

'I gave him the evening off. He's gone to see his mum. I think maybe we both need a break. It's been a bit lively, the last few days.'

'And,' Eileen said, 'it's different actually cohabiting with someone rather than seeing them, even if it's every day.'

'Yeah, I guess. Have I got time for a bath before we eat? My bones are aching.'

'Yes, that's fine. Why not have an idle evening? You look as if you need a good rest.'

Natasha came down from her bath in her dressing gown, with her hair wrapped in a towel. She took her supper on a tray and curled up on the sofa in front of the television. She was quiet and inward-seeming, as if digesting an unusual amount of new information. Eileen left her to it; Natasha never responded well to pressure.

Eileen sat at the kitchen table, next to her sleeping dog, and started to read. She felt a need to meet with Universal Truth incarnate in human guise, and found her way to the eighth chapter of John. Here Jesus was speaking, not to the hostile Pharisees, not to the fickle crowds, not to the hardened sceptics, but to his followers.

"So Jesus said to those who believed in him, 'If you obey my teaching, you are really my disciples; you will know the truth and the truth will set you free.'" *This includes me.* She felt her brain wake up and take notice.

"'We are the descendants of Abraham,' they answered, 'and we have never been anybody's slaves. What do you mean, then, by saying, 'You will be free?'"

People still are that literal. Most of them, anyway. Jesus must have been baffling: not only a prophet, but a poet. And all when they were hoping for a warrior leader.

"'Why do you not understand what I say? It is because you cannot bear to listen to my message. You are the children of your father, the Devil, and you want to follow your father's desires. From the very

129

beginning he was a murderer and has never been on the side of truth, because there is no truth in him. When he tells a lie he is only doing what is natural to him, because he is a liar and the father of all lies. But I tell the truth, and that is why you do not believe me. Which one of you can prove that I am guilty of sin?"'

Those poor bewildered Jews. So superior they reckoned themselves, with Abraham as their ancestor. And maybe they really were, in Old Testament times, compared with the neighbouring citizens of Moab and Ammon, the worshippers of bloodthirsty gods. They were offended to be called slaves, but all people were slaves to sin. The trouble was so often in the terminology. If she mentioned sin to the person-in-the-street, a woman of around her own age, for example, that woman would think she was talking jocularly of chocolate. So was the language debased, following the concepts it was modelled by. But sin was not a joke. Sin was grovelling greasily before the great god Self and its sickening, ego-massaging smallness. It was such an offence, somehow, knowing that only by hitching themselves to God's chariot could people become the spiritual beings he destined and equipped them to be. She felt it too, that sense of affront, and it was a constant battle to remind herself that it was he, "the father of all lies", who fostered that desire to go it alone, to achieve something in her own strength. She knew it was all illusion, and shattered in a moment by difficult circumstances, or ill-health, perhaps: but the illusory desire was deep-rooted.

Between one thought and its fellow she was interrupted by the door opening and Natasha appearing, rubbing her hair lazily with the towel.

'I'll put the kettle on, Mum.'

'All right.' Eileen closed her Bible.

'Funny thing, I was telling Sean what you and I were talking about the other day, you know, the stuff you said you could find in there.' Natasha waved a hand. 'And he said you were right, it makes a lot of sense.'

'So does he,' Eileen said. 'You two haven't fallen out, have you?'

'No, not at all. I'm a bit hacked off with his mum, though.'

'Oh? Why?'

'She's been ringing a lot lately, wanting him to do jobs for her. I don't mind that so much, but she doesn't seem to like it when I answer the phone. I don't know what I've done to her.'

'Luckily it's not her you have to live with.'

'Too right. But it's hard on Sean, all the same.'

'I'm sure he will cope, somehow.'

Natasha sighed. 'Probably,' she said, putting two cups of tea on the table and flopping down in a chair. 'How did you get on with Dad?' she said, after a few sips.

'All right, I suppose,' Eileen said. 'Actually, he wanted to know if I was going to Scotland with him.'

'What? You mean, for ever?'

'So it seems.'

'He's crazy. You'd never do that.'

'As it happens, you're right. But what makes you say so?'

'Well, I don't know.' Natasha floundered. 'But you're not exactly keen on the whole marriage thing, are you?'

'I was once, or thought I was. I don't quite know when it all began to change.'

'I do,' Natasha said with surprising firmness. 'It was when Dad started taking the mick out of you going to church.'

'Hm. That didn't help, I grant you, but I think things were getting a bit unglued even before then. Anyway, I don't know if he told you on Sunday, but there is another woman on your dad's horizon.'

'Really?' Natasha goggled. 'Cheeky old thing, he never mentioned that. I wonder if Christie knows.'

'I doubt it. It looks as though that little snippet was for my ears only.'

'So who is this fancy woman?'

'I know nothing about her, except that her name is Margaret.'

'Do you mind?'

'I can hardly complain, can I? Your dad was probably lonely. He is a normal man after all, even though you probably think he is old and past caring.'

Natasha smirked. 'Old, young, if they're not at it they're thinking about it.'

'And you should know.'

Natasha burst out laughing. 'And I should know. Oh well, if I'm knackered I've only got myself to blame. The laugh is, Sean's dead on his feet as well. He's been caught kipping through his lunchbreak with his head on the desk.' She giggled, suddenly looking half her age. 'That's why I thought we'd better both have an early night.' She got up. 'Still, it is rather nice, you know, Mum.'

'I do have a vague memory, actually,' Eileen said drily, 'despite my advancing years and dimming intellect.'

Natasha's expression was suddenly all seriousness. 'Joking apart, Mum, don't you get lonely and fed up sometimes, wish you had someone to keep you company?'

'Sometimes I do, of course. But it's not enough to make me want to change things. Not nearly enough.'

'Mm. Oh well, I'm going to make the most of my little breather and get an early night, with nobody but my teddy bear. Goodnight, Mum.' She came over to Eileen and gave her a hug. She was taller than Eileen by a couple of inches. Her skin was smooth, and she smelled of soap.

'Goodnight, love. I hope you have pure dreams.'

'Wouldn't that be something!' Natasha was still sniggering as she went up to bed.

Something about her daughter's mood cheered Eileen. Natasha's relationship with Sean seemed to have opened the door to an easier interchange with her mother; she was no longer so prickly and suspicious, and this time Eileen had few misgivings about her choice.

I forgot to tell her about Tillie and what the vet said. I'd better mention it in the morning. I don't want her to have too much of a cold dousing, but she needs to be warned.

She bent down and stroked the dog's soft ears. 'Are you going out, old dear?' she whispered. 'No, I haven't the heart to disturb you.' Tillie opened one eye and closed it again. 'Goodnight, dear old dog.'

Thursday 30th May 1996

Eileen came down the stairs the next morning feeling bleary and woolly-headed. It seemed to her that she had picked up some low-grade bug whose symptoms had not yet fully manifested themselves. She was brought back to reality with an unpleasant jolt by the state of the kitchen. Tillie had obviously had a spectacular accident, and now stood by the back door, whining, dishevelled, the epitome of hangdog.

Eileen, after the initial sinking of her heart, felt a rush of pity. Even dogs who had never been blamed for such occasional lapses managed to look guilty and cowed.

'Never mind, old dear,' she said. 'You just go out into the garden for a minute while I clean up.'

For the next half hour she was busy with mop, bucket and disinfectant. She cleaned the bed, washed the bedding, washed and dried the dog herself. By the time Natasha came down, dressed for work, the room was cleaner than it had been for a while, even if it did smell rather clinical.

'What's up?'

'Tillie. She had an accident. I forgot to tell you last night. She's quite ill, I'm afraid.'

'Why, what's the matter?' Natasha asked, all concern, as she bent to stroke the dog, now curled up again in her basket.

Eileen reported her conversation with the vet. 'There's not a lot can be done, it seems, except injections to make her feel better, but even they won't last for ever. I suspect she's had this condition for some time, but it's only now it's beginning to show.'

'Poor old dog,' said Natasha sadly, still squatting by the basket. 'It's no picnic, getting old.'

'You'd better have some breakfast, if you're having any, or you'll miss the bus. Are you coming home again tonight?'

Natasha poured herself a skimpy bowl of cereal. 'I don't know yet, Mum. I'll call you.'

Eileen smiled, her eyebrows faintly raised. 'I guess you need to find out just how rested Sean is.'

'Yep, that's it,' Natasha said with a broad and brazen grin. 'See if the poor dear's up to round two!' She put her bowl in the sink and picked up her bag. 'Bye, Mum, see you whenever.' And she was gone.

An hour later Eileen again made her way to the woods. She left Tillie behind. The dog seemed more comfortable and relaxed, but inclined to do nothing but sleep. *Later today I will take her to the vet for an injection. I have to make her life more bearable, while it lasts.* Her feeling of deep sadness, the threat that at any moment she might weep uncontrollably, gradually lifted as she walked down under the green canopy of the trees to Christopher's camp, carrying another bag of supplies.

As she approached she called out to him softly. There was no reply. In the bivouac his gear had returned, but there was no sign of its owner. She stood, uncertain for a moment. Then a tiny sound made her look up. She saw him sitting on a branch above her head, legs dangling. He had taken off his shoes, and his bare feet were encrusted with dirt. He was wearing only jeans and a shirt, open by several buttons. Under his clothes he was clean, his skin pale and smoothly muscled. Suddenly an awareness of him as a man flashed across her mind, and she banished the thought, feeling hot and uncomfortable.

'What are you doing up there?' she said. 'You look like someone out of Robin Hood.'

He jumped down before her and dusted his hands. 'I like to keep out of the way till I know who's coming.'

'Do many people come down here?'

'Not many. But one's enough to blow it for me. Is that my breakfast?' His gaze was unnervingly intense.

'Yes, help yourself.'

Again for ten or fifteen minutes she watched him eat. He was clearly ravenous. How had he coped before she brought him food?

'You weren't here yesterday afternoon,' she said.

'No, I nearly decided to move camp.'

'Why?'

'I don't know. I got scared. But I couldn't find anywhere better, so I came back. Then I found the stuff you'd left. Thanks.'

She watched him as he finished his meal. 'Do you really like living in the woods?'

He looked at her from under his dark brows. More and more he seemed wild, prehistoric, fey. 'Some things are good. Like being free, with no one at you, or nagging you. Like going wherever you want. But I don't like being dirty and smelly.'

134

'You could come up to my house, if you liked,' Eileen said. 'For a bath. I could even wash your clothes. Do you have anything clean to change into? I've got no men's clothes.'

He nodded warily. 'I've got some other stuff, in case I have to go into town again.' He paused. 'Do you really mean it, that I could wash?'

'Of course.'

He was silent for a moment, considering. 'Do you have a television?'

Eileen was startled. 'Yes. Why?'

Christopher shuddered. 'Would it be turned on?'

'I hardly think so. It's only Natasha and Michael who watch it much, and that's in the evenings.'

'Who's Natasha?'

'My daughter.'

'Does she know about me?'

'She knows there was someone in the woods, that's all. She's probably forgotten all about it by now.'

'Is she indoors?'

'No, she's gone to work. She probably won't be back tonight either. I expect she'll go to her boyfriend's.'

'How old is she?'

'Twenty. I have another daughter. She's away at university.'

Christopher digested this. 'I have twin sisters. I told you. They are sixteen. Girls are scary.'

'Why do you say that?'

'They are so knowing, they can trap you. They are like hunters, very clever.'

'Have you had girlfriends?'

Christopher seemed to draw himself together in a tight ball. 'Please, don't ask. It was too horrible.'

'Sorry. I'm being nosy.'

'I don't really mind that. I ask you a lot of questions, don't I? I think of you as normal, so maybe I think I can find out what normal life's like. It's like something to compare myself with.'

'Don't you think you ever had what you call a normal life?'

'I looked as if I did, when I was still at home, but it didn't feel normal to me.'

'How do you mean?'

'To me,' he said slowly, as if thinking about every word he uttered, 'it all seemed weird, like a dream, only sometimes it turned into more of a nightmare. Yet I guess if you had seen me, you'd have thought I was a normal person, doing normal things.'

135

'Such as?'

'I worked in a couple of places after I left school. My grandad died just before I took my exams, and I failed them all, even the stuff I was good at. Some I didn't even take. I just hung out in the fields by the school, looking at the room I should have been in, but I couldn't make myself go. What a mess I was.'

'Were you ill then?'

'Not like I am now. That stuff came later. Why am I telling you all this? Isn't it really boring?'

'No, it isn't at all.'

'Do you mean that?'

'Yes.'

'OK. Anyway, even the exams I took, when it came to it I couldn't write anything, I just sat there like a blank. All I could think about was my grandad, and the way his coffin disappeared behind those awful plush curtains at the crematorium. I felt as if I was with him, slipping down a long, greasy, black tube into a pit full of darkness.'

'Didn't anyone notice how you were?'

'Maybe. But they were all really upset too, I suppose. Or just busy arranging stuff. They sold his house. I used to go back there sometimes, afterwards. I'd hang around in the street, looking in at the windows, imagining him still living there.'

'What a grim time that must have been.'

'Well, as I said, I failed everything. Even before that my parents had written me off as a bit of a no-hoper at school, and my exam results clinched it, from their point of view. I left school and got a job in a factory, packing office supplies. It was there I first began to realize how ruthless and predatory girls are.'

'What happened?'

'Nothing really terrible, I guess, but I felt hounded. There were a group of them, three or four, from the office, they used to call out to me, stupid stuff at first, then when I didn't answer it got very crude. I felt guilty and embarrassed.'

'Didn't anyone try to stop them?'

'There were one or two, older guys, who used to tell them off. But mostly they all thought it was funny. Then one day I went berserk.' He was sitting on the ground telling her this, his knees drawn up. Now he seemed to hug himself more tightly, to become smaller and more hunched.

'What did you do?' Eileen asked.

'They'd been at it as usual, calling out as I went past. "Hi, Chris, how's your love life? Who's the lucky girl then? Bet you put it about a bit, eh? It's always the quiet ones,'" he mimicked savagely. 'Then they got worse. "Got your end away last night, did you? Give her a good seeing-to? Bet you're a big lad, aren't you? How about giving us a look?" Then they'd collapse into giggles. That day somehow I couldn't stand it any longer. I grabbed one of them round the neck and screamed at her. I can't remember what I said now. But there was a horrible shocked silence all around us. I am not a violent person. I know I am not.' He looked up at Eileen, as if pleading for recognition. 'I hated the way they talked. It made me feel filthy.'

'So what happened then?'

'I left, before I could be sacked. Some of the blokes there were quite sympathetic to me, I think, but there wasn't much they could do. Anyway, a while later I got another job. It wasn't much, but it suited me better, because I was left alone. I worked in a butcher's shop, cleaning up. It was pretty revolting, and it gave me bad dreams, really bad sometimes. But I had my own money, and they left me alone.'

'It sounds like a lonely life.'

'It was. My mum used to try to get me to go out. But I had no friends, so I used to hang around in my room. If things got bad at home, like when my Aunt Deborah came to dinner, I went out. Sometimes I used to go on the bus into Osewick, just to hang around the streets. Sometimes I went to the cinema.'

'What's so bad about Aunt Deborah?'

Christopher shrank back into himself, and began almost imperceptibly to rock on his heels. 'She's my father's sister. She's big, loud and bossy. I absolutely hate her. She is a newsreader on local TV; you might have seen her.'

'Yes, I think I have. A rather glamorous lady, in her forties, with a deep voice, terribly cultured.'

'That's her. It's why I hate television. I can't watch the news. I feel totally terrified. Sometimes I think they're all in on it, my aunt and all the other people in the studio, they know about me and laugh.' His breathing had become loud and ragged; now he made a visible effort to control himself. 'You must think I am stupid,' he mumbled. 'I know they can't really see me, but I can't help being scared.'

'I don't think you are stupid. Far from it.'

'When she came to our house she was always trying to sort me out,' he said bitterly. 'Her and my sisters, sharp cocky little know-alls.' He shook his head suddenly. 'I shouldn't talk about them like that, but they are a bit like the girls in the factory, only not filthy, of course, my parents

137

wouldn't have stood for that. They used to treat me as if I was completely dumb, like some subhuman creature. The less I said, the nastier they got. Only it was all so witty and amusing, and they almost never got done for it. Aunt Deborah encouraged them. She likes clever girls, not stupid boys.'

'But you were happier at the butcher's shop.'

'Yeah, it was OK. There was Ken, the guy who owned it, and an old man called Ernie, who used to come in part-time when it was busy, and they mostly left me alone. They were OK, they didn't keep asking me stuff.'

'I get the feeling that a big "but" is coming,' Eileen said.

'You could say that. I don't know if I can tell you this. It is so humiliating and sick.'

'You don't have to.'

'I want to somehow. Nobody else knows this bit, except Dr. Partridge. He made me tell him. But the stuff he said didn't make much sense to me.'

'It's your life, your story. Tell me if you want to, don't if you don't.'

He was silent for several long moments, staring intently down at his bare feet in the damp brown leaves. 'One Christmas time Ken got really busy in the shop. Ernie couldn't come in because he was laid up with the flu, and Ken asked me to help him serve. I didn't really want to, but I did it because he'd been good to me and I didn't want to let him down. This girl started coming into the shop. I couldn't help noticing her. She was really pretty, and I was seventeen and in some ways I was still a normal boy. I was scared of girls but I still fancied them. And she seemed nice, not like the girls in the factory, all loud-mouthed and tarty, the sort who go to work with everything half hanging out and skirts up to their knickers, daring you to look, no, she seemed a quiet, nice sort of girl, a bit young for her age. She used to blush when she asked for a pound of sausages.' He laughed softly, his eyes distant as if he was indeed reliving the past. Eileen almost held her breath, afraid that if she moved or made some comment the spell would be broken, and he would revert to his suspicious, hard-eyed self and tell her nothing more.

'She used to come into the shop quite a lot,' he said, 'on errands from her mum. I think she was a relation of Ken's; he had a big family. Anyway they were quite familiar with each other. Looking back I guess she was coming in to see me, but I didn't cotton to that at the time. In my own mind I was an ugly freak, so I couldn't believe any girl would want anything to do with me. Then one day she was there, outside the shop when I finished work. She asked me, ever so shy and sweet, if I would walk her home. Of course, I did. After that I used to walk her to the corner of her street a few times. She was nice, chatty, she seemed just an ordinary, innocent girl. Fourteen, she was. I began to feel that perhaps I wasn't such a weirdo, if Wendy liked me. I think Ken knew about it, but he didn't say anything. Then one evening when I dropped her off I got really brave and asked her to go out with me. Looking back now, I wish, how I wish I hadn't.'

'What went wrong?'

'It was all right at first. We went to the cinema, then we got the bus home. We had to wait for a while in the bus shelter. It wasn't so late really, but it was raining and the bus didn't come for ages. We were holding hands, and she started getting a bit affectionate, and I was alarmed but excited as well, because although she seemed so young and naïve and little-girlish she was all woman under the pink jumper, I was painfully aware of all that. Then it was obvious she wanted me to kiss her, so I did, and then something seemed to explode inside me, all the loneliness, and I started to grope her, a bit roughly, I guess. I can remember now how it felt, it was a kind of horrible excitement. Then she was crying and pushing me away, and I was in tears and apologising. Eventually we both calmed down and I tried to make excuses. Thinking about it now, if she had really been the nice, innocent, well-brought-up girl I thought she was, she would probably have given me the push there and then. But she didn't. She gave me a prim little lecture on self-control, and said if we were to continue seeing each other I would have to behave.' He laughed bitterly. 'What an idiot I was. After that it was as if she was a little queen and I was her humble, adoring slave. But really she was a tease. She was using me to experiment on. We used to go back to that lonely bus shelter sometimes, then when the weather was better we'd go for long walks. She would encourage me, then she would switch me off. "No, Christopher," she would say, looking up at me with her big baby-blue eyes, "you know we mustn't go *too far.*"' He mimicked her soft, lisping voice. 'But I noticed her jumpers were getting tighter and her skirts shorter. She was driving me mad. At work all I could think about was having her. I nearly chopped my thumb off with a meat cleaver once. I was absolutely obsessed, riddled with lustful thoughts, my body was in a state of permanent excitement, my brain was whirling, I was tense and confused, I didn't know what it all meant. It all had to end in tears, as they say. One spring evening we went to Morden Chase. We lay down on the grass. There was nobody else about. She let me kiss her a few times, then when she knew I was well and truly raring to go she pushed me away and started undoing her buttons. She had a white lacy

139

bra on underneath. She must have seen my eyes popping out of my head because she said, in that high-pitched voice of hers, "No, Christopher, don't get silly. You can look, but you mustn't touch." That's one thing that used to make me sick, she was full of bloody cliches. But then, it all seems so extraordinary now, she reached out, took my hand, and put it on her breast.'

'Little minx,' Eileen said.

Christopher grinned, like the grin of a skull. His eyes were deep, dark and glittering. 'You can imagine, perhaps, what happened next.' His every word spoke of humiliation and shame. 'I flipped, I went crazy, I very nearly raped her. Not quite, though. Her tights got in the way, so our little drama was more of a farce. But it changed my status in her eyes. I was no longer the obedient, lustfully-admiring but controlled little lapdog, but a savage beast threatening her girlish defences. No tears now, except mine. She was cold and cruel and quite composed. She said if I ever came near her again she would tell her father I had assaulted her. For her, that was the end of it. But for me, it was the beginning of madness. It doesn't seem much, does it? But I guess I was half way there already. Not long after that I began to slide down from reality into, well, something else. It was the dreams that were the worst part.' He shivered suddenly, as if a cold wind had arisen, although the morning remained calm and fine. He scrabbled among his things, fetched out a sweatshirt and put it on. 'Are you sure I'm not boring you with all this pathetic drivel?'

'Positive.'

'When I told Dr. Partridge about the dreams he dismissed them with some trite psychiatric rubbish, but for me they were the worst part. Night after night I used to dream. It was all about Wendy, but it was mixed up with my job at the butcher's. I would dream about her, lying naked with her legs apart, beckoning me, drawing me down to her, then she changed, she became a mess of gory stuff, lights and guts and bones and blood, like the stuff we threw out. It was disgusting, I was disgusting. But at the same time it was exciting. I was just flying out of control.' He was shuddering convulsively, his arms wrapped round himself, rocking jerkily. 'I hated her, I hated myself, but I was helpless. I couldn't work there any more. Every morning I had to face it, looking at the meat, the blood, the guts, and thinking of her.' Slowly he raised his head and looked at Eileen, searching her face, trying to see what was written there, expecting, dreading, to see disgust and revulsion, pleading for acceptance, fearful, hopeful, a mess of contradictions. 'What do you think? Am I a pervert, beyond redemption, a repellent apology for a human being?'

'Of course you aren't,' Eileen said. 'From all I have heard, you were a lonely, unhappy young man thoroughly ill-treated by a bunch of manipulative little witches. Who, I guess, had no idea at all what they were doing.'

'But someone else, someone not like me, tougher, maybe, or more worldly-wise, it wouldn't have driven them mad, would it? What does that make me? Weak in the head?'

'Nobody reacts like anybody else. You lost your grandfather, failed all your exams, and maybe your family weren't as observant as they might have been. You were alone in your own world. Those are pretty heavy pressures, by any standards. All the usual muddle and misery about sex didn't help either, I imagine.'

'You had a tough time too, you were telling me, your parents died.'

Eileen nodded. 'Yes, that was a dreadful blow, to lose my mother. We all depended on her so much. After that, although I was terribly sad to see my father so ill, it wasn't unexpected to have him depending on me.'

'Did you get on with your dad?'

'Well, yes, I suppose so. We didn't row or anything, particularly.'

'Did you feel you were ever a disappointment to him?'

'Not really. I don't think he ever had very high expectations of us, except perhaps to earn our own living and provide him with descendants. I know you feel you've been a disappointment to your father, though, don't you? Is that really from him, or is it something you assume?'

Christopher shrugged. 'Who knows? He never seemed to take a lot of notice of me. He was always so busy. We moved around a fair bit when I was very small. I can remember being glad when we landed up at Barnwell because it was near my grandparents. My grandmother was alive then. She was lovely. She died just after I started school, not long after we came to Barnwell. My parents wanted more children after me, but there were problems. I don't know what, they never really discussed it, not when I was in earshot. I think Mum may even have had some fertility treatment. Anyway when the twins were born they were premature and quite sickly for a while, so everyone was fussing over them. I spent a lot more time with my grandfather. He was a newish widower, so maybe he was lonely too. What I didn't get at home I got from him. He was like my dad in lots of ways, not surprising really, but he was much kinder, at least that's how it seemed to me as a small boy.'

'Is your dad really unkind?'

'He's distant, dismissive, rather mocking. Maybe he thinks he's being amusing. He's very bright, a bit of a success in his own circles, altogether

141

a gifted sort of man. Perhaps he can't understand how I could be his. Perhaps I'm not. Perhaps my mum had a fling and he nobly adopted me. I certainly don't look like any of them. My mum is blonde, and dad and the twins are gingery. Look at me—I could be a gypsy changeling. Though I can't see my mum dropping her knickers for some didicoy.'

'They have really hurt you, haven't they,' Eileen said.

'Maybe I am punishing them by being mad,' Christopher said bitterly. 'But I could be doing a better job of it. I could still be at home, being embarrassing before their eyes, couldn't I? I could be dribbling at the dinner table, running around naked, refusing to wash or flashing in front of the neighbours. Or even the bishop.'

'I can't imagine you doing any of those things. But you certainly seem very angry with them, especially your father.'

'When I got really ill my mum did at least finally do something about it. He just withdrew as if I was something distasteful he didn't care to touch. He makes me feel like a worm. I put that together with his pronouncements from the pulpit—I had to endure that for years, remember—so it's not surprising I am anti-religion. It's just a euphemism for control. My dad couldn't control me, so he mocked and despised me and wrote me off.' He sighed, and got to his feet. 'I've had enough of thinking about him. It's a depressing subject. Why don't we go for a walk?'

'Where to?'

'Just round the woods.'

'All right. I'll go the long way home. But I need to get back soon. I want to take Tillie to the vet again, to see if an injection will help her. I'll come back and look for you later, if you like.'

He pulled on his shoes, then paused, thinking, and took them off again. He left the camp, hesitated, looked back at her shyly, then smiled. It was the first simple, unaffected smile she had seen on his face, untinged by bitterness, sadness or anger, and it transformed him. He struck a pose. 'I'll be Robin Hood. Or a merry man.'

'OK. But don't stand on any thorns.'

She followed him curiously as he darted down the path, in and out of the trees, ahead, then doubling back, laughing and whooping, swinging on the branches, tumbling in the leaf mould. Once, hearing voices, he stopped quite still, listened, then climbed up an oak, and sat on a low branch, panting, his dark hair sticking to his forehead with sweat. The voices died away without approaching nearer.

Later, when he had calmed down and was walking soberly beside her, Eileen said, 'Christopher, do you still have vivid dreams?'

142

'Yes. But, I am happy to say, not about meat.' He shivered.

'What are they about?'

'Silly things. Some nightmares, not often now. Angels.'

'*Angels?*'

'Yes. They do exist, you know. God's bright, golden, flaming messengers. I've seen them, and I was awake.'

'How extraordinary.'

'Haven't you ever seen an angel?'

'I wouldn't know one if I saw one.'

'But you would! They are very big, about eight feet tall, and they have huge, translucent golden wings folded down their backs. They are beautiful. And alarming.'

'Do you see them or dream about them often?'

'Oh, yes. There was one actually with us just now, at the camp. But I guess you couldn't see him.'

'No. I confess I thought there was just the two of us. What was he doing?'

'He was in a tree, looking down at us.'

'What do they do, these angels?'

'They lie in wait for me. They're always there, or the threat of them. They pursue me sometimes. Usually they accuse me. It's when they all shout at once I find it hard to take.'

'How many are there, then?'

'Oh, hundreds, I would guess. But usually I only see one or two.'

'So they aren't there to help you?'

'No. Quite often they rant and rave over something I have done or not done. I don't always understand. Sometimes they talk in a weird language, probably just to make me confused. Sometimes I think they are the voice of my conscience, but they can also be very sly. If I do what they say, usually they quiet down or go away for a few days. I wonder why that one turned up just now. He's probably keeping an eye on me, in case I say something to you that I shouldn't.'

'I don't think I would care to be surrounded by angels. Not if they're like that.'

'I don't much like it either. But sometimes it can be quite comforting to have a big bright angel nearby, especially in the middle of the night when something really horrible is creeping out of a badger-hole to get you.'

'So,' said Eileen, amused. 'Angels not only have a cosmic battle to fight, but they have to perform mighty feats in the woods as well.'

'Now you're taking the mickey.'

'A bit, perhaps. It's a bizarre thought, that I might meet an angel in Holton woods. I'd better go home now, Christopher. Maybe I'll see you later.'

He waved to her a little forlornly as she went up the hill by a sandy path edged with straggling gorse bushes. She waved back to him as she turned towards home. Then he was out of sight.

The trip to the vet proved physically exhausting and emotionally harrowing. Tillie was very unwilling to be parted from her basket, and seemed weak in the legs. In the end Eileen, with some difficulty, carried her to the car and laid her gently on a blanket on the back seat. Listening to Christopher had distracted her from her own condition. Now she was again aware of her aching eyes, her heavy legs, her tiredness. She wondered again if she was brewing up for something.

At the vet's Tillie was anxious and restless, adding to Eileen's discomfort. They had to wait for some time to be seen, while a stream of other creatures were attended to, many of them younger and healthier than Tillie. Seeing pups at the beginning of their lives, with shiny coats and bright eyes and eagerly lolling tongues, bounding with energy as Tillie once had been, gave Eileen a stab of inconsolable pain.

Finally the injection was administered, and Eileen was told that she should see a distinct improvement within twenty-four hours.

'We can give her this once a week,' the vet told her. 'Then she will need it more and more frequently as her general condition deteriorates. A lot is up to the individual animal.'

'Do you think she has had this condition for some time and I just haven't noticed it?'

'It's possible. At her age she is slowing down a lot anyway, of course. Be in touch if you are particularly worried.'

'I will.'

When she got home she felt shattered. It wasn't until she had settled the dog down again and made a cup of tea that she noticed Natasha's jacket and bag slung across the back of a chair.

She went upstairs. The bathroom door was locked.

'Tash? Are you in there?' An inarticulate groan told her that it was so. 'What are you doing home at three in the afternoon?'

'I'm not feeling so good. Daphne sent me home. I passed out in the shop at lunchtime.'

'How did you get here?'

'On the bus. I rang you for a lift but you weren't here.'

'Sorry, love. I was at the vet's with Tillie.'

'Why? Is she worse?'

'No, I took her for an injection.'

The door opened and Natasha emerged, clutching the edges of her bathrobe round her middle. She looked grey, and her eyes were baggy and bloodshot.

'My word, Tash, you look grim. What do you think it is?'

'I don't know, flu maybe. But I feel sick as a parrot as well.' She looked at Eileen under her brows, glowering 'And Mum, don't ask me if I'm pregnant. Daphne did that and I nearly hit her.'

'It never occurred to me.'

'Well, if I am, I'll handle it. Right now I'm going to bed.'

'Best place for you. Can I get you anything?'

'No, I'm OK. I'll shout.'

'Right.'

The house was quiet. Both Natasha and Tillie were asleep. Eileen felt an overpowering need to talk to someone. Not feeling especially optimistic she dialled Marie's number. There was no answer.

She reluctantly sorted out a pile of laundry, and thought of Christopher and his dirty clothes. *He can't come and wash today, even if he is ready to do it. Not with Natasha at home.* She felt restless and irritable. Looking down the garden she saw the bright sunshine, the trees moving lazily in the breeze. She put on her shoes and quietly, almost stealthily, left the house.

It was cooler under the trees. Her soft shoes made almost no sound on the path. As she arrived at the camp Christopher appeared suddenly in front of her, making her heart contract with momentary alarm. He seemed to be standing very close to her. She imagined she could even feel his breath on her skin.

'Hello.' His voice was hesitant. 'Did you bring me anything to eat?'

'Goodness, no! I'm sorry, Christopher, I forgot.'

He looked bewildered. 'You don't have to, of course, but I thought that's what you came for.'

Eileen began to feel strange, somehow dislocated. *Something weird is going on here.* 'Yes, it was. Or so I thought. Right now I just came to see you, I guess.'

'That's nice.' He sounded guarded, as if not quite believing her. 'People don't usually just want to talk to me. They usually want to do something to me or get me to do something.'

145

'Look, Christopher, I can't stay long. My daughter has come home early. She's not well. If you like I can go and fix you something to eat now, and leave it just at the entrance of the woods for you to collect.'

He looked down, shuffled his feet, now back in dirty trainers. 'Yeah, OK. But it doesn't matter about the food.'

Without thinking she laid her hand on his arm. He flinched, then looked up. His eyes were a dark, intense blue, full of secrets.

'Chris, I'm really sorry. I'll come down tomorrow if I possibly can. As soon as Natasha is better and back to work you can come and have that bath.'

He smiled then as if he could not help himself. His eyes crinkled at the corners, he beamed. Eileen noticed what beautiful teeth he had. Young people often had excellent teeth from all that brushing and good diet. She smiled inwardly at the sheer inappropriateness of her ungoverned thoughts.

'How is Tillie?' Christopher asked.

'She had her jab. I'm hoping she'll pick up.'

'Maybe she can come to the woods again.'

'I hope so. I'll have to go. But I'll leave the food. You have to eat. In half an hour?'

'Thanks. Thanks for everything. See you tomorrow.' It was a confirmation of their arrangement, but it was also a plea. As she walked home Eileen felt a twinge of anxiety, but it was very fleeting. Seeing Christopher smile, seeing his suspicion and self-hating misery recede, made her feel simply happy. The gremlins lurked at the corners of her conscious mind, warning, threatening, predicting the worst; but she banished them scornfully.

As she went indoors the phone was ringing.

'Hi, Eileen. It's Marie. Did you call earlier?'

'Yes, it was me.'

'I was in the bath. Philip is collecting me in a minute. It's such a glorious afternoon we thought we'd go for a drive. I'm getting sick of four walls. You all right?'

For a moment Eileen almost told her about Christopher, but then she checked herself. He belonged in the woods. He was a secret, and common sense would shatter him. She told Marie about Tillie, about Natasha.

'Oh dear. What a shame,' Marie said. 'Michael's back on Saturday, isn't he? Maybe I'll pop over and see you all. I'm a lot stronger these days.'

'It would be great to see you. It seems an age.'

Marie sounded surprised. 'It isn't really, you know.'

'No. Perhaps not.'

'And I want to hear all about David.'

'Oh, all right. That seems a long time ago as well.'

'Eileen, I think you are losing it. You are obviously missing my steadying influence in your life.'

'Obviously.'

'Got to go, I hear the car. See you soon.'

'Bye, Marie.'

The afternoon seemed interminable, the good weather a mockery. There was no need to walk the dog, there was no one to cook for except herself, and everyone seemed shut off from her in his or her own secret cell of private activity.

Eileen opened her Bible, and with the aid of a concordance noted down every reference to angels. She found that they had many roles and that there were distinct personalities. An angel saved Isaac from being sacrificed by Abraham. The Angel of Death slew the Egyptian firstborn, passing over the Israelite homes that had been daubed with blood, sparing their sons. An angel led the Israelites from bondage, and the "Angel of the Lord" killed 185,000 soldiers of the Assyrian army, thus saving King Hezekiah and his Israelites from the vengeful might of Sennacherib. Daniel was saved from the hungry lions when an angel shut their mouths. Guardian angels also appeared, one assigned to Greece, and to Israel the great Michael. Gideon also saw the Lord's angel—or was it God himself? Scripture was vague. Angels prayed in God's presence, and they were countless. Angels appeared in a dream, ascending and descending on a ladder as Jacob slept, his head upon a stone. Angels were named as workers in the harvest, presumably of souls. They ministered to Jesus after his temptation by Satan, and in Matthew 26 Jesus claimed he could call upon the protection of "twelve armies of angels." Satan too had his angels, who, according to Peter, would be thrown into hell at the end of time. Angels reflected God's priorities, rejoicing with him over one sinner who repented, but even they did not know the time of his second coming, and they could be rebuked by their Lord. Gabriel announced Jesus' birth to Mary; a great host of angels appeared to the shepherds; angels carried Lazarus to Abraham's side in the parable; Michael and his angels fought against the great dragon in Revelation, and an angel was sent to announce the message to the churches. Stephen at the moment of his martyrdom had the face of an angel; but Satan too could disguise himself as an angel

147

of light. An archangel would announce the end of time; and yet was it not also written that mere humans would judge the angels? And Peter said that salvation was something the angels would very much like to understand. They were servants and messengers of God, greater and yet lesser than men.

And what of Christopher's angels? What semi-manufactured beings were they? He had described them as huge, with translucent golden wings, yet at points in Scripture they appeared in manlike guise: to Abraham, promising a son to Sarah, and to Lot, to warn him of Sodom's destruction. The personality of Christopher's angels seemed suspect too, more a construct of his chaotic psyche than anything strictly Biblical, where they are servants, messengers, some lesser, some greater, imbued with God's power, and serving both him and, at his command, humanity. In various places there seemed some ambiguity: whose voice was it that spoke to Jesus from heaven, which many in the crowd took for an angel's, in John 12?

Eileen lay back on the sofa, still holding her Bible, and closed her eyes. Her head was throbbing gently like some great animal at rest, or an idling engine. The afternoon sun warmed the room. There was no sound except the periodic buzzing of an indolent fly. One hand on the book that lay heavy on her chest, the other trailing on the rug, Eileen drifted away into unlooked-for sleep.

The great being stood before her, close enough to touch, surrounded with a hazy golden light. His wings were partly open, and his body was draped in folds of white. Fire flashed from his eyes. His voice was like a gong, and just as incomprehensible, and in his hand he held a huge shining sword with a hilt of gold. She was immobilized by utter helpless terror. The angel—for what else could it be?—was speaking, his voice was loud and ringing, yet she could not understand a word he was saying. It was as opaque to her understanding as a donkey braying, and as musical. She noticed that his fiery eyes were black, bottomless pits, and that he had a curly, golden beard, like a painted statue of an ancient Greek athlete. Above all he looked and sounded fierce and pagan, not like a being under God's jurisdiction at all, and she realized that this was the source of her fear. She was lying, barefoot, on the sofa in her sunny room, helpless before a huge, ungovernable creature from someone else's imagination. As she stared up, the angel raised his sword arm and brought it slowly down. Convinced she was about to be slaughtered as a sacrifice, she opened her mouth to scream, but then the arm slowed still further and the sword was laid gently on her, its point at her throat, its hilt across her abdomen, like a great golden cross symbolically transfixing her inert body. Transfix, crucifix, the words whirled chaotically in her brain as the angel disappeared, upwards towards the ceiling, with a huge, rushing roar, like a jet taking off or a hurricane-force wind.

The Bible falling to the floor woke her with a sudden start. For a moment she lay still, bewildered by the vividness of her vision and its resistance to understanding. Vague quotations floated around her memory: "...the sword of the Spirit, which is the Word of God...","...and sorrow, like a sharp sword, shall break thy heart..." She shook her head impatiently, willing herself to get up and do something, anything, to banish the growing anarchy of her thoughts, but a deeper heaviness crept over her, and this time there were no dreams.

Friday 31st May 1996

Eileen slept late the next morning, and was awakened only by the sunlight streaming through the curtains and falling on her face. As she put her feet to the floor she became aware of a curious feeling of light-headedness. *I can't be ill. There is too much to do.* But she didn't feel exactly ill, more peculiar, as if at one remove from reality. She went downstairs and put the kettle on. The kitchen was awash with light. Tillie raised her head, yawned, and wagged her tail. She seemed brighter, but still a bit dopey. Eileen heard a door bang above her, and the sound of retching from the bathroom. Shortly afterwards Natasha emerged. She called down the stairs, her voice harsh and croaking. 'Mum, I still feel terrible. Can you ring Daphne later?'

'Sure. Go back to bed now, love. Is there anything you want?'

'A glass of water.'

'Right.'

Eileen gave Tillie some biscuits, and was delighted when she managed to eat them. The phone rang. 'Eileen, it's Sean. How's Natasha?'

'Not feeling very well, I'm afraid. She looks like she's got a dose of flu but she's throwing up as well.'

'Oh, dear. Poor old thing. Should I come sick-visiting?'

'I'll ask her. But you don't want to catch it, if it is catching. And it's just possible Tash won't want to see you in the state she's in.'

'I don't care what she looks like.'

'No, but she does.'

'I've got to get to work. I'll ring again later, if that's OK.'

'Of course. You're still all right, I hope?'

'Yes, just a bit tired.'

'I'm sure she'll be fine soon. Don't worry.'

'No. Well, thanks, Eileen, maybe I'll speak to one of you this evening.'

150

Eileen took a glass of water up to Natasha's room. Natasha had fallen asleep. She put the glass on the bedside table and crept from the room.

As Eileen walked softly under the trees she could feel the warmth on her arms and back. Her shoes made almost no sound on the tender spring grass, but Christopher must somehow have known she was coming. He was sitting on the damp ground, leaning up against the tree stump, his arms behind his head, his legs stretched out, his eyes half-closed against the sun's sharp rays, a thin cigarette between his lips. 'Good morning.' He spoke without moving, smiling slightly.

'Hello.'

Slowly he got up, offered her the tree stump with the air of a gracious courtier showing his queen to her throne. 'How are you?'

'I don't really know,' Eileen said.

'That's funny. I thought it was only me that couldn't answer simple questions like that.'

'I feel strange, kind of detached, not quite real. I keep thinking I am going to go down with something, but it never happens.'

Christopher smiled. 'It sounds as if you are catching my disease. I didn't realize madness was catching.'

'The more I see of you,' Eileen said, 'the less mad you seem. Don't you sometimes think it is you who are sane, and the whole world off its rocker?'

Christopher shook his head. 'No, I can't think that. It would make it even more confusing. And anyway, you only see me now. You don't know what I used to be like.'

'What were you like?'

'Do you really want to know?'

'You know I do. But it's always your choice, you know that too.'

'Can I have some breakfast first?' he asked, a glimmer of amusement in his deep-set blue eyes.

'Of course. Sorry, Christopher, I told you, I am not entirely with it this morning. I hope you like bacon sandwiches.'

'I love them.' He unrolled his thin grey blanket and sat on it. Eileen handed him the bag. For a while he ate, she watched, and there was silence. Then he said, 'How is your daughter? And the dog?'

'Natasha is still poorly, and at home in bed. Poor dear, she really does look rough. It seems like some kind of stomach bug. Tillie is a bit brighter. I took her for her injection yesterday, as you know, and it seems to be having some effect. She actually ate a few biscuits this morning.'

'I'm glad.' He dusted off crumbs, and downed a cup of coffee.

151

'Thank you, that was lovely. Would you like to continue with my life story now?' There was a hint of self-mockery in his voice; it was as if, each time she saw him, he was a little less mad and afraid and strange and a little more human, in touch with himself and his surroundings, even to having a sense of humour. Was it all pretence, illusion, magic? Was the hurting, crazy creature still there beneath the civil, well-bred surface? Was he not still living in the woods?

'Of course,' she replied, with due solemnity, sensing that any humour must be his.

'Where did we get to?' He shivered. 'Yes, it was that dreadful episode with Wendy, wasn't it? Why is it that the females in my life were so terrifying, I wonder?'

'All of them? You said your grandmother was good to you. And your mother wasn't all bad, as far as I can tell.'

'Mothers are supposed to care for you, aren't they?' Christopher suddenly sounded like a nine-year-old. 'And my grandmother *was* lovely, but she was an old lady. You couldn't call her predatory. Anyway, she died, so she couldn't help.'

'No.' Eileen realized she had strayed into very tricky territory. 'So what happened after Wendy left the scene?'

Christopher was silent for several moments, and Eileen began to wonder if she had said something to discourage or alienate him. But as it turned out he was thinking, running his past before the eyes of his present, testing it gingerly before he began. 'I began to get very ill. At first nobody seemed to notice. But I knew something terrible was happening. I started dreaming then. I told you about Wendy and the meat, didn't I? I felt I had to somehow get her out of my system. It was as if she was lodged in my brain or my blood stream, like a virus. I had to get her out. There was only one way I knew. I expect you can guess. I hope you don't find this part too sickening, but I couldn't stop thinking about her, even though I really quite deeply disliked her by then, with the bit of my mind that was still rational. It was still there, just, fighting for its life, I guess.' He hunched his shoulders and stared moodily at the ground. 'Because she had wound me up so much, because despite myself I still wanted her, no, not her, her body was all I wanted, I just needed to…well, you know. I don't have to spell it out, do I? I felt it was like a disease, and I had to cure myself. So I did what many lads do at that age, shut up in their bedrooms with loud music playing, only for me it was for mad reasons, not just rampant lust. I felt I had to purge myself of everything to do with her.' He sighed. 'Then I started having different dreams. That was when the angels started. I dreamt about them when I

152

was asleep and they appeared during the day as well. I remember once I woke from a dream about angels fighting with swords to see one standing at the foot of my bed.'

'Wow. That must have been alarming.'

Christopher grinned, but it was the Death's Head smile, bleak and savage. 'I thought he was there to punish me.'

'Did the angel speak?'

'No. He stared at me, but his gaze got so bright I had to shut my eyes, and when I opened them he was gone. But later, when I got used to them, the angels did speak.'

'There were more than one, then?'

'Yes, there were several different ones. They were a team, and they had a purpose. It was to do with me, but I never understood what it was. It was as if the angels' thought-processes were too far above mine to be comprehended by a mere human. But I had the clear idea that they had been sent.'

'By whom?'

Christopher shuddered, and his voice dropped to a mutter. 'By God, I suppose.'

'Oh.' Eileen could think of nothing to say. Her imagination had taken her to that lonely, darkened room and a young boy fighting for his sanity, and she felt dazed.

'You probably think of God quite differently,' Christopher said. 'But I have heard him speaking, and he can make his voice fill the whole universe, till you are deaf to anything else.'

'What did he say to you?'

'I can't tell you. It wasn't exactly words. But his voice was huge, deafening, like the percussion sections of a hundred orchestras, but all out of tune, syncopated, booming, clanging, crashing, screeching. There were no clear words, but I got the message, that was plain enough.'

'What was it?'

'It was all full of damnation. I was hounded, accused, threatened till I was just a quivering wreck. That was the worst time, when I felt filthy, worthless, totally terrified and helpless.'

'It sounds unbearable. Don't talk about it if it upsets you.'

'No, I want to. It helps to get it straight. Anyway, that bit's history now, thanks to medical chemicals.' He laughed gloomily. 'Later, a lot later, when I was calmer and saner, one night at my place in Denbigh Street, while the others were all watching TV, I decided to check it out.'

'What do you mean?'

'I still had my Bible. It was the one they'd given me at Sunday school

153

when I was ten, and I kept it even though I felt it was terribly dangerous, like a bomb. I wanted to see if my idea of God was right, or if it was just a product of my illness. But it's all there, you know.' He looked up at her, and the lost, bleak, bewildered look on his face cut her like knives. 'All those prophets, threatening doom and destruction if the people didn't toe the line, all the stuff about killing them in all sorts of horrible ways, including the babies and the animals. Even the land itself didn't escape the curse. God was threatening to turn it into a desert inhabited only by owls and jackals. It's all there. You must have read it too. It goes on for page after page. He really is like that. No wonder my dad is like he is. He is a servant of the cosmic monster.'

Eileen could not answer him, though she felt he was waiting for her to say something, if only to pounce on her every word, to refute and reject. She said nothing for several long moments. 'Something had to break, I guess. What happened then?'

He nodded. 'My mum noticed I was peculiar. Finally. I wasn't eating or sleeping. Then she heard me talking in my room, loudly, but it was rubbish, she said. I don't remember. Maybe an angel was there. Maybe I was yelling back at Big Voice, pleading to be left in peace. She heard me shouting, and she came in. It wasn't something she usually did. Anyway, I used to bolt the door. I must have forgotten that day. Later, when I was getting better, she told me about that time: how thin I was, and the crying bouts, and the smell, because I forgot to wash.'

'So what did she do?'

'They must have had some kind of family conference, her, my dad, Aunt Deborah. My mum must have made an appointment with the doctor. She persuaded me to take a bath. She washed me like I was a baby again. I liked that; it felt very calming. She was afraid, my mother, I think. Afraid of me, and for me. Anyway, she was very kind and gentle, I remember that.' Again there was a long silence. Eileen could hear the birds calling, the breeze rustling the leaves, her own breathing. 'I was driven to the doctor's surgery. I don't really remember much. It was all a bit dreamlike, with lots of people in white coats, bright lights, and hushed voices. They must have thought I was in a bad way, because the next thing I was in hospital, in the psychiatric ward, tucked up tightly in a hard white bed. I guess they gave me something, because I don't remember much at all. I just slept for ages, and the dreams I had were vague and unthreatening, like wispy clouds on the horizon. I was grateful for that. I didn't care what muck they pumped into me, if it got rid of that terrible voice.'

'Poor Christopher. It all sounds absolutely horrific.'

'I got better. Or at least I calmed down. The drugs kicked in, and I didn't feel so scared. But I used to cry a lot. I was terribly depressed. I felt my life was over, and I was only eighteen. I thought it would always be like that, a life full of quiet nurses in white, and crazy, sad people who couldn't cope, like me, for ever, with no let-up. My brain felt foggy. All I could do was cry, and sleep, and submit to whatever they did to me. I changed, I was like a child again, helpless. The nurses used to bath me. Thinking about it now, there were some very pretty nurses there, as well as butch hairy blokes and old dragons, but even if I was lucky enough to be scrubbed by a gorgeous young blonde it never turned me on. I had no interest in sex any more. Perhaps it was just as well.' He looked at Eileen, a small frown gathering between his brows. 'I'm not offending you, am I?'

'Of course not. Don't feel you have to put on an act for my benefit. I may not know much about mental illness, but I'm learning. And I hope I'm not a prude, either.'

'Thank you,' he said. 'If what I am saying makes you sick, please tell me to shut up.'

'So what happened then? Were you in hospital long?'

'I honestly don't know. Time seemed unreal. I didn't know if it was Wednesday or Christmas. It's a long story and not very edifying, so I'll cut it short. I saw a psychiatrist, Dr. John Partridge. He's still got overall charge of my case. At first I didn't understand what he was saying, then, later, when I began to improve, I realized that from where I stood he was spouting pure drivel. He just didn't seem to cotton to me at all. Some of the staff were very nice, very kind, but others were bullies. The other mad people were scary too, not in themselves necessarily, but in what they were letting the system do to them. There were some terribly sad cases in there, so many dreadful stories. Terrible things had happened to them. I couldn't help them, but I learned something in there.'

'What was it?'

'That I had to get out, and be my own master. If I stayed I would go under, cease to exist.'

'How did you get out?'

'The drugs helped. They got rid of what they call the positive symptoms, the visions, the voices, all that. It left me with the negative ones, the blankness, the not talking or moving for hours, the lack of willpower, the dependency. But all that got mixed up with the depression. I felt such a weight of silence, as if I was muffled. I had to prove I would be all right. It wasn't easy, but I had to find my rational self again. It was there, in hiding, very small.'

'Did you manage it?'

'Yes, after a long while. They let me out, and I went home. My room had been cleaned and redecorated. They all treated me with great care, even my sisters. I think I had scared them. And they were still scared. They probably thought I might go mad again. It made me feel a bit triumphant, but sad as well. At least, for then it kept them off my back. I went to a day hospital twice a week, to see a psychiatric nurse. I remember her, her name was Abby. She was a little redhead, very freckly. It was then I knew I must be getting better, because I fancied her. I used to undress her in my imagination while we were talking. Sorry, I seem to be back on the subject of sex again. Anyway, I liked going to see her, and I was beginning to feel better about women generally. I got to the point where I was able to go to the hospital by myself on the bus, so then they decided I didn't need to go any more, and instead they sent a CPN to visit me at home. His name was Rob, he was Scottish, a big fellow with tattoos, a nice enough bloke I suppose, but I felt intimidated, and I definitely couldn't fantasize about taking his clothes off, so I went down again then, and got quite depressed. Although I was a lot better, it was a lonely life. Also my family, especially my darling sisters, began to lose their fear of me. I guess I wasn't so obviously mad, just their poor, drippy, miserable failure of a brother, and they got back into their old ways bit by bit, sniping, joking at my expense, talking as if I wasn't there, or ignoring me completely. I guess they were just nasty, spoilt little girls, too clever for their own good. They were twelve by then and they'd done really well and got into Osewick Grammar. They thought highly of themselves, too. What a contrast to their mad, useless brother. They had high-flying careers planned, and I couldn't work at all. They were just hitting puberty, and used to flaunt their skinny bodies despite what my mum said. You would be disgusted to know what fantasies I had, the revenge I wanted to take.' He winced, as if in pain. 'I hope I haven't shocked you. You must think I am a real sicko. Well, I guess I am.'

'Maybe you're just more honest than most.'

'Do you think so? Do normal people have horrible thoughts?'

'I am sure they do. Whatever normal is.'

Christopher smiled faintly. 'Well, you will be glad to know I am coming to the end of this long, tedious chapter. I got very depressed at home. I was going nowhere. I thought my family were, as usual, sitting in judgment on me and finding me wanting. A place came up at the house in Denbigh Street, and Rob thought it would be good for me to live

156

more independently—with discreet supervision, of course. They knew I was good about taking my medication, and that was a point in my favour. There was a sort of trial period, a few months, when they monitored things to see if we were all getting along OK together, which was a bit daft because people came and went anyway. It was lonely, but no worse than with my family. I came to realize I was lucky. Compared to many other mad people, I was still in touch with my rational self, my real self, I like to think, even if he was often very quiet and weak. I was depressed a lot, but I could cope. I had a new CPN, Sandra, and a nice lady called Jackie who does stuff for me and will help if I am in trouble. Social Services had to get in on it too. That's Mick, I told you about him. In my worse moments I get very paranoid, and I think they are all talking about me and plotting, which they are in a way. Then I get scared and hide for a while.'

'Is that what you're doing now?'

Christopher glanced at her, then immediately looked away again. His expression seemed to freeze, and his voice almost disappeared. 'No. I meant I hide in my room. This is different. I can't talk about it. Not now. Please don't ask me.'

'It's OK, Christopher, you don't have to say another word. Please, don't be afraid. I am not one of the plotters, I promise you.'

He looked at her intently for a while, then a small smile appeared, hesitant and still suspicious. When he spoke his voice was different, almost as flat and dull and toneless as when she had first spoken to him. This reversal shocked her, more than the meaning of his words. It taught her again how fragile were the bridges she was building.

'Please,' he said. 'Please understand. I want to trust you. I need a friend. But what do I know? I don't know how to trust people.'

She swallowed, and took a deep breath. 'I know. All I can tell you is, I don't want to hurt you. I hope I can be trusted. I keep my promises, even when I have made them in haste and foolishly.'

His tense shoulders relaxed a little. 'All right. I will try not to be paranoid. But it is hard.'

'Yes, I can see it is. Look, Christopher, I'd better go. Please be patient. Natasha is not well, so I have to see if she is all right. And tomorrow I have to collect Michael, and when he is around I won't be quite so free to come and see you.'

Christopher nodded. 'Where is he?'

'He's with his family. It's quite possible that very soon he will go back to live permanently with them.'

'What are you to him, then?'

157

'His foster-parent.'

'That means you have to go to Social Services.'

'Occasionally, yes. But I have never mentioned you there, nor will I.'

'I don't like them, all the officials, the hierarchy, the social workers, the psychiatrists, the self-important conspiring busybodies.'

'But I am not one of them. I am a friend, if that is what you want.'

'OK.' He was grudging, sullen, would not look at her directly.

'Christopher, look. I won't be so free over the next few days. Please, be patient, suspend your disbelief. I will come when I can. And if I can't come, I will leave food by the tree at the top of the path. Things will settle down. It will be all right.'

He nodded, but his shoulders were hunched, his eyes downcast. 'Yeah. I'll see you.'

There was no more she could say. The whole situation was as fragile as a breath. But now it was she who was powerless, and it was he who held all the decisions. 'Goodbye, Chris. I'll see you soon. Look after yourself.'

Walking away from him was harder than she would have believed possible. She felt that she had, for a time, accompanied him into his world, and it disturbed her to find that world so difficult to leave.

After the last few days of communicating, however tentatively, with a universe that seemed so alien, choir practice came as a shock of normality. Eileen left Natasha wrapped in her duvet on the sofa, sipping a mug of soup in front of the television. She was feeling better, but very weak. She spoke to Daphne on the telephone, and was told that on no account was she to appear in the shop until Monday morning at the earliest. Eileen made sure she was comfortable and walked the short distance to church. It felt odd to be alone, with no Michael at her side. Over the past week she had deliberately not thought about him much. Imagining him with his family was hard, and with all that was happening with Christopher, and Tillie's illness, Eileen felt that it would be too much for her overloaded brain. But very soon she would have to put Michael back at the forefront of consciousness. Tomorrow he would be back, full of…what? She had no way of telling. And on Monday there would be a meeting with Denise, Andy and Charley. Michael's future, her future, would be debated. It had to be done, thought about, prepared for; but not yet. The short walk to church was not long enough. As she pushed open the creaking ancient door, stepping from the warm sunlight into the soft shadows of the church, Eileen felt keenly the need of someone to help her bear the burden, to bat things against, to make it all clearer. But she could not share it all. Christopher, the hardest and

158

heaviest part, had still to be a secret, bound by an undertaking that had been made in haste. And Marie seemed unprecedentedly distanced from her, whether by her own preoccupation with Philip or by Eileen's barely-admitted wish. As she stepped inside the church a pang of conscience struck her. *I have let myself go adrift, I have forgotten you, Lord. Thank you that you do not forget me.*

Her thoughts were interrupted by a burst of childish laughter from the vestry. As she went in it subsided into giggles. The little girls were clustered round Georgina Quilley at one end, while some of the adults, sorting out music, cast disapproving glances. Eileen exchanged greetings absentmindedly, startled by the change in Georgina's appearance which was, so it seemed, the source of the younger girls' fascination. She was wearing shiny black ankle boots with three-inch heels, making her tower over the nine-year-olds, who looked up at her with awe and admiration. Her skirt was tight and short, revealing a great length of bare leg, and her blue top, spangled with stars, was equally tight, showing every nuance of puppy fat and straining breasts. Her hair had been cut short, stiffened with gel and adorned with multi-coloured clips, and her face was caked in makeup. It all seemed a bit over the top for choir practice, and was no doubt intended as a statement. Her still-innocent round face showed alternately smug acceptance of the little girls' adulation and sulky defiance of the adults' less rapturous reactions.

Eileen felt a grip of fear clutch her between heart and guts, and a wave of sympathy for both Georgina and her anxious mother. But she decided to behave as if everything was normal, which in a way it was. Was Georgina not the same young girl she had been at last week's choir practice, only done up for battle like some new-fledged Indian brave?

'Hello, girls. Hi, Georgina,' she said, helping herself to a pile of music. 'Had a good half term?'

The younger ones were soon telling her about sleepovers and swimming sessions. Georgina simply smiled and said nothing, and Eileen sensed with growing unease that she was nursing some very precious and inflammatory secret. What was she up to? Fourteen was too young for dangerous secrets. She was too tender and vulnerable; she would be blown away. But what could Eileen do? Nothing.

Georgina was not to be the only surprise that evening. A few minutes later, as they were beginning to take their places in the choir stalls, Philip arrived. He too looked different, but the changes were more subtle. He had obviously had a haircut, and his clothes had at least been brushed, or perhaps over half term he had had little contact with chalk dust. But there was something unfamiliar about his whole demeanour. The slouch

159

had gone, he spoke almost boldly, he looked at people directly, giving out an air of quiet confidence. It was as if Philip the musician, competent, masterly, in control, had begun to cross over to Philip the man. As choir practice continued Eileen watched him with astonished fascination. Was this the transformation of love, of sexual release, of growing self-belief? Or all of these? Whatever it was, it was intriguing. Again Eileen felt the need to talk to Marie, but with a stab of sadness she remembered that, as far as she knew, the situation had progressed beyond scurrilous conversations full of unseemly hilarity. *It's all gone serious and private now. Their gain is my loss. Well, I wish them all joy. Whatever it is, Marie is having quite an electrifying effect on Philip. What power we all have to build up and energize, or to tear down and trample. And most of the time we aren't even aware of it.*

Eileen sang automatically. Her mind was elsewhere. They practised for Sunday, and for the induction. The music was coming along satisfactorily, and Philip had little cause to detain them long. Eileen saw him cast a quizzical glance at Georgina, who blushed and scowled. Then he looked away, obviously dismissing her appearance as of little importance. He was in a hurry to get away, back, no doubt, to that new source of strength and power over a world which must have been for him, till now, so often hostile or disappointing. Eileen watched him walk down the churchyard path, get into his car and roar off down the village street. Mentally she saluted him, and said goodbye, with an unwelcome sense that he was going where she could not follow.

When she got home Sean's car was parked outside in the road. The light was fading; the merest streak of pink remained in the sky, just above the tree line. Sean and Natasha were sitting on the sofa. She was still in her dressing-gown, and he was holding her gently as if she were a small child. Eileen was touched. *This man's a treasure, don't let him go.* He looked up and smiled when she came in. 'Hello, Eileen. I had to come and succour the sick.'

'So I see,' Eileen said. 'How do you find the patient?'

'A bit feeble. But improved.'

'Do you mind,' Natasha said in muffled tones, her face half-hidden in Sean's jumper. 'I am actually here, you know. I haven't died, or lost my marbles.'

'Or your voice, I notice,' Eileen said. 'I think you must be feeling better. Do you two want a cup of tea?'

This offer was accepted by Sean but rejected by Natasha, whose stomach was still fragile and unpredictable. They drank their tea and talked lightly of very little. Then Sean said he would go home, solicitously tucked the quilt round Natasha's recumbent body, which was taking up almost all the sofa, kissed her and left.

'I'm going to have a bath, OK, Mum?' Natasha said. 'I feel smelly and disgusting. Then I'm going back to bed, to see if I can fight this thing off.'

'All right, love. Shout if you need anything. Goodnight.'

Confuting every expectation, Tillie rose from her basket, yawned, stretched, and stood by the back door, looking at Eileen expectantly, her long black plume of a tail slowly waving from side to side.

'This is a surprise, old dear,' Eileen said, opening the door. 'Whatever was in that jab must be working.'

Tillie cruised the garden for several minutes, sniffing around, checking that all was as it should be. She seemed livelier than she had been for a considerable time. Coming back in she looked at Eileen enquiringly. Eileen gave her a modest bowl of food which she ate slowly but with evident relish. Then she drank some water and lay down again in her basket, sighing contentedly. Her eyes seemed brighter. She was regaining her old self, and Eileen was gladdened, even though she knew it could only be temporary. She stroked the dog's head and ears. 'Look reasonable for Michael. He's got enough going on in his life, without having to come home to find you pegging out. Maybe tomorrow, if you're up to it, I'll give you a bath. It's good to see you so much better, dear old thing.' Tillie licked her hand gently in appreciation.

The house was quiet. Only the soft soughing of the wind in the apple tree could be heard in the garden, occasionally punctuated by the call of a hunting owl. It was a warm night. Eileen stood at the open back door, looking down the garden towards the dark woods, imagining Christopher wrapped in his blankets, among the leaf mould under the creaking oaks. Despite the warmth she shivered, turned and went indoors, contrary to her usual habit closing doors and pulling curtains shut, as if she were trying to shut out the uncomfortable thought of the young man sleeping alone under the trees. She sat at the kitchen table, took down her Bible but did not open it. Her eyes were aching. It was late, and she needed sleep. But she needed guidance too. People in the church tried to keep things going, but there was no continuity, no direction, no one with overall charge of their spiritual welfare, no one paid to pray for them daily and preach to them weekly. Maybe the home-groups were still running. She didn't know. She was beginning to sense she was drifting, going astray; she needed discipline and regularity. It was like swimming in a vast ocean out of sight of land. It would be good to have a minister again, someone to take responsibility for that invisible but weighty charge, the cure of souls. She opened her Bible randomly. *I don't even know what to look for in here. Maybe I need a study guide. Perhaps I can get one in Caxford tomorrow when I go to pick up Michael, if the bookshop runs to such things.*

She flicked a few pages, and began to read where her eye fell. It was a familiar passage.

"Finally, build up your strength in union with the Lord and by means of his mighty power. Put on all the armour that God gives you, so that you will be able to stand up against the Devil's evil tricks. For we are not fighting against human beings but against the wicked spiritual forces in the heavenly world, the rulers, authorities, and cosmic powers of this dark age. So put on God's armour now! Then when the evil day comes, you will be able to resist the enemy's attacks; and after fighting to the end, you will still hold your ground."

St. Paul was right about the dark cosmic powers. Maybe that was why people often felt so confused and helpless. Maybe they were battling against the wrong enemy. She had a series of mental pictures then, one after another like frames of a slow-moving film: of Stephanie in the darkened night-club; of shadowy figures round the bar; of clusters of people huddled together doing who knew what illicit business; of stereotypical gangsters in gloomy garages. The whole scene was clouded with the vapours of mysterious substances, and interspersed with faces in pools of sudden light, among them the innocent face of Georgina Quilley, surrounded by the forces of darkness. She shuddered involuntarily. Her mental scenery shifted, and she seemed again to be inhabiting Christopher's universe, encircled by great glowing winged creatures bearing down upon him. Surely angels were not creatures of evil? Yet in Christopher's experience they were agents of a great tyrant, howling hounds that drowned out his weak human voice. Perhaps this passage from Ephesians might help Christopher, the idea of buckling on spiritual armour as a defence against demonic attack. If she got a chance, she would mention it to him.

She decided to go to bed. Natasha had finished with her bath. There was a dim light from her bedroom, but all was quiet.

Saturday 1st June 1996

Both Eileen and Natasha slept heavily and late, and it was only Tillie's whining that finally dragged Eileen to confused consciousness. After letting out the dog, who was clearly anxious not to repeat her *faux pas* of a few days earlier, she looked at the clock. Nine fifteen. It was almost unheard-of for her to rise so late. She ate breakfast quickly, took Natasha a cup of tea, and decided she just had time to give Tillie the promised bath. Getting the dog clean took less time than washing down the bathroom afterwards. Wet black hairs and muddy splashes seemed to have reached every wall and corner. Tillie lay on the grass outside, recovering from her ordeal, letting the warm sun dry her coat. Eileen hastily assembled food for Christopher, and left it by the prearranged tree, out of sight behind a gorse bush, in case some early-strolling dog should find it first. What if she had met a dog-walking villager, an acquaintance, how could she have explained her eccentric actions? Crossly she dismissed the thoughts. There was no time, and no answer.

She arrived at Caxford Social Services and parked. Caxford seemed livelier than usual. People crowded the pavements, dressed for summer. As Eileen entered the building Charley waved to her. She was speaking to someone on the phone in the office on the ground floor. Eileen waved back and made her way up the stairs to the family room. There was no one there. She sat down in a threadbare armchair by the window, looking out over the car park. Five minutes later a large but battered and extremely noisy saloon roared in and parked in a welter of exhaust fumes. At once five people piled out, banging doors and talking loudly. Eileen watched the parents organize the children, picking up fallen toys, smoothing hair, holding them back from approaching cars. *This is Michael's family now, but he still doesn't look quite like one of them.* That transformation, she guessed, would take a bit longer. Then there were pounding feet on the stairs, and shouting voices, and Michael, hesitating for a fraction of a second in the doorway, raced across the room and flung himself on her, hugging her tightly. As his parents approached he disengaged himself, and stood by her chair, smiling broadly. He looked

163

rounder and pinker. *Rubbish, not in a week, I have just let his image slip.* She had not been prepared for the feelings that welled up in her when she saw him, the simple gladness to have him back, and the pain, following swiftly after, of knowing that it could not be for long.

Then the room was full of noise and greetings and bundling children. Charley followed them up the stairs, giving Eileen a private and sympathetic smile. 'Well, you lot,' she said, addressing the children in her ringing voice, 'have you had a good time? Managed not to fight too much?'

The two younger ones answered her together, and above the clamour their parents just smiled. They seemed relaxed. Evidently the week had gone well. Michael said little. Eileen knew that he would report later, when they were quiet, and it was his thoughts she wanted to hear.

Andy put Michael's suitcase by the door. 'We're not stopping,' he said to Charley. 'We've promised the kids a trip out, so we need to make a reasonable start. We'll see you on Monday, anyway, won't we? Eleven, wasn't it? Come on, kids, don't get too involved with the toys, we need to get a move on.' Denise bustled around, peeling children away from toys, smiling rather apologetically. Among the confusion Eileen watched Michael, and Charley watched Eileen. 'Well, cheerio, son, we'll see you dead soon, no worries.' Andy and Denise both hugged Michael at once. For a moment he was surrounded in a charmed parental circle, and he stood there quite passively, but the conflict of joy and embarrassment was plain to see.

'Cheerio, Eileen,' Andy said heartily. 'See you Monday. Don't let him misbehave.' He cuffed Michael, who blushed. Eileen found herself echoing Denise's weak smile. The two boys gave each other a brotherly punch, Denise scooped up Ellie, and they were gone, with Charley following. Eileen and Michael watched them roar away.

'You ready to go, Michael?' She forbore to say 'home'; perhaps he no longer knew where home was.

Michael nodded. Eileen picked up his suitcase, and he took her free hand as they went down the stairs. They said goodbye to Charley in the car park, and a few minutes later were on their way back to Holton.

They were quiet for a while, then Eileen glanced at him. 'Had a good week?'

'Yes, it was OK. The kids are a bit of a pain, but they went to bed earlier than me. I got to stay up and watch films and stuff.'

'Right.'

'And I had my own room. I didn't have to bunk in with Harry like I

164

thought. There's a kind of little room they used to use for junk, only they made it for me, painted it blue and put a bed in there. It was small, but nice.'

'They've worked hard for you.'

Michael nodded. 'Dad says, when we move to Lambury, I can have a bigger room. I might have to share with Harry, but it'll be big enough. And,' he said, the rising excitement in his voice uncontainable, 'when we have a garden, Dad says we can get a puppy.'

'That would be lovely. What sort of dog do you think it will be?'

'I don't know. But he says we can all go and choose it. And he promised to make a new hutch for Bill. He does need one, doesn't he?' he asked, anxious suddenly that he might seem to be belittling their joint effort.

'Of course he does. I expect your dad is a more expert carpenter than we ever were.'

Michael was quiet for a moment. As they slowed down, coming into the village, he said, 'Is everybody all right?'

'Tasha has been unwell, she's been off work, but she's getting better. Tillie hasn't been too well either, but I took her to the vet and she's perked up. I gave her a bath in your honour.'

Michael smiled. 'Can I call Christie later?'

'Yes, if she doesn't ring first.'

He got out of the car and manfully hauled his suitcase out of the boot. He looked up at her, his face serious. 'Have you seen Chris?'

'Yes. I have given him some food and blankets. He is all right. But we mustn't mention him, except to each other. He wants to stay out of sight.'

'I won't say anything. After lunch can I go and see Steve?'

'Sounds like a good idea. He's probably missed you.'

'Yeah, he had to play with his stupid little sister, I expect.'

There was an air of cocky bravado about Michael which Eileen had not seen before, even in the playground or with Stephen. She shrugged, fighting down a pang of disappointment. She was just a caretaker now. But this was hard for a boy of eight, and she must try not to make it any harder.

They went into the house. Natasha was up and dressed, looking fragile but determined. 'Hello, stranger.' She enveloped Michael in a bear hug. 'It's been very quiet round here without you. Oh, Mum, I nearly forgot, Marie rang. She can't come over today after all. She's going out somewhere with Philip.'

Michael flew round, greeting Tillie, fetching Bill out, throwing clothes on his bedroom floor. Eileen noted how clean and beautifully pressed they were, as if they hadn't been worn. Lunch came and went, then in a whirl he was gone again.

'Back to normal, but not,' Eileen said to Natasha.

Natasha looked up and nodded. 'Everything's changing, Mum. So many things on the move. It's a bit scary, in a way. But at least you'll still be here, and this place is always the same.'

Eileen went to the sink and started to wash dishes, thinking about what Natasha had said. *Not even that is certain. Nothing is. All we have are temporary certainties to act on day by day, at the end the certainty of death, and beyond that the biggest uncertainty of all.* She shook away her gloomy thoughts. Feeling the need of merriment, a hearth against the dark, she said to Natasha, 'Why don't you ring Sean? As you're feeling better, he could come over for supper, meet Michael.'

'Yeah, why not. I'll even help you cook.'

'Don't overdo it.'

'No chance of that.' Natasha grinned and went to the phone.

In the end it was a happy evening, if tinged with the sadness of things coming to an end, at least for Eileen. For the others, there was also the hope and excitement of new things beginning. After they had eaten, Sean and Natasha went out, obviously, though they hid it politely, starved of private time. Eileen read to Michael for a while, then she said, 'So, tell me a bit more about your half term. What did you do?'

'Lots of stuff. We went swimming. Mummy took the little ones in the baby pool, but I was allowed in the big pool with Dad. He said I was a really good swimmer.'

'So you are.'

'We went and had a look at the new school I might go to. Not inside, because it was shut for the holidays. It's a big place, like a mansion, with loads of grounds round it. You had to drive in, it was so big.'

'It sounds quite something.'

'We went to the beach one day. Dad and Harry and I made a castle, and we had fish and chips.'

'Sounds like you had a really great time, Michael. Do you think it will be nice to live with Mum and Dad and Harry and Ellie all the time?'

'I felt funny at first, but I am getting used to it now. And I do really belong to them, don't I?' he said earnestly.

'Of course you do. The important thing is for you to be happy.'

'I am OK.' He took her hand. 'But will you be OK?'

'Of course I will. I told you before, I will miss you very much, we all will. But knowing you are getting on all right will help.'

A thought struck Michael. 'Mum, I meant to tell you. Steve and I went to the woods.'

'For a change.'

Michael ignored this. 'We thought we might see Chris, but he wasn't there.'

'Did you go to his camp?'

'Yes, but his stuff was all gone.'

'Maybe he's gone to another part of the woods. He sometimes does that. He might come back. But we needn't worry about it now. I hate to remind you, but you've got church in the morning, and school on Monday, so it's time for a little shut-eye.'

Michael turned over, and pulled the quilt up round his shoulders. 'It's nice to be back,' he mumbled sleepily. 'It's nice to be here, but I like to be there too. Life is hard.'

Eileen laughed. 'You sound like an old man. Life is all right, yours is all right. Go to sleep.'

Later she went down the garden. It was almost dark. Tillie followed her, looking at her puzzled as if half-expecting a moonlight walk. Eileen retrieved the bag from behind the bushes. It was untouched. She felt a moment of horrible panic. Where was Christopher? What was going on in his mind? Had the little headway she felt she had made with him all been undone? Most importantly, was he all right? She felt a compelling need to find him, and reassure herself. But Michael was asleep indoors, the woods were dark, and she was powerless.

She lay in bed, awake and alert, waiting for sounds. Only the owl spoke to her from the shadowy trees. She dozed. Presently she heard Sean and Natasha return. There was a discreet clinking of cups, murmured voices, long intense silences. Eileen tried to stop herself thinking about what was happening in those silences. She told herself crossly that it was none of her business. But she wished Sean and Natasha would take their erotic aura elsewhere. It was highly disturbing. Despite herself she imagined them downstairs, lying in each other's arms, whispering, making up for lost time. She punched her pillow which suddenly felt lumpy. And Michael: he was there, but not there. Everyone was moving on, but she was standing still. And where, where was Christopher? She felt abandoned, even while knowing the feeling was irrational. *I am getting crazier than he is.* But the demons would not let up, and sleep was long in coming.

167

Sunday 2nd June 1996

The day passed in a blur. Church, lunch, animals, Natasha, now back to normal, in and out of the house. Christina rang, worn out but relieved that her exams were over. She spoke to everyone, but longest to Michael. In church all the talk was of the new vicar, his family, the induction. Philip was brisk, everybody was busy. Eileen felt as if she were on a little island, something small, dead and post-volcanic, alone in a vast bright sea on which many vessels, big and small, purposefully sailed. Some passed the island, sometimes someone waved, but nobody ever dropped anchor.

In the afternoon she went to the woods, accompanied by Tillie. Michael had already gone, back to Stephen's.

Christopher's camp was indeed empty. As she stood in the little clearing, she heard voices. A party of Sunday strollers went noisily past, a young woman with a small boy, a man with a baby on his back, two dogs, an elderly couple, all chatting and laughing loudly. Eileen explored a little further but there was still no sign of Christopher. A sense of deep foreboding settled on her, however hard she tried to rationalize it away. Then she had to turn for home, because Tillie was tiring.

The evening came. Michael was bathed, his school uniform laid on the chair. Sean and Natasha were out. The silence became oppressive, and Eileen felt her restlessness rise to almost unbearable levels. She could neither read nor pray. Her spiritual machinery was grinding, oilless and noisy; cogs were shrieking in protest.

Sorry, sorry. I can't talk to you, not now. But please, please Lord, take care of him, don't let him come to harm.

168

Monday 3rd June 1996

The morning brought with it a heavy dew. The grass in the back garden was long, well overdue for mowing, and Tillie came in from her early foray wet up to her belly. Natasha was away to work before her mother had vacated the bathroom. Eileen felt dishevelled, baggy-eyed, heavy and sluggish. Getting Michael to school was an effort, and they were almost late. Returning home she soaked in a hot bath for half an hour and nearly fell asleep. By the time she was ready it was past ten o'clock; there was too little time to go and look for Christopher. She felt a need to arrive at Social Services at least reasonably calm. To talk to Christopher needed more resources than she at that moment had.

In the event, the meeting proved something of an anticlimax. When Eileen arrived the meeting-room at the back of the building had been set out neatly with chairs and a jug of water. Someone had even put a tiny vase of flowers on the table. Denise, Charley and Eric Delaney were already there, chatting in low voices.

'Hello, Eileen,' Charley said, obviously relieved to see her. 'We're just waiting for Andy, then we'll get started.'

Presently Andy arrived, heralded by the noisy car. He was in his greasy blue overalls. 'I've come straight from the garage. They've given me a bit of time off.'

'All right,' Charley said. 'We're all busy, so let's get rolling. You've all met Eric, I think. I've filled him in on what's been happening to date, so we all know where we are. Andy, Denise, how do you feel the week went?'

Andy and Denise looked at each other briefly. Denise said, in her rather hesitant and apologetic way, 'Michael was kind of quiet to start with, so I was a little bit worried, but I realized he was just checking things out, like he didn't want to do anything wrong.'

'That was just the first day, though,' Andy said. 'After that he was fine, mucked in with the kids, enjoyed all the stuff we did.'

Charley said, 'How do you feel he related to you two as parents?'

169

'He was funny at first,' Denise said, 'ever so helpful and polite.'

'Yeah, like a little old man,' Andy said. 'Even with his brother and sister. But after a day or two he was acting more like you'd expect.'

'How do you mean, Andy?' Charley said.

'Oh, you know, a bit of rough and tumble, boy stuff.'

'OK. Do you feel there were any problems that arose?'

Denise shook her head. 'Not really. He seemed a bit shy to start with, like I said, then after a while it was Mummy this and Daddy that. He seemed quite happy.'

'How about from your point of view? Did it all go as you both hoped?'

'Well, he's our boy, isn't he?' Andy said. 'We want him back, whatever he's like.'

Denise smiled nervously. 'But he's such a good boy. Really nice manners and everything.'

Eric Delaney, silent and observant till then, shifted in his chair. 'So, Eileen. How have you found Michael since he's been back with you?'

Eileen thought for a moment. 'He's obviously had a lovely time. He enjoyed all the outings, and he's very excited about the prospect of getting a puppy. He also seemed proud that he and Andy would be making a new hutch for his guinea pig. He does have mixed feelings, of course. He was very pleased to see me, and Natasha, and his friend Stephen, and to talk to Christina on the phone. But overall he feels as Andy does, that he belongs with them.'

Charley nodded. 'OK. So far, so good, then, would we all agree with that? So where do we go from here?'

Andy was evidently concerned about getting back to work, and there seemed little to argue about. The end of the summer term, seven weeks away, seemed a convenient and appropriate time for Michael to move on. Meanwhile he would continue to live at Holton during the week for the sake of his schooling, and go to his parents at weekends. They asked that he be brought to them on a Friday evening, rather than Saturday. It hardly signified that he would be missing choir practice when that part of his life would soon be over. Eileen wondered if he would remember any of it after a while. When the years had rolled on, would he remember that he could sing when he was a child? Did any of it matter?

Practical details were mentioned, then Andy got up to go. He paused in the doorway. 'Oh yes, I forgot to tell you,' he said, with an air of triumph. 'We got a letter from the council this morning. We get our new house in a month, garden, three bedrooms, no worries.'

'That's excellent, Andy,' Charley said. 'It all seems to be working out. And the school is still prepared to take Michael in September.'

'Yep, that's sorted.'

'Right. Well, before you go, please remember, if there are any problems, anything you feel concerned about, however small, and I mean both you two, Andy and Denise, and you, Eileen, you must let me know. We can't afford to get this wrong, for Michael's sake.'

The meeting broke up. Eric Delaney, after a few civil remarks, disappeared to his own office. Andy took Denise away.

'Don't go for a minute, Eileen,' Charley said. 'I'll make us a cup of coffee.' Eileen followed her downstairs to the tiny kitchen. Charley made two mugs of coffee and handed Eileen one. She perched on the edge of the table. 'So, how did Michael seem?'

Eileen shrugged. 'As I said, he had a good time. I get the feeling there are things he's not saying, as if he's still mulling it all over. He's still committed to the whole idea, though. I'm a bit concerned that he hasn't taken in the finality of it all yet.'

'Hm. We must keep an open mind, see how things go. I'm relying on you a lot, I know, and it can't be an easy time for you.'

'No. Anyway, I'll do my best.'

'I know that. Keep in touch, Eileen.'

Driving home Eileen felt as if a muffling blanket were weighing down her spirit. It was not just the prospect of losing Michael, but the thought of what might lie ahead for him. Andy was, or so it seemed, still sold on the role of fatherhood, and to date Michael was his only natural child; but there was every possibility that he and Denise might have other children in the future. Where, then, would be the unique position that was clearly so important to Michael? She sighed. It was none of her business and there was nothing she could do about it. Like every other family, they would have to work it out in their own way. But for her Michael was not any boy, and the thought of him coping with a new family and a new life without her support was painful and worrying. *I have to cut this cord. It's getting stretched and strained. I have to stop worrying when it is so pointless.*

Driving back into Holton her other worry resurfaced with urgency. Arriving home she at once made some sandwiches and went down into the woods. Now, being a weekday, the ramblers were gone and all was quiet, but Eileen felt the peace deceptive, almost threatening.

For more than two hours she searched for Christopher. The sun grew warm. She took off her jumper and tied it round her waist. She combed

171

the woods, all the paths she knew, but there were many places he could hide, and he had had plenty of opportunity to explore very thoroughly. Perhaps he had even gone back to Caxford; but somehow she felt that he had not, that he was somewhere to be found.

In the end it was he who found her. She had crossed the rape field near Annette's house, and had just plunged back into the trees on the other side. Her feet were aching, and she was hot and sticky. She kicked off her shoes and cooled her feet in the long, soft grass of a tiny shady clearing. Then she saw him, a few feet away up the path, standing quite still, his dark eyes intently upon her. Seeing him gave her a heart-constricting shock. He was wearing the striped jumper he had on when she first saw him, and for a passing second it seemed that time had reversed, that she had never met him before, that she knew nothing about him. She felt both foreboding and profound relief, and she was astonished to feel tears come into her eyes. 'Christopher. There you are. I have been looking for you.'

He did not reply. He laid a finger on his lips, and turned back down the path, beckoning her to follow. After a few yards he stopped and turned back. As she approached he took her arm and drew her off the path into the shadow of several large oaks. Here, among the piles of last year's acorns, long abandoned by the foraging squirrels, he had evidently made another camp. But his things were packed and rolled, as if he was again ready to run.

She looked at him, bewildered. 'Christopher, where on earth have you been? Why did you move so suddenly? Why didn't you take the food I left?' These were not the questions she wanted to ask, but they were all the words that presented themselves.

He cleared his throat. His eyes were still fixed unblinking on her face. 'I had to run.' His voice was growly. 'He was coming after me again. I had to hide. You were not there, you had withdrawn your protection.'

'What? What are you talking about? Who was after you?'

'Him, of course. Big Voice. He is back.'

'Oh, no. This is terrible, Christopher. Why? What has brought this on?'

He shrugged. 'Sometimes that's the way it goes.'

'But I was worried about you. I thought something had happened to you. Or maybe you'd gone for good.'

'Would that matter?'

She struggled with herself. 'Yes, it would.'

He was silent for a moment. Then he said, 'Why don't you sit down? I can unroll my blanket. It's a bit damp here after the dew.'

172

He sounded so normal and practical suddenly that her confusion intensified. She felt as if things were slowly but inevitably going out of control. She sat down. He too sat, a few feet away, his arms round his drawn-up knees. He began to rock very slightly backwards and forwards. The movement was almost hypnotic.

Breaking the silence, she said, 'Aren't you terribly hungry?'

'I forgot about food. But now that you mention it, yes, I am.'

He ate and drank what she had brought. Watching him she fought with herself, trying to bring her thoughts back into some semblance of order and sense. 'Why do you think it has happened now, Christopher? I mean, getting that voice back.'

'I don't know. But it's OK, he won't shout at me while you're here.'

'I don't understand why my presence would make a difference.'

'Nor do I. But it does. You remind me I am a human being.'

'What do you feel like when I'm not here, then?'

'A very shy, timid animal, like a rabbit, something that has few defences, except for running.'

'But you have gone so far away. Why don't you come back, nearer, like before?'

He shook his head. 'I am afraid. It's too near people. I have to hide.'

'I wish I knew why. I wish I could help you.'

'I can't tell you yet. And you are helping me.'

She looked at her watch. 'I've got to get back. It's nearly time to collect Michael from school.' She paused, thinking. 'Christopher, do you still want that bath we talked about?' He looked interested, but wary. 'You could come tomorrow, if you like. After Michael has gone to school. I'll be home soon after nine. Come up the back path. You'll be OK. Most of my neighbours go to work, and old Mrs. Corbett is almost blind, so she won't see anything. And bring your dirty clothes. I'll wash them for you.'

With a darting movement, as if unsure, he took her hand and squeezed it. 'Thank you.'

'Will you come?'

'I don't know. I want to do it, but I am afraid.'

'Well. It's up to you. I'll be there.'

'All right. I'll try and make it.'

'I've got to go. Please, look after yourself.'

He nodded slowly. She got up, took the bag, and backed out onto the path. His brooding eyes followed her, his face serious and intense.

'Goodbye, Christopher.'

He raised his hand, then let it fall. Silently he watched her go.

Tuesday 4th June 1996

Standing in the playground waiting for the children to go in, so that she could wave to Michael as she always did, impatience bit into Eileen, making her feet fidget, distracting her from the chat of the surrounding mothers. As soon as the bell clanged she was away, smiling vaguely where she would often have paused to exchange meaningless but amiable comments. What if Christopher, conquering his terror, came to the back door and found it locked? Did he have a watch? She couldn't remember.

Arriving home, there was, of course, no sign of him. It took her fully five minutes to get her breath back. She put the kettle on, fed the dog, and sat in a kitchen chair with outstretched legs. Inside her Bible was the sheet of paper on which she had written out the list of references to angels. Something occurred to her as she got up to make a cup of coffee. *I will write out that verse from Ephesians. About buckling on armour. And I will look up everything I can find which shows God as not only harshly just but merciful, tender, sorrowing. Christopher has this image of retribution, of God as a destroying, vengeful force, of the angels as his tormenting agents. I will try to find stuff from the Old Testament especially. Then maybe, if I get the chance, I can move on to Jesus. Christopher can't say he is violent, full of revenge, out for blood and punishment, can he? I won't load him up with it all at once. I'll go very easy. But it won't hurt to have it to hand.*

She sat down again with pen and paper. She sipped her coffee. The clock ticked softly as she worked. Her search was fruitful, as she knew it would be. After a while she looked up, blinked, and eased her stiff neck. A thought struck her. She went upstairs to where she kept her books on a set of shelves on the landing. There she found a leather-bound Revised Standard Version which had belonged to her mother. Taking it downstairs with her she looked up a few references at random. The language was different, plain enough but powerful, more poetic, less pedestrian than her own version.

"Say to them, 'As I live, says the Lord God, I have no pleasure in the death of the wicked, but that the wicked turn from his way and live; turn

174

back, turn back from your evil ways; for why will you die, O house of Israel?'"

"He will feed his flock like a shepherd, he will gather the lambs in his arms, he will carry them in his bosom, and gently lead those that are with young."

The image of the loving shepherd reminded her of another image, the words of Jesus himself: "'Come to me, all who labour and are heavy laden, and I will give you rest. Take my yoke upon you, and learn from me; for I am gentle and lowly in heart, and you will find rest for your soul. For my yoke is easy, and my burden is light.'"

She looked at the clock. It was ten past ten. She sighed. Perhaps she had hoped too much. Perhaps she had underestimated what a huge effort of will it would take for him to leave his sanctuary. She got up, stretched, looked out of the window, down the garden, towards the woods. The trees stood there, timeless, innocent, moving slightly in the breeze, apparently devoid of lurking madmen. With a kind of desperation she went back to her reading.

She lighted on John's Gospel, and within ten minutes Christopher had receded to the back of her consciousness, although it was he who had inspired her search. Here it all was, everything, as she thought, he needed to know. She read with such urgency that she had no time to write anything down; words and phrases and images unrolled themselves before her eyes. All of them were familiar, yet seeing them through Christopher's eyes made them new, marvellous, radical. *This is what he needs to read. This, and some of the Psalms. I'll look at them next.*

For a moment the tiny sound did not penetrate into her conscious mind. Then it came again, a timorous tapping. She had been so rapt in her studies that when she realized what it was she felt a moment of fear. Then, as it evaporated into relief, she pushed back her chair and opened the door.

He stood, flattened against the wall, nervously twitching. She ushered him inside and closed the door. He was panting, like a fox pursued by hounds; his eyes flicked, yet she felt he was taking in nothing. In the face of his fear and distrust, palpable, almost physical, she felt her confidence, the gracious, enabling influence of John, recede.

'You made it, then,' she said. 'I had almost given you up.'

He looked at the books and papers on the table, shuddered slightly. 'You are reading your Bible.' His voice was thick from lack of use.

'Yes, I often do. I was looking up stuff for you.'

'Me?'

'Yes. There's things in there you might need to know, things that might help. But not now, I think. Would you like some breakfast?'

175

He nodded. He was jerky, like an automaton, and his eyes seemed clouded, almost blind.

'Sit down, Christopher,' she said gently. 'Try not to be afraid. You are safe here.'

Gradually he seemed to become calmer. She made him coffee and toast, put marmalade back on the table, scrambled some eggs. By the time he had finished he was beginning to look a bit more human, and he even managed a small, tremulous smile.

She smiled back at him. 'Shall I go and run your bath now? Did you bring your clean clothes?'

'Yes.' He indicated a bundle at his feet.

'All the stuff's there in the bathroom, towels and so on. You can use my old bathrobe. It's hanging on the back of the door.'

'OK.'

'Just dump your dirty stuff outside and I'll wash it for you.'

'Thanks.'

As she went to the stairs she patted his shoulder gently. She felt his muscles stiffen, then relax. She went up to the bathroom, ran water into the bath, feeling absurdly cheerful, as she had not done for a long time. The weight of irritation, frustration, the sense of powerlessness, was lifted, at least for now. She set everything to hand for him, and turned off the taps.

'Go ahead, Christopher,' she said, returning to the kitchen. 'It's all ready for you.'

She busied herself with the washing up. The bathroom was oddly silent, and she felt a tiny twinge of alarm. Then there were languid splashes, telling her he hadn't fallen asleep or drowned himself. She collected his dirty clothes and put them in the washing machine. She paused at the foot of the stairs. Among the splashes there came an unexpected sound: Christopher was quietly humming. Her own delight amazed her. Right or wrong, it seemed that for this moment he was happy.

He was a long time in the bath. Finally he emerged and called down to her. 'I've tried to clean up after myself, but I don't think I've made too good a job of it.'

'Don't worry. I'll sort it out later.'

He appeared in the kitchen, and she looked at him with a sudden shock. He was wrapped in her old threadbare bathrobe, his wet hair clinging in dark curls round his neck. He had managed to shave off the stubble, and had nicked his chin. There was a trail of blood, and she had to resist an impulse to wipe it away. His eyes were back to bright and blue. Clean, he was quite unexpectedly beautiful. The slap of sensation in her stomach was so strange and powerful that she shrank from putting a name to it. She thrust the crowding thoughts back.

'It's wonderful to be clean,' he said. 'Thank you for this.'

'You're welcome.'

'Will you tell me some of the stuff you've been finding out for me?'

'Of course, if you want.'

'Yes, yes I do.'

'Come into the living room, then. It's more comfortable there.'

He hesitated. 'You won't put the television on, will you?'

'No, of course I won't.' A thought struck her. 'What about music, are you OK with that?'

'Oh yes, I love music.'

They sat down.

Eileen said, 'You know, I've been thinking about what you told me about your angels.'

'Oh?'

'Did you know Satan has angels too? Could it be his you are seeing?'

Christopher shook his head doubtfully. 'I don't know. I always connected them with Big Voice, and I'm sure he is God.'

'When I looked up angels in my Bible, I didn't find any that seemed like the ones you described. I found angels who saved people from death, like Isaac when Abraham was going to sacrifice him, and Daniel, when he was in the den of lions. And angels looked after Jesus when he had been fasting in the desert. They are messengers, there to serve God.'

'But I am so bad,' Christopher said, almost in a whisper. 'Maybe that's why they, and he, are so angry.'

Eileen shook her head. 'I don't think so. Would you like to hear some music with an angel in it?' Christopher looked alarmed. 'It's not frightening, I promise. It's calm, joyful, reassuring.'

'What is it?'

'It's from Elgar's "Dream of Gerontius." The old man has died, and the angel, his guardian angel, is taking him to the Judgment Seat. But he's already saved. There's a wonderful duet. Towards the end they sing different words as well as different melodies, all interwoven. It's quite lovely.'

'All right, if you think so.'

'I've only got an ancient record player, so it will probably be a bit crackly.' She turned on the set, got the record out, dusted it. 'While you're listening, I'll get some lunch, shall I? If you want to, you can easily turn it off. Just flick this switch.'

'Can I look at the picture on the box?'

'Sure. The words are in there too, written by John Henry Newman. He was a Catholic cardinal.'

'Do you suppose he knew what he was talking about?'

'Probably.'

She left him sitting on the living room rug, in front of the dead fireplace, and went into the kitchen. Presently Elgar's music filled the house, transcending the inadequacy of the old equipment and the scratchy disc. She paused in her preparations, listened with satisfaction to the superb diction of the tenor as he sang of the profundity of the rest that comes when the soul is wrested from the body. There was no other sound from the living room. Then the voice of the angel came, powerful, warm, compelling, announcing the end of his work as he took the saved soul home to God.

She smiled to herself as she put things on the table, trying not to clatter the crockery. The angel and the soul of Gerontius sang their beautifully-timed dialogue, until they came to the glorious conclusion, separate and yet together, their themes interwoven, mutually sustaining. The angel spoke of the joy of knowing that heaven is at hand, and the old man's soul replied in confident serenity.

As the last notes died, she remembered with a jolt what came next. She didn't think Christopher was quite up to the demons' chorus, and she decided to switch the music off. Lunch was ready, anyway. She went through and turned off the set.

Christopher was asleep on the rug, curled up. Cardinal Newman's poem was in his hand, which lay limply at his side. His breathing was deep and quiet, and he looked completely at peace.

She studied him for several minutes, while a tide of indescribable feeling rose up from her stomach through her chest to her throat, threatening, she felt, to choke her. Asleep, relaxed, he had the tranquil beauty of a child. His skin was white. Against it the dark hairs stood out starkly, and long black eyelashes lay against his flushed cheekbones. He had wrapped the bathrobe so carelessly round himself that large areas of bare leg lay exposed. *He is trusting of me in that one way, at least. I am not threatening to him like one of his predatory females.* The thought was both sad and touching.

She looked at the clock. It was after one. She would have to wake him. If he was to get dressed and eat lunch and be away before she had to go to collect Michael, he needed to wake. She bent down, suddenly reluctant, and shook him gently by the shoulder.

'Christopher,' she said in a low voice. 'It's time to wake up.'

He stirred, rolled onto his back, his arms flung wide. The bathrobe fell away, revealing the white skin of his chest, the soft furring of dark hair. He opened his eyes, slowly focused them, and seeing her bending over him, smiled. It was for Eileen a moment of heart-constricting intimacy.

She backed away as he sat up. 'Lunch is ready. It's after one. You'll want to be away before Michael gets home.' He nodded. 'Why don't you go and get dressed?'

'All right.'

When he reappeared in the kitchen, she felt that both he and she were safe, protected by a conventional barrier of clothes. But the unnamed feeling in her stomach was still strong, and she found it difficult to eat. He, however, was almost blithe. He seemed unaware of any possible tension or discomfort, and ate heartily.

'The music was lovely,' he said. 'I wish I hadn't missed so much by falling asleep. It was so sunny there, so peaceful.'

'You can always listen to it again.'

'I would like to. Eileen, may I borrow the words? Take them down into the woods when I go? I would like to read them. I promise to keep them clean.'

'Of course.'

He finished his meal, pushed back his chair, stacked dishes on the draining board like a dutiful, well-raised son.

'You don't have to do that.'

'I don't mind.' He turned to her. 'I will go now, Eileen,' he said, suddenly serious. 'Thank you for the bath, and the food, and the music. I hope I haven't made too much work for you.'

'No, of course not. Shall I fix you something to take for your supper?'

He stood by the window, looking down into the sunlit woods, frowning slightly, while she swiftly prepared sandwiches, fruit, a flask. She handed the bag to him, and he put Newman's poem in with the food. 'I'll get your clothes dry. It won't take long, with this weather.'

'Thank you.' He hesitated. 'Will you come and see me tomorrow?'

'If you want that.'

'Yes. I want to hear about the stuff you have been looking up for me. I know you won't tell me anything frightening.'

'I'll try not to. Where will I find you?'

'The same place I was yesterday, near the rape field.'

'All right. I'll come in the morning, if nothing happens to stop me.'

'I will be looking out for you.' Suddenly he leaned over, brushed her cheek with his lips. She stopped breathing. 'Thank you, Eileen. For everything.'

179

The back door banged; the house was empty.

For some minutes Eileen stood there unmoving. Her brain was reeling. She flushed hot and sweat trickled down from her hairline. Gradually she came back to herself. It was as if she had been moving in a stately dance, or dreaming a long and complex dream. Now reality, the ordinariness of her familiar surroundings, began to filter through her dazed consciousness. She busied herself cleaning the bathroom and clearing up the lunch things. She would not let herself think, not for the moment. It was all too much, too much information, too much confusion. A headache threatened, throbbing at the base of her skull. She took some painkillers. Then she locked the back door and went to the school to pick up Michael.

Around five o'clock the phone rang. It was Annette Dyer.

'Hello, Annette. How are you doing?'

'Well, not too bad, all things considered. Whatever is all that noise?'

'Oh, that's Michael and Stephen. They're in the garden, making papier mache. There's a lot of wet newspaper and paint flying around out there.'

'They seem to be having fun.'

'Yes, don't they.' Eileen cradled the receiver between her shoulder and neck as she tried to wipe sticky bits of newspaper off her hands.

'Rather you than me. Eileen, I was wondering if you'd be very kind and take me to Caxford tomorrow.'

'Certainly I will. Usual time?'

'Yes, please.'

'How is it going?'

'Rather well, actually. I'll tell you all about it tomorrow.'

'All right, Annette. See you at one thirty.'

'Thanks, Eileen. Very soon I think I might be able to brave the bus.'

'Don't worry about it. I don't mind driving you. I can always do some shopping.'

Then Natasha rang. 'Mum, I'm staying over at Sean's. I'll see you tomorrow night.'

'OK. How is Sean?'

'Fine. He says hello.'

'Hello back.'

There was a pause. 'I might have something to tell you when I see you.'

'Oh?' Eileen smiled to herself. 'Might I be able to guess what it is?'

'Maybe.'

'I'll just have to wait, then, won't I?'

'Got to dash, Mum, we're going out. See you.'

After Michael had gone to bed and the chores were done, Eileen flopped in an armchair. For a while she idly watched a gangster film on the television, then she sickened of its inane dialogue and turned it off. The Elgar was still on the turntable. She turned the record over, dusted it, and dropped the needle down gently. She sat down again, stretched her legs and closed her eyes. For a while the noisy surface of her elderly record irritated her. *I must get a decent system. One day.* Then the music broke through, and technological deficiencies ebbed.

The voice of the Angel, deep, portentous, sounded a solemn note, warning of the approach of judgment. Eileen felt a shiver pass through her body, prickling the hairs on her arms. There followed the beatific innocence of the choir of angelicals, music full of confident delight, words exploring the mystery of the Incarnation and the God who sacrifices himself, the yet deeper mystery of divine love, so difficult for a human imagination to grasp. Then came the set-piece by the bass Angel of the Agony, pleading at the foot of God's throne for the souls of men and women, putting the sufferings of Christ between the sins of humanity and the just wrath of God, with that chilling moment when his voice drops to plead with Jesus, followed by the faint tones of the tenor Gerontius, dead now to his earthly existence, as he prepares to go before his judge.

Eileen shook herself, got up, switched off the record before it got to the purgatorial cleansing. She did not feel in the mood for the postscript. She pondered the notion of judgment. The soul of Gerontius was no longer afraid, because, the Angel implied, he had feared enough during his life in the body to live as he should, to circle round God as the centre of all things. *Have I done that? Am I doing it now? Should I be afraid of judgment? Am I completely off-beam? I just don't know, and there is nobody to ask. I have to do what seems to be right. My Governor reached out to the pariahs in his own society, didn't he? He cast out demons and restored the afflicted to health and sanity. Am I doing his work? Or is it my own agenda I am following? I cannot say. And what about Christopher?*

She felt again a sense of urgency, as if time was running out. Perhaps it was. Perhaps soon someone would miss him from his house in Caxford, and start asking questions. Perhaps his mother would call in unexpectedly. Did she do such things? Or maybe even one of his house-mates would realize he was not around, and say something. Were any of them sufficiently aware to be worried about him? She had no idea. She felt a tension rising, between the need to be patient, gentle, and unthreatening with him and the lack of time and leisure to tell him all she felt he needed to think about, or perhaps to rethink, because he had obviously given the whole subject of God if not thought, then great attention. She was troubled by the sudden cold idea that his very soul might be at stake. No, that could not be right. That was the God he saw, not hers, not he whose body and heart were broken for sinful humanity, who forgave right to the end.

She sighed, went to the window for a moment, and peered out into the dark. There was nothing to see. She made a cup of coffee, and opened her Bible where she had left it, marked at John's Gospel, her eyes falling on a passage that she had read many times.

"'Let not your hearts be troubled; believe in God, believe also in me. In my Father's house are many rooms; if it were not so, would I have told you that I go to prepare a place for you? And when I go to prepare a place for you, I will come again and take you to myself, that where I am you may be also.'"

That was it. That was what he needed to know, how much loved and treasured he was, that there was a place for him, in time and in eternity. How could someone as needy as he was possibly resist the compelling power of that love? She would tell him. But she would be careful. She knew that much.

She finished her coffee and let the dog out. A warm breeze blew gently up from the garden, bringing with it the earthy scent of the woods. She locked up, switched off the lights and went to bed.

She had died, she had passed through judgment, and been taken up into the very courts of heaven. And yet it was a strange, unexpected kind of heaven, crowded, noisy, full of colour and movement, with many beings milling about energetically. These creatures were odd, with squashed and faceted faces, jerky movements, grey skin, lopsided features. They looked like the boys' papier mache models. The throne of God was not there, but there was a sense that his presence was all around, or that he had not long departed. In her dream she was with Christopher. They were both wearing long, richly-embroidered robes, and he was taller, brighter than she, alive with laughter and flamboyant gestures. They were in the midst of a huge, pillared room, hung about with tapestries, like the great hall of an ancient castle, but warmer and full of light. The beings all around them were dancing, talking excitedly, though no meaning could be distinguished, and she and Christopher began to dance too, part of the moving mass of people, to the sound of gongs and harps and drums, fiercely percussive. He turned to her suddenly, his eyes bright, smiling, and took her round the waist, holding her hand in his free one, and whirled her round in a rhythmic, foot-stamping dance. He held her ever closer, and she could feel the heat and hardness of his body through the stiff material of his clothing, until she too began to feel hot, waves of heat rippling up from the ground through every part of her till she flushed up to her brows. And all around the noise grew more deafening, the music clanged louder, the dancers whirled, as Christopher bent over her, his bright eyes hypnotic, his smiling mouth inches away from her face. The erotic charge was strong and yet diffuse, a kind of universal fire crackling through her veins.

The dream shocked her awake, and for a few brief moments as she swam up to consciousness she felt a most intense happiness and mental clarity, as if all understanding and all joy had been conferred on her at a stroke. Then, as she came fully awake, the bitterness of reality struck her with cold, sickening force. Nausea and shame gripped her as she looked on the antics of her own unconscious, and heard the messages it was sending her. It seemed then that all good intentions, all innocent love, all spiritual striving, were stained, corrupted, self-indulgent. *Is that all this is about? Is that all it is, the fantasy of a frustrated middle-aged woman?* It was as if all her tentative and well-meaning communication with Christopher had been cruelly reduced to the tawdry level of a scandal-sheet. Her stomach churned.

Her first impulse was to run, back away, escape, disappear. *But I cannot. I promised him. And how is he at fault here? Not at all. So why should he suffer even more because I am guilty, of self-delusion if nothing else? Dear God, help me here, I am in over my head, drowning, too far from shore to be seen.*

She got up and put on her bathrobe, the same one that Christopher had worn earlier. Weariness engulfed her. She went downstairs, made some tea, and gathered herself together as she sipped it. She would just have to be even more careful. Perhaps this dream was some kind of warning, a message. She was not in heaven yet. There was still a long way to go, and many traps set for unwary feet. She must not give her destructive self any leeway; no, the rational self must be in charge, the part that controls and civilizes the savage. She could not afford the luxury of letting go, or she would take Christopher down into the dark.

It was two in the morning. She went back to bed, and lay with her eyes open. The moon had risen, half full, and it sent thin white light through her curtains onto the end of her bed. She watched it, mesmerised. Gradually the sense of horror and fear released by her dream subsided, and her reasoning self returned. But she had smelt the stink of corruption from her own soul, seen the darkness within, and it made her wary, almost timid. Here she was, trying to draw Christopher

183

out into the light, without even looking to see where she herself was standing. She ran the risk of drawing him out of his pit into her own. *Lord, I have been very stupid, very blind, perhaps even arrogant. I have got myself into a mess I cannot handle. Shine through me as if I were transparent; let Christopher see you, because you are irresistible. And if that cannot be, then show me a graceful way out, a way that will not harm him, or set him back, or lose the little way he has made. I wanted to save Christopher for you, and now I am asking you to save him from me. I am part of that world of corruption which has already done him damage, and I did not know it till now. What did I think I was? Something pure and disinterested?* She shook her head in disbelief. Her dream had revealed her own dark self, a being if not evil then at the least weak, proud, deluded and unwise.

Her mind strayed back to Christopher, sleeping in the woods under the moon. As sleep took her he seemed to change in her eyes. He was no longer a frightened, muddled man but a glorious heavenly being, untouchable by desire or decay. The moon slipped behind a bank of cloud, and the soft light faded.

Wednesday 5th June 1996

As soon as she had delivered Michael to school, she went to the woods as she had promised, taking a circuitous route to avoid meeting anyone she knew, though it was unlikely. *I am catching Christopher's paranoia.* When she arrived at his camp she found he had made little attempt to conceal himself. He was waiting for her, and greeted her with an incautious whoop and a broad smile, which Eileen found disconcerting.

'Hello, Christopher,' she said, putting her bag down on the ground. 'Did you sleep all right?'

'Funnily enough, I did. I don't know why, but I am feeling better. It might be because I haven't been taking my pills.'

Eileen was alarmed. 'Why not? I thought you were dead set on taking all your medication.'

He shook his head. 'I wouldn't go without my injections. That might be a disaster. But the pills don't do much good. They just make me dizzy and woolly and give me headaches. It's like they wrap me round in blankets, insulate me from any real feeling. I feel now I want to get back in touch with reality, even if it's bad. If I'm going to be miserable, that's tough, but I want to know what's going on in my own head, not be a protected zombie.'

Eileen raised her eyebrows. 'This is a great step.'

'Isn't it right, though,' he said, his eyes dark and glittering, 'it's danger that makes people feel alive?'

'So they tell me,' Eileen said, 'but you can take that theory too far.'

'I'll be sensible.'

'I hope so. Here's your breakfast, if you want it.'

'Thanks. I am starved.'

He seemed restless, and full of unusual vitality. As he munched, he paced round the tiny space between the trees, kicking up the damp brown leaves, inspecting the new growth, humming under his breath. He ate and drank quickly, almost bolted, like an animal on the run; but he was not fearful, as he had been, glancing all about as if afraid of being watched, hunted, trapped, but simply as if he could not contain the

185

energy pulsing through his body. Eileen found this puzzling. She wondered if it was another feature of his illness.

'OK,' he said, swallowing the last mouthful, 'tell me about all this stuff you've been tracking down for me. Oh, yes, here's Cardinal Newman. I kept him clean.' He handed her the printed booklet with the glowing yellow sun-surrounded angel on the cover. 'I liked the bit at the end, where the old guy's soul has to be washed. It's very peaceful. Stern, but reassuring somehow.'

Eileen smiled fleetingly. 'Don't forget, not everyone believes in Purgatory. But you are right, the end is amazing.'

Christopher dropped down and sat beside her on the blanket which he had spread for her to sit on. He was friendly and confiding, like a puppy or a small boy, and Eileen found his closeness disturbing. Although he was, of course, young enough to be her son, she could not think of him as a child. She wrapped her arms round her knees, as if holding something in, something powerful and unpredictable. She took a deep breath. 'Have you got your Bible with you?'

Christopher shook his head. 'No, I left it behind in my room in Denbigh Street. I thought it might be dangerous, maybe lead the angels to me.' He smiled sheepishly.

'Oh. Well, I've brought one of mine. It belonged to my mother. If you want you can borrow it and maybe read it when I've gone.' She hunted in the bag, found the RSV, and handed it to him. He took it gingerly, as if he was afraid it would suddenly show its teeth.

She told him where to look, and quietly he read, a frown of concentration between his brows. Once he exclaimed softly, and looked up at her. 'I have never felt the support of the everlasting arms.' He went back to his reading. 'This is a good bit,' he said presently, showing her the passage from Isaiah. 'Is he really gathering me up in his arms like a lamb?'

'I believe so.'

'How come I never knew that?'

'We all erect barriers, I think. The experts, of whom I am not one, would probably tell you that it is people's inherent sinfulness that gets in the way.'

'I can believe that,' he said, suddenly gloomy.

'There's another bit about the Good Shepherd,' she told him. 'Later on in John's Gospel. But I wanted you to see some of the stuff in the Old Testament where God is seen as merciful, kind, tender-hearted, grieved by his people's sufferings.'

He finished reading the references she had given him, and sighed.

186

'Does it mean everybody? I mean, if you are really bad, surely you are outside for ever.'

'Well, according to Ezekiel, God wants the wicked to turn from his wickedness and live.'

'Is that right?'

'I believe it is.'

'It seems like I've missed a lot. I know a lot of stuff, because I spent long enough hours at Sunday school and in my dad's churches, but somehow that never filtered through. Why do you think that is?'

'I don't know. But there's another one I found. Shall I read it to you? It comes from the prophet Hosea. He had an unfaithful wife, and he used his marriage as a sort of symbol of God's relationship with his people.'

'Read.' He handed her the Bible.

She found the page. '"When Israel was a child, I loved him, and out of Egypt I called my son. The more I called them, the more they went from me; they kept sacrificing to the Baals, and burning incense to idols. Yet it was I who taught Ephraim to walk, I took them up in my arms; but they did not know that I healed them. I led them with cords of compassion, with the bands of love, and I became to them as one who eases the yoke on their jaws, and I bent down to them and fed them. How can I give you up, O Ephraim? How can I hand you over, O Israel? My heart recoils within me, my compassion grows warm and tender. I will not execute my fierce anger, I will not again destroy Ephraim; for I am God and not man, the Holy One in your midst, and I will not come to destroy."'

He was silent when she finished. Then he said, 'Eileen, this is very weird. How can this guy be the same as the one who shouted accusations at me all day and half the night?'

'How indeed.'

He shook his head. 'I don't get it. But maybe I will find out. Is there more?'

'Of course, reams. Some of the Psalms might speak to you, and they are poems as well.'

'Will you read them to me? You have a peaceful sort of voice.'

'All right, if you like. I'll just read bits from different Psalms. You can always look them up again later.' She cleared her throat. '"I waited patiently for the Lord; he inclined to me and heard my cry. He drew me up from the desolate pit, out of the miry bog, and set my feet upon a rock, making my steps secure. He put a new song in my mouth, a song of praise to our God. Many will see and fear, and put their trust in the Lord."'

187

'"Up from the desolate pit,"' Christopher quoted softly. 'So he's been there too.'

Eileen continued. '"I waited patiently for God to save me; I depend on him alone. He alone protects and saves me; he is my defender, and I shall never be defeated."' She paused and looked at Christopher. He sat with his knees drawn up, his eyes closed. She went on. '"Whoever goes to the Lord for safety, whoever remains under the protection of the Almighty, can say to him, 'You are my defender and protector. You are my God; in you I trust. Father of the fatherless and protector of widows is God in his holy habitation. God gives the desolate a home to dwell in…he leads the prisoners to prosperity…'"'

Christopher was silent for several moments. 'So who, or what, is that terrible voice that tells me I am useless, rotten, corrupt, filthy, and should be punished?'

'I guess it's someone your mind has invented.'

'Not real?'

'I don't think so.'

He scratched his head, his brows creased. 'Is there anything else?'

'Yes, lots. But don't try to take it all in at once. Your brain won't be able to cope with it. Give it a rest for now.'

'All right. But I can read it later.'

'Sure. I'll leave you my Bible. Read St. John's Gospel. There's a lot of stuff in there for you.'

'For me?'

'Why not?'

'OK. I will read it. Will it make me afraid?' His eyes searched her face, as if for answers.

'I hope not. You don't seem afraid now.'

'You do that. You make me feel safer.'

A ripple of fear chased coldly across her skin. 'I can't be here all the time.'

'I know. But you are here now. Tell me something about your life.'

'I've told you a lot. I would much rather talk about you.'

'Like what?' The wariness came back, as a faint edge to his voice.

'I am concerned about you. Doesn't anyone know where you are?'

'Only you.'

'But what about your parents? Don't they ever visit, or phone?'

He shrugged. 'My mother phones sometimes.'

'What will she think when you are never at home?'

'The others will just say I'm out.'

'Won't she get worried?'

'I shouldn't think so. She's a very busy woman.' He laughed bitterly. 'They're all just glad I'm safe out of their way. She tries to do what she thinks is right, I suppose.'

'So what about your carers, your…what is it, CPN? Your social worker?'

'I told you, I make sure I am around for appointments. They think I am OK, I look clean, I chat to them as if nothing is wrong.'

'That must be difficult.'

'Not really. They are easy to fool. They are thinking of other things, and glad I seem all right and not a problem.'

'What about the other people at your house? Won't they notice your absence?'

'Maybe. But they won't say anything.'

'I can't help being worried about you, holed up here in the woods. The weather could change. Wouldn't you be better off at home?'

He shook his head fiercely. 'No, I wouldn't. Please believe me.'

'I believe you feel that, of course. But why, Christopher?'

'I can't tell you.' His voice was tight.

'You said you felt safe, that you trusted me.' As she said this she felt she was daring a great deal. He shuffled closer to her, until their shoulders were touching. His eyes, deep, dark, like a bottomless well, were on a level with hers. He took her hand. His hand was very warm, and she felt its heat travel up her arm.

'I do, you know that,' he said. 'I will tell you. I will, soon. Please be patient with me.'

He was too close. His eyes were too bright. She felt an overpowering impulse to hold him in her arms, to feel his warmth not just in her hand and arm but over her whole body. The feeling was no longer shocking, but it terrified and depressed her. She stood up quickly and dusted herself down. 'I'd better go now, Christopher.' The world seemed at one remove, and she could hardly hear her own voice. She gathered herself up with a great effort. 'I am taking my friend to Caxford this afternoon. I'll leave you with your reading. There's some more food in the bag for later.'

'OK. Thanks. Will I see you tomorrow? If I read what you said, I'll need to ask you about it.'

Feeling odd and faint, she leaned on a tree trunk. 'All other things being equal, I'll be here. But please, don't think of me as any kind of expert. I am on the same road as you.'

'Only further along.'

'Maybe, in some ways. Probably not in others.'

He too stood up, standing close enough for his sleeve to brush against hers. She backed away, and almost stumbled on an exposed root.

'Till tomorrow, then.'

On the way home she felt her normal, sane, earthbound self gradually return. With Christopher, among the trees, she was in another universe, a bubble out of time, and it was only with a struggle that she had not let herself drift with the powerful pull of her ungoverned impulses. How easy it would be, and how catastrophic, to seek from Christopher the strength and consolation that he sought from her, to rob him of his little peace. She had not thought herself so needy.

Once indoors and busy with mundane tasks the disturbing feelings receded. But, thinking about the next day, when she had promised to go to the woods again to talk to Christopher about his reading in St. John, she was filled with a terrifying mixture of elation and dread. What was going on? How much longer could she cope? Something, someone, she felt certain, was going to give way. Something would force a change. He seemed to be getting stronger, calmer, even saner, but she was going the opposite way. It was as if his illness had been some kind of protective barrier which was now crumbling away. *I am so afraid, so unsafe, so untrusting of myself, and yet I cannot stop this process, wherever it may lead. Perhaps I should tell someone, or run away, but who, and where? And I am bound to him. I promised to help. How could I explain? It would be such a betrayal, to abandon him now. I must go on. But help me, help me. I am weaker than I knew.*

Annette was waiting for her at the end of her drive. She looked a trifle anxious, but poised and smartly dressed. 'What do you think?' she said as Eileen got out of the car. 'I had that hairdresser woman over again. I got her to cut it short.'

'It suits you, makes you look younger.'

'That's what I thought. I'd let it go such a long time, and it was terribly out of condition, so I thought, why not, let's start again.'

'Good idea. Are you ready?'

'I'll just go and make sure I've shut the front door properly. I don't want Sam escaping.' Sam was visible through the window of the front room, his paws on the sill, looking forlorn. 'How's Tillie?' Annette asked as she got into the car.

'Hanging on, but more by the effect of the jab than anything else, I think,' Eileen said. 'There's not a lot more we can do for her.'

Annette patted her hand awkwardly. There was silence for a while as they pulled out into the village street and drove off in the direction of Caxford.

'So, what did Richard think of the new haircut?' Eileen asked.

'What does Richard make of the new Annette!' She smiled wickedly. 'Richard is confused, baffled even. I get the distinct impression he preferred me as I was. At least, from his point of view, when I was depressed he knew what I was up to.'

'You are horribly cynical, do you know that?' Eileen said. 'And what, if I may ask, *are* you up to?'

'Well, I have certain possible plans,' Annette said. 'Sorry if I sound mysterious, but they are still at the preparatory stage.'

'You're not thinking of running off with that chap at the group, Mark Pepper, are you?'

Annette hooted with laughter. 'He's only in his twenties, Eileen, do be serious. What would he be doing with an old trout like me, even if I have had my hair done? Anyway, nice fellow that he is, and believe me, I'm ever so grateful for his help, he's a bit too intense and dedicated for me. I am in the mood for a little fun these days.'

'So who is he then?'

'Who is who?'

'The man that's changed your life.'

'No, no, it's nothing like that. I'll let you know when things pan out. If they do.'

'I look forward to it. It's good to see you so much happier, anyway.'

'Well, you know, dear, something had to break, and I thought, why should it be me?'

'Quite right.'

Just before two she dropped Annette off at the corner of the street, waved goodbye, and drove to the car park. There were few people about. She did a bit of shopping, stowed the things in the boot of the car, had a desultory browse round the shelves of the library, but found her mind distracted, unable to settle on anything. She came out again into the High Street, and decided to stroll up to the tea shop where she and Christina had gone a few weeks ago. She crossed the access road to the Hotspot nightclub. All seemed quiet at a quarter to three in the afternoon. Nobody was about, but a dusty windowless black van was parked outside. Eileen shrugged, went into the café, bought a cup of coffee and sat down on a seat in the window to drink it and watch the torpid Caxford world go by.

She was thinking of nothing in particular, enjoying a generalized sleepy emptiness of mind, when she heard the roar and rattle of a

191

damaged exhaust and the black van appeared at the entrance of the access road and turned up the High Street towards her. For a few moments it was held up, still loudly revving, by minor roadworks, and Eileen had a clear view inside. Farthest from her the driver was in partial shadow, a man in dark clothing with either a very short haircut or a shaven head. On his left hand, resting on the steering wheel, she noticed a chunky gold ring. But her attention was not long on the driver, because the passenger, only a few feet away from where she sat, was Georgina Quilley.

At that time of day Georgina should have been in school, and she was still in her school uniform, except that she had removed her green-and-maroon striped tie and undone her white blouse by several buttons. She had also found time to put on several layers of makeup and do her hair in a way Eileen was sure would not have been approved by either her school or her parents. Georgina looked directly at Eileen, but she obviously didn't see her. Before they roared away, Eileen saw her turn to the driver with a smirk, at the same time lighting a cigarette and tugging down her blouse to reveal still more youthful cleavage.

Oh, no. Eileen felt slightly sick. What did the stupid little fool think she was doing, bunking off school to keep company with some highly dubious character from the local dive? There was no way Georgina could cope with the snake's nest she was stirring up. No wonder Angela was worried.

Annette was chatty on the way home. 'You'd never credit it, but that poor girl with all the kids and the husband who knocks her about is pregnant again–and with twins!'

'How does she feel about that?'

'Well, she seems permanently down, and who can wonder at it? But what I can't understand is how she can let the bloke who beats her up knock her up the next minute. She loves him, she says. Funny kind of love, if you ask me.'

'What about the old guy with the long hair and tobacco teeth?'

'Oh, you mean Neville. He wasn't there today. The word is he's found some fancy woman to console him and keep him in vodka. I can't imagine who'd want him. He's perfectly hideous.'

'And Mark? How is he?'

'Poor Mark is going through it a bit at the moment, I think. It seems he has a ghastly old bat of a mother who wears him down. I do wonder if he is going back into depression. He won't be able to run the group then, will he?'

For a mile or two they travelled in amicable silence. Then Annette said, 'Do you know, dear, I really think I will be able to take the bus next week. If I don't ring you, assume I've gone under my own steam.'

'This is great progress, Annette. Whatever next?' She drew up outside the Dyers' house.

Annette got out of the car and leaned on the door-frame. She grinned. 'Watch this space, is all I can say at present. Thanks for the lift.'

At six o'clock Natasha came home from work with her usual noise and flurry. The front door banged, there was a loud halloo and feet pounded up the stairs. Presently she came down into the kitchen where Eileen was cooking the supper, and slapped her left hand on the table. 'How do you like it?'

'Like what?' Eileen said, obtusely ignoring the rock on Natasha's finger.

'Mum, wake up, will you. I just got engaged, that's all.'

'I had my suspicions. Congratulations, darling. It is Sean, I suppose, is it?'

'Don't be daft, Mum, of course it's Sean.'

'Where is he?'

'He's on a course. He'll probably be over later.'

'We should celebrate.'

'We are. We're going over to Lambury, to the County, very posh, for a few drinks.'

'Nice. The meal's ready. Could you find Michael?'

'Where is he?'

'In the garden somewhere.'

When they were eating, and Natasha had silenced Michael's teasing remarks about her engagement with a few crushing rejoinders, Eileen said, 'So, what are your plans? Huge frothy wedding, morning suits, etcetera? I can just see Sean in a top hat.' Michael sniggered loudly and sprayed crumbs all over the tablecloth. 'When will it be, do you suppose?'

Natasha gave Michael a meaningful look. 'No idea, Mum. It won't be for ages yet. We've got to get some money together, and find a house. I don't suppose there'll be much over for a posh wedding.'

'I've got a few bob tucked away. You can have that if it'll help, though it's not much of a dowry.'

'What's a dowry?' Michael asked.

'In the old days,' Natasha said to him, staring fiercely, as if daring him to laugh, 'brides had to bring money or property into the marriage.'

193

'What?' said Michael. 'You mean she had to pay the bloke to marry her?'

'Not exactly, Michael,' Eileen said, smiling. 'And I'm sure Sean would have Natasha tomorrow, with or without the family fortune. Come on, let's leave Tash to get ready while we wash up.'

Michael said reflectively as he took down the tea towel, 'I didn't know you could get a girl to pay you to marry her. I must tell Steve.'

'Have either of you a bride in mind?'

'Well, Steve quite fancies Kelly, I don't know why. Maybe he just likes the way she screams and runs away when we chase her round the playground.'

'Why do you do that?'

'It's fun. We sing, "Smelly Kelly, legs like jelly," and she runs off. She doesn't mind, though, not really.'

'I hope not, poor child. What about you? Do you like anyone in particular?'

'No, girls are dumb. Anyway, I'm not even nine years old yet.'

'Sorry, I was forgetting that.'

'Mum, I have to learn some spellings.'

'OK, go and get them and I'll test you.'

'I hate spellings.'

'I know, but with any luck your new school will help you with reading and spelling and all that stuff till you are quite expert.'

'Dad says he'll help me too.'

'I'm sure he will.'

Thursday 6ᵗʰ June 1996

That morning it seemed warmer than ever. There was a tense stickiness to the atmosphere, somehow faintly ominous, as if a storm was coming slowly to the boil in some distant cosmic cookhouse. The sun broke blearily through a hazy pall of cloud. When Eileen went downstairs, cooling her bare feet on the kitchen tiles, Tillie whined from her basket. She looked anxious, and held herself at an odd angle, as if in discomfort. Staggering slightly from her basket she drank deeply, but refused food.

'It looks like another trip to the vet,' Eileen said to the dog with a sigh. 'If only going to the vet didn't seem even more traumatic than being ill. I hate it when animals are ill. People mostly get moderately sick, suffer for a while and get better, unless it's something really dire. But animals seem to be either perfectly all right or on the way out.' She stroked the dog gently. 'Never mind, old girl, we'll do our best for you.'

Looking round she decided she had neglected the domestic scene too long. Housework was not her forte but the dust and grime were beginning to clamour for attention. She wondered how Christopher could read down in the woods in the dark. Did he have a torch? She decided to do some chores before she went, to give him time to read in daylight.

Seeing Michael in at the school gate she said suddenly, 'Be nice to Kelly today, Michael.'

He looked at her blankly. 'Why?'

'Because.'

He shook his head; clearly he thought she had gone barmy. 'Don't worry, Mum. Everything's under control.' Then he was gone, into the milling crowd of shouting children.

Eileen smiled as she walked home. Her fears for Michael had lessened. Perhaps Charley was right; perhaps he could cope with all the changes better than she knew.

The heat and heaviness slowed her down. She kicked off her shoes, switched on the radio, and found a station where there was no talking,

195

just a rather frenzied violin running up and down what sounded like scales. *Maybe this will ginger me up. I need it.*

For the next two hours she worked determinedly, washing floors, stripping beds, inaugurating mountains of laundry, swiping dust from obvious surfaces. She ironed Christopher's dry clothes and put them in a bag with his supplies. Then she glanced at the kitchen clock. It was time to go and find him.

As she closed the gate at the bottom of the garden he stepped out silently from the shadow of the trees, making her gasp and step back. He seemed tense; his fists were clenched by his sides, his eyes were hard and shining. 'I thought you weren't coming.'

'I had to do some housework. The place was a pigsty.'

'I thought you'd forgotten me.'

'I don't think I could do that.'

Under the trees it was more sultry than ever. Christopher turned, dived down the path, and led her by devious routes. As they neared his camp he suddenly reached back and pulled off his grubby T-shirt. Seeing his slender nakedness, the muscles moving under the white skin, the sheer youthful smoothness of his body, made her feel momentarily faint. *For pity's sake, get a grip. How did Annette describe herself? An old trout. That's how I must seem to Christopher.*

But the feeling did not go away. Eileen was reluctant to face it, to analyze it, but ignoring it had not helped. Somehow, in the fecund darkness of her unconscious, where the critical light of reason had not shone, it had grown and thrived. It was not simple lust, she decided, it was more complex than that, although lust was clearly a factor. Her head swimming in the gathering heat, she berated herself. *You are quite ridiculous.*

By the time they arrived she felt exhausted, but Christopher apparently had energy to spare. As she flopped down on the blanket, he paced restlessly round, humming, stretching, squinting up into the leafy canopy.

'Christopher, have you got a torch?' she asked.

'Why?'

'I wondered how you could read down here in the dark.'

'I do have one, but I am saving the batteries for emergencies.'

'So?'

'It gets light very early. I wake up then. I've been reading since it was light. That's why I was waiting for you. I wanted to talk to you about it. I nearly came and knocked, but I couldn't quite get up the courage to come up the path, in case anyone saw me.'

196

'You should have. It's more comfortable than in the woods.'

'I thought you loved these woods.'

'I do. But I am getting too old to be sitting on tree stumps or damp ground for hours on end.'

'I don't think you are old.'

'Don't you? Well, I am quite.'

'No, you are no age at all to me. You are just yourself. It doesn't matter how old or young you are, it's what you have lived and learned that matters.'

'Maybe, but as you will probably one day find, your body gets older and starts protesting when you abuse it.'

'Do you think of me as young?'

'Yes,' she said, and before she could stop herself, 'young and beautiful.'

'You're kidding. I am an ugly weirdo.'

'That's nonsense.'

He looked at her, or rather in her direction, long and hard in silence, obviously thinking deeply. She felt her face begin to burn. Then he blinked, and shook himself as if dismissing an unproductive train of thought. 'I've been reading what you suggested. You're right, there's some amazing stuff in there. I must have heard a lot of it before, but somehow it didn't mean anything to me then.'

'And now?'

'Well, I can see like a glimmer of light, but it's too much. I can't see how it hangs together. I need help.'

'I'll do my best, if that will serve.'

'Who else have I got?' he said simply.

'OK.' She sighed, smiling, though her heart felt like a great weight in her chest. 'Let's get to work. The reason I thought you should read this gospel is that I think your view of God is skewed, and maybe it would put you right. The bits about judgment are there, of course. They are telling us we are all accountable. And you're right, we're all pretty rotten, even if we haven't done anything obviously terrible like murder. We're all self-serving and small-minded and lazy and mean-spirited and distractible. Even at our best we're nothing like we should be, what our creator intended us to be.'

'So what's the sense of trying?'

'You don't need to. All you have to do is accept the gift.'

'What do you mean?'

'Jesus has done it all, paid all our debts.'

'But why?'

197

'Because he is love.'

'Oh.'

There was a pause for a moment as he turned this over in his mind. Then Eileen said, 'Look, you seem to see God as a vengeful tyrant. But John says that if you have seen Jesus you have seen God. It's in John 14, when he's speaking to Philip.'

'Yes, I remember that bit.'

'So, if you want to find out what God is like, you need to find out what Jesus was like. It's only logical.'

'I suppose so.'

'So what is he like?'

Christopher thought. Then he said in a low voice, 'He was astonishing. I don't think human adjectives are adequate really.'

'Yes. He was radical, and I would guess very charismatic. The gospels are all written in plain unemotional style but Jesus comes through the pages somehow. I think if you really see him he is irresistible.'

'So why do so many resist?'

'Eyes tight shut, I would guess. Spiritual eyes, I mean. How can I say? I can't speak for anyone else.'

'Tell me some more.'

'No, you tell me. What does Jesus say about himself? What bits really struck you?'

Christopher grinned. 'This is like a scripture exam.'

'Sorry.'

'No,' he said. 'You're right. I wrote a few things down so I wouldn't forget.' He took a crumpled scrap of paper from his jeans pocket, smoothed it flat, and opened the Bible she had lent him. He flicked pages and began to read, slowly, with long pauses. She felt her eyes grow heavy, but it was not from tiredness or boredom; it was more like hypnosis.

'"I am the light of the world; he who follows me will not walk in darkness, but will have the light of life."' He looked up, searching her face. She nodded without speaking, and he turned pages again. '"If you continue in my word, you are truly my disciples, and you will know the truth, and the truth will make you free."'

'I am glad you found that bit,' Eileen said. 'The truth is hard, but it releases you from so much rubbish.'

'He says he is both food and drink,' Christopher said. '"I am the bread of life; he who comes to me shall not hunger, and he who believes in me shall never thirst." Hang on a minute, there's more. "Everyone who drinks of this water will thirst again, but whoever drinks of the water that I shall give him will never thirst; the water that I shall give him

198

will become in him a spring of water welling up to eternal life.'" He frowned, evidently perplexed. 'Eileen, is this true?'

'Certainly, in my experience.'

'So why didn't I ever catch on to all this from my dad? All those other people?'

'How can I say? I've never met them. But it's a sad fact that some people can put you right off, not draw you in. People, all of us, are very inadequate witnesses at the best of times.'

'You aren't.'

Eileen shook her head. There was nothing she could think of to say. 'What else did you find?'

'Guide me.'

'Well, what about the miracles of healing? There aren't that many in John, actually. The other gospels record more, if I remember right.'

'Could it really be that he brought his friend back from death?'

'What, Lazarus? Why not? He had power over life and death even as a human being. But look at the paralyzed man, who found he could walk, and the sick child who was cured, and the blind man who could see. What does that say to you?'

Christopher hesitated. 'That I might be healed too?'

'Isn't it possible?'

'I've never dared to think about it.'

'So what else leapt from the pages of John?'

'I liked the bit about Jesus as the Good Shepherd. If I could only believe it was true. It would be lovely to be a lamb carried in the shepherd's arms.'

'I think you are a lamb.'

'What about you?'

'Me, too.'

Christopher was silent, staring thoughtfully into the distance. Then he jumped up and began to pace. 'So, where do we go from here? What is the outcome? What do we have to do?'

'Did you read the bit about washing his disciples' feet?'

'Yes, but I'm not sure I understood it.'

'It was really quite a shocking thing to do. But I think he was trying to make them, and us, understand that that is the distinguishing sign of belonging to him—loving and serving one another.'

'Is that what you are doing for me?'

She swallowed. 'That's what I wanted it to be, Christopher. But who knows? Like I said, people, me definitely included, are pretty poor vessels. They, I, are all he has to work with, and we're not brilliant.'

199

'I think you are brilliant.'

She shook her head sadly. 'We're all in the same boat, you, me, everyone. Struggling to get it right. The only difference is that if we have him, we have help.'

'But he is dead, he is not here.'

'No, he is alive, his spirit is here, now, with me, with you.'

He gazed at her in puzzled fascination. 'Do you really think so?'

'If I did not have him, life would be worthless. There would be no point.'

'But you have a life, family, friends.'

'Even so.'

'I've got to think about all this. I'm getting a headache.'

'So am I.'

'Maybe it's time for breakfast. Or is it lunch?'

'Sorry, Christopher. I forgot you hadn't eaten. Here.'

She handed him the bag. He insisted on sharing the food with her, and it was a companionable meal. She felt shattered, as if they were the exhausted and only survivors of some overpowering cataclysm. For a few minutes, as they ate and drank in the green quietness among the trees, there was peace between them.

She broke the silence. 'I will have to go soon.'

He nodded. 'Will you come again?'

'Yes. Tomorrow.'

'OK. What shall I read while I am on my own?'

She smiled. 'Psalms.'

'All right.'

She got up, dusted the crumbs off, and stretched her stiff limbs. 'Give me the Bible a minute.' She looked for the verse. 'Listen to this— it's very short. Joel 2 verse 25: "I will restore to you the years which the swarming locust has eaten."'

'That's poetry.'

'A lot of it is. The Psalms are.'

'Can that happen? Will my locust years be restored?'

'I don't know. But I know it's possible.'

'I will read some more, and think. Thank you, Eileen. See you tomorrow.'

Friday 7ᵗʰ June 1996

Eileen woke feeling sluggish and heavy. The night had been sultry, the air thick and still, and she had slept poorly, tossing in her damp and wrinkled sheets, her dozing brain tormented by fleeting and chaotic images to which she could ascribe no meaning. Michael too seemed tired and irritable. Even the prospect of a weekend with his family and carpentry with his father seemed insufficient to jolly him out of his uncharacteristic sullenness.

Tillie seemed no worse, but she was still not eating. Under the dry coat Eileen could feel her ribs, and it gave her such a pang of sadness and worry and guilt that her stroking hand recoiled. She rang the vet, and made an appointment for the afternoon. She sighed deeply as she hung up; it was not a trip she could look on with any pleasure or anticipation of anything but temporary alleviation, and even that bought at a price. She felt dragged down, weary and dejected, and as she put food together for Christopher she was suddenly impatient, even resentful. *How am I supposed to cope with all this alone? Who am I, what can I do? It is too much. Maybe I brought it all on myself. But what else could I have done? I am out of my depth, and I am afraid. It's like walking on thin ice, and the cracks are running away out of control with my every foolish step.* She blinked away tears of tired self-pity, and doggedly set off for the woods.

He was waiting for her in his first camp, barely a quarter of a mile down the track. She was startled as he materialized from the shadow of the trees. 'What are you doing back here? Did you think I wouldn't come?'

'No, I knew you would.' He smiled, laid a hand on her arm, making her shiver. 'I thought I would save you a long walk. You are looking tired.'

'I suppose I am.'

'Come and sit down.' He guided her gently to the tree stump as if she were a convalescing invalid. His solicitude touched her, made her feel weaker, and the temptation to rest on him, especially as he seemed so normal, so in control, grew perilously strong. An overpowering desire simply to lean against his shoulder and sag, both physically and mentally, welled up in her. Passively she resisted it, letting it recede, telling herself, not fiercely but dully and repetitively, that however it seemed, he was the sick one, he was the needy one. She drew in a deep breath, steadied herself, and sat down, smiling up at him faintly. He looked at her with concern. 'Are you all right?'

'Sure. Of course I am. I don't sleep well this weather, I guess that's it.'

He nodded. 'You'd probably be better off in the woods. It's cooler here.'

The thought of sleeping with Christopher under the trees did not help. The sudden hot surge of longing that leapt up from feet to head nearly knocked her off her perch. She swallowed down a spasm of nausea. With a great effort she said, 'Have you been reading?' Her voice did not sound as if it belonged to her, but Christopher did not seem to notice.

'Listen to this,' he said. 'The first bit is good, but then it gets scary. I'm glad I read it this morning, in the daylight, not last night. OK, John 5 verse 24: "...Truly, truly I say to you, he who hears my word and believes him who sent me has eternal life; he does not come into judgment, and has passed from death to life. Truly, truly I say to you, the hour is coming and now is, when the dead will hear the voice of the Son of God, and those who hear will live." I can cope with that bit, that's OK, but the next bit is worrying. "Do not marvel at this; for the hour is coming when all who are in the tombs will hear his voice and come forth, those who have done good, to the resurrection of life, and those who have done evil, to the resurrection of judgment."'

'So what is it that bothers you about that? Is it the thought of the dead waking? It is a bit spooky, I suppose.'

'No, not really,' he said. 'I think it's the idea that even when you are dead you aren't safe. He is still on your case.'

'Of course. But it doesn't have to be scary. The outcome is in your power. I told you yesterday, all you have to do is turn to him, turn your life around, accept what he has done for you.'

'You think my life can turn around?' Christopher whispered.

'Yes.'

He fell silent, obviously plunged in a deep well of thought. He was sitting on the blanket at her feet; he shuffled into a more comfortable position, leaned up against her knees, and closed his eyes. The sick feeling in her guts returned in force.

'Read to me, Eileen,' he said. 'Read me bits you think might help.'

'All right.' She cleared her throat. 'Here is the bit that tells us we are not alone. "I have much more to tell you, but now it would be too much for you to bear. When, however, the Spirit comes, who reveals the truth about God, he will lead you into all the truth…the Spirit will take what I give him and tell it to you.'"

'The words sound different,' Christopher said without moving.

'That's because I have a different translation, a bit more modern,' Eileen said. 'It doesn't matter; it's still the same message. Shall I go on?'

'Yes, please.'

'Here's the bit where Jesus is praying for his disciples, not just the ones he had then, but the ones he would have in the future.'

'Like you.'

'Yes, like me. It's long, so I'll pick bits out. You can read all of it for yourself if you want to, later on. "I pray for them. I do not pray for the world, but for those you gave me, for they belong to you…And now I am coming to you, and I say these things in the world so that they might have my joy in their hearts in all its fullness…I do not ask you to take them out of the world, but I do ask you to keep them safe from the Evil One."' Christopher exclaimed something unintelligible. She went on. '"I pray not only for them, but also for those who believe in me because of their message…Father! You have given them to me, and I want them to be with me where I am, so that they may see my glory, the glory you gave me; for you loved me before the world was made."'

Neither spoke for a while. There was no breeze, and the leaves hung limply in the stillness. Even the birds were silent. Despite the heat, Eileen shivered. 'It is said he is still doing that. Praying for us sinners, pleading at the foot of God's throne.'

Christopher shifted and sat up. 'He certainly seems to be the key to everything, as far as I can tell.'

'Yes.'

'Is there any more?'

'Aren't you getting fed up with it?'

He shook his head. 'No, I could go on listening to you all day.'

She sighed. 'I haven't got all day. My poor old dog seems to have slipped down again. I'm taking her to the vet this afternoon.'

'Oh. I'm sorry.'

'Just a few more verses, then. You can find them all again later. I've written them all down.'

'Thank you.'

'Here we are. "See how much the Father has loved us! His love is so great that we are called God's children—and so, in fact, we are…this is how we know what love is: Christ gave his life for us…this is what love is: it is not that we have loved God, but that he loved us and sent his Son to be the means by which our sins are forgiven.'"

Christopher turned to face her, and gazed at her intently. 'Why did you pick that particular bit?'

She shrugged. 'I suppose it seemed to me you needed most of all to know how much God loves you, not that he wants to hound and pursue and torment you.'

'Is that how you understand love?'

'Yes, I suppose so, if I understand it at all.'

'But what about loving people?'

'That's supposed to flow from the love of God, isn't it? It says it in here, about loving and serving one's brothers and sisters.'

'Do you do that?'

'I try to. Perhaps not very successfully.'

'Is that why you are here, helping me, wasting your time on a useless headcase? Does it mean that you love me?'

Eileen felt her breath choked out of her body. A tight band of fear closed around her chest, and there was a singing in her ears as if she was going to faint; but nothing happened. 'I guess so, if you are thinking in that way.'

Christopher was absorbed in his own train of thought, apparently unaware of the turmoil he was causing. Then, suddenly, a look of sheer panic crossed his face, and he gripped her wrist so hard it hurt. 'Eileen, tell me, quickly.' His voice rose in alarm. 'I've just thought—oh, no, what an idiot I am! What day is it today? Tell me.'

Eileen was taken aback, so sudden was his change of mood. 'Whatever is wrong? What does it matter what day it is?'

'It does, believe me.'

'It's Friday, the seventh of June,' she said.

He sagged, slumped, sighed with relief, his face breaking out into a beam. 'Thank God for that. For one terrible moment I thought I had cocked it up. No, it's OK, don't worry. I have an appointment with Dr. Partridge. I must keep it. It's on Monday at twelve, so I'll have to travel back on Sunday night to be ready for when Jackie comes to fetch me.'

'What, walk all night like before?'

'Yes. Then I'll walk back here on Monday night. So I won't see you till Tuesday.'

The thought of his absence brought both relief and disappointment. 'I could drive you to Caxford.'

'No. Thanks, but no. I daren't be seen. My whole cover depends on it.'

204

'Your clean clothes are in here,' Eileen said, indicating the bag. 'I can leave food for you tomorrow, if you like. But I won't be able to come down here. Michael will be away, but there's every chance Natasha and Sean will be around, and with them I never know when.'

'I understand. It will be strange, not seeing you for three whole days. Will you be all right?'

What does he mean? Has he seen something, does he know? 'I'll be fine. How about you?'

He nodded slowly. 'I've just got to keep calm, follow my plan, and not get agitated. I can't afford to let Jackie or Dr. Partridge suspect anything.'

'Wouldn't it be better to tell your psychiatrist what's bothering you? Couldn't he help?'

'You don't understand,' Christopher said, his dark eyes fathomless. 'None of them can help. They just want me quiet. I'll explain it all to you, I will, I promise, soon, when I am brave enough.'

'Why do you need to be brave?'

'Because you might not like me any more,' he said, his voice barely audible. 'If you knew how bad I am.'

'I am pretty bad myself.'

'I can't believe that.'

'I'm afraid it's true. But we can all be forgiven. Do you believe that yet?'

'I don't know. That's what I'll be thinking about over the next few days.' He stood up, and she too got to her feet. He was very close to her; his eyes, hands, mouth were on a level with hers. 'Don't forget me.'

'Of course I won't.'

There was silence then for a long moment, a silence full of questions, crackling with contradictory possibilities.

'You'd better go. You've got to take your dog to the vet. I hope she's OK.'

'Yes. Goodbye, Christopher.'

But she did not move. It was as if her feet had taken root.

'Goodbye, Eileen.' He gently patted her arm in farewell. His action broke the tension, and she backed off.

'See you on Tuesday,' he said.

She nodded, found her way back to the path, and looked at him with difficulty.

'Take care of yourself, Christopher.'

'I will.'

205

When Eileen parked at the vet's, with Tillie on her blanket on the back seat, the receptionist came out to speak to her. 'Mr. Ballard says bring her in the side door. Then he can just give her the shot and you can put her back in the car. It'll save hanging about in the waiting room with all the other animals.'

'Thank you,' Eileen said. 'That's very thoughtful.'

She carried Tillie into the surgery. She felt light and insubstantial, her coat dry and rough. The vet examined her briefly and silently, then sank the needle into the loose skin at the back of her neck. 'She seems to have gone down again quite quickly. I would guess that after this time there won't be a lot of point in keeping up the injections.'

'Do you think, then, she is worse than we realized?'

'It looks that way, I'm afraid. This shot will help for a few days, maybe a week, then I would expect it to be a case of nature taking its course.'

'Will she be in pain?' Eileen asked.

'I don't think so, but if she seems distressed you can bring her back in.'

'But then that will be that.'

The vet nodded. 'I'm really sorry. The only thing is to tell yourself what a long and happy life she has had.'

Which is more than you can say for many humans.

She put Tillie back into the car, paid her bill and drove back to Holton. She collected Michael from school in the car.

'Why is Tillie with you? Why aren't we walking?' he said.

'I've taken her to the vet for another jab.'

'Is Tillie going to die?'

'Sooner or later, I'm afraid so, Michael.'

He was quiet for a few moments. 'Why do animals have to die?'

'Well, I suppose one way to look at it is, if none of the old dogs died and people kept getting puppies the whole world would soon be overrun with dogs.'

Michael looked at her, his mild blue eyes bright with tears. 'You will be terribly sad, won't you, Mum?'

'You bet I will. But right now we just have to make her as comfortable as we can, don't we?'

Michael nodded.

'Are you playing with Stephen?'

'No, he's going to his auntie Mandy's for tea.'

'All right. I've got to get you to Caxford by five, then you'll have your supper with your family. I've got your bag packed, so what shall we do till then?'

'I want to have a bath.'

206

'You *want* to have a bath?'

'Yes, so I can sail paper boats.'

'I can't believe I am hearing this.'

'It's not because I want to wash. But if I sail my boats I will get wet anyway, so I might as well be in the bath with them.'

'Devastating logic. Go on, then. I'll be up in two minutes.'

In the end it was all rather a rush. She dropped Michael off at Social Services where his father was waiting for him in the noisy car. Andy and Michael roared away. Eileen and Charley waved.

'Does he seem OK?' Charley asked, looking at Eileen with her shrewd sideways glance.

'Yes. I have to say he seems to be coping remarkably well.'

'And you?'

'I am glad Michael is out of the way really. The dog is ill and not likely to improve. There's no point in Michael being upset.'

'I'm sorry.'

'Well, one jolly happening, my Natasha has announced her engagement.'

'Congratulations. Does that mean you'll be busy?'

'I hardly know. Anyway, it's probably all a long way off.'

'Do you approve of her fiancé?'

'Very much. Twenty years ago I'd have had him myself.'

Charley laughed. 'I think you might want to rephrase that, Eileen. Well, it's time to knock off. I'll be in touch.'

Eileen picked up Natasha from the florist's, drove her home and cooked them both a hasty meal. Natasha disappeared upstairs to prepare herself for Sean's arrival. Eileen left the dishes in the sink and went to choir practice. The sky was darker than it should have been, the air was leaden, and she thought she heard the soft distant rumble of thunder. By the time she arrived at the church door she was sweating. *I'll welcome rain. But not for Christopher.* Thinking of him, even in passing, brought back a faint reminder of the feelings he had evoked in her earlier, and she felt that same lurching of her stomach, the faintness, the sense of unreality. It was a relief to step into the lighted church and hear the chatter and laughter from the vestry.

Ten minutes later most of the choir members had arrived, greeted one another, collected music and assembled in the choir stalls. The little girls had been brought to order, and were now drawing and writing notes on little bits of paper, huddled together at one end. At the other, smiling to herself, apparently in some other dimension, sat Georgina Quilley.

207

'Philip is late,' said Gillian Clayton. 'It's not like him.' The church door creaked on its hinges. 'Goodness, it's Marie back! How nice to see her up and about.'

Eileen said nothing, but she was surprised. Marie had not said anything, but then, Eileen had not spoken to Marie for several days. Surprise intensified when, immediately afterwards, Philip arrived, closed the door behind him, took Marie's elbow and tenderly guided her up the nave to her place. Amid the chorus of greetings he remained silent, a small, inscrutable smile on his face; and Eileen knew that she was not the only one to have registered that Philip and Marie had gone public. She heard Gillian Clayton murmur, 'Well, well.' Then Marie slid into the choir stalls beside them, her cheeks tinged with pink.

'Hello, stranger,' Eileen said *sotto voce*. 'Good to have you back. Are you well?'

Marie smiled rather guiltily. 'Yes, I am, thanks, Eileen. Sorry if I've been a bit neglectful lately. Things OK with you?'

'I'll talk to you later, if there's time,' Eileen said. 'It looks like Philip wants to start.'

As it happened, there was no time to talk. After choir practice Philip whisked Marie away in his car. Gillian Clayton evidently wanted to discuss this latest development, but Eileen made an excuse and went home. She felt oddly dislocated, an alien in her own country. It was as if everyone was blithely abandoning her—Michael, Marie, Christopher, even Tillie. *Don't be ridiculous. Self-pity makes fools of us all.* Nevertheless as she approached the house she was relieved to see Sean's car parked outside. Company would be nice. She let herself in. The dirty dishes she had left had all been washed. Sean's jacket was hanging in the hallway. But there was no sign of life. For a moment she was puzzled. Then, with a jolt, she realized that they must be upstairs.

For a long moment, standing in the dark hallway, she battled with a wave of misery so intense that it threatened to swamp her. She gripped the stair rail so tightly that it hurt her hand; the strength of the feeling almost robbed her of breath.

After a few minutes she went into the kitchen, said hello to the dog and put the kettle on. Then she went into the living room, switched on the television and turned the volume up. As she drew the curtains against the gathering dark, Sean and Natasha appeared, talking unnaturally loudly, and looking flushed and uncomfortable. After a few moments of neutral chat they went out, and Eileen was left alone.

The pain ebbed to a dull, throbbing ache in her throat. *It's not only Christopher that needs a prop.* She turned to the Psalms.

"Lord, you have examined me and you know me.

You know everything I do; from far away you understand all my thoughts.

You see me, whether I am working or resting; you know all my actions.

Even before I speak, you already know what I will say.

You are all around me on every side; you protect me with your power.

Your knowledge of me is too deep; it is beyond my understanding…"

Eileen closed her Bible before the next verses. She let a tear run down her cheek; but the words had calmed her.

Then the phone rang. It was David. 'You'll be getting a letter from my solicitor. I just wanted to tell you about it, so it didn't come altogether out of the blue.'

'Thank you.'

'I'm assuming that you haven't changed your mind, had second thoughts.'

'No, it's all as we left it.'

'Well, we might as well be businesslike. I'm going to pay the usual sum into your bank account until the end of the year, when it will be cancelled.'

'Fair enough.'

'But I'm proposing to sign the house over to you. It was mostly your money that bought it anyway.'

'That's generous of you.'

'If you have any problems with the arrangements, will you talk to me before you instruct your solicitor?'

'Yes, of course.'

'It must be best for everyone to keep things civilized.'

'I quite agree.'

'All right then, Eileen. That's really all I wanted to say. I'll be in touch again.'

'Goodbye, David.'

It was what I wanted. What I said I wanted: even now I hardly know what I want. But it was still a body blow. She felt unnaturally calm, as if all feeling was suspended, in some untouchable place, too raw and tender to be lightly approached. She turned off the lights and went to bed. She was beyond words, beyond prayer, alone in the swallowing dark.

She was in a dark room, in a cottage with bare plaster walls, devoid of furniture or any adornment, damp, with a floor of hard-packed earth. The door, hanging on broken hinges, and painted a dry, cracked powder-blue, hung inwards, sagging open. Pouring in through the opening came many tiny golden creatures, brilliantly shining, chattering and chirruping. At first Eileen took them for tiny angels with sharp swords; they swarmed around her feet, stabbing at her with many painful pinpricks. She could not move: her ankles were chained to iron rings set in the floor. Then, looking more closely, she saw that they were not angels at all, but insects, with hard clattering wings and brittle carapaces, and what she had thought were swords were in fact stings, sharp golden shafts of venom, piercing the skin of her bare feet. She cried out in pain and protest, and the creatures backed away, forming a chittering circle round her, moving restlessly. Then the noise sank to a dull resentful mutter. A deep-shadowed doorway led to an inner room, and in the gloomy space stood a dark figure, dressed in homespun with a wide leather belt. His face was in shadow, but Eileen knew it was David, because on his gauntleted wrist poised a huge, beautiful owl, unmoving save for its round orange eyes. The bird, without leaving David's hand, reared up and spread its wonderfully striped and speckled wings, and the insect-creatures turned and ran, squeaking, through the crumbling doorway. Eileen sank down on the cool, damp floor, her pierced feet throbbing. As she half-lay in the same position, the scene changed. She found herself on a grassy hillside, up each side of which many people were steadily climbing. All of them were looking up into the sky, shading their eyes with their hands, and when Eileen also looked up, she saw the sharp black bite in the side of the sun and realized she was looking at an eclipse. The gathering people gave a shout in unison, so loud that it shook her awake, long enough to contemplate the dream before she sank back into sleep.

Sunday 9th June 1996

She woke after a night of fitful sleep to a heavy dew and a feeling of chill, but by mid-morning the heat and humidity were building again. Marie was in the choir for the morning service. As Eileen slid in beside her Marie smiled conspiratorially. In the vestry afterwards, unbuttoning her cassock, she said, 'I haven't seen you for ages, Eileen. If you're not busy, pop down for a chat tomorrow.'

'OK, I'll do that.'

She picked up Michael at five o'clock. On the way home he was full of chat about the new hutch for Bill, and scornful of the help offered by Harry. 'Dad said he was too young to bang nails in, so Harry went off in a mood and got told off for pinching Ellie.'

'Oh. And where was your mum in all this?'

'Mummy doesn't like it when we're arguing and fighting.'

'That's understandable.'

'But Harry is a pain. He's just a kid.'

'So are you just a kid, Michael.'

'But I am bigger and more sensible. That's what Dad says.'

'Poor old Harry. Wouldn't it be better if you and your brother could get along?'

'Maybe.' After that he fell silent, looking out of the car window. 'The grass is looking all brown.'

'Mm. We need some rain. It keeps trying, but nothing much has happened yet.'

Natasha and Sean appeared briefly during the evening, chiefly for Natasha to collect clean clothes, as she was planning to spend at least some of the following week at Sean's. They seemed in good spirits, but were soon away about their own affairs.

Monday 10th June 1996

Eileen took Michael to school, and then spent an hour sorting out his bedroom and his laundry. On her way down to Marie's she decided to call in at the village shop for a few forgotten items. Mrs. Pickett was alone behind the counter, looking rather strained.

'Good morning,' Eileen said. 'How are things?'

Mrs. Pickett shook her head. 'Reg is not so good. Nora is out the back now, seeing to him. Not that we're especially busy. I can manage on my own. What can I do for you, dear?'

Eileen made her modest purchases and after a few sympathetic remarks she left the shop. She met Marie coming in, followed by Angela Quilley and Kit Muldoon.

'I won't be long,' Marie said. 'I just thought I'd get us some decent biscuits.'

'All right. I'll wait for you outside.'

Marie was longer than she expected. When she came out she took Eileen's arm, and they strolled slowly down the main street before turning into Marie's lane.

'You were a long time getting a few biscuits,' Eileen said.

'I know. Kit Muldoon was stirring things up as usual, and Mrs. Pickett and Angela were talking about that chap you saw in the woods. I didn't know he was still about.'

Eileen's stomach lurched. 'Is he?' she asked. Her voice shook slightly but Marie seemed oblivious.

'Apparently someone, one of the Muldoon boys I think,' Marie said, 'saw him last night, crossing a field as you go out of the village towards Caxford. It was dark, but he saw him in his motorbike headlights.'

'How did he know it was the same person?'

'No idea. But if it was, he's been hereabouts for quite a while. I wonder why he's hanging around down here.'

'Who knows?'

Marie looked at Eileen thoughtfully. 'You haven't seen him again then?'

Eileen shrugged, but said nothing.

'If it is the same person,' Marie said, 'surely someone should be told. I can't believe nobody has realized he's missing.'

'Mm.' Eileen felt a pang of acute disappointment. *I would have told her. At least I would have told her something. Not everything, of course. But now, somehow, I can't. She won't understand.*

They reached Marie's door. Marie let them in and put the kettle on.

'So,' Eileen said, smiling, gathering herself up. 'What's the latest on the Philip front? You two caused quite a stir on Friday, you know, coming in together like that.'

Marie grinned. 'Yes, I imagined it would have that effect, if only on Gillian Clayton. Was she after more information?'

'Naturally. But I'm afraid she was disappointed.'

'Gillian is a good soul really. She just hates to think she's missing anything.'

'Her own life may possibly be on the dull side. Unlike yours, it seems. Are you going to tell me or not?'

Marie handed her a cup of coffee. 'Well, things are certainly moving, I'll say that, and I am hoping that there will be developments to Philip's advantage. He's wasted here, of course.'

Eileen nodded. 'And for all we know our new rector may want to change all the traditional music and have kids on bongo drums or a bagpipe ensemble.'

Marie shuddered. 'Please, spare me. It's more likely he'll ask you to play if Philip goes.'

'If?'

'I can't really say more until things are all official. You understand.'

'Of course. But I don't fancy trying to fill Philip's shoes in any capacity. Music aside, where do you fit into all this?'

'With Philip, I hope.'

'So if Philip went, you'd go too. Is that how it is?'

Marie leaned on the kitchen counter and sipped her coffee. 'I only rent this place. And Stephanie's hardly ever around. You couldn't say she needs me. There's only you I'd miss here.'

'Goodness, don't even put me in the equation.'

They ambled into the lounge and sat down in the squashy armchairs.

'Whatever happens, I won't be far away,' Marie said. 'We can still see each other.'

'So I should hope. It's got beyond the bodice-ripping stage, then, has it? More the cosy cocoa in front of the fire?'

Marie laughed. 'Perish the thought. I may be an old bag, but Philip is not quite ready for the carpet slippers and pipe routine. And I'm happy to say there may yet be a few more bodices to bite the dust.'

'I'm glad to hear it. It's time you looked after your own interests. I wish you both more than well.'

'I know you do. Thank you, dear. And what about you?'

'The latest is, Michael is returning to his family permanently at the end of this school term. Things seem to be going OK there, I think. My poor old dog is on her last legs, though.'

'Oh dear. I am sorry. Poor old Tillie.'

They fell silent for a moment, each busy with her own thoughts.

'Natasha and Sean are engaged, did I tell you that?' Eileen said.

'No, indeed you didn't. Well, how delightful. When's the wedding?'

'I've no idea, neither have they.'

'Still, something to look forward to.'

'I suppose.'

'You sound a little jaded. Aren't you pleased about it?'

'Oh yes. If Tash is happy, that's good enough for me. Sean is a lovely fellow. I can't fault her choice.'

'So?'

'Oh, perhaps I'm a bit off "happy ever after" just now.'

Marie smiled sympathetically. 'Is it final then, you and David?'

'It is.'

'Your choice?'

'My choice.'

'Not easy even so, I'd guess.'

'No.'

'Perhaps I shouldn't be crowing about Philip so much, in the circumstances.'

'Nonsense. Crow away. I don't begrudge you a thing, you know that, and I hope it lasts forever, for your sake. But if I am completely truthful, the only part I really envy you is the occasional bout of rampant lust.'

Marie smiled wickedly. 'Well, who knows what, or who, may be lurking around the corner? And don't tell me you're too old. That's what I thought. And I was wrong.'

Walking home an hour later, having thoroughly discussed Michael's future, the possibility of Eileen's getting another dog, and sundry ideas on the likelihood of weddings, Eileen pondered this remark of Marie's, and was startled to find the thought sobering, even depressing. *I've had enough of uncertainty. Of not knowing. When I thought I was past it, too old to care, I was glad. I can't wait to feel that way again. Love, or one of its myriad substitutes, is a great disrupter of order and reason. It brings wild hope in its train, and that's*

214

usually untrustworthy. No. Let me get old unnoticed, and keep my own counsel. I want to be done with life, and love, and fecundity, in all its forms. I want to be left in peace.

Tuesday 11th June 1996

The way through the woods that morning, carrying a bag, to Christopher's second camp near the Dyers', seemed long and weary. No freshening breeze lifted the heavy-hanging leaves, and the woods seemed strangely silent, as if even the birds were too worn out to sing. For Eileen it was less a walk than a trudge. By the time she approached the grassy pathway to where she hoped Christopher was hiding, she was damp with sweat, and even her hair and clothes seemed to fall limp and heavy.

At first, in the green shadow of the overhanging trees, she could not see him, and for a moment she thought he was not there. Then she saw him, curled up very small in his grey blanket, which he had pulled up over his head. A spasm of panic gripped her like a cold fist in her stomach and for a horrible second the thought flashed through her brain that he was dead.

She squatted down, and shook him gently. 'Christopher, wake up. It's Eileen. Wake up, don't be afraid.'

He pushed the blanket off his head and with the same hand gripped her wrist painfully hard. His face shocked her. His eyes were red and baggy, his expression wild, and his cheeks were flushed against a background of extreme pallor. His chin was stubbly, his hair damp and stuck to his forehead, and his breath was rasping.

'Christopher, what is it? You look awful. What has happened? Are you ill?'

He did not reply. With a sudden, jerky movement he threw the blanket off and rose to his knees, still holding tightly to her wrist. His breathing was laboured, and his chest heaved. He groaned softly several times, then he said haltingly, 'He's coming for me, Eileen, he's so close, he knows where I am, I can hear him crashing in the woods. Can't you hear him?' Eileen shook her head. 'But he's so loud. He's not pretending any more. I've really blown it. He won't let me off this time, I'm for it, I know. Even you can't help me now.' His dark blue eyes welled with tears.

216

'But Christopher, what on earth has happened? For goodness' sake, tell me.'

He shook his head, unable to speak. Sobs rose uncontrollably, painfully, and he began to shake.

Aghast and bewildered, with no real idea what to do, she put her arms round his shoulders and drew him close. He flopped against her, his head on her shoulder, crying like someone broken in pieces. She held him tightly. A sour unwashed smell rose up from his body and hair. She did not care.

After a few minutes he seemed to quieten. He knelt, his hands limp in his lap, his head bowed, leaning against her shoulder, breathing deeply. Then, with an effort, he raised his head and looked at her searchingly. Appalled by his appearance, she looked back at him without blinking or turning away. 'Are you going to tell me what's wrong, Christopher?'

He hung his head. 'I will have to.' His voice was croaky. 'Even if you end up hating me. I can't cope with it any more on my own.'

'Why should I hate you?'

'I have this mental picture,' he said, 'of you leaping to your feet and pushing me away in disgust and never coming back.'

'But why?'

'Because you have discovered what I am really like, degenerate, slimy, like some horrible creature that's just crawled out of the sewers.'

'Hadn't you better just say what's been happening and leave me to make my own judgments?'

He shuddered. 'All right.'

She stood up, and found a more comfortable log to sit on. 'Have some coffee and something to eat. It might make you feel more human.'

'I ran, you know,' he said.

'Ran?'

'All the way from Caxford to here, last night. Almost all the way, that is. I had to stop a couple of times when I had a stitch.'

'You *ran* here from Caxford? That's nearly seven miles!'

'I know. I didn't know I could do that. But it felt like all the armies of hell were after me, gaining on me every minute, growling and howling and baying.'

'You mean you could actually hear those noises? It wasn't just your imagination?'

He nodded. 'But I can't hear them now. Maybe he has gone too.'

'Who? The voice that pursues you?'

'Yes. Him. But I don't think he has really gone. He's just quiet, waiting.'

'Christopher, tell me why you ran. No wonder you look so terrible. You must be exhausted.'

'I had to run.'

As he ate and drank he seemed to become calmer, and his voice dropped to its normal pitch. She said no more. After a few minutes' silent chewing he looked up. 'I went to see Dr. Partridge. You know about that. I went back to Denbigh Street and let myself in. There was nobody around but Sylvie. The others were either out or still asleep. I had a bath and made myself presentable. Jackie came at eleven fifteen. She didn't seem to see anything unusual, and she chatted away in the car as she always does. I was nervous and quiet, but I am when I have to go to the hospital.' He looked at her, waiting for some comment, but when she remained silent, he went on. 'I saw Dr. Partridge. That was just the beginning. He didn't ask me many questions, but he kept going on about me becoming withdrawn, and talking about changing my medication, and taking me into hospital so he could monitor me, and then there was something about a new group starting up that I could join, and I panicked. I couldn't cope with all that. I don't want change, I don't want to be noticed, studied, singled out.' His voice rose hysterically and he began to pant.

'OK. So what happened next?'

'He said I should go away and think about what he'd said, and we'd discuss it further at our next appointment. I couldn't wait to get out. I found Jackie. She was talking to someone she knew while I was with the doctor. I dragged her out of the hospital. I was probably very rude but I was desperate to get away. Anyway Jackie had another person to see so she just dropped me at the gate. I let myself in. I didn't have time to get upstairs to my room when the living room door opened and out he came.'

'Who?'

'Maurice.'

'Who?'

'I didn't tell you about him, did I? I guess I'll have to now.'

He took several deep breaths. Eileen could see he was trembling, and his voice shook as he spoke. 'Maurice Bentley is the sixth inmate at Denbigh Street. He is in his fifties, I guess, always very smart-looking, with well-pressed suits, and he smells of cologne. Thinking about it here, now, he is a very sick man, but he is brilliant at covering it up. If you didn't know, you'd think he was a bank manager or something. He speaks softly, and he is very thoughtful and sensitive to other people's feelings. If anyone in the house was upset, they'd always turn to Maurice.

218

He used to make them cups of tea and listen to their troubles. He was a sort of father-figure, I suppose.'

'So why was he there?'

'I don't know much about his background, neither did anyone else. I think he'd been in hospital quite a few times, but before that he had a life, a good job, someone told me. He was a very intelligent man, and well read. I didn't get to know him for quite a while when I was first at Denbigh Street. He seemed so retiring, so modest and self-effacing. Now, looking back, I think he was just biding his time.'

'For what?'

'To take me over, to make me his slave.'

'What?'

Christopher nodded, his face a rigid mask of misery. 'You mustn't blame him. He's obviously quite ill, I see that now. And I let him do all those things. It's me that is to blame.'

'What things?'

'After a few months, Maurice and I got quite friendly. He is an interesting man to talk to. The others are OK, but they can be very weird, and they don't know much. Maurice was kind. He seemed to take an interest in me. I trusted him. I am such a fool, Eileen, such a baby. I deserved it all.' He was silent for a while. 'Gradually I started to realize that his behaviour was changing, but it was so slow and subtle, I wasn't sure, and I thought that perhaps I was just being paranoid. By the time I knew for certain it was too late. I was caught, and I felt confused and helpless, like a rabbit in the middle of the road, hypnotized by the glare of headlights, about to be mown down, but unable to move.'

'Didn't you tell anyone?'

'I couldn't. I was kind of frozen. Do you understand? I became like a mechanical thing, a robot. I think what was happening made me sicker, though I didn't know it then. I was on those pills that made me spaced out. Most of the time I didn't really know what I was doing. Oh Eileen, this is just too horrible.' Still kneeling in the grass, he began to rock back and forward.

'Go on.'

'Well, it went on for quite a long time, eight or nine months, I guess. I know now I could never be what Maurice wanted, but he managed to persuade me, and himself, that I would fit the bill. I became like a sort of bond-maiden to him, available whenever he wanted to act out his fantasies. He was never unkind; he was always fatherly and gentle and protective, but he had me in a kind of trance. One part of me knew what

219

was happening, but the rest was almost paralyzed. I can't tell you why. He even gave me a girl's name. Tess, he called me.'

'Christopher, this is horrific. How come nobody found out?'

He shrugged. 'Maurice wasn't going to say anything. And even in my moments of lucidity, I was too scared. That's the awful part. In the end I didn't know what I felt or thought. I didn't even know if I felt excited or revolted. Somewhere, at the back of it all, I knew something was terribly wrong, but I couldn't think straight long enough to sort it all out. Big Voice was after me a lot then, of course. But when I was with Maurice, he seemed to take a back seat. Now, I don't know what was worse.'

'So, are you telling me that's why you came here, to the woods, in the first place?'

'Yes. To escape from Maurice.'

'How did you get away from him? From what you have told me, it was almost as if he had you under a spell.'

'That's just how it felt. But then, Maurice had to go away for a few days. His old aunt had died, and he went up north for her funeral. That's what he told me. Maybe he had to go into hospital and he didn't want me to think he was crazy. I was the crazy one, that was understood. He explained all this to me very solemnly. He made me put on the girl's clothes, all the pink, frilly stuff. I must have looked grotesque. He put makeup on me, and he carefully brushed my hair. I was never allowed to have it cut, so by then it was half way down my back. He made me promise not to go out while he was gone, and he said sick stuff like, "You must save yourself for me, Tess. Be a good girl, then I will be good to you, very good, when I come back." Now, telling you this, I want to throw up. How did I just give in? It was like I was mesmerized.'

Eileen shook her head. 'So what changed? What happened to break the spell?'

'I began to have the really bad dreams again. Only they were different. They were all highly explicit sexual dreams, thrilling, repellent, terrifying. Big Voice had a field day, of course. Every waking moment he was shouting at me, calling me a filthy pervert, degraded, fit for nothing but pitchforking into hell. Only I was already in hell. And that was the moment my mother chose to ring.'

'Go on. I'm listening.'

'Dave called me to the phone. He looked at me very oddly. No wonder: I was done up like the fairy on the Christmas tree. His sniggers and sly remarks must have set something going in my mind, because when my mother asked me how things were I went crazy at her. I told her she was rubbish as a mother and why hadn't she kept me safe as a mother should, etcetera. No wonder she hasn't called again or come to see me. She's probably still offended. Anyway, that did it. I can't tell you how, but the spell was broken. I ran upstairs, tore off the girl's clothes, scrubbed off the makeup, and put on my normal stuff. I must have been in a wild state because when I went into the living-room with a pair of scissors in my hand they all jumped up and screamed. They thought I wanted to stab someone. Actually all I wanted was for one of them to cut my hair. In the end I persuaded dopey Sylvie to do it. Then I collected my few things and came here. I walked overnight so no one saw me, and found my hiding place in the boys' camp.' For several moments he was silent, staring at the ground. 'I was free here. I started to get my sanity back. I felt as if I was getting to be more in charge of my own life. I thought I would feel better when I was alone, and I did. And then I met you, and found that perhaps after all I was not such a hopeless case, if you thought I was worth befriending. I never knew before, that it was possible to have a friend like you.' He paused, still not looking up. 'That's why I was afraid to tell you about Maurice, in case you hated and despised me and thought I was disgusting. I wouldn't have blamed you; I despised and disgusted myself.'

'But that man used you, Christopher. He took advantage of you. You were vulnerable and confused, and he preyed on you.'

'He is a sick man too. And I went along with it, didn't I?'

'No wonder seeing him again yesterday had such a violent effect on you. Did he say anything to you?'

'It was horrible. He said, "Tess, darling, you're back. Where have you been? I've missed you." And he said it with a really sick, knowing look. I just ducked, ran upstairs, collected my things and bolted. I was in such a panic I couldn't stop running. I'm sorry, I think I'm going to throw up.'

He jumped to his feet, took a few steps, turned away from her and retched violently several times, leaning against a tree. When he turned back to her, his face was grey.

'Christopher, you are ill. You should see a doctor. You can't just stay down here like this.'

'I'll be all right now. It's over. I've got away from Maurice. He has no power over me any more. And I've told you everything, and I think you are still my friend. You are, aren't you?'

'Of course.'

'I'll be all right. I'll sleep now, and then I'll have something more to eat, and maybe later I'll move back to my first camp. I think if I am close to you Big Voice will keep his distance.'

'I am very worried about you, Christopher.'

'Don't be. I am feeling better already. Come down to the boys' camp tomorrow. Maybe we can talk some more about what we were discussing before I left. I will be OK. Don't worry.'

I can't do anything. I am as helpless as he is.

She left him curled up again in his blanket. It was one of the hardest things she had ever done. She had come to a point where her human ingenuity had run out, like the sand in an hourglass, and now her only resource was prayer. *It should be the first, not the last resort.* She tramped home through the sultry woods. *Maybe that's all I can do for him now. Pray.*

She turned at random to one of the paper markers she had left in her Bible. It opened at a psalm she had read to Christopher, psalm 40. The last six verses had the title "A prayer for help."

"I am surrounded by many troubles—too many to count!

My sins have caught up with me, and I can no longer see; they are more than the hairs of my head, and I have lost my courage.

Save me, Lord! Help me now!...

I am weak and poor, O Lord, but you have not forgotten me.

You are my Saviour and my God—hurry to my aid!"

She sighed. *Amen to that.* And she was thankful for her salvation, of course she was. She wanted Christopher to know it too. But what had she done? Had she helped him or harmed him? She couldn't really help him, that much was plain; there was too much in his life that needed healing. He was too much for her inadequate resources. Only God could pull him out of the pit where he lived, heal his wounds, surround him with love that could not fail.

She rested her head in her hands, trying to still her thoughts and clear her mind. *Lord, I lift Christopher up to your all-wise eyes. In his muddle and misery help him to know that you are the Good Shepherd, and he is a lamb of your flock. He is your beloved child, as we all are. Help him to know and feel and accept it for his own healing and hope. Lord, help me to do the right thing. I am very afraid for myself and for Christopher. Please don't abandon us, even if we deserve it.*

Wednesday 12ᵗʰ June 1996

But the next day, when she found Christopher in the woods, her concern intensified. He had moved back to his original camp, as he had said he would; he was sitting on the tree stump, the grey blanket round his shoulders. His eyes seemed sunken, and his face was pale and sweating.

'Christopher, you still look ill. How do you feel?'

'Cold. No, hot. A bit out of it.'

She laid a hand on his forehead; it seemed all right. But he was shivering.

'It's not a virus, you know,' he said. 'I am sick with shame. It's like an inner corruption, working its way outwards.'

'I'm more inclined to favour the germ theory. Come up to the house, have a hot bath, something to eat, sleep in a warm bed for a few hours. See how you feel then.' He hesitated. 'Nobody will see you. I'm not expecting anyone. Everything is quiet.'

He was silent, looking at her, a frown gathering between his brows. Then he seemed to relent. 'All right.'

He let himself be led, childlike and docile. When they arrived at the back gate he glanced around automatically, in case there were any ramblers about, or villagers with dogs, but the paths were deserted, and the gardens were empty.

In the kitchen he stood vacantly, as if helpless, drained of strength. 'Will you read to me later?'

'When you are fed and clean.'

'I'm not very hungry.'

'All right. I'll just do you some tea and toast.'

She left him eating very slowly while she ran his bath. He seemed in a trance. She had to chivvy and guide, almost bully him. Eventually he was clean and wrapped in her bathrobe.

'You can sleep in my bed,' she said to him, trying to sound matter-of-fact and motherly. 'I'll wash your clothes while you sleep.'

He gripped her arm. 'Don't go. Stay and read to me like you did in the woods. It makes me calm.'

'Read what?'

'Bits out of your Bible. Anything.'

'All right. Dry your hair a bit. I'll be back in a minute.'

She put his clothes in the washing machine. When she went back upstairs he was in bed, the damp bathrobe flung on the floor. Despite the heat he had pulled the covers up, and only his bare shoulders were visible.

She sat down carefully in a cane chair opposite and looked at him. 'How are you feeling?'

'Sleepy. Read to me, please.'

She opened her Bible, and cleared her throat. 'OK. "Everyone whom my Father gives me will come to me. I will never turn away anyone who comes to me, because I have come down from heaven to do not my own will but the will of him who sent me. And it is the will of him who sent me that I should not lose any of those he has given me, but that I should raise them all to life on the last day."' She glanced up. She thought he was asleep; his eyes were closed and his breathing even.

Then he said, 'I wonder how you have found so many bits like that, that seem right for me.'

'I did my homework. Do you want to hear more?' He nodded. 'OK, here's some thrilling stuff from Revelation about the end of time. "I heard a loud voice speaking from the throne: 'Now God's home is with human beings! He will live with them, and they shall be his people. God himself will be with them, and he will be their God. He will wipe away all tears from their eyes. There will be no more death, no more grief or crying or pain. The old things have disappeared.'"'

There was a long pause. Then Christopher opened his eyes. 'Do you really believe that, Eileen? It sounds almost too good to be true.'

'I believe he keeps his promises, yes.'

'Always?'

'Always. Not always as fast as I'd like it, but yes, that's my experience. Always faithful. Shall I continue?'

'Please.'

'Another gem from Revelation, then. The very end, or nearly. "The angel also showed me the river of the water of life, sparkling like crystal and coming from the throne of God and of the Lamb and flowing down the middle of the city's street. On each side of the river was the tree of life, which bears fruit twelve times a year, once each month; and its leaves are for the healing of the nations. Nothing that is under God's curse will be found in the city.

"The throne of God and of the Lamb will be in the city, and his servants will worship him. They will see his face, and his name will be written on their foreheads. There shall be no more night, and they will not need lamps or sunlight, because the Lord God will be their light, and they will rule as kings for ever and ever."' She finished reading, and looked up. 'Christopher.' But he was asleep. She took her Bible and went quietly out, pausing in the doorway to look down at him. He slept peacefully, and the grey pallor of his skin was tinged with a slight pink flush around his cheekbones. He looked very young.

That is how he is. Barely more than an adolescent, really. My daughters' generation. And he sees me as a sort of motherly friend, obviously. That's how it has to be. That is at least appropriate, that can be handled. Maybe. How could I have let any other thought enter my brain?

Feeling stronger, more in control, she busied herself with laundry. She hung his clean clothes out to dry with her own and Michael's. In the afternoon a gleam of sun broke through the oppressive layer of cloud. She prepared Christopher some supplies, then went to wake him. 'Christopher, I have to go and get Michael.'

He opened his eyes and smiled at her, a smile so sweet and trusting that for a moment her resolve faltered, followed instantly by hot shame. She swallowed hard. 'Are you feeling any better?'

'Much better. Thank you. You are my good angel.'

'Hardly. I'll get your clothes.'

By three o'clock he was gone, bag in hand, flitting like a noonday ghost down the garden and back to the shelter of the woods.

Eileen was awakened in the night by a choking, whining sound. Instantly alert, she knew it was the dog. She threw on a dressing gown, stuffed her feet into slippers, ran downstairs. Tillie's eyes were glassy, her breathing ragged. Eileen knelt by Tillie's basket, laid her grizzled head in her lap, stroked her, spoke to her gently. After ten minutes the dog seemed calmer, her breathing more even. Eileen laid her head back in her bed and warmed a little milk. Tillie lapped it slowly, with difficulty but as if she was thirsty. Then she sighed, snuffled, licked her lips and settled down. She looked at Eileen with gratitude, a look that cut her. 'Your faith in me is sadly unfounded, dear old thing,' she whispered, stroking the dog's ears. 'I can't really help you any more. I wish I could.' Tillie yawned. 'You too? Well, if you're OK for now, I'll go back to bed.'

She was in the back seat of an open-topped car, a car being driven at breakneck speed by Philip, and Marie was in the passenger seat beside him, her hair held down with a scarf, wearing a polka-dot dress and huge

225

sunglasses like some fifties film star. They were laughing and talking loudly as the car careered along what seemed to be the road out of Caxford towards Osewick. Eileen was wrapped in several blankets. She knew that she was very ill, and that Marie and Philip were taking her to the hospital. Then Christopher was standing by the side of the road, waving. She shouted to Philip and Marie above the scream of the wind to stop and pick him up, but they simply laughed even more loudly and sped away with a screech of tyres.

Then she was in a hospital bed, propped up by pillows. Everything around her was white and silent. A white-coated doctor came into the room and leaned over her as she lay. It was Christopher. She began to question him as to how he had got there, how he had fooled everyone into believing he was a doctor; then she realized that he really was a doctor, that he had a cure for her disease, but that he had to act in secret, because they—who were they?—were trying to prevent him. As he bent closer to her she had an overpowering feeling that something extraordinary was about to happen.

She woke up suddenly, and as she recalled the dream before it faded a hot blush burned her cheeks. *How humiliating to find my unconscious is full of such tacky junk.* She drifted back to sleep.

Thursday 13ᵗʰ June 1996

When she came to full consciousness she felt an icy grip around her heart. Prepared yet unprepared, she forced herself to go downstairs, holding her breath as she entered the kitchen, expecting Tillie to be stiff and cold. But the dog blinked and yawned and lazily wagged her tail. Relief was swamped almost at once by apprehension. The worst was yet to come.

A little after nine Christopher startled her with uncharacteristic boldness. She had barely kicked off her shoes, coming into the hallway after dropping Michael off at school, when there was a tapping on the back door, and there he was.

She raised her eyebrows. 'You are getting very brave all of a sudden.'

'Not really. I don't think I have ever been brave. Unless it is brave to run away. I seem to have done a lot of that.'

'How are you feeling?'

'I feel all right.'

'Do you want some breakfast?'

'No, thanks. A cup of coffee would be good, though.'

Again he seemed restless, pacing the room, picking books off shelves, looking out of the window, running his hands through his hair, his eyes bright and always moving.

She handed him a mug of coffee. 'What do you want to do?'

'I am not stopping you doing something, am I?' he asked 'Sometimes I forget, you have stuff to do. I only have to think about myself.'

'It's OK.'

'Could we listen to "Gerontius?" Another part? I missed a bit by going to sleep.'

'All right. I'll play the first part for you, where he sets out the main themes.'

For half an hour they sat without speaking. Christopher half-lay on the sofa, arms and legs languidly draped, head back, eyes closed. Eileen watched him covertly. The music took them to where the old man struggled as his soul parted from his body: the quiet, mysterious

227

beginning, the volume suddenly intensifying, then his dismay at the disintegration of his mortal being, and the pleading prayers. When the tenor began to sing of the hideous being flapping, cursing, tainted, she watched Christopher even more closely, but he did not seem to react. Then came the bass Angel, full of God's authority expressed in the sonorities of Latin, making the final division and sending the naked soul to its eternal destiny, confident, triumphant, yet ending quietly, a line drawn under a life.

The music came to an end. There was silence in the room. Then Christopher opened his eyes. 'That was truly amazing.'

'Did you find the references to demons and creatures of hell disturbing?' I wondered.'

'I didn't get to hear the demons when I was here before, did I? I fell asleep.'

'Actually, I switched it off, thinking it might be too much for you. But you were already out for the count.'

'I read that part, though,' Christopher said. 'Down in the woods, very early in the morning. I read it all. I couldn't imagine how the music would be, but I quite liked the demons' words.'

'Funny, I've thought that too. I can quite relate to the idea of the demons' disgust at what they feel is their rightful place, as spirits, being usurped by flesh and blood. You know the part where they describe the believers as full of cant, pious cheats, bootlickers without pride. They got it wrong, of course. But somehow you can understand why.'

'It was never demons that pursued me, anyway,' Christopher said. 'I could have understood that. It was because it was angels that made it hard, the idea of God himself hounding and tormenting me because I was so bad. But I think I got it wrong too, like the demons.'

'How do you mean?'

'Well, I am not really afraid of judgment any more. I thought I wouldn't stand a chance. But—I think this is right; please tell me if I've got it wrong again—it seems not so much what I am that counts, but what he is.' His voice sank to little more than a whisper, and he looked at her searchingly.

'What you are matters too, of course,' she said. 'But I think you have found out something very important. And you don't have to be afraid. He has defeated the forces of darkness on your behalf.' She let him digest this for a moment. 'Do you want to hear some more, or do you want to read?'

'You read.'

'OK.' She took up her Bible and opened it. 'I found a few bits for you to think about. "Now the message that we have heard from his Son

228

and announce is this: God is light, and there is no darkness at all in him. If, then, we say that we have fellowship with him, yet at the same time we live in the darkness, we are lying both in our words and in our actions. But if we live in the light—just as he is in the light—then we have fellowship with one another, and the blood of Jesus, his Son, purifies us from every sin.'"

'I have been in that darkness,' Christopher said.

'I think it's referring to the darkness of sin. Surely your darkness came from your illness.'

'Sick or well, I have done a lot of wrong things.'

'So has everybody. But those things can be renounced. And maybe you were more sinned against.'

Christopher shook his head. 'Do you really think so?'

'Who can say? Anyway, it's not yesterday that matters now, it's today and tomorrow, it's what you do with your knowledge and the time you've got left. That's the point of these verses, isn't it? That no profession of belief is any good unless it results in change, change to how you behave. Anyway, there's a bit more.'

'OK. Go on.'

'"If we say that we have no sin, we deceive ourselves, and there is no truth in us. But if we confess our sins to God, he will keep his promise and do what is right: he will forgive us our sins and purify us from all our wrongdoing. If we say we have not sinned, we make God out to be a liar, and his word is not in us."'

'What does that mean?'

'I think it means that even for the converted, sin and wrong remain an active force in them and they need to keep going back to God for restoration.'

'So is it really as easy as that? You just say, "Sorry guv, fair cop, guilty as charged?"'

'More or less. But the next bit is tougher. "If we obey God's commands, then we are sure that we know him. Those that say that they know him, but do not obey his commands, are liars and there is no truth in them. All those who obey his word are people whose love for God has really been made perfect. This is how we can be sure that we are in union with God: those who say that they remain in union with God should live just as Jesus Christ did."'

Christopher whistled. 'Who could manage that?'

'Who indeed?' Eileen said. 'Not me, anyway. But look further on. It says, "Do not love the world or anything that belongs to the world. If you love the world, you do not love the Father."'

229

'What? Not the good bits? Not the woods, the sunshine, the seasons, the sea?'

'I don't think it means the world as creation. I think it's talking about the corrupt situations created by humanity.'

'Oh.'

'I read once another translation which was rather more resounding than mine. It speaks of "the lust of the flesh, the lust of the eyes, the vainglory of life." It stuck in my mind.'

'I understand that bit. That's what so much of this world is like— vain, stupid, shallow, cruel, tainted, everybody out for himself.'

'I'm afraid so. This passage ends with a warning: "The world and everything in it that people desire is passing away; but those who do the will of God live forever."'

'Heavy stuff.'

'Well, that's what I used to think. But now I have come to see it isn't like that. Listen to this bit. "…our love for God means that we obey his commands. And his commands are not too hard for us, because every child of God is able to defeat the world. And we win the victory over the world by means of our faith. Who can defeat the world? Only the person who believes that Jesus Christ is the son of God." I used to find the idea of obedience distasteful, but it isn't just miserable submission, giving in because we have to, because he holds all the cards. The truth is, obeying God is our only way of rising above evil and death.'

'This stuff could really freak you out.'

'Is that how it makes you feel?'

'No. But the thought of eternity is a bit double-edged.'

'Only if you think of it in terms of our earthly life. I don't think "eternal life" means just going on living for ever. That would be a kind of hell, wouldn't it?'

'What is hell, Eileen? What is it like? Will I go there? I thought I had already seen hell.'

'Well, if eternal life is the fullness of joy in God's presence, hell has to be knowing that you could have had this wonderful gift but blew it, threw it away, and relegated yourself to the outer darkness.'

There was silence. Christopher seemed sunk in thought, a slight frown between his brows. Then he looked up suddenly. 'What was that?'

A rasping, gurgling sound came from the kitchen, then a loud whine. Eileen felt her scalp prickle. 'It's Tillie. She had a funny turn in the night.'

She jumped up and ran into the kitchen, closely followed by Christopher. Tillie was standing up in her basket, all four legs stiff and straight, her head held at an unnatural angle, her tongue lolling. Eileen sank to her knees beside her dog and gently put her arms round her neck. Tillie seemed to buckle and collapse against her. Her thin chest heaved.

'What's the matter?' Christopher asked.

Eileen shook her head. She could say nothing. Gradually the stertorous breathing quietened. Tillie's whole body sagged, she gave something between a cough and a sigh, and lay still, her head resting against Eileen's side. There was silence for several moments.

'I think she's gone, Christopher.'

'Are you sure?'

Eileen nodded, unable to articulate, unprepared for the shockwave of feeling that flooded her. Had she not known that death was imminent? Somehow knowledge made no difference; for here was reality in all its mystery, that sixteen years of life were ended, another line drawn between past and future.

Christopher knelt down beside her, and put a hand on her shoulder. She looked up at him. His dark blue eyes seemed huge and bright, his face inscrutable. 'Eileen, I am really sorry. Would you like me to bury her? I could save you that job at least.'

'No, Christopher. Thank you, you are very kind. But if you don't want to be seen here, digging a sizeable hole in the garden is probably not a good idea.'

'It doesn't matter. Not really. You have been such a good friend to me, and this is a little thing I could do to help.'

She rose to her feet, and shook her head. 'It isn't practical, here on the edge of the woods. No, I'll call the vet, have them take her for cremation. I'll do it now, then I can put all her things away before Michael gets home from school. There's no sense in upsetting him any more than is necessary.'

'I'll get back to my camp now, then. If you're sure I can't help. Will I see you tomorrow?'

'I don't know yet. Whatever happens I'll leave you some supplies at the top of the path.'

He went to the back door, and stood there, looking at her as if reluctant to leave. He turned away, put his hand on the door handle, hesitated, then quite suddenly and unexpectedly turned back, and in one swift movement crossed the few feet between them and put his arms around her, hugging her close to his chest. She was startled, knocked off balance. She could feel his warmth through the thin cotton shirt. In another second, before she had time to gather herself, he released her. His eyes, on a level with hers, were bright with tears.

231

'Poor Eileen,' he whispered. 'You are almost as alone as I am.'

Then he was gone. The back door banged, she heard the sound of light running feet on the garden path, and the silence rolled back to fill the space he had left. For several long seconds she stood, dazed and shaken, unable to face what had passed there between them. Then she took a deep breath, and let it out in a long sigh. *So nearly undone. That's just how it feels—that I am becoming unstuck, unglued, about to fall into a thousand useless shards. I have to handle this better, but I don't know how. Oh God, hold me together, because I am in danger of falling apart.*

The horrible deed was done. As soon as Christopher had gone, she telephoned the vet and made the arrangements. She carried Tillie's body, light and frail, wrapped in a blanket, through the side door of the surgery, where sympathetic hands bore her away. Blindly she filled in a consent form, paid her bill, drove home. Still mechanically she put all Tillie's things out of sight in the shed. Now she sat at the kitchen table, nursing a cooling mug of tea, and the empty silence of the house rolled round her like waves of the sea, clamouring for attention with cruel childlike voices, telling her with relentless repetition that her life was as empty as her house, and as friendless. A great weight seemed to settle in her stomach, dragging her down into a place of complete darkness.

With an effort of will, as if every bone ached, she got up and tipped the neglected tea, now stone cold, into the sink. She noticed on the shelf an old photo of Tillie which she had forgotten. She picked it up and wiped off the dust with her hand, looking at it with a faint smile. *I won't put it away. Why shouldn't I remember her?* She placed it carefully back.

She took her Bible in her hand, but did not open it. Instead she sat down in an armchair, staring down the garden, but seeing nothing, fighting to bring her scattered thoughts to order. Gradually a lifetime's habit of stony stubbornness began to reassert itself, as if with a bugle-call riding to her rescue, and with some submerged part of her consciousness she recognized it.

To be able to think again was an intense relief. She put her Bible down, went to the window, looked critically at the overgrown garden, then turned, casting an appraising eye over the house. Everything needed attention. The windows were going rotten, and the place was generally shabby, full of creaking ancient appliances on their last legs. The train of thought began inexorably to build. By the end of the year she would have no income, only a house in need of repair, costing money she wouldn't have. Christina and Natasha were effectively out of the picture; they were no longer dependent and only minimally resident. She no longer needed to provide a home and a life for them; they could and must do that for themselves. Then, David. She didn't doubt the next thing she heard from him would be something official and legal. So be it. Michael was on his way too, and very soon he would be gone. She had a fleeting memory of a poem by Yeats about his infant son, foreseeing a future when the child would be grown and gone from him. Marie too would soon be gone, gathered up into a new life with Philip. Even her dog was dead. Eileen herself needed a new life too. She would have to work anyway, for how else would she survive? Even if she stayed where she was she would have to work. But what was there now to keep her there? Not much. She would see her friend and her daughters wherever she was. Some loves were whisked into the past, others, for the time being, continued. The plan grew in her mind, alarming and liberating, not to be denied. *I'll spruce the place up a bit. Clear the garden, slap on some paint. Then I'll sell up, move, get somewhere more practical for one person, find work, I don't know what. What skills I had are superannuated now. No matter. It's not a question of choice, but of necessity.*

And what of Christopher? He was the hardest part; and yet her thoughts for her future might also go some way to solving the huge problem that he was becoming. She felt as if a chink of light was beginning to break through a heavy layer of cloud, the light of reality, cold, bleak, necessary. With a sense of loss she recognized that Christopher also could not continue as he was, that he too must carve out a life for himself. *Maybe one day, when we are gone from here, set up somewhere else, we can still have some kind of friendship. No. If I am very pragmatic, it will not survive the current situation.* She saw then with horrible clarity, knowing that until that moment she had not allowed herself to see it, how their present condition, if prolonged, would be catastrophic for both of them, and especially for Christopher. *I will tell him. I will try to explain gently.* She didn't want him to feel rejected or betrayed. But she had to hold on to sense and sanity, for his sake.

She went into the kitchen to make herself a sandwich. Her thoughts began to bring her relief and a measure of peace, but it was a bleak and miserable sort of peace all the same, and the future that she envisaged seemed devoid of joy. That was how it was when you let yourself wander off into some half-baked dreamland. Things got broken. *Just be grateful you have woken up in time to patch something together.* She pushed down the thought that gratitude and sanity and reality made poor fare for a spirit as ravenous as hers; but the hollowness remained.

Friday 14ᵗʰ June 1996

All Friday the mood of emptiness persisted. She woke, feeling leaden, to a grey sweltering morning without air. There was a heaviness in her limbs and a dull throbbing in her head. Like many others in the south of England that day, she longed for rain: heavy, wild, lashing, windswept, blowing the wall of stickiness away. But still the weather did not break, and she had to force herself to do the things she had to do. Coming down that morning to an empty kitchen brought another wave of bleakness, yet with it also a sense of relief, that there was one thing she no longer had to worry about. Her eyes ached and itched. Michael's grief at Tillie's death had broken her own control, and they had wept together.

From somewhere she barely knew existed she summoned up the determination to get something done, even if it was only household chores. After dropping Michael off at school she drove into Caxford and shopped for food. Back at home she dispatched a pile of ironing. By then the heat and humidity were overpowering. Her hair stuck to her forehead and her clothes were damp with sweat. At midday she sat down with a sandwich. Most of all at moments of idleness she missed her dog. Her thoughts were fragmented, barely coherent. She did not want to talk to anyone, especially not to Christopher. She left his food at the top of the path, hastily, almost furtively; she was glad there was no sign of him. She could not yet say to him what she knew must be said. Finishing her lunch, she took up her Bible which was still lying on the coffee table. She opened it idly, without particular purpose, and was not surprised when it fell open at Psalms.

"God rises up and scatters his enemies.

Those who hate him run away in defeat.

As smoke is blown away, so he drives them off; as wax melts in front of the fire,

So do the wicked perish in God's presence.

But the righteous are glad and rejoice in his presence;

They are happy and shout for joy.

234

Sing to God, sing praises to his name; prepare a way for him who rides on the clouds.

His name is the Lord—be glad in his presence!"

Her eyes began to blur, and the small print danced fuzzily.

In her jumbled and senseless dream a phone was ringing, insistently, intrusively. She came out of a sticky doze to find that it really was ringing. She heaved herself out of the chair. Her Bible fell to the floor.

'Mum? You OK? You were ages answering.' It was Natasha, ringing from the shop.

'I dropped off in the chair. It's so hot, it saps your energy.'

'Just thought I'd let you know I'll be home tonight, and tomorrow probably.'

'All right. I could pick you up after work if you like. I've got to drop Michael off at five.'

'Thanks, that would be great. How's Tillie?'

'I'm afraid she died, love. Yesterday morning.'

'Oh, Mum. I'm sorry I wasn't there with you.'

'No matter.'

'What have you done with her?'

'I let the vet take care of it. I thought it was the practical thing to do.'

'Yes. All right, Mum, don't brood, will you? I'll see you later.'

Looking at the kitchen clock, she realized with horror that she had only five minutes before Michael came out of school. The rest of the afternoon seemed a bit of a blur: getting Michael ready for the weekend, driving him to Caxford, collecting Natasha, preparing a hasty meal.

She had half an hour to spare. She lounged in a cool bath, thinking that it would be nice to have a shower, especially in hot weather. Quicker. Perhaps she would get one some day. *No, no I won't. Because I'm not staying. It's not worth changing anything.* Remembering her resolve, remembering what she had to tell Christopher, brought back the leaden lump of fear in her stomach. Suddenly the bathwater felt cold. She shivered, got out, and wrapped herself in a towel.

'Tash, are you expecting Sean over later?' she said as she dried her hair.

'Yes, some time. We might pop out to the pub.'

'Right. Maybe I'll see the pair of you then. Now I'd better get to choir practice. It's the induction tomorrow.'

'The what?'

'The new vicar, remember?'

235

'Oh. Yes.' Natasha sounded vague. 'Sing well, then, Mum.'

As Eileen walked up the churchyard path she could hear, but not see, the four little girls shrieking somewhere among the leaning gravestones. It was already seven o'clock. Eileen smiled to herself as she pushed open the ancient door. *Gillian will be out here in a minute. Bringing them all to order.* As she closed the door behind her she became aware how quiet it was. There were no bell-ringers milling about, and from the vestry came only the most subdued of murmurs. When she went in to join them she was surprised to find half a dozen of the adult choir members and a sprinkling of bell-ringers in a huddle, looking very serious.

'Hello, everyone, what's up?' Eileen said.

Gillian Clayton detached herself from the group. 'Actually, Eileen, none of us know. But we think something is. Haven't you noticed the police cars? No, I guess you wouldn't have, living this end of the village.'

'Police cars? Why?'

'Well, there have been cars in and out for the past hour or two. I noticed one parked outside the Quilleys' house when I popped to the shop, and Bill here saw something else, didn't you, Bill?'

Bill Mottram was leaning against the wall, his arms folded over his considerable stomach. 'I was just coming down here about an hour ago. Thought I'd do a bit of tidying up round Mum's grave before choir practice, and I saw them coming out and getting into the police car.'

'Who?'

'Angela Quilley, looking terrible, and young Georgina wrapped up in a blanket.'

'Goodness knows what's happened,' Gillian Clayton said. 'Bill says he spoke to them but they ignored him.'

'Just got in the car and roared off down the road,' Bill said. 'Off towards Caxford.'

'And Philip's quite late,' Gillian said. 'It's not like him. You haven't seen or heard anything, then, Eileen?'

'No,' Eileen said, shaking her head. 'Not a thing.'

The news troubled her, linking it in her mind as she could not fail to do with the change in Georgina over the past few weeks and Eileen's sighting of her in the black van with the man from the Hotspot.

The door creaked again, and closed gently. A moment later Philip appeared, hand in hand with Marie. Both were looking very grave.

'Hello, Philip, Marie,' Gillian said. 'Shall I call the girls in?'

'No, Gillian, please don't,' Philip said, raising a hand to stay her. 'What I have to tell you is not for children.' He looked at them for a moment with his dark gaze. 'I have had a telephone call from Peter

236

Quilley. You will have noticed that neither Arthur nor Georgina is here. Something terrible has happened this afternoon. We are not sure yet exactly what, but Georgina has been taken to Lambury police station. Angela is with her. Peter and Neil are holding the fort and looking after Arthur, who is very distressed. Georgina isn't talking, but it appears there has been some kind of attack on her here in the woods.' There were gasps and horrified murmurs. 'According to Peter, Georgina appeared on the doorstep this afternoon, when she should have still been on her way home from school, covered in scratches and bruises and dirt, in a hysterical and incoherent state, her clothes torn. Since then she's gone completely silent and won't tell the police anything, but it's fairly obvious that something dreadful has happened, and she's been taken to the police station to be examined and questioned.'

After a moment of silence everyone began talking at once.

'Poor kid! What a terrible thing to happen.'

'But what was she doing out of school? What was she up to in the woods?'

'The way she's been acting and dressing lately…'

'Poor Angela, it's a mother's worst nightmare.'

'Is she badly hurt?'

Philip waved away their questions. 'I don't know any more than what I've told you. And we can't achieve anything by discussing it now. We have an important service to prepare for tomorrow. Luckily I think all we need to do tonight is just add a bit of polish, so we'll have a short practice. Gillian, would you call the girls in now, please?'

They practised for forty minutes. For once everyone concentrated on what they were doing, or seemed to. The little girls, catching the sombre atmosphere, glanced at each other with round eyes.

Afterwards, nobody seemed in any mood to linger, and after a few minutes Philip, Marie and Eileen were alone. Marie and Eileen paused outside while Philip switched off the lights and locked the door.

'Did Philip really tell us all he knew?' Eileen asked.

'Well, yes, factually speaking,' Marie said. 'Peter sounded completely distraught. Reading between the lines it's clear he suspects some kind of serious assault.'

Eileen sighed. 'I think Georgina's been keeping some dubious company lately,' she said, and she told Marie about seeing Georgina in the black van.

'But she's not old enough to go to that nightclub,' Marie said. 'They wouldn't let her in.'

'Her brother is, though. And we saw a whole crowd of them, Neil, the Muldoons, Georgina, and a couple of heavies, in the layby on the Caxford road a few Sundays ago. It was the weekend Christie was home.'

Marie shook her head as Philip joined them.

'Let me know if you hear anything, won't you,' Eileen said as they parted.

'Yes, I will. Oh, and Eileen, in case you forget with all this going on, we will be in trouble with Gillian if we don't bring something for the bunfight after the induction.'

'Thanks for reminding me.'

Sean's car was parked outside. Remembering she was early she entered the house with as much clatter as she could muster and hailed them loudly from the hallway. They were sitting sedately on the sofa. Natasha switched off the television.

'Hello, Mum, you're early.'

'Yes, Philip ran a short practice and sent us home. Hi, Sean.' She told Sean and Natasha what Philip had told the choir. 'Have you two been to that club lately?'

Natasha shook her head. 'Not since Christie was with us. And that was the first time for ages.'

'My first time ever,' Sean said. 'The last, I hope.'

'I don't really like it that much any more,' Natasha said. 'It was all right when it was just local kids having a good time, but when that other mob arrived it changed. I'll tell you who'd know everything that goes on there, though, and that's Stephanie. It's her patch.'

'I wonder how she takes to competition,' Eileen said. 'Do you think one of these out-of-town types might be responsible?'

'Well, who else would it be?' Natasha said. 'I can't see any of the local lads doing harm to a young kid they've known since she was in her pram. Unless it's this tramp, or whoever he is, that's been lurking in our woods. But that doesn't answer what Georgina was doing there in the first place.'

Until now, Eileen had not consciously thought of Christopher, but the implications of Natasha's remark made her go cold. She knew that Christopher would not hurt anyone, but would he automatically be suspected? She thought of Georgina, undergoing who knew what torment in Lambury police station. *Talk, Georgina. Tell them what happened. For yourself, and for him.*

Saturday 15th June 1996

The vestry was crowded. The choir, after robing, had been temporarily shunted to the bell tower where they tried to keep away from the ringers.

'Who are all these foreign bodies?' Eileen whispered to Marie.

'Visiting clergy, I gather, the rural dean, various others, and we're still waiting for the bishop.'

'I didn't realize the bells were so deafening.'

Eventually, at the designated time, everything came together. The organ fell silent, the rural dean announced the opening hymn, and the choir processed slowly up the nave, singing heartily and trying to look solemn, followed by a bevy of ecclesiastical dignitaries in starched surplices.

The bishop, flanked by his chaplain, sat in a seldom-used velvet-covered chair. Before him stood two unknown men in suits, and between them a tall, slim young man in robes. His light-coloured hair was curly and undisciplined, and a pair of steel-rimmed glasses rested on his aquiline nose.

'Bishop, we have prayed and consulted together and I now present to you the Reverend Edward Jescott to be instituted as rector of Holton.'

Edward Jescott replied to the bishop's greeting; his voice was an educated tenor. Eileen found herself glancing covertly round the packed church. In the side pew at the front sat a dark-haired young woman and three small children, the youngest boy on her lap. Eileen felt a pang of sympathy for the new rector's wife, for whom, to judge by her nervous smile and lowered glance, the occasion was one of potential humiliation rather than rejoicing, as well it might be, with three bored young children done up in their Sunday clothes.

The service proceeded: readings, hymns. The anthem passed off well enough. The bishop gave Edward the cure of souls. *What a burden for a mortal man to bear.* Then there was a march round the church and the ringing of a bell. Eight times Edward rang it, once for each year of his incumbency, so tradition claimed, as if such a thing could be predicted. Various parish worthies presented him first with a service book, then

239

with water, a Bible, a paten and chalice, representing respectively worship, baptism, preaching the Gospel, and Holy Communion. All these things Edward promised to uphold.

Prayers, hymns, more from the choir. A wail from Simon Jescott, an apologetic smile from his mother. By this time the two older ones were under the pew, drawing. Edward greeted his parishioners, his brother clergy, civic dignitaries. Then at last the blessing, the final hymn, and it was over. The organ thundered out a complicated fugue. As instructed by Frank Aherne, the choir made itself scarce until the visitors had disrobed. Meanwhile a handful of ladies were busy transforming the space at the back of the church into a running buffet. A tea urn steamed, plates clattered, children, finally released, gave vent to mirth or misery. Edward, his surplice ditched, his face flushed, grappled with the tempestuous Simon while a stream of people tried to introduce themselves to his wife. She, meanwhile, was trying to locate her other children, who had escaped to the churchyard with the little choir girls.

Once the queue had abated Eileen and Marie helped themselves to a slice of cake and a cup of tepid tea and tried to be inconspicuous behind a board displaying posters of missionary activity in Africa. Gillian Clayton, done for the moment with fussing over crockery and personally greeting all the visiting clergy as if they were long-lost friends, joined them. 'What a crush! Thirty in the Sunday congregation, then this lot appear from nowhere.'

'They've come to cast a critical eye over our new rector,' Eileen said.

'He seems a nice young chap,' said Marie. 'I feel sorry for his wife, though.'

'Why?' asked Gillian.

'Three young kids, and you have to share your husband and your home with a load of pushy strangers. I'd rather work nights in a rat-infested sewer.'

Gillian looked startled. Marie merely smiled sweetly and Eileen stifled a snort.

'Marie, you are a tease,' she said when Gillian turned back to her catering.

'Somehow, when Gillian is around, I can't help it,' Marie said.

Philip had finished his closing voluntary, much of whose splendour and technical wizardry had been lost beneath the babble of voices. Eileen said as much. He smiled and shook his head. Marie procured a cup of tea for him and one of the last remaining sandwiches. Edward Jescott materialized beside them. He had shed his fractious son who was even now being taken home by his mother. He shook hands with Philip whom he had clearly met before. Philip introduced Marie and Eileen, mentioning that Eileen also played the organ on occasions.

'I play very little now, and I could never aspire to Philip's level,' she said hastily. Edward simply smiled graciously, and moved away to meet other parishioners.

Marie said, 'I got Philip to ring Peter Quilley this morning.'

'Oh?' Eileen was all attention. 'Any news?'

Marie nodded. 'I don't think we should talk about it here. When we can, we'll slip away. Come over to my place and I'll fill you in.'

The three of them walked up to Marie's cottage through the sultry evening. Nobody had much to say. Eileen noticed great banks of cloud, battleship grey, piled up above the tree-tops.

'Is it going to break soon?' she asked.

'The weather men have been telling us for weeks to expect storms,' Marie said. 'I'll be glad of it.'

'I think we all will.'

They went indoors. Without a word Philip disappeared into the kitchen and put the kettle on. Marie and Eileen subsided into armchairs.

'I won't stay long,' Eileen said. 'I want to catch Tash before she goes out.'

'All well there, I hope?' Marie said. 'And Michael?'

'Yes, fine. But before you ask, Tillie finally gave up the struggle on Thursday.'

'I'm sorry, Eileen.'

'Yes. The house seems very empty. Well, what of poor Georgina?'

'According to Peter, she finally did start talking, but not to the police, not yesterday when she was having to go through the whole horrible routine, no, it was when she got home late last night. They were finally able to let the poor child have a bath, and then she broke down and told the whole story to Angela. I guess she must have been in a state of total shock.'

'No wonder. So?'

'Apparently she'd been seeing this man on and off. He's part of a crowd that's been coming down from London. That's where the police are searching for him now. She couldn't give them much information, but at least she knew his name. Of course she's said nothing all this time, because she's been bunking off school to meet him, and she knew Angela and Peter would have grounded her.'

'How come the school didn't get suspicious?'

'I don't know about that. But it seems it's been going on for a few weeks. Anyway for whatever reason they decided to come down here, to the woods. And that's where it happened.'

241

'What, exactly?'

'Philip didn't press Peter, understandably, but it seems that Georgina had no real clue what this fellow was like and just got in way over her head. But yes, I'm afraid it looks like she was raped as well as knocked about.'

Eileen sighed. 'Poor kid. How absolutely horrific.'

'I guess this man will say she asked for it, but of course he's on a loser with her being only fourteen.'

'Yes. And you couldn't really say she looked years older, could you? Despite all the clothes and makeup and high heels she's been fooling around with lately, she still looked like an adolescent experimenting. Well, let's hope they catch him.'

'I'm sure they will. Apparently the local police have been keeping an eye on the Caxford scene in case of trouble, and they've found out some of this lot's London haunts. Besides, they're presumably liaising with their colleagues in London, and it may be this Pountney person is already known to the law.'

Philip came in with a tray and handed them each a cup of coffee.

'Thanks, Philip. What did you say his name was, Marie?'

'Darren Pountney. Not that it means anything to me.'

'Nor me. But it might to Stephanie.'

'Yes, it probably does,' Marie said. 'I haven't heard from Stephanie for quite a while. I hope she's not mixed up in all this.'

Eileen shook her head. Who knew what Stephanie was mixed up in?

'Anyway, that wasn't the end of it,' Marie said. 'Georgina said something else to Angela and she reported it directly to the local law. It seems there was an independent witness to the attack.'

'A witness?'

'Yes, a young man. Up a tree, apparently. It sounds like our tramp, doesn't it?'

Eileen felt herself begin to flush and sweat. The hairs prickled on her arms, and momentarily she lost hearing and sight.

'Are you all right?'

'Yes, of course,' Eileen said, recovering herself.

'Only you went a bit pale then.'

'I think it's the heat. Not to mention this quite harrowing story. Was this witness on the scene all the time?'

'I don't know. He must have followed Georgina and the man into the woods, and at some point Georgina noticed him up a tree. Then later, afterwards, when Pountney had already left, this chap came down and approached her.'

242

'How extraordinary. What did she do?'

'Well, she totally panicked. She picked herself up and ran. That's when she turned up on her own doorstep and gave her mother and poor old Arthur a terrible fright.'

'Arthur will be shattered. He is very close to Georgina.'

'That's just it, isn't it? The fallout is indiscriminate, like a bomb.'

Eileen finished her coffee. 'Thanks, that was good,' she said to Philip. 'I must go home and see what Tash and Sean are up to, if anything. I'll probably see you in church tomorrow.'

'Poor Edward Jescott. What a start to his work here.' Marie accompanied Eileen to the door. 'I feel I should warn you,' she said, her voice low. 'Philip has resigned from his job as organist here. Tomorrow will be his last service. He hasn't made it public because he hates fuss. But be prepared to be asked to stand in.'

'I'm terribly rusty.'

'There's only one answer to that, and it's called practice.'

'Until you get to Philip's level, and then you can do it standing on your head with a foot in your ear.'

'Sounds like something out of ancient Indian erotica,' Marie said, opening the door.

'Here we go—it's raising its ugly head again.'

'Sorry. I do try to rein it in.'

'Oh, sure. You're a paragon of restraint.'

They walked down the garden path together.

'So what would you say if he asked you?' Marie said.

'No.'

'Just like that?'

'Well, probably not. I expect I'd mention my lack of qualifications and plethora of commitments.'

'Hm.'

Walking slowly home in the gathering dark she thought of Christopher, trailing after Pountney and Georgina into the woods. Why had he done that? He, who was so anxious not to be seen? Had he been spying? It seemed unlikely, but there may have been something in his mind connecting Georgina to his own ill-fated Wendy. Was that a possibility? Was his interest prurient, even vengeful? Or did he somehow fear for Georgina, and follow them to offer protection? He must have been horribly afraid. From what she had seen of the man in the black van, Darren Pountney was at least six feet tall and built like a brick wall. And why had Christopher approached Georgina after the attack? Eileen felt sure it must have been to offer assistance, but how ill-judged, if so. His cover was now completely blown. Eileen could, perhaps, just imagine his chaotic state of mind, his lack of rational judgment, especially if he had witnessed the attack on Georgina. But now, what was he thinking now? Eileen could not begin to piece together in her own mind what must be going on in his, except she felt sure he would be very frightened. What exactly had he seen? And where was he?

Eileen filled Natasha and Sean in on the latest news, leaving out the parts she had no wish to air. Sean finally went home around ten thirty, and soon afterwards Natasha went to bed.

'Don't worry, Mum,' she said. 'I'm sure they'll catch the bastard really soon. I don't think we need to shake in our beds.'

'I wasn't planning to,' Eileen replied with a hint of acidity.

Natasha paused on the stairs. 'Do you think they'll call that tramp into the witness-box?'

Eileen shuddered and shook her head. Christopher could not possibly cope with any of that. He would go totally to pieces. He would rather die than stand up in a court of law and tell a bunch of lawyers that he had seen a young girl raped and battered. A cold dread rose in her; her palms sweated, and her heart raced. *Yes, he really would rather die, literally.* She imagined him in a state of panic and despair, guilt and fear. Would he think it was all too much to bear, not worth the effort?

Under the heavy cloud the night was dark. No star relieved the stifling pall of gloom. There was no sense at all in going to look for him. She twitched back the curtains, stared down the back garden, hoping to see him dart up the path from the woods. But the night wore on, and he did not come.

She could not sleep. Her bedroom seemed hotter than ever. In the early hours she came downstairs, registered again with a pricking of her eyelids the absence of Tillie. She flopped on the sofa. It was cooler, fractionally, downstairs. The night was quiet, the hunting owl elsewhere. She thought she could hear a tiny breeze begin to move in the trees at the bottom of the garden. She prayed for Christopher. *Keep him safe, Lord. Keep him stable. Help me to help him.*

But the gremlins were waiting in the musty cellars of her unconscious mind, and as soon as she drifted off to sleep they opened the trap doors and with a triumphant whoop were capering and posturing, thumbing their noses at all rationality, all attempts at altruism or wisdom. Fragments and tatters of dreams, full of bizarre, distorted images, floated in and out of her restlessly sleeping brain, slipping from her mental grasp at the moment when it seemed they might yield some meaning. She woke in the night, and lay still, blearily listening to the sounds of the house. A wind was rising. The boughs of the apple tree were creaking, its leaves rustling. The air was distinctly cooler. She closed her eyes and sank into a deeper sleep.

Sunday 16ᵗʰ June 1996

She awoke to the sound of the wind, a sound she had not heard for weeks. She had slept wrapped only in her threadbare bathrobe; now she drew it around her, shivering. She went into the kitchen, and made tea for herself and Natasha. It was already nine o'clock. The house was quiet. She took the tea up to Natasha, an invisible hump under the bedclothes. She merely growled in acknowledgement.

'I'm going to have a bath, then get off to church,' Eileen said. 'I'll see you later.'

The church, while not as packed as the evening before, was fuller than usual.

'Our new rector has novelty value,' Eileen murmured to Marie as she slid into the choir stalls beside her. 'That won't last long.'

'There are people here I've never seen,' Marie whispered. 'Where have they all come from?'

Eileen shrugged, and glanced around. Towards the back sat Penny Jescott, pretty, dark, anxious, surrounded by her milling children. Today, mercifully, the youngest was asleep in her lap.

Edward's style was friendly, conversational, but brisk. He mentioned the Quilley family in the prayers, but tactfully, letting little out. When he stepped into the pulpit, however, his attitude seemed to change, and Eileen remembered his reputation as a powerful preacher. She looked at her service sheet. He had entitled his sermon 'Making a difference', taking as his text Matthew 5 vv13-16, which he read in full.

'"You are like salt for the whole human race,"' he said in his pleasant tenor voice. '"But if salt loses its saltiness, there is no way to make it salty again. It has become worthless, so it is thrown out and people trample on it.

'"You are like light for the whole world. A city built on a hill cannot be hidden. No one lights a lamp and puts it under a bowl; instead he puts it on the lampstand, where it gives light for everyone in the house. In the same way your light must shine before people, so that they will see the good things you do and praise your Father in heaven."'

246

If only it were that simple. But most people didn't want to know. It never seemed to occur to them that they might have needs other than health and wealth and human love. The nearest many people got to worship was the care of their family. There was nothing wrong with that, but it was only a part of the story. It was as if their spiritual senses were dulled. What a good thing it was that no one was physically immortal. For many people the shock of death was the only thing that brought them face to face with the deeper levels of their being.

Edward was developing his theme, talking about how Christian faith should be lived out in the home, in the workplace, in the community. Gently he touched on the idea of making a contribution on a global scale, the reverberation of a single life through eternity.

He was good. Given the proper response, he would be very good. But there was the rub: soon he'd be bogged down in piffling questions and people would bombard him with their own pet issues, and between him and his real gifts would come Sunday School and Parochial Church Council and flowers and bell-ringing and the bishop, and in twenty years' time he'd be a very different man. She raised her eyes from her hymn book to where Simon Jescott, now awake, was writhing, red-faced and loud, in his mother's restraining grasp. At least by then the children would have left home. *But I won't see any of this.* A tiny shock rippled through her as she remembered. *I won't be here. I wonder where I will be.*

The service ended. Marie and Philip were dashing off somewhere to lunch, and made a hasty exit. Eileen, divested of her robes, paused to shake Edward's hand.

Unexpectedly he said, 'Would it be all right to drop by and see you this evening?'

Eileen was startled. 'Yes, do. I'll be in. Do you know where I live? Just over there, number five.'

'Thanks.'

She strolled slowly home, realizing that she would have to tell him, even though her plans were still vague. She didn't mind filling in, but she couldn't take on the responsibility for the church music, not after Philip. *Anyway, I won't be here, will I?*

The wind had risen even more. All through the service she had heard it moaning among the gravestones, whipping the trees and bushes that edged the churchyard. The massive grey clouds that had built up over the past few days were now being chased across the sky, fleeing in rags and tatters. The wind brought coolness with it, but only a little, and the humidity was still overpowering.

247

Natasha was up, and Sean had arrived. 'Can he stay for lunch, Mum?'

'Of course, if he doesn't mind eating any old thing.'

'He's used to that, with my cooking.'

'I finally got to meet the mysterious Mr. Draycott,' Sean said over lunch. 'I went over to Mum's to fix a leaky window, and he turned up.'

'So he is real, then,' Eileen said.

Sean smiled. 'Yes, and he isn't a midget either.'

'What are you on about?' Natasha said, frowning. 'Why did you think he might be a midget, for heaven's sake?'

Sean grinned even more broadly. 'Just a daft idea your mum and I had, love. As it turns out Mr. Draycott is tall and thin with big glasses and very little hair. He seemed a nice enough bloke, and mother behaved well when he was there, I noticed.'

'A good influence then, you think,' Eileen said as she got up to clear the plates.

'I hope so,' Sean said. 'We'll wash up, won't we, Natasha?'

'OK, if I must,' Natasha grumbled. 'Don't hang about, though. We're meeting Paddy and Lisa at three.'

When they had gone Eileen let herself think about Christopher. Her unease was growing. There had been no sign of him, and more and more she was convinced that he had seen everything that had happened to Georgina. If so he would have spiralled down, back into his world of terror and confusion. He would need help, he would need calming and reassurance. Who else was there for him but herself? She decided she just had time to look for him before collecting Michael, and was putting some supplies into a carrier bag, when the phone rang.

'Eileen, it's Marie.' Marie's voice shook slightly; she sounded as if she was trying to control it, and failing.

'What's up?'

'I've just had the police on the phone.'

'The police?'

'Yes. It's Stephanie. All these years I've dreaded a call like this, and now it's come. I used to get calls from her school, telling me what she'd been up to and asking me what I was going to do about it. But this is much worse. She's really excelled herself this time.'

'So what has happened?' Eileen could sense her friend was making a huge effort to be calm. But as soon as Marie began to speak her voice cracked, and she was unable to go on.

'Marie, shall I come down? Is Philip there?'

After a pause Marie whispered, 'Yes to both. Thank you, Eileen.'

With a last look down the empty garden Eileen sighed, put on her shoes, locked the door and walked briskly down to Marie's. The front door was open as usual. She let herself in and went into the lounge. Marie was sitting on the sofa, a damp handkerchief clutched in her hand. Eileen sat beside her and put her arm round her shoulders. Philip came in from the kitchen. He put mugs of tea in front of them, patted Marie's arm, and vanished upstairs.

'I'm sorry about this, Eileen,' Marie said. 'Were you doing something important?'

'Not in the least. But I do have to go and collect Michael later.'

Marie nodded. 'Of course you do. Philip is great, of course, but when it comes to Stephanie I think he feels a bit out of his depth.'

'So what has she done to have the police call?'

Marie took a gulp of tea. 'It seems there was a fracas at the nightclub last night, you know, the one Stephanie frequents in Caxford. I told you, didn't I, there have been some louts there from out of town, London I think, heaven knows what they see in a one-horse place like Caxford, but anyway, it turns out there was some kind of argument. The police hinted that drugs were involved, which wouldn't surprise me in the least, but that wasn't the worst of it. The row turned into a screaming match with Stephanie in the middle. I still don't know exactly what her involvement was, but I guess it was territorial, because she seems to regard that place as her little kingdom. She was yelling and one of these London people was going back at her and everybody was egging them on, the way they do when they've had too many drinks and who knows what else, and suddenly Stephanie pulls a knife and stabs this man.'

'Good grief! He's not dead, is he?'

'No, thank heaven, he tried to defend himself, and she gave him a nasty gash on his arm. Bad enough for stitches, though. By that time the nightclub manager had phoned the police, and they arrived in time to stop the mess turning really ugly.'

'So where is Stephanie now?'

'In the police station at Lambury. She's been in the cells all night. But that's not all. Apparently when the police arrived Stephanie just gave herself up, admitted everything, handed over the knife and went with them like a lamb.'

'That doesn't sound like Stephanie at all. Did the police tell you all this?'

'No, they were very brief and businesslike as you'd expect. After they had rung off I telephoned Colin Muldoon.'

'Oh? Why him?'

'Well, I thought maybe he and his brother had been there. I couldn't really call Neil Quilley, could I? Not at a time like this. Anyway, after I managed to persuade that old witch Kit to get her son, he was very helpful.'

'So what was his story?'

'He didn't want to say too much, I guess for fear of involving himself. But the interesting thing is, from what Colin was hinting, the whole thing may have been partly about Georgina.'

'How come?'

'Colin seemed to think that Stephanie knew something, and that something she said started the row in the first place. Do you know, it was almost as if she wanted to get caught. As you say, it's not like Stephanie to give in without a fight, and she's never been exactly enamoured of the police. But she didn't even utter a single swear-word, according to Colin.'

Eileen shook her head. 'So what happens next for Stephanie?'

'She's asked me to go down there tomorrow morning, the policewoman said. They suggested nine-thirty. Will you take me? Philip would, of course, but he's got work to go to.'

'Of course I will. I'll hang around if you want.'

'Yes, please. I'm bound to be flummoxed and not take anything in. Poor Stephanie. She's turning out like her father after all.'

'Let's not make any judgments till we've heard the whole story, OK? Has she got a solicitor?'

'The police organized someone.'

'Good. Look, Marie, try not to worry. We'll sort something out tomorrow. Till then there's nothing much we can do. Is Philip staying with you? Will you be all right?'

'Yes. He'll go straight from here to school. Thanks, Eileen. You're a rock.'

'I'd better go and get Michael now. I'll pick you up tomorrow as soon as I've dropped him off at school. I'm in this evening, if you want to phone. But you'll have Philip.'

Marie accompanied Eileen to the door. 'I'll see you about nine, then,' she said. Her face was pale, her eyes puffy. Eileen turned to wave briefly from the gate. What would she be feeling like now if it had been one of her own instead of Stephanie? *Just as Marie does now, of course. Shattered, fearful, guilty, dreading what might come, feeling responsible but unable to help.* And for Marie it was worse. Her instinct was to rush to Stephanie's side. But what reception would she get? That, too, must have been in her mind, what she saw as her failure as a parent. Poor Marie. But she had Philip. Eileen hoped that he, too, was a rock.

She went quickly home. The bag full of food for Christopher was still on the kitchen table. She took it down the garden, out of the gate, and left it in the usual place. The bag that she had left there on Friday afternoon was gone, but of Christopher there was no trace. The wind had dropped a little, but it was still strong enough to cause a rush and sway among the uppermost branches.

It was time to collect Michael. Again she locked up, and drove out of the village. Along the road the trees that bordered open fields, unprotected by houses, danced wildly in the wind.

Michael and Andy were waiting in the car park. Eileen parked and got out of the car.

'Hello, Andy,' she said. 'Hello, Michael. Had a good weekend?'

Both seemed quiet, even sullen. Andy shrugged. 'This is all getting a bit of a pain. I don't see why he can't just come home and have done with all this backwards and forwards stuff.'

'That's what we all agreed, wasn't it?' Eileen said. 'Including you and Denise.'

'Yeah. Well, OK. See you next week, Mikey.'

He ruffled Michael's hair, got back into the car and roared away. Eileen took Michael's bag and put it into the boot. 'Shall we go?' He nodded and got in beside her. They were silent as she negotiated the back streets of Caxford. Then, as they came out onto the open road, Eileen said, 'Is that how you feel too, Michael? Fed up with toing and froing?'

'It doesn't matter,' Michael muttered. 'Dad's just in a mood.'

'Who with?'

'Mummy, the kids, everything. Don't worry about it.'

'All right, I won't. How's Bill's hutch coming along?'

'It's really good. We've nearly finished it. I'm letting Harry help. I had to show him how to hit nails in straight.'

'Bill won't know himself.'

Sean and Natasha appeared in time to eat sandwiches and drink tea. Then they were away again. 'I'll be at Sean's for a few days, Mum,' Natasha said. 'I'll ring you. Bye, Michael. Be good.' Michael made a face.

Soon after eight he was bathed, read to and asleep. Eileen began to sort out his clothes for school. The wind had risen again, and was howling round the corners of the house. Something made her feel watchful, almost apprehensive. Perhaps it was just the wind, gusting, rattling loose palings, dying to a growl, then building again to something like frenzy, loud and wild. She put the kettle on and made coffee. Then,

251

among the crashing and battering, came another sound, a thud on the back door. She glanced up, and her heart nearly stopped. At the uncurtained window was a face: Christopher.

With a soft exclamation she hurried to the back door and opened it. The wind almost pulled the handle out of her hand as he tumbled inside. He looked windswept, wild-haired, almost feral, his eyes a dark blaze, glancing from side to side. He breathed heavily, as if he had been running. For a few moments he just stood there, trembling. Eileen closed the back door. Then he said, his voice thick and furred, 'It's started to rain at last. Big, fat drops.'

'Come in and sit down, Christopher,' Eileen said. 'Do you want some coffee?' He nodded.

She took her time in the kitchen, waiting for him to calm down. As she gave him the cup his hands shook. He took a sip, then a gulp, and spluttered. He put the cup down carefully on the floor. 'Everything is changing. It's really going to rain tonight. There's going to be a storm. Can you smell it?'

'You will get wet in the woods,' she said, then, suddenly reckless, added, 'Do you want to stay here tonight?' He looked at her warily. 'Natasha isn't coming back. Michael is asleep; I doubt he'll wake. We're alone. You can be gone early, if you want.' He was silent, staring at her. The silence lengthened. She registered the spectral moaning of the wind, the rattle of rain on the windows. 'What is it, Christopher?' she said. 'Hadn't you better tell me?'

He was perched on the edge of the chair. Suddenly he bunched himself up in a ball, clutching his head in his hands, and began to rock jerkily back and forth.

'Come on, Christopher,' she said. 'Whatever it is, share it with me. Is it what you saw in the woods?'

He looked up. 'How do you know?' he whispered.

'Of course I know. What happened to poor Georgina is all over the village. And she saw you, you know she did.'

'I wanted to help her,' he said, his voice a strangled moan. 'I wanted to, but I couldn't. You do believe me, don't you? I really wanted to help her, but I was so frightened, I just couldn't. Then, when that man had gone, she was just lying there in the dirt, she had blood on her, and she was crying. Eileen, I tell you, it was a terrible sound. Then I came down from the tree, because I wanted to help, but when she saw me she jumped up, and screamed and ran away. Eileen, tell me, will she be all right?'

'Who can say, Christopher? She has been damaged, abused and hurt, physically and psychologically. You understand that.'

He nodded. 'Yes, I do. I wanted to tell her that I understood. It was the wrong time though, wasn't it? I just scared her even more.'

'Did you see everything that happened to her?'

'Yes. They didn't notice me. I was in the tree.'

'Why? Why did you follow them? Weren't you afraid you'd be seen?'

He looked at the floor. His face flushed dark red. 'I am ashamed.' His voice was low and husky. 'I am a bad person. But I did want to help her. When I realized what was happening, I was horrified. I wanted to rescue that poor girl, but I was too scared, I just couldn't move.'

'But what about in the beginning? Why did you follow them at all?'

'Because I am bad,' he said. His voice was odd, flat, without inflexion; he spoke as if he were reading from a script. His eyes were glassy. 'I am corrupt. I can't escape from the rottenness that is inside me. It's taken over.'

'Christopher, you're not making sense.'

To her horror he began to sob. 'Eileen, don't you understand? I followed them because I wanted to watch. I am a pervert, a freak, I wanted to see what they did, I am surrounded by filth, I am tainted, like rotten meat, like the stuff we threw out at the butcher's, and she, that girl, she made me think of Wendy, so young, so innocent, but with such knowing eyes, and all that bare flesh on show, don't you get it, I wanted to see, I wanted to see him pull her knickers down and push her up against a tree and do it to her. But when it actually happened and I saw how terrified she was I wasn't excited any more, I was appalled and sick at myself. Then I really wanted to help, but all I did was make it worse.' He looked up at her, his flushed face streaked with tears and dirt. 'Oh, Eileen, what have I become? I am not a human being, I am some crawly, slimy thing, I am sick. What can I do? I am so ashamed. I am not fit to live.'

She took his trembling hand in her own. For a while she did not speak, searching for words. 'Has that voice been after you as well?'

He smiled bleakly. 'Of course. He never misses a trick. But I don't really need him any more. I say all those things to myself now. I don't need him to curse me. I have cursed myself.' He began to cry again. 'That poor girl. I could have saved her, but I was too pathetic. I am so sick, I was prepared to enjoy it—can you believe that anyone could be so twisted? It's almost as if I did it to her myself.'

'That's nonsense. I don't believe you would ever willingly hurt anyone.'

He shook his head. 'Who can tell what I might do? I am a monster, didn't you know that?'

Before she could answer, the doorbell rang. Christopher looked at her, bewilderment in his eyes.

'Oh, no,' she said under her breath. 'I'd forgotten he was coming.'

'Who? Who is it?'

'It's the new rector. He asked if he could call. I'd completely forgotten.'

Christopher jumped to his feet, pushing her aside. 'I can't see him! He has been sent to judge me, he is like my father, they are all the same, agents of the shouting tyrant, let me go, I can't see him!' He ran to the back door, and fumbled with the handle.

Eileen ran to the door after him. 'Christopher, don't be stupid, it's pouring with rain! Can't you just hide? He won't be here long.'

He turned to face her. He was trembling, but she could see he was making a huge effort to control it. 'No more hiding, Eileen. No more.'

He wrenched the door open. A gust of wind and a fine spray of rain beat on them. Then he was gone, leaving the door banging. The doorbell rang again.

Eileen went to the front door and opened it. Edward Jescott stood there, the collar of his jacket turned up.

'I'm sorry to call so late,' he said. 'I had a phone call at the last minute—'

'Forgive me,' Eileen said. 'I can't talk to you right now. I will explain.' And she shut the door in his startled face.

She ran to the back door again, and held it from banging while she stuffed her feet into shoes. Then she was out in the wind and the rain, running down the wet garden path, lit only by the light from her own living room. The wind whipped her skirt round her legs, and the rain plastered her hair to her head and trickled down her neck.

She reached the back gate, and held on to its rough, familiar wood. 'Christopher!' she yelled above the pounding, lashing rain. 'Christopher, don't be a fool! Come back! Christopher, it needn't be like this! Please, come back!' She listened, but only the elements answered her.

What can I do? It's dark, the weather is foul, and Michael is indoors asleep. What can I do?

Around midnight the wind dropped suddenly. Like some fierce, shambling monster tired of playing at havoc it fell to a dull rumble, muttered, and ceased. But the rain went on falling all night, steady, heavy, pounding the earth in straight lines, relentless, like a barbarian army, without understanding or mercy. It ran off the dry fields, hissed down the gutters, bubbled into drains. Eileen lay awake, listening to what would in other times have been elemental music. Now she pictured Christopher huddled under the trees, soaked, shivering, despairing and alone. She was angry, with him, with Edward Jescott, with herself, with fate, with God.

Where would Christopher be now, if Edward, seeing the weather, noting the late hour, had decided to call another day? *He would be here, with me.* She beat her pillow in fury. Perhaps he would be lying here asleep beside her; perhaps he would even be sleeping in her arms. He would be dry, and warm, and safe. She would stand between him and the demons.

But then she laughed at herself, a miserable parody of laughter. She ridiculed herself for her vanity, her pitiful proud resistance to the truth. *I can't even fight off my own demons.* The bleak fact was that Edward Jescott, whether she liked it or not—and she didn't like it at all—had been God's own angel that night. He had saved Christopher from Eileen, and as a side-effect he had saved her from herself. *What a poor fool I am.* Her anger evaporated, and she felt only weak and helpless. Tears rolled down her face unchecked.

Very early in the morning the rain eased. It ceased to thunder and drum and became gentle, bathing the shocked ground with showers. Worn and battered, she slept, and for the moment some strong and merciful hand kept the mocking imps from the doors of her mind.

Monday 17ᵗʰ June 1996

At nine twenty-five the desk sergeant at Lambury police station showed Marie and Eileen into a small, sparsely-furnished room with pale blue walls. Marie shivered. 'It's like a slightly up-market cell.'

The door opened and a middle-aged man in a suit came in. He was well-fed, well-groomed, sleek, with just a whiff of oiliness. He looked from Marie to Eileen. 'Mrs. Clements?'

'I am Mrs. Clements,' Marie said. 'This is my friend, Mrs. Harding.'

The man shook hands. 'Robert Marshall, of Moreton, Stanley and Marshall. Miss Clements expressed no preference for a particular solicitor so the police have asked me to advise her. She has asked me to fill you in on the facts of the matter before she meets with you herself, and of course to answer any questions you may have. I am sure you have no wish to prolong this meeting more than is quite necessary, so shall we begin?' He opened his briefcase and took out papers which he laid on a low table to one side. 'There are two separate, but related, charges against Miss Clements. One is connected with the supply of certain illegal substances, the other is of wounding. Miss Clements has fully admitted her involvement in these offences, whose gravity she understands. In fact she has been very helpful to the police, which may go some way towards a shorter sentence eventually. In particular she has provided names, places and dates which, it is hoped, will help to bring to justice a number of individuals wanted by the police. In addition she has furnished information about another offence committed recently by someone else.'

Marie digested this, struggling a little with the solicitor's circumlocutions. 'So all these events are connected. Is that what you are telling me?'

'So it would seem.'

'Perhaps you could start from the beginning, Mr. Marshall.'

'Of course. Miss Clements has, it appears, been involved in supplying certain drugs in the Caxford area, using as a base a nightclub there. As I understand it, this activity has been going on for some considerable time.

256

Some months ago a group of people from London began to frequent the Caxford nightclub. These people were known to the police in London, and it appears that they came here because the law was getting too close for comfort. In other words, they were keeping a low profile. Miss Clements felt antagonized by their presence, and there were some disagreements. This gang came and went, and your daughter kept a close watch on them, believing that they were planning to take over her territory, as it were. One of the members of this group, all of whom are known to the police for offences involving drugs and minor violence, has been implicated in the other crime of which I spoke earlier. You will understand that I cannot name any of these people at present. In a nutshell, that is the background to this case.'

Marie sighed. 'I always did wonder where she got all her cash from. Now I know. I can't pretend I am surprised. I am afraid my daughter has always been a wild child, Mr. Marshall.'

Robert Marshall nodded, not without sympathy. 'It seems, Mrs. Clements, that last Saturday night the tensions that had been simmering between your daughter and her associates on the one hand and the London gang on the other came to boiling point. By then the other crime was known about, and remarks were made, deliberately in your daughter's hearing, as if to goad her, by one of the more callow members of the rival group, which tipped Miss Clements over the edge. Up to then, despite everything, she had held on to her self-control; but her hatred for her competitors was aggravated when she heard of the offence committed against a young person of her acquaintance. Forgive me if I seem to be going all around the houses, but I have to be very careful not to breach confidentiality which would prejudice the ongoing investigations. I am sure you know to what I am referring.'

'Of course. Please go on, Mr. Marshall.'

'A quarrel broke out, and the young man who made the remarks was wounded. That's really all I can tell you. Your daughter is undoubtedly guilty of the charges brought against her, and she is not denying them. But, as I said, she has been helping the police, not only with evidence against the London group, but also with information regarding her own suppliers. As to her evidence relating to the other crime, it is more or less superfluous, since other evidence should be sufficient to bring the offender to book, which I fully expect to happen sooner rather than later.'

'What will happen to my daughter now, Mr Marshall?' Marie said, her voice rather faint.

'The question of bail probably won't arise,' Marshall said. 'In any case, Miss Clements does not wish to be bailed. This may be partly

257

because she is not confident as to her safety while any of her rivals remain at liberty. Obviously nothing will happen immediately. Meanwhile your daughter will remain in custody. That is also her wish. Naturally I will keep you informed of any developments, assuming that you are agreeable to retaining my services.'

Marie waved her hand vaguely. 'Yes, I can't see any reason not to. Will she go to prison, do you think?' Eileen could hear how hard Marie was trying to conceal her anxiety.

'I'm afraid a custodial sentence is inevitable, given the gravity of the offences,' Marshall said. 'However, as I mentioned earlier, her assistance to the police in catching other offenders will go some way to reducing her sentence. That part of it is, as you will understand, at the judge's discretion. But her custody now will also count against her sentence. I would not wish to second-guess the judge, of course, but I would say she might serve between three and four years if she behaves well.'

Eileen saw her friend go pale and lean back in her seat. She squeezed Marie's hand reassuringly, but there was nothing to say.

'Now, Mrs. Clements,' Marshall said briskly, 'your daughter has asked if she could speak with you after I had briefed you.' He collected up his papers and put them back in his briefcase. 'If you have no further questions at this point I think I need not detain you any longer. Here is my card: please don't hesitate to contact me if you have any points which you wish to raise.' He stood up, and shook hands again. 'Goodbye. The duty officer will take you to see your daughter.' He left the room, closing the door quietly.

Marie looked at Eileen, her blue eyes round. 'Well! What do you make of that?'

'It answers a few questions, doesn't it, about Stephanie's mysterious movements,' Eileen said.

'I wonder why she wants to stay banged up. It all seems a little odd, don't you think?'

'Hm. You'll have to find that one out from Stephanie herself.'

The door opened, and a smiling young policewoman invited Marie to follow her.

'Do you mind waiting, Eileen?' Marie said. 'I'm sorry to mess up your day like this. I'll try not to be long.'

'Don't worry, Marie. Go and talk to Stephanie.'

When Marie had gone Eileen stood up and went over to the window. The police station occupied several floors of a modern office building, and she looked out over the roofs of Lambury. This was where Michael would be living. She did not know Lambury well. It was a fairly modern town, a place where people worked, with mushrooming housing developments on its outskirts. Over the top of Lambury she looked eastwards to the sea. If she had been on the other side of the building she might have looked west to Caxford and north-west to Holton. But there was little to see. After the night's rain the air was heavy with moisture, and a haze obliterated the further view.

In her mind she travelled back the thirty miles to Holton, down her garden path, out of the gate, down through the familiar woodland walks. Hidden among those trees was a life as precious to her as that of her children. Fear twisted and cramped her guts into actual physical pain. A clock ticked softly on the blue wall. Minutes lengthened into hours, hours away from Christopher, and she was helpless to help him. Removing her physical presence was equal in her mind to taking away all his protection. She thought of him as naked and defenceless, with all the inimical spiritual powers around and over him poised to strike. It took all her willpower not to rush down the stairs, out of the building, into her car waiting in the car park, and out onto the road home, to stand beside Christopher as his sword and shield.

Had she ever shown him that passage on the whole armour of God? She couldn't remember. In her confused state, her agony of fear and impatience, she did not think to surround him with prayer.

Marie was gone about half an hour. Returning, she gave Eileen a timid smile. 'Let's go home. I'm sure you are anxious to be away. I can tell you about Stephanie in the car.'

Eileen felt as though fetters and manacles had been cut away from her. She concentrated on getting out of Lambury onto the ring road, and said little to Marie until they were speeding westwards through the orchards.

'Are you all right, Eileen? You seem tense.'

'Oh. Do I? Tell me about Stephanie.'

'Eileen, it's so odd. Stephanie is different.'

'How different?'

'Well, she looks relatively normal, for a start. No weird hairstyle, no heavy makeup, no aggressive clothes or peculiar footwear, just a girl in a T-shirt and jeans. I almost didn't recognize her.'

'Go on.'

'And her attitude, as well, she is unlike herself, so quiet and calm, relaxed, even humorous. I have to say I quite liked her.'

'One would hope so.'

'I don't know if I ever did before, you know. She wasn't exactly likeable, if we are very truthful.'

259

'Perhaps not. Well, what did she say?'

'She told me that when she heard what had happened to Georgina something happened in her own mind that changed everything. She said she had an overwhelming vision of herself as a kind of channel of evil. She is quite convinced that she is the cause of all the bad things that have happened. That's why she wants to go to jail: she wants to pay, to atone.'

'I can hardly credit what you are saying.'

'Neither can I. But she isn't dramatic, there are no great statements or tears, just quiet, convinced determination. She said when she stabbed that young man, Jamie Sloman his name is, only Stephanie calls him Slimy Sloman, she said it felt wonderful, that she did it for Georgina. She told me about the fight in the nightclub, Eileen, and I have never heard her speak with such bitter hatred, not in all the years of quarrels and boasting and general nastiness. Apparently this Sloman character was leaning on the bar, and every time Stephanie was within earshot he would say something calculated to infuriate. What was it she said? Yes, I remember. I can hardly blame Stephanie for losing her temper. He called Georgina "Daz's jailbait," said Pountney preferred "fresh meat."' Marie shuddered. 'You can't comprehend it, can you? Just thinking about it makes me feel nauseated. Poor Georgina. Whatever possessed her to get in with such a pack of sewer-rats?' She sighed. 'Well, back to Stephanie. The odd thing was, Eileen, it was like an interview, or an audience: I hardly said a word. She said to me, "You'll see, Mum, when I come out of prison I am going to be quite different, someone you might want to know. Don't worry about me, just get on with your life. I'll be fine." I don't quite know what to make of it.'

'Will she, do you suppose? Will she make something of herself? Hold on to her resolve?'

'Well, as you know, Stephanie is nothing if not an extremist. Perhaps she will amaze us. The odd thing is, I feel I ought to be terribly upset, but I'm not.'

'Why do you think that is?'

Marie smiled sadly. 'Maybe it's partly because I know that for a while at least she'll be safe, out of trouble, and I won't have to worry about where she is or what she's up to.'

They were silent for several miles. The air was still again, but from time to time the sky darkened and a shower whipped round the car and was gone in minutes.

'Will you come in for a moment, Eileen?' Marie said as they drew up outside her house.

'No, I won't, thanks, Marie,' Eileen said. 'There are things I must do.'

260

'Of course. Thanks for today. Having you there made all the difference.'

'No problem.'

Marie paused, her hand on the car door. Eileen looked at her enquiringly.

'Philip has asked me to marry him,' Marie said, her voice sounding strange.

'Has he? Well, good for him! And are you going to?'

Marie looked at her in amazement. 'You bet I am!'

'Did you tell Stephanie about this?'

'Yes, I did. She came over and hugged me, and said she was delighted. I can't cope with the new Stephanie. It's almost surreal.'

'But you won't be staying here, will you?'

'No. That's the other thing. Philip has been offered his old job back, as organist and director of music at Osewick Abbey. He was headhunted, actually. When Philip left the Abbey originally, it was all down to church politics and in-fighting. Even Philip's replacement, a chap called Dalton, got the same treatment, which is why he moved on so quickly. He didn't even stay two years. Apparently he's got a job at a cathedral somewhere in the Midlands, so the Osewick job fell vacant again.'

'Who was causing all the trouble, then?'

'It's a sickening story, especially when you think such people ought to know better, so I'll spare you the details, but it was the dean who was the source of all the poison. As it turns out quite a lot of people are glad to see the back of him.'

'What's happened to him?'

'Well, he was getting on towards retirement anyway, but this Dalton fellow's resignation letter made it damningly plain why he was going, and when the dean received it I guess his blood pressure went through the roof, because not long after he had a stroke. I think he's recovered up to a point, but it's obvious he'll never work again, and so he's retired a few years early.'

'All change at Osewick.'

'Yes, for the better. It's not what you'd call an uplifting tale of Christian witness, is it? Anyway, it's all behind us now, I am thankful to say. Philip's got his old house back in the Close. It's really quite lovely. You must come and visit.'

'I will. One thing, Marie, if it hadn't been for the Demon Dean, you and Philip would probably never have met.'

'I did think of that. I am sort of glad I didn't wish any horrible fate on the old toad.'

'I am really pleased things have changed for you, Marie. Go forth and multiply. Figuratively, I mean.'

'I should hope figuratively, at my age.'

'So when's the wedding? Another wedding! I might even have to buy a hat.'

'There's nothing fixed yet. I'll let you know. We could have had it in the Abbey, but that's a bit grand for me. I don't much care, to be honest. I'm not interested in the trappings. We're thinking of going away for a while; I'm looking forward to that. Away from dramas and secrets and worries, just to be peaceful with Philip.'

'Enjoy it while you can.'

'I hope to. Thanks, Eileen. I won't hold you up a second longer.' She got out of the car.

'I'm going too, as it happens,' Eileen said.

'What?'

'By the end of the year I'll be broke. There's nothing to keep me here now, is there? I'll sell the house. And I'll have to find work.'

'What will you do?'

'No idea. Watch this space.'

'So much change, Eileen. We'll talk again soon, won't we?'

'Of course. Bye, Marie. Look after yourself.'

She headed home. She parked the car, let herself in and paused only to change her shoes. Then she was out again, down the back path, through the gate, into the woods. The long wet grass soaked her bare legs, but she waded through it uncaring. Fear and elation danced together. She could feel her heart pounding against her ribs. It was not happiness she felt, it was freedom; the dread and apprehension were still there, but springing up irresistibly was also joy. Why? Where was it coming from? Was she finally losing her reason?

After the heavy rain the going was hard. The paths were slick with mud, the grass and ferns were long and weighed down with water, and with every movement of air the trees shed their load of captive raindrops on her head and back. The warmth and wetness of the air made it difficult to breathe, and negotiating the slippery paths in unsuitable shoes was exhausting. The high winds of the previous night had wrought some damage: dead and shallow-rooted trees had been blown down, some across paths that she needed to take, so that she had to find detours. Her shoes were soaked and covered in mud, her clothes clung with damp and sweat, and after an hour of slipping about and climbing over fallen logs, scratching her legs, she was still a fair way from where she expected to find Christopher. Somehow none of it mattered. The sense of urgency which impelled her grew, combining in almost equal measure the joy of a free woman going to meet her lover with the terror of someone facing an unknown danger. She did not allow herself to consider the rationality of her actions; she blanked thought from her mind, except to solve the immediate problem of negotiating the storm-battered woods. At that moment neither reason nor physical exhaustion nor caution nor anything else could have prevented her from searching for Christopher until she found him.

And she did find him finally, in the hidden clearing on the other side of the rape field, not far from Annette's. It was where she thought he would be.

As soon as she saw him an icy terror made her skin prickle as the sweat cooled on her body. She stood looking at him, and within seconds the anticipation, the crazy euphoria, evaporated as her returning reason took in what her eyes were showing her. He lay among the leaves, curled up under his grey blanket. One foot, in a dirty unlaced trainer, lay uncovered at an awkward angle. Beside him in a neat pile were his few belongings, and on the top, her mother's Bible, pinning down a square of damp white paper.

Time slowed down; it seemed to become unpredictably elastic. How long she stood there, trying to grasp it all, she did not know. Eventually she tiptoed over to him, and knelt down beside him. In an agony of fear she touched his shoulder. There was no movement. She shook harder. He rolled back from her, and the grey blanket fell away. His body was limp and cool, his legs drawn up. There were deep shadows round his closed eyes, and his lips and fingers were tinged with blue.

'Oh, dear heaven, Christopher, what have you done?' she whispered. Under him as he lay on his back was revealed a half bottle of vodka, most of which had gone, and in his right hand, the fingers tightly curled, was a brown plastic medicine bottle, empty.

The realization that he was dead hit her with tremendous force. She felt like someone trapped in a building that was being demolished; she could hear the booming and crashing, and see the falling masonry and the cloud of dust as darkness enveloped her. As disbelief gave way to certainty sobs of panic rose in her throat. She hauled him clumsily onto her lap and held him close in her arms, as if to warm his cold flesh with her living heat. She rocked him like a baby, tears pouring down her face. After a while a germ of thought found its way through her muddled brain. She knew that it would be useless, but she tried to resuscitate him, trying to remember what she had been taught in a first-aid course years ago. But her efforts were fruitless, and the touch of his cold, unresponsive mouth brought only fresh anguish.

'Oh, Christopher, you stupid boy, why didn't you wait for me?' she whispered to him as he lay, head flung back, in her rain-soaked lap. 'You lost what little faith you had.' She brushed the hair away from his forehead with her fingers, and studied the pale young face now completely at rest, no blaze of life from his restless dark eyes, no agitated speech ever to fall again from his stilled lips. She laid him down carefully on the sodden leaf-mould, replaced the medicine bottle in his hand, and wrapped the blanket round him as if to keep the cold from a sleeping child. Dull and mechanical, she thought of protecting both of them from inquisitive minds, and she took her mother's Bible from his pile of belongings. Under it, on top of a few other pitiful things, were three letters. Two were in envelopes, addressed "To my family" and "To the authorities." The third was simply a piece of lined paper, folded in half. She took it and opened it.

"My dear friend," she read in his spiky writing, and at this greeting tears sprang to her eyes. She wiped them away with her hand.

"My dear friend,

I will not name you in case anyone else should find me, although I think it very likely that you will find me. You found me when I lived, and now you have found me when I am dead. Please forgive me for the shock of what I have done. When at last you have time and peace to think about it, I know you will not be surprised. Perhaps you will be sad, and I am sorry for that.

I wanted you to know that I am not going in despair, only in the certain knowledge that I cannot cope with this world and my life as I see it stretched out before me. I am going to see for myself whether there really is a room set aside for me in our Father's house.

Thank you for everything you have done for me over the past few weeks. I have nothing to give you back except a word from your favourite book—'...the darkness is passing away, and the true light is already shining.'

I have left letters for my family and the authorities which I hope will explain and make things easier. This letter is only for you. I hope I will not cause you any trouble.

The pills I stole from Maurice are beginning to work now and I will not be able to write much more. Just remember that if you are right, this is not the last time we shall meet.

With love,
            Christopher."

For a long time she knelt there, holding the scrap of paper in her hand, and wept as she had not done for nearly thirty years, when she stood in a sunny churchyard, watching her mother's coffin being lowered into the earth.

But eventually sense and sanity came creeping back. She heard voices in the distance, and realized that she could hear the shouting of the children in the school, let out to play after their midday meal. The thought of Michael and the other children yelling and running round the playground, while she knelt beside a dead man in the woods, brought her back to a sense of what she had to do. She bent over Christopher and kissed his cold, still face. Then she got to her feet stiffly, taking his note and her mother's Bible in her hand. As she backed away from him, the pain of leaving him there, alone among the trees, was almost more than she could bear. She turned quickly and stumbled down the slippery paths towards home.

Afterwards, Eileen could remember nothing of how she had retraced her way through the woods and arrived at her own back door. But once there, cold and blank, she washed and changed and telephoned the police. Then she phoned Nancy Potter, asking her to collect Michael from school and take him home. 'Do you mind? Something urgent has come up. I'll tell you about it later. Thanks, Nancy.'

When the police arrived, accompanied by their medical officer, she made them tea. Then she took them by the shorter route, via Marie's lane and the footpath along the rape field. As they passed, people stared from their gardens, but she ignored them. She took the two policemen and the doctor to where Christopher lay, but she went no closer than the end of the path. She could not look at him again. The police were sympathetic, understanding how distressing it must have been for someone taking a stroll in the woods, as she so often did, to find a dead body.

They emerged from the trees. One of the policemen contacted his superiors.

'Yes, life extinct,' the medical officer said to Eileen, shaking his head regretfully. 'Early this morning, I'd say he took the stuff. Only a young chap, too. Did you say you'd seen him around, Mrs. Harding?'

'Once or twice, yes.'

'Can't think why anyone in their right mind would want to live rough out here. Though I dare say the poor fellow wasn't in his right mind. Well, we shall see.'

'What are the police waiting for?' Eileen asked. 'Do you need me any more at this moment? You know where I live, if you need me for anything. I really don't want to see him carted out in a body-bag.'

'Quite understandable,' the doctor said. 'You might as well cut off home, but check with the sergeant first. I expect you'll get a call from the coroner's office.'

Eileen was alarmed. 'What will I have to do?'

'Oh, don't you worry, it'll be just routine. Tell the coroner what you told us. There'll be no problem. It's not as if you had any connection with this chap, did you, apart from having the misfortune to discover the body.'

At home, she sat in the kitchen and thought. Although she had blanked out the feeling part of her brain, her thought processes were clear and decisive as she reviewed her options. She knew she had to tell at least Marie and Natasha, and from there the village would get to know. The biggest problem was Michael. She would have to handle him with great care.

Later that afternoon she went up to the Potters' to collect him. Before anything else she drew Nancy aside and quietly explained what had happened. 'I want to take Michael home and tell him calmly, just the two of us. I think perhaps we need to be careful. After all, these two boys got to know this man, if only a little, and I wouldn't want them unduly upset.' Nancy Potter saw the wisdom of this and agreed to talk quietly to Stephen later.

Michael had never given much thought to the idea of self-destruction, and it was the puzzle of suicide that worried him more than the fact of Christopher's death. In the end he seemed to accept that to kill oneself may be an understandable, if deplorable, reaction for someone whose mental health was so seriously disordered. All he said was, 'We did try to help him, didn't we, Mum? I guess we couldn't really have, though, could we? Not if he was crazy like that. But he didn't seem crazy.'

'I don't think you can always tell, Michael. Don't forget, will you, that no one knows we knew poor Christopher, only you and me and Stephen.'

'Steve doesn't count. He was too scared. He won't say anything to his mum, though, because he doesn't want anyone to know he's a bit of a baby.'

'Let's keep it quietly between ourselves, then. It's better that way.'

Michael had agreed, but for Eileen he was still a source of worry. Had he really accepted what had happened, or was he hiding his feelings, trying to be tough when in fact he was worried and upset? And would he say anything? The thought of her involvement with Christopher becoming public property was intolerable. At that moment she did not ask herself why. She only knew, beyond reason, that he must remain her secret.

July 1996

She went to the inquest, a brief affair that opened, only to be closed again till a later date, to give Christopher's family the chance to take charge of his body. Then someone came and took a written statement from her, a document that did not lie, but did not tell the whole truth either. Eileen felt like a criminal, but to the young woman who interviewed her it all seemed routine.

She went to his funeral. The service was held at Lambury Crematorium, to be followed at some future time by an interment of ashes at his father's church, All Saints, Barnwell. She crept into the back of the little chapel, tastefully decorated with sombre maroon hangings, a thin discreet music coming from the tiny organ. By then she could already feel the beginning of her inner disintegration, but she maintained her self-control somehow, glued together by her anger. She wanted to see the family that had so neglected and marginalized him, the remote and disappointed father, the busy mother, the sniping sisters, the domineering aunt. But when she saw them, occupying the front row of seats in the chapel, she could not hold on to her bitterness. They all seemed so much smaller than she had anticipated. His father, though a man of more than average height, seemed bowed and shrunken. His mother was an effigy in marble. His sisters clung to each other and wept, and his aunt handed out tissues and looked old and lined, nothing like the well-fleshed, confident woman who read the local news. Though at that moment of despair Eileen could not have said she felt pity for them, the evaporation of her rage left an echoing space which later, perhaps, might be infiltrated by softer thoughts. Forgiveness she could not contemplate; but her sudden inability to hate the Arrowsmiths began also to erode her loathing for Maurice Bentley.

Christopher's funeral was a turning-point for Eileen. It broke down her defences as she finally acknowledged that he was dead, his body encased in blond wood on which rested a single bunch of white lilies. The moment that seemed to pierce the very joints of her bones came when the officiating clergyman, in his brief address, said something quite unexpected.

267

'Christopher left a message for his family which they have shared with me,' he said, 'and in which he asked for a certain Bible passage to be read. It is my solemn privilege to carry out one of his last requests. I read to you Psalm 25.

"To thee, O Lord, I lift up my soul.
O God, in thee I trust,
let me not be put to shame;
let not my enemies exult over me.
Yea, let none that wait for thee be put to shame."'

The shock of the words, and what they might imply of Christopher's last thoughts, dazed Eileen, and the rest of the psalm filtered into her brain in shreds and tatters.

"'Be mindful of thy mercy, O Lord;
and of thy steadfast love…
For thy name's sake, O Lord,
pardon my guilt, for it is great.
My eyes are ever toward the Lord,
for he will pluck my feet out of the net.
Turn thou to me, and be gracious to me;
for I am lonely and afflicted.
Relieve the troubles of my heart…
Consider how many are my foes,
and with what violent hatred they hate me.
O guard my life, and deliver me…
for I wait for thee."'

Eileen left the chapel after the reading of the psalm. She could bear no more. She felt that it had been a clear message to her, intending to reassure and comfort her, but knowing that he had been so close to understanding made his death all the more unendurable. In her anguish she was plagued by hollow thoughts of what might have been, and they served only to increase her torment.

With her anger went her anchor and her control, and she saw a black pit gaping before her feet, a pit into which she fell headlong, feeling something akin to gratitude as its suffocating depths engulfed her.

For almost four weeks she existed in a lightless chasm. All outer life seemed to depart. The only activity was within her mind, and that was intense and chaotic. Almost overnight, she ceased to be able to function normally. She lay awake all night and slept for much of the day. When she was awake, she stared sightlessly into the distance. Michael phoned Natasha, Natasha spoke to her boss, and came home to be a mother to

268

her mother and Michael. She then phoned her sister, who postponed her trip with her friends and came up from Exeter. Eileen looked at her blearily and said simply, 'Hello, Christie. Aren't you supposed to be on holiday?' The girls called the doctor. He came, but Eileen would not, or could not, cooperate.

Looking back on this episode, what memories she had of her outer world were vague and insubstantial, but the thoughts and the dreams were like fireworks by contrast, loud, vivid, electrifying, fearful. One night she dreamed that she was somewhere on the ceiling, looking down at herself lying in bed, wrapped in a wrinkled sheet, unmoving. It was as if she could *see* the passage of time: a child appeared in the bedroom, spoke soundlessly to the inert figure, and went away. Then a man got into bed beside her, slept, got up, and left. The scene was repeated several times. At a point she clearly recognized, then and after, she saw herself die; there was a kind of atmospheric 'click'. She witnessed with horrified fascination her own deterioration and decay. Still the child visited, still the unknown man took his nightly place beside her. It was as if she were invisible, as if no one knew she was dead, or even that she was there. There welled up in her a sense of horror and injustice at her own insignificance, her lack of substance, her non-existence. Yet somewhere her mortal voice was crying, 'I was here, I was alive, my life mattered, I was sick, I died, didn't you notice? Can't you see I am falling apart before your eyes?'

People came to speak to her. It was a struggle to understand what they were saying, although she knew that all their intentions were kind. Sometimes Michael would come upstairs and sit on the bed beside her and hold her hand, and at a huge echoing distance the sight of his troubled face gave her pain.

Then there came a morning when she woke from a dream of horror to something even more horrible: reality. She had dreamed that she was in her own kitchen, and suddenly Christopher had appeared from nowhere, wrapped in a greyish sheet like a shroud, whey-faced, sunken-eyed, looking as ill as he could have looked this side of death. She had remonstrated with him, knowing his illness to be critical, trying to persuade him to go back to where he belonged—bed? the hospital? she did not know. Again the dream was permeated by a sense of dislocation, of wrongness. Waking to the knowledge that all hope had died was worse than the dream. She clung forlornly to her own illness as it irresistibly escaped her, wishing Christopher rather ill than dead, rather mad or miserable than dead, rather anything than dead. She put her arms over her head and sobbed.

269

Not long after this Michael came upstairs and lay down beside her with his head on her arm. She was unresisting. 'Mum, you've got to listen to me, OK? Mummy and Daddy are saying things about you.'

'Mm.'

'They want to take me away. They say you can't look after me. They keep asking questions. I said you aren't well. Mum, you've got to help me.'

She looked at his face, and his anxiety pierced her, breaking the spell, releasing her voice. 'You know, it's nearly time anyway, Michael. Time for you to go home.'

'I know. But I don't want to go until you are better. I want to help Tash take care of you.'

'You are all doing a great job, Michael. Thank you.'

'Mum, is it because of Christopher that you are sad?'

'Yes, I guess so, Michael.'

'You will get better, won't you?'

'Yes, I will. I will start today.'

He turned to her and hugged her, his eyes bright. 'I am glad. Shall I get Tash to make you a cup of tea? I will bring it.'

'All right.'

The end of July arrived, and they came for Michael. Eileen made a convincing invalid, wrapped in a blanket in the armchair, pale and gaunt but rational. Michael shook hands with Sean and hugged his sisters, then came over to Eileen and put his arms round her neck.

'Goodbye, my darling,' she said softly. 'Be happy.'

He stood back, a strange smile on his lips, and somehow she knew that Christopher would always be a secret that lay between them, that he would never tell, that perhaps as he grew up the knowledge would sink and fade and be relegated to the unimportant past.

Michael picked up the new carrier which had been bought for Bill. They all waved to him from the front garden. Eileen was weak, and leaned on Sean's arm. Christina and Natasha wept a little, but Eileen said, 'You know, Michael has been gone for a while now. And he always wanted to be with his real family.'

She began to feel better: to eat, to sleep without dreaming. She still could not read. The printed word refused to stand still and blurred before her eyes. Once or twice they told her that Edward Jescott had visited, but she would not see him. 'Tell him I am not ready for visitors,' she said. 'It's not just him.' This was only half true, but she felt he deserved a kindly lie. Then there came a day when she felt she could get

270

up, get washed and dressed, take part in life again in a small way. She got out of bed, put on her old bathrobe, and went shakily downstairs. There were voices coming from the kitchen: Natasha, Christina, Marie and Sean. Something made her pause and listen.

'I don't really get any of this,' Natasha was saying. 'I mean, Mum has always been so strong. I can understand her being upset; anyone would be if they found a body when they weren't expecting it, but to go completely to pieces, it just isn't her.'

Christina said, 'I was really amazed when you rang me, Tash. I just couldn't believe what I was hearing. Mum was the last person on earth to have a breakdown of any sort. What I'd like to know is how her faith has helped her. It doesn't seem to have done much good, does it?'

'Wait a minute,' Sean said. 'You can't tell what's going on in another person's mind. And your mum has had a hell of a lot happen to her in a short time. There's Marie and Natasha getting married, there's Michael gone, she's getting divorced and having to sell up, and even her dog died. I guess finding this body was just the last straw. And none of us has really paid her much attention until now, have we? Shouldn't we have seen something coming?'

In the silence that followed came Marie's quiet, hesitant voice. 'I thought I knew Eileen pretty well. Now, I wonder. But you are right, Natasha, your mum is strong, one of the strongest people I know. Maybe people like that fall harder when they do fall. I feel guilty that I wasn't there for her a bit more. She was always there for me. I guess I was so wrapped up in my own affairs. I feel badly about that. But I wonder, I do wonder, whether there wasn't more to this so-called tramp than we know.'

'What on earth do you mean, Marie?' Christina said.

'I don't know. I can't put my finger on it. But I can't help thinking there's something she's not telling us. I wonder how she came to be in that part of the woods that day. I mean, it's not as if she had a dog to take out any more. And then it just seemed such an almighty reaction, didn't it? But perhaps you're right, Sean, perhaps it was just on top of everything else.'

Eileen crept back up the stairs. Then she came down again, coughing and treading heavily. The voices ceased. Natasha came to the bottom of the stairs.

'Mum! What are you doing up?'

'I am feeling a lot better. I just came down to tell you that I am going to have a bath, and I don't want anyone pounding on the door, desperate for the loo, while I am wallowing in foam. And I thought it would be

271

nice to give my wonderful cooks a night off. Sean, my dear, how would you like to drive to the take-away? My purse is on the dresser. Help yourself. I think it is about time I started living again.'

Despite the brave words, she did not get better overnight. But just as anger had kept her together in the days immediately following Christopher's death, so now the need to keep the secret fuelled her recovery. Perhaps somewhere in the deep layers of her mind she knew it would not be a permanent cure; for an affliction so profound something more dedicated and prolonged was needed. But it would serve for now. She had a mission again, however small, and it gave her enough of an illusion of control to take up her life and carry on.

August 1996

When she was a lot further along that road, they told her of a sad and peculiar happening in Holton.

'You know, for a while the story of you finding the body was all over the village,' Natasha said. 'Everybody was speculating. Then when you started going to pieces it all intensified. I couldn't go to the shop without having to field a load of questions, and not all of it sounded very sympathetic. I was just glad it wasn't you at the receiving end. I began to get quite worried about how they would be when you got well enough to go out yourself. But then they found poor old Nora Meadows in the churchyard, and your story was old news.'

'What do you mean, found her?'

'Well, apparently she went up to visit her son's grave. You knew she had a little boy, didn't you? He died when he was a toddler. It was years and years ago, but she used to go up there regularly and take flowers. About a fortnight after you were taken ill they found her there, dead as a doornail, leaning against his headstone.'

'Good heavens. So what's happened to poor old Reg?'

'He had to go into a nursing home. Isn't it queer? We all expected him to go, not her. Anyway, you were a nine-day wonder after that.'

'I am relieved to hear it.' *Now Christopher has taken another step back into neglect and obscurity. Apart from his family, it will only be me that remembers him.* She started to think again about the psalm read at his funeral. She felt sure that it was meaningful, a message, but her brain was still too weak and weary to work on it, and she left it for another day.

She put the house on the market. The Milners came and within a week had agreed to buy. Christina, finally satisfied that her mother was on the way to recovery, joined her friends in Europe. Marie, though full of her own plans, visited often, and Sean and Natasha hovered like anxious parents until she sent them packing to take up their own lives again. 'You two have been great. I'm truly thankful you've been around. I couldn't have managed without you, I know that. But I am OK now.

273

We can all get on with whatever it is we have to do. No more worry, all right? I am back to normal.' It was not entirely true, of course; but perhaps normality was an illusion anyway, and what she had would be good enough.

One last odd thing happened which gave Eileen another jolt into taking control of her life. She was at the front gate, tying knots in plastic sacks, when a car drew up, and out of it stepped Annette Dyer. To Eileen's eyes she was transformed: smartly dressed, makeup, sophisticated hairstyle, long red nails.

'I phoned, you know,' she said. 'I heard you were ill. I'm so sorry, dear. Are you quite all right now?'

'Yes, thanks, Annette. I'm fine. But you, you look wonderful.'

'I am leaving, Eileen. I had to stop by and tell you, and say thank you for your part in it all. I am leaving Richard, and Holton. I told him last night. I had it all planned.'

'Good grief, Annette! How on earth did he react?'

'For once, he was so stunned he had very little to say for himself.'

'Are you absolutely sure about all this?'

'More than absolutely. As I said, I've got it all planned. It's a long story, but I bumped into a friend of a friend, and then the second friend, Adele, phoned me and the upshot is I'm going to live with her in London and help her with her business. She runs a mail-order company dealing in fine china. She started it up twelve years ago, after her divorce, and it's doing very well. It's on a trial basis, of course, but if we are both happy with the arrangement I'll stick with it. She's lent me her car to take the last of my stuff. Nice, isn't it?' She waved a hand at the sporty white saloon. 'Whatever happens, I won't be back. But I had to come and say goodbye, and please, dear Eileen, let's keep in touch.'

'I hope so, Annette.'

'So what are you going to do?'

'My plans are a bit vague at present. I have to work too, though I doubt I'll find a job quite as dazzling as yours.'

'I wish you all luck, Eileen.'

'And you.' She hugged her friend. 'Goodbye, Annette.'

September 1996

Philip and Marie married on a weekday in the middle of September, a day which marked the beginning of an oasis of calm weather. The civil ceremony at Osewick Register Office was followed by a simple service of blessing in the quire of the Abbey, and a garden party at their house in the Close, one of a beautiful eighteenth-century terrace from whose upper windows the Abbey could be seen across the green. It was a modest party, the guests, apart from Eileen, mostly friends of Philip's, but the quiet delight of Marie and Philip at their new status warmed the entire gathering. And Stephanie was there, escorted by a prison officer who, despite being out of uniform for the occasion, still looked exactly what she was. Stephanie's presence lent a bizarre note to the chiefly churchy ensemble, which she and her mother evidently found amusing. Eileen knew very few people there, but she strolled round the sunlit gardens contentedly enough, glass in hand, while photographs—Marie, Philip, Stephanie—were taken. She came across the prison officer, a short, stout, youngish woman with large glasses, hovering awkwardly by a wall up which scrambled a yellow rose-bush still resplendent with nodding flowers.

'This must be a strange sort of working day for you,' Eileen said.

The woman seemed relieved to be spoken to. 'Well, it beats some of the stuff I have to do. And it's very nice here, of course. But I do feel a bit like a sore thumb, I have to admit. And there's just that little worry about keeping a close eye on my charge.'

Eileen raised her eyebrows. 'Are you afraid she might try to escape?'

'These things do happen, you know. And then it would be my head on the block.'

'I feel sure Stephanie has no such plans,' Eileen said. 'I spoke to her earlier. She is very happy to be at her mother's wedding. I don't think she expected it.'

'Well, to be honest with you, she is being rewarded for good behaviour. She is a model prisoner, actually.'

'It's strange,' Eileen said. 'She's the second person I have known

275

who's gone to prison and both of them seem to have benefited from the experience. And yet I would have said that despite many good people's efforts the majority of convicts come out worse than they went in.'

The officer bristled. 'We have a very good system at Allerton. We pride ourselves on having good relationships with our inmates, and I can assure you it isn't easy.'

'I don't doubt it,' Eileen said. 'You're obviously doing a fine job with Stephanie.'

Stephanie was allowed to stay long enough to wave her mother off as she and Philip departed. An unmarked secure van was parked discreetly at the end of the Close, and when Philip's car had vanished round the corner the prison officer attached herself smartly to Stephanie with a pair of handcuffs and took her away. Eileen found herself standing next to the bishop's chaplain, a man she recognized from Edward Jescott's induction.

'Bit unusual, that,' he remarked, sipping his champagne. 'Having your convict daughter at your wedding. I hear she was a drug dealer or something. Quite young for all that sort of thing.'

Eileen looked at him without smiling. 'Stephanie is eighteen. Young enough to change.'

Suddenly things began to move in the lumbering machinery of conveyancing, and contracts were exchanged with the Milners, a middle-aged couple whose only son was living abroad. They were keen ramblers and bird-watchers and possessed many do-it-yourself skills. *Just as well.* They were enthusiastic about the house, keen to take part in village life after living for several years in the suburbs, and talked of acquiring a dog, or even, in one flash of inspiration, a goat.

Eileen, galvanized into frantic activity, was appalled at how much junk she had accumulated over the years. Ruthlessly she divided it into piles, and made many journeys to the charity shops in Caxford. Now it was the turn of the rubbish. On this bright, hazy afternoon she had built a bonfire in the back garden. It crackled merrily in the still air, gobbling up long-forgotten useless items, things that were broken, yellowed newspapers, all the debris of more than a quarter-century's careless living. Rubbish that could not be burnt she put into tough plastic sacks and dumped at the front, ready for the rubbish collectors. Leaning at a perilous angle by the front fence was the sign which told the world that her house now belonged to someone else.

Marie's cottage was also empty, except for the decorators who were preparing for the next tenants. Thinking of her friend, Eileen smiled to herself. Marie and Philip were now in Italy. That morning Eileen had received a postcard of a church set among rolling hills in Umbria, with the brief message, "I think I have arrived in heaven ahead of time."

Eileen threw another bundle of rubbish onto the fire. She wiped her dusty hands as she watched the flames hungrily take hold. Then she went indoors and put the kettle on. The house was like a transit-camp, the living room full of boxes and crates, the kitchen reduced to bare essentials. Upstairs, there was nothing left except a suitcase of clothes, a few necessary items for washing, and a fold-up camp bed. She made a cup of tea and went back into the garden to watch the fire.

She worked until it was almost completely dark. She did not want to stop. There was so much to do, and it was a positive pleasure to feel strong again. Around nine o'clock she called it a day. She concocted a hasty meal, and sat in her denuded lounge on the one remaining chair to eat it. The curtains were open, and she could see the embers of the dying fire still glowing in the darkness of the garden.

In the soft light of a small table-lamp she read verses from Isaiah.

"A voice says, 'Cry!'
And I said, 'What shall I cry?'
All flesh is grass,
and all its beauty is like the flower of the field.
The grass withers, the flower fades,
when the breath of the Lord blows upon it;
surely the people is grass.
The grass withers, the flower fades,
but the word of our God will stand for ever."

A wave of sadness washed over her, and she brushed a tear from her cheek. She thought of Christopher withered like the grass, faded like the flower under God's fiery breath; and yet she herself, though broken and damaged, still lived. What did it mean? And what was Christopher's message in Psalm 25? Could she take it at face value? Did he mean what he said in his note to her, or was he merely offering her a scrap of comfort in a dark moment? She had no idea what he had read and thought during the long hours alone in the woods; she knew only what he had chosen to discuss with her. Perhaps it was true, perhaps he had seen through his fear and recognized the light of eternity filtering through the trees, the outstretched arms waiting to receive him. And if this was so, shouldn't she be rejoicing? She should, and she told herself she was, and yet, if she was cruelly honest, was this what she wanted, what she would have chosen? She wanted him to live. But another voice echoed, 'For what?' and she could not answer. She felt her face burn hot as the thought came to her that perhaps indeed God had stood aside while Christopher destroyed himself in order to rescue him from Eileen. It was as if the voice in her mind, contending against her own familiar inner voice, was saying to her, 'What you want is not right, and I will not let you harm a servant of mine, even if that servant be yourself.' She felt shame then, but it was not bitter, for was that love not directed also at her? Did it not say somewhere in the book she now clutched in her lap that God not only guides and directs but also punishes those whom he loves? She had travelled a long, blind journey into the country of self, but tonight she had stopped, and turned round, and begun the long haul back. She turned to the last chapter of Job.

"Then Job answered the Lord.

'I know, Lord, that you are all-powerful; that you can do everything you want. You ask how I dare question your wisdom when I am so very ignorant. I talked about things I did not understand, about marvels too great for me to know.

'You told me to listen while you spoke and to try to answer your questions. In the past I knew only what others had told me, but now I have seen you with my own eyes.

'So I am ashamed of all I have said and repent in dust and ashes.'"

She read no more, though she knew that at the last God restored to Job his years of the locust, and heaped upon him the wealth of his heart. She did not want to think about pleasure, or happiness, or restoration, or reward. Those things might come, or they might not. For now, knowing that she was on the way back was enough. She closed the book and went to bed.

The end.